An Act of Kindness

Ray Hobbs

Wingspan Press

Cover hand model: Chloe Wood

Published in the United States and the United Kingdom
by WingSpan Press, Livermore, CA

The WingSpan name, logo and colophon are the trademarks of WingSpan
Publishing.

ISBN 978-1-59594-521-1 (pbk.)
ISBN 978-1-59594-860-1 (ebk.)

First edition 2014

Printed in the United States of America

www.wingspanpress.com

Library of Congress Control Number

1 2 3 4 5 6 7 8 9 10

This book is dedicated to prisoners of conflict everywhere
and to those who keep faith with them.

Sources & Acknowledgements

Waite, C. with La Vardera, D., *Survivor of the Long March* (Stroud, Spellmount, 2012)

Gilbert, A., *P.O.W.* (London, John Murray, 2006)

Doyle, P., *Prisoner of War in Germany* (Oxford, Shire Books, 2011)

Rollings, C., *Prisoner of War* (London, Ebury Press, 2007)

Longden, S., *Hitler's British Slaves* (Moreton-in-Marsh, Arris, 2005)

Pape, R., *Boldness Be My Friend* (London, Elek Books, 1953)

Castle, J., *The Password is Courage* (London, Souvenir Press, 1954)

Batstone, S., *Wren's Eye View* (Tunbridge Wells, Parapress, 1994)

Houston, R., *Changing Course* (London, Grub Street, 2005)

Scott, P., *The Battle of the Narrow Seas* (London, Country Life, 1945)

Dickens, P., *Night Action* (London, Peter Davies, 1974)

Sweet, M., *West End Front* (London, Faber, 2011)

Thomas, D. A., *Malta Convoys* (Barnsley, Pen & Sword, 1999)

Fearnley-Whittingstall, J., *The Ministry of Food* (London, Hodder, 2010)

Braithwaite, B/Walsh, N/Davies, G., *The Home Front* (London, Leopard Books, 1995)

BBC, *WW2 People's War*, recollections published on the internet (2003-6)

. . .

I am indebted also to the following for their invaluable assistance: The Archives Department of the British Red Cross Society; The Imperial War Museum, London; Dover Public Library; Mr R. B. Williams, Hon. Librarian, Dover Museum; Capt. T. Rowbotham, R.N. retd., Coastal Forces Heritage Trust; 'The Wren' magazine; the late Mr Albert Marshall for his memories of prison camp and work camp life in Upper Silesia; Mr Dudley Ridgeon, sometime First Lieutenant of MTB 354, and Mrs Joyce Baker, sometime P.O. Wren, for their wartime recollections of HMS Wasp and HMS Lynx; Ms Susan Scott, Archivist, Fairmont Hotels and Resorts, and the obliging staff of the Savoy Hotel's American Bar, for information regarding the layout and decor of the bar in 1945; Dover Harbour Board for allowing me to explore Lord Warden House, where much of the story took place; Mrs Susan Mosley for her help with the glossary; Miss Chloe Wood for her part in the cover

Ray Hobbs

illustration; the Director and Archivist of Eden Camp Modern History Theme Museum for allowing me to use the photograph of the observation tower; my wife Sheila for tolerating my long absences, for answering a great many silly questions and for helping me put together a typical Next-of-Kin parcel. Finally, I should like to thank my brother Chris, who acted both as soundboard and as a ready source of ideas from planning to final draft, and who helped fuel my enthusiasm throughout.

RH

Glossary for Readers outside the UK

Wren	member of the Women's Royal Naval Service
MTB	motor torpedo boat
ML	motor launch
RAF	Royal Air Force
Shilling or 'bob'	12 old pennies. Worth 20 US cents during WW2
Blitz	the nightly bombing of British cities
Coupon	(ration) ticket proving entitlement to rationed goods
'Blackouts'	navy-blue, elasticated drawers, sometimes altered by Wrens into French knickers. An allusion to the cloth used to darken buildings at night against bombing
Suspender (lingerie)	garter
Vest (underwear)	T-shirt
Balaclava (helmet)	knitted garment that covers the ears, neck and throat
Queue	Line
'Jack' ('Jack Tar')	any British sailor
'Pusser'	[1] anything officially naval [2] strictly according to naval regulations
Wardroom	naval officers' mess
'The Andrew'	The Royal Navy, but no one really knows why. It is possibly an allusion to Andrew Miller, a prolific 18th C press-gang officer, or to St Andrew, Patron Saint of fishermen and sailors
'Bootneck'	Royal Marine
'Marrer'	(Tyneside slang) 'buddy'
Chips	fried potatoes
'Cuppa'	cup of tea
'…Got a cob on'	(Liverpool slang) angry
NAAFI	Navy, Army & Air-Force Institute – a retail/catering facility, equivalent to the American PX
'Oppo'	friend (lit. 'opposite number')
ATS	Auxiliary Territorial Service – women's army
WAAF	Women's Auxiliary Air Force
'Civvy'	civilian
'Blighty'	home (the UK)

Ray Hobbs

'Bookie's Runner'	a collector of off-course bets. Illegal until 1960
'Doodlebug'	V1 flying bomb
'Randy'	'horny', eager for sex, therefore not used as a name (at least, not a polite one) in the UK
Anderson shelter	outdoor air-raid shelter for family use
Scouse	native of, or pertaining to, Liverpool
ENSA	Entertainments National Service Association
Solicitor	attorney
WVS	Women's Voluntary Service
'Hoolie'	(Liverpool slang) party or celebration
'Sweetie' (sweet)	piece of candy
'Party'	boy/girlfriend
Barrage balloon	large balloon moored by a steel rope, flown to impede low-flying aircraft
Pavement	sidewalk
'Queer Street'	financial ruin
'Goffers'	non-alcoholic drinks

1

Tamowicz Work Camp
Poland
1943

Freddie had no intention of admitting he was in the wrong, at least for the time being. It was the kind of defiant gesture that had become his habit, although he wasn't sure exactly when it had begun. It was as if, having forfeited his freedom, he felt obliged to defend every decision and stance, however unworthy, simply because he had lost far too much already.

On this occasion, however, his obstinacy was tempered with guilt. The girl had written the letter out of kindness and therefore deserved his gratitude. She was also blameless and a thousand miles away, unlike the instigator of the letter, who currently occupied the bunk beneath his. Freddie leaned over to speak to him.

'Len?'

'Yes, mate?'

'Why did you do this?'

There was a meaningful silence, the disagreement having run since the arrival of mail that morning, and then his companion said wearily, 'Joyce and I reckoned you needed an interest beyond the wire. We thought it might buck you up a bit if someone wrote to you with news for your eyes alone, and perhaps bunged you the odd pair of socks.' He levered himself upright and punched his flattened pillow into shape. 'It still might if you let it.' He was plainly tired of the argument, because he said, 'I'm going for a stroll.' He added almost as an afterthought, 'Are you coming?'

'All right.' Freddie swung his legs over the side of his bunk and slid with

1

practised ease to the floor. The two men donned their greatcoats against the early winter chill and left the hut.

'I'm sure you did it for the right reason,' Freddy conceded after a while. 'I just feel, I don't know … awkward about it, I suppose.'

'Awkward my foot.' Len kicked at a mound of earth in frustration. 'I know fate's played a rotten trick on you, Freddy, but you've got to break out of that shell of yours some time, if only for your own sake.'

'I know that.' In spite of Freddy's whims, their friendship had survived almost two years in Italian and German prison camps, and he was used to Len's direct manner.

'In any case,' said Len, 'letters make life behind the wire worth living. They're a reminder that we won't always be half-starved, eaten by lice and herded by goons.' When they had walked a little further, he asked, 'What does she have to say?'

'Basically that you told Joyce I never get any letters, and they both think it's a bugger – my word, not hers – and she'd like to write to me regularly.' He added, 'To be fair to the girl, she sounds very pleasant.'

'If I'd told Joyce what a miserable sod you can be she'd never have got her to write to you. What's her name, by the way? Joyce told me but it's slipped my mind.'

'Sylvia.'

'I remember now. It's a nice name.'

'Her address is in Leyburn. It's in the Yorkshire Dales.'

'That's a stroke of luck, isn't it? You won't need a translator.'

Freddy ignored the jibe. 'She wants my measurements so that she can knit things for me.'

'And you're still dithering?' They stepped aside to make way for two morose guards, who were too involved in their conversation to notice the two prisoners.

Len watched them disappear into the orderly hut. 'What was all that about?'

'Nothing much. They were just having a moan about the duty roster.'

'Even the goons have their problems.' Len smiled briefly at the thought before returning to the original subject. 'What are you going to do about that letter?'

'I don't know. I need to think about it.'

'Well, don't spend too long thinking about it. You're going to need those woollies.' The previous winter in northern Italy was difficult for either of them to forget. 'Just out of interest, what's the date on the letter?'

'The twenty-second of August.'

'Two months, same as Joyce's. Still, I suppose they had to come via Italy. Like us, really.' He held up his hand to cover an expansive yawn and said, 'I'm going back to the hut.'

Okay, I'll walk that way with you.' Sunday was their day off and leisure time was too precious to waste so they returned the way they had come. In taking that route they could also stay upwind of the latrine, known somewhat starkly as the *Abort*.

Physically they were very much alike: clean-shaven but with dark, roughly-trimmed hair, their features gaunt after months of prison camp rations. Each wore a greatcoat too. Len's matched the RAF uniform and sergeant's stripes to which he was entitled, but Freddy's was khaki, and beneath it he wore a nondescript navy-blue battledress tunic with khaki trousers, the Red Cross store having been short of naval uniform when he was kitted out. His flying overalls were at the bottom of the Mediterranean.

More than anything, their accents told them apart. Len was a native of Balham in South London, whereas Freddy's flat vowels were born of Yorkshire's East Riding.

'If it helps,' said Len, 'I reckon Sylvia might need someone to write to as much as you do.'

'What makes you think that?'

'Her chap was killed in action last year. Joyce says they were very close, so it must have been hell for her.' He gave Freddy a straight look and said, 'You're not the only one with a problem, mate, and she's only nineteen.'

'Poor kid.' It was impossible to imagine. At nineteen Freddy and his contemporaries were still enjoying the novelty of legal drinking and the tantalising possibility of sex. In those days war had seemed no more than a passing threat.

He left Len to his siesta and continued walking. The hut was noisy and reeked of wood smoke and stale sweat. It was easier to think in relatively fresh air.

Len and his wife had acted in good faith. It was a shame he found their gesture intrusive, but reticence was an essential feature of camp life; a prisoner's thoughts and feelings were part of his private self, the ultimate citadel that neither the enemy nor anyone else could penetrate. There had been no privacy at Veano, and neither Tamowicz nor the main camp at Lamsdorf offered any improvement in that respect. He'd told Len about his family because he'd been in the hut when the news arrived, and that was a measure of their friendship, because he had told no one else.

Even so, Len was probably right. It was time lower his guard, at least to some extent, and he had to reply to the girl's letter out of politeness.

3

Even if their correspondence ended there, he owed her that. He was also uncomfortably aware that her personal tragedy had touched him where he was most susceptible.

He walked and pondered for some time before returning to the hut, where he measured himself with the tape from his sewing kit and a little help from Len. Then he took out a letter-form and pencil, laid a bed board across his bunk as a makeshift writing desk, and set about the easy part.

31st October, 1943.

Dear Sylvia,

Thank you very much for your letter, which arrived today. It was very kind of you to think of me. It's also generous of you to offer to knit something for me but I don't want you to be out of pocket. If you really want to do that I can write to the Paymaster at the Admiralty and arrange for money to be sent to you, so please let me know what I owe you. Here are the measurements you asked for:

Length 26 inches, sleeve seam (I imagine that's shoulder to wrist) 20 inches, and my shoe size is 10.

Then he was stuck. Life in camp and at the railway yard was too sordid and banal to interest anyone. The main features of his day were work, hunger and insect bites. In any case, according to Len, nothing he wrote about camp life would make it beyond the censor.

He wondered a little about Sylvia. She worked with Joyce, and that meant she was in signals, so she might be a coder or telegraphist, or maybe a visual signaller. Otherwise, all he knew was that she was a nineteen-year-old Wren earning less than three shillings a day and she was offering to send him parcels.

He thought for a while about her coping with the loss of her boyfriend, and it seemed to him that to shy away from the subject once might create a taboo as hard to break as to ignore, so he had to say something. Also, he wanted to repay her kindness in some way, and sympathy was all he had to offer. He picked up his pencil again.

Len told me about your loss and I'm truly sorry. People say the most ridiculous things. They tell you they know just how you feel, and most of them haven't a clue. I believe I can sympathise with you, though, because I lost my parents and sister last year in the Blitz. My home was on the outskirts of Hull, so the risk was always there, but that kind of knowledge doesn't help us when it happens, does it? We only know that it hurts. We know as well that people learn to cope with the hurt, but the coping sometimes seems a long way off. I hope it starts happening for you very soon.

He looked at what he'd written, relieved that he'd felt able to say those things, and suddenly the task that had seemed so daunting was much easier.

People do terrible things to one another in wartime, but some are capable of true kindness, as your letter shows. Please tell me about yourself, the things you like to do and what you did before the war. It should be fun to compare notes. I'll go first to start things off and then it's your turn.

2

Dover Naval Base HMS Wasp
November

The hand on Sylvia's shoulder was 'Will' Hay's. He was one of the leading telegraphists on her watch and she liked him because he was good-natured and helpful. Also, he came from Middlesbrough and didn't poke fun at the way she spoke.

'What have you got there, Sylvia?'

'Just one "Routine".' She finished logging the six pages of four-letter coded groups and looked up at the clock. It was nearly 0200.

'Take it through to Coding and then you can have a wet.'

'Thanks, Will.' She was ready for a mug of tea. Her last one had been before she came on watch at 2300 and that seemed a lifetime ago. She removed her headphones and vacated the chair for him.

HMS *Wasp* was a base for coastal forces. The motor torpedo boats, gunboats and motor launches operated from the submarine basin at the eastern end of the harbour; accommodation, signals, plotting and operations took place on the western side, in the former Lord Warden Hotel on Admiralty Pier. There was no hotel luxury, however, in the junior Wrens' mess. It's bare, dull-green painted walls and uncared-for appearance led Sylvia to imagine that the room had been a utility area or dining room for the hotel staff. It couldn't have looked very cheerful then, and four years of naval service had done nothing to improve it. Also, the building was inhabited by cockroaches. She wasn't sure when they had invaded the place but they were now part of the establishment. One wag had even suggested painting them blue before the next inspection.

She joined Joyce at the tea urn, having spotted her immediately. Even in their pinned-up state, those ginger curls were impossible to miss.

'Hello,' she said, 'what have we got tonight?'

'Herring or pilchard. I suppose we'll never know which, but I'm going to have one anyway.'

'Me too.' They took their tea and sandwiches over to the nearest table.

Joyce took a sip of her tea before giving way to curiosity. 'Tell me about the letter.'

'It's a nice letter.' Sylvia smiled as she took it from her shoulder bag. ' "Leading Airman F. W. Hinchcliffe",' she read. 'He's from Hull. I don't think I've ever met anyone from the East Riding. Still, it's quite a coincidence that he's a Yorkshireman, isn't it?'

'You mustn't say too much about where you live,' said Joyce. 'The censors are quite strict about that.'

'Yes, I saw that in the stuff that came from the Joint War people.'

'Len and I have a sort of private code that we use for odd bits of information. It's just references that mean something to us but to no one else, and it's quite useful. The prisoners have their own slang words as well but I imagine the Germans will know them all by now.'

Sylvia nodded. 'They can't be as obscure as some of the naval jargon we've had to learn.'

'No, it's nothing like that. There's a new word though. It must have something to do with them being in a German camp now because I don't recall Len using it when he was in Italy.'

'What is it?'

' "Kriegie." It's what they call themselves, so I imagine it means "prisoner-of-war." '

'Yes, it'll be short for *Kriegsgefangene*.'

'Who's a clever girl, then?'

'Not really. It says *Kriegsgefangenenlager* on the outside, here.' She held the form up to show her. A *Gefangene* is a prisoner and a *Lager* is a camp.'

'Well, I never.'

'He was a photographer before the war.' Sylvia moved the conversation on so as not to appear too clever. 'He took pictures of animals as well as people. He says cattle are particularly photogenic because they have such large, appealing eyes.'

'I suppose someone has to love them.'

'Well, I respect a man who likes animals. He likes dancing as well, and he played clarinet and alto sax with a band called the Humber Rumba Boys.'

'Is he serious?'

'I think so.'

'I wonder what they were like. There were so many awful bands around before the war.'

'And lots of good ones too. Be fair.' Sylvia looked at the first page of the letter again and her smile faltered. 'He was really nice about James,' she said. 'Len must have told him.' She finished her sandwich while she re-read the paragraph.

'It's good that you can talk about it now,' said Joyce, 'even with a stranger.'

'Yes, and he doesn't go on about it. He just says … well, he says enough.'

Joyce gave her wrist a sympathetic squeeze. 'What else does he say?'

'Oh, lots more. His writing's really tiny.' She smiled again. 'He says that as we're not allowed to send photos he wants me to describe myself.'

'Ah, but has he described himself?'

'Yes, he's got dark hair and grey eyes, and he used to be five-feet-eleven but he thinks he may have shrunk in captivity. He says it's either that or his ducking in the Med that caused it.'

'So he hasn't lost his sense of humour after all. Len's been quite concerned about him.'

'Yes, you said so.' She looked again at the second paragraph. 'He certainly has plenty to feel sad about.'

Joyce smiled playfully over her mug and said, 'Tell him about your lovely brown hair and those pretty blue eyes. It'll give him something nice to think about instead.'

'He could be disappointed if we ever meet.' She lit a cigarette and drew on it without inhaling. Smoking was just something that everyone did because duty-frees were so cheap. She kept telling herself she would stop before her teeth turned black like the First Lieutenant's.

'He won't be.'

'Ah well, it's not as if it's likely to happen.' She folded the letter and put it carefully in her bag. 'Tell me,' she asked, 'has he got absolutely no one to write to him?'

'He has an uncle and a cousin somewhere, but they stopped writing ages ago, when he was in Italy. They were never close.'

'That's awful.' Sylvia glanced at her watch. 'Oh dear,' she said, 'It's time to go back.' They rinsed out their mugs and returned to work.

. . .

After breakfast she fell into bed and slept until after half-past three in the afternoon. On her return from the bathroom, she was surprised when Dorothy, a new girl from Liverpool, told her about the shelling.

'Surely you can't have slept through it. Do you mean you never heard a thing, like?'

'Nothing at all. I was exhausted when I turned in. Was it bad?'

'It was terrible. Some of the shells landed in the town. I can't imagine how you slept through it all.'

'I've been sleeping better lately.' She was also getting used to the regular shelling from Sangatte. She and Joyce had recently stood in the Signal Station at the end of the pier and watched the muzzle flashes across the channel, but gunfire was a new and startling experience for Dorothy.

'You'll get used to it,' Sylvia told her. 'Everyone does.'

'I hope so.' Dorothy looked inconvenienced rather than scared. She was quite plain, and Sylvia wondered in her nineteen-year-old wisdom if Dorothy's stiffness might be rooted in insecurity.

When she was dressed she took out a letter-form and wrote:

Dear Freddy,

Thank you for your letter. You said some lovely things that I found helpful, and you naturally have my sympathy too. Maybe we'll both begin to feel better soon.

I really enjoyed reading about your life before the war, and we have so much in common! I love dancing too. Can you do the slow foxtrot? It's my favourite dance, and most men I've met haven't a clue. If I'm honest, I haven't known all that many men, but I expect you know what I mean.

She had been thinking hard about the next bit. Somewhat self-consciously, she wrote:

I've never described myself before, but you asked what I look like, so here goes. I'm quite ordinary really, not glamorous or anything special. My hair is medium brown, my eyes are blue and I'm five-feet-five. My sister Audrey says I'm skinny but I'm not really. She's jealous because she's expecting a baby in two months' time and it's created havoc with her figure. Oh yes, and people say I smile a lot. Well, it's better than scowling, isn't it? I hope that helps.

I've got lots of interests, including films and reading, and I'm glad you like animals, but instead of telling you about it all now I'll do it in instalments.

I'm going to send you some things, hopefully by Christmas but I suppose that's in the lap of the gods. I'll keep writing, but in case my next letter

9

doesn't reach you before Christmas, let me wish you whatever happiness you can find in spite of everything. I'll be thinking of you.
   Yours with warmest wishes,
   Sylvia

.

   She read the letter twice before she was satisfied, and then considered her next job, which was to organise some knitting.

3

Walter Charlesworth took his eyes off the *Yorkshire Post* crossword for a moment to ask, 'What are you knitting, Jessie?'

'A pair of socks.'

He peered over his glasses at the bottle-green wool his wife was using. 'Not for me, surely?' He never wore green socks.

'No, they're for the boy our Sylvia's writing to, the prisoner-of-war.' She paused between stitches to say, 'You know, I just don't know what to think about that.'

Walter shrugged. 'It's Sylvia being Sylvia. You wouldn't want her to be different, would you?'

'No, of course I wouldn't, and if it helps her to get over that poor lad James it'll be a good thing, I suppose. I've told her to send the labels and all the literature to me. She has to use this address anyway as she has to keep quiet about being in the Wrens, so I'll send the parcels. There'll only be one every three months.'

'I see, but where's all this stuff going to come from? I suppose she's considered rationing and shortages?'

'There are special allowances of cigarettes and chocolate for prisoners and she'll get extra clothing coupons for him as well.'

He lit his pipe and smiled. 'I think I know who's going to pay for all this.'

'Yes, that's your job, Walter.'

'I thought it might be.' He took his pipe from his mouth and blew out a cloud of smoke. 'I often wish I had a wealthy father too. I'm told they can be very useful.'

They sat quietly for a while, the only sounds in the room being the soft click of Jessie's needles, the ticking of a log in the grate and an occasional squall that rattled the window panes. The house was double-fronted and built of stone, and it had defied more than two hundred Dales winters.

After a while Walter said, 'I fancy that old fishing jersey of mine is about to die of old age.'

'Well, it didn't help when you caught it on that nail. It's certainly past its best.'

'I shan't need one until next spring but I've been wondering about the situation with the clothing coupons.'

'I should wait and see what happens at Christmas, Walter.'

'Oh really?' He peered more closely at his wife's knitting and said, 'Jessie, that's my old fishing jersey, isn't it?'

'Well, it was.' Jessie finished the line she was on and put her knitting down. 'But as you said, you won't need one until next spring.'

. . .

Sylvia sat on her bed embroidering the initial 'A' on a handkerchief, a Christmas present for her sister; Dorothy was unpicking the thread from a broken suspender, and Joyce, the other inhabitant of the cabin, as they were obliged to call their accommodation, had stopped knitting briefly to reminisce.

'I once had a suspender break on a date,' she told Dorothy. 'It was before Len and I were engaged. We were just coming out of the Gaumont Palace Picture House in Streatham when it happened.'

Dorothy paused from her work and asked, 'What did you do?'

'Len gave me a fruit gum to use.'

Dorothy's eyes widened.

'We went into a shop doorway and he stood in front of me while I fastened it. It worked nicely, but when we got to the bus shelter in our road he asked for it back.'

'Was it his last one?'

'No, he just wanted a fumble.'

Dorothy scowled. 'Men are only interested in one thing.' Her thoughts seemed forever poised on the edge of that alarming prospect.

'There.' Sylvia finished her embroidery and held it up to admire it.

'I wish I could do fine stitching like that,' said Dorothy. 'Mine always ends up tatty, like.' She held up her suspender belt with a fatalistic shrug.

'It's easy if you're careful,' Sylvia told her. 'Let me have it and I'll show you.'

'All right.'

'We swap favours, remember,' said Joyce. 'We help each other.'

Dorothy seemed at a loss but Sylvia had the answer. 'Can you knit?'

'It depends what it is.'

'A pair of mittens for a man.'

'If I've got a pattern.'

'I'll give you a pattern, the wool and the needles.'

'All right then.'

Sylvia threaded a sewing needle and said, 'Right, now you've unpicked it I'll show you how to sew one on without making it look a mess.

She took her work down to the Wireless Telegraphy room when she went on watch at 1800. It was a good idea to have something to do when things were quiet.

Third Officer Fuller was impressed. 'You girls are all so talented,' she said, 'You make me feel ham-fisted.'

Sylvia asked, 'What are you best at, ma'am?'

'I'm afraid my needlework is very basic.'

'Can you knit, ma'am?'

'Yes, I used to knit. Perhaps I should take it up again.'

'I think you should, ma'am.' Third Officer Fuller was the most approachable of the officers, and Sylvia felt confident enough to ask, 'Could you knit a man's scarf if I gave you the wool and the needles?'

Miss Fuller hesitated only briefly and said, 'Yes, I could. I take it you have a particular man in mind?'

Sylvia told her story and the deal was made. Now, all she had to do was find the wool.

. . .

Her opportunity came on her next day off. The YMCA were holding a jumble sale at their hostel in Folkestone Road, and Sylvia, who had never been to one in her life but had taken advice on the matter, was there in good time. Even so, she found when she arrived that a queue had already formed and that many of the people in it seemed to be old hands. Some of them were poorly dressed and appeared ill-fed, and she imagined they must be living on very little. Simply being there made her feel quite guilty until she reminded herself that the man whose needs had brought her there was currently a jolly sight worse off than they were. It also crossed her mind that many of them would be there for the wool, as she was, and that sort of equalised things.

A woman next to her said, 'They're nice. I suppose you get them free.'

Sylvia realised that the woman was looking at her artificial silk stockings, which must have looked impressive, considering no one else was wearing stockings at all. 'We have to pay for replacements,' she said.

'Do you, now?' The woman sniffed. 'At least you can get hold of 'em. No one else can.'

All the conversation was about shortages, rationing and, inevitably, the daily shelling of Dover, huge areas of which were already reduced to rubble. It was heart-rending to see what was happening to these people and their homes.

The same woman asked her, 'Are you from down the Lord Warden, then?'

'That's right.'

The woman was eyeing her category badge with open curiosity. 'What is it you do down there?'

'I'm afraid I can't say. "Careless Talk" and all that.'

'Fair enough.' The woman seemed satisfied.

'She's a signaller.' An elderly man joined the conversation, pointing to her badge. 'That's what she is. Isn't that right, dear?'

'Yes, but I really can't talk about it.'

'It's amazing what they train these young gels to do.' The woman blinked in disbelief.

'That's right,' said the old man, 'and they're doin' a grand job. All our boys and girls are. We've got the job weighed off now and we're ready for anything.'

As a general principle it was possibly true, but Sylvia was not prepared for what happened next. Someone in the queue had seen a face at the window, and that gave rise to a murmur of excitement that reached its peak on the stroke of ten, when the doors opened and the queue surged through.

Scarcely able to keep her feet, Sylvia was carried along by a tidal wave of determined humanity until she found herself in a hall set out with long tables of the kind paperhangers used. Each was laden with clothes, boots, shoes and bric-a-brac, through which the shoppers, who had waited so patiently in the queue, were now rummaging voraciously. It was too much for a girl of Sylvia's polite upbringing. Her parents had taught her always to stand aside for others and to wait for her turn, and now, as she struggled to reach one of the tables she was elbowed out of the way. She had no idea what she might have done had fate not intervened at that moment in the most violent way.

There was a screeching roar like the noise of an express train, which continued for several seconds before terminating in a thunderous explosion. It must have been some distance away but it shook the YMCA building so that the windows and doors rattled violently. The shelling siren was now wailing its belated warning, and one of the YMCA people pointed to what looked like a cellar door. She called, 'The shelter's this way!'

Immediately, the jumble hunters, who had been jostling, shoving and grabbing only a few moments earlier, formed a brisk procession to the door, leaving behind only Sylvia and the helpers.

One of them asked her, 'Aren't you going to shelter, dear?'

'Yes, please. That's very kind of you.' Sylvia completed her search and held up three thick woollen jerseys. 'How much are these?'

As another shell came screaming over the helper said somewhat anxiously, 'They're a penny each, dear, but you can give it to me down the shelter.'

Shells continued to fall but Sylvia was happy. She had found the knitting-wool she needed.

4

December

The cabbage soup was thin, and three thin slices of black bread didn't go far, but it was the main meal of the day and the kriegies awaited it eagerly. They also welcomed the fifteen-minute break that accompanied it. Mail had arrived for most of the *Arbeitskommando* at the railway yard, including Freddy and Len.

'She's going to send me a parcel,' said Freddy. 'I don't mind if it arrives after Christmas. It'll still be something to look forward to, but I can't help wondering how much she can knit in a few weeks.'

'Oh, some women are like lightning with their knitting needles.' Len folded his letter and put it in his pocket. 'What else does she say?'

'She's given me a description of herself, just as I asked.'

'Go on then.'

'She says she's quite ordinary and not glamorous or anything special, but I don't care.'

'She's modest as well, Freddy mate, because Joyce says she's pretty.'

'Does she?'

Len took out his letter again to consult it. 'She says, "Sylvia is pretty in a nice sort of way", whatever that means.' He put the letter away again and said, 'I think the world of my other half and I really appreciate her letters, but I have to say that she talks fluent bollocks sometimes. What is "pretty in a nice sort of way", for heaven's sake?'

'It makes a kind of sense. She says that Sylvia's pretty but not glamorous. She could be pleasing to look at but not in a way that makes women sharpen their claws.'

16

'You could be right, now I think of it. She could be pretty in a pleasant sort of way, I suppose.'

A guard terminated their conversation by shouting, '*Arbeiten!*' It was time to return to work.

'I imagine they shout all the time, even when they're at home,' said Len. 'You've got to feel sorry for their wives.'

'I don't. It serves 'em right for marrying goons.'

'*Stille!*' The guard called for silence and the prisoners marched back to their various jobs.

The railway yard was rich in opportunities for sabotage. The kriegies had to be careful that nothing could be traced back to them, and it would be unwise to attempt anything too ambitious, but any little hitch that hindered or frustrated the enemy made the risk worthwhile. Freddy and Len had the task of loading freight on to the outgoing trains, and in the short time they had been at the camp they had consigned several cargoes to some highly inappropriate destinations. The trick was to do it selectively and infrequently.

'What sort of preservative do you reckon this is, Freddy? There are two cases of it.' Len was peering at a case in the gloom of the wagon they were loading.

'Let me see.' Freddy crouched down to look. '*Präservativ*,' he read. 'Believe it or not, each of these cases contains one thousand contraceptives and they're going in this wagon to Leipzig. At least, they were.'

'Two thousand spoggies,' said Len. 'It makes you think, doesn't it?'

'It's better not to.'

'Right enough.' He grinned mischievously, 'Where do you think we should send them?'

Their heads turned simultaneously towards the train on the next track. They had spent the past two days loading it, so they knew it was due to leave that night for the Russian Front. Freddy jumped down and looked around. There was no sign of a railway worker or guard, so he beckoned to Len, who threw both cases down to him before joining them. Quickly, they crossed the track and stowed the cases in an enclosed wagon, pushing them out of the line of sight of anyone looking through the open doorway. Len gave them a farewell pat, saying, 'There you go, all the way to the Eastern Front, but I don't think they'll get much use out of you there.'

· · ·

Sylvia was pondering the pros and cons of service in the Wrens. 'Join the Wrens and Free a Man for the Fleet,' the posters said, but they made no mention of heavy shoes, starched collars with studs, and the worst

17

bugbear of all, which was squad drill. Everyone had done it in basic training but the Admiralty nevertheless insisted that all personnel serving in shore establishments must undergo regular sessions of foot drill. Therefore at odd times the First Lieutenant ordered off-watch personnel – Wrens alternating with ratings – to muster on the parade ground, formerly the hotel's car park, where they marched back and forth, performing complex manoeuvres unrelated in any way to dance steps or any other worthwhile pedestrian activity that Sylvia could call to mind. Moreover, she was convinced that nature had not designed women for marching. There was something unnatural about walking in a straight line whilst staring straight ahead. If women were intended to do that, why on earth, she wondered, had shop windows been invented? Worst of all, though, was man's inability to speak coherent English once he stepped on to a parade ground. The man in question on this occasion was an ebullient, newly-promoted petty officer from the submarine basin.

'Squad, with intervals, by the righ', dress!'

It was a good start. The order was in reasonably plain English, and each girl spaced herself by performing a little sideways shuffle until the tips of her right fingers touched the left shoulder of the girl on her right.

'Squad, squad, 'hun!'

They came to attention, and their performance might have passed without comment had Elsie Crabtree not dithered, thereby bringing herself to the petty officer's notice.

'Squad, 'tan' at heise!'

Guessing correctly, they stood at ease and waited whilst he eyed Elsie up and down.

'You've got two left feet, darlin'. What 'ave you got?'

'Two left feet, darling … sorry, I mean "PO". Silly me.' Looking down at her feet, she said, 'I suppose they are very similar. I can't say I've ever thought about it much, but I was actually trying to avoid this puddle.'

'Were you now? Well, when you've quite finished tiptoein' round the rock pools, per'aps we can get on with the drill. I realise that it must be hard for you gels to step into a man's world an' do all that we have to do, but you'll just have to try your hardest, an' that includes you, my dear.'

'Oh yes. Yes, of course, PO.' Elsie played an excellent dizzy debutante.

'Squad, squad, 'hun!'

Guessing correctly again, they came to attention.

'Squad, move to the right in threes. Righ' turn! By the righ', quick march!'

The squad moved off. When ordered to do so, they turned to the right and the left, they wheeled and they halted, all of which attracted the petty officer's criticism, although Sylvia thought they were doing quite well and that their drill master was just being fussy. After all, marching was men's work, as he had pointed out, and he demanded very high standards.

They had almost reached the perimeter when they heard the order, 'Squad will turn about, squad haybout turn!' They completed the manoeuvre but the petty officer was far from satisfied. 'Squad will halt, squaaad, halt! Lef' turn! ''Tan' at heise!' He stood in silence for a moment with his eyes closed, struggling to find the appropriate words. Eventually, they came to him. 'Dear, oh dear, oh dear,' he said, 'what a shambles. It's so simple my little boy of three could do it smarter than you lot.' He breathed deeply again and looked around the squad. 'There was one of you, just one, who had more or less the right idea.' His eye came to rest on Iris Dean. 'I want you,' he said, 'to show the others how to do it properly. Come and stand beside me, dear. Don't be shy.'

Sylvia stifled a smile. Iris was the last girl anyone would call shy.

The petty officer placed his hand on her shoulder and said, 'Go ahead.'

'Yes, PO.' Addressing the squad, Iris began her demonstration. 'The word "turn" comes as your left foot goes down. You bring your right heel to the left one to make a letter "L", rather like Charlie Chaplin but without the silly walk. Then left in front of right, and you go sort of pin-toed, to make the letter "T", like this,' and she demonstrated, lifting her knees high like a soldier. 'Then bring your right heel to your left to make a nice, neat "V", and off we go. Actually, PO, it helps if you say "L-T-V" as you do it.'

'Does it now? And which expert gave you that piece of advice?'

'My brother.'

The PO blinked. 'Your brother. And he is?'

'An officer in the Grenadier Guards.'

'I see.' The petty officer licked his lips uncertainly for a moment and said, 'Right, we'll try it again, and you can say, "L-T-V", as the officer said.'

Iris rejoined the ranks and the petty officer marched them off again. As they approached the perimeter fence he gave the order, 'Squad, haybout turn!'

The squad responded lustily. 'L-T-V! Left, right, left, right....'

'All right, all right, all right. I give the orders around here.' He halted them again to speak to them. 'That was a lot better. Not perfect but better. One thing I will say, however, is that you are not required to slam your heels the way ... What is your name, dear?'

'Wren Dean, I.M., nine four two one seven six ....'

'All right, never mind all that.' He addressed the squad again. 'You are not required to slam your heels the way Wren Dean showed you. It is not necessary and could even be harmful to the female anatomy.' The last two words were barely audible as he muttered them with some embarrassment.

Iris was quick to ask for clarification. 'What could it harm, PO?' Her expression was one of innocent enquiry.

'I was referring,' he said, articulating the words hurriedly out of the side of his mouth, 'to the female parts. It suffices to say that there is no need to slam your heels. Right…'

'What harm can it do the female parts, PO?' Elsie Crabtree snatched the baton eagerly.

'The PO coughed, 'I am referring to the … *moving* parts.'

'What moving parts?'

'The parts that move independently.' His face was crimson and he was about to give an order when Elsie delivered the knock-out blow.

'But PO, don't men have parts that move independently?'

He looked around in near-panic. 'Squad, squad, 'hun!

But no one could, because they were all helpless.

When Sylvia went on watch at a little before 1800, she asked Will Hay why sailors never slammed their heels.

'Oh yes, I heard about you lot giving that PO a headache this afternoon. Did he tell you it might do you a mischief?'

'Yes.' Sylvia was still amused.

'That's what I heard, but seriously, can you imagine watchkeepers trying to get their heads down with all that stamping going on up top?'

'Fair enough, it would be impossible.'

'They don't let bootnecks do it either, and drill is their department. Mind you,' he chuckled, '*they* say it's because it damages the brain.'

'Oh no.' For the second time that day, Sylvia was helpless with laughter.

'But silly stories apart, what's all this about Iris Dean's brother being an officer in the Guards?'

'That was a daft story too,' she said, recovering. 'He's only twelve and he's a boy scout.'

It was good to have a laugh. It was just a shame she couldn't tell Freddy about it. He might have enjoyed the story.

At the end of the watch she went down to the mess for cocoa before turning in. She had with her Freddy's latest letter, which she read again.

Dear Sylvia,

Many thanks for your 20th November. I'm allowed to write two letters and four postcards each month and, as mail takes anything between three and five weeks, things could get confusing unless we refer to each other's by date. Do you agree? As a rule, I'm not keen on numbers, even though they're occasionally useful. I only just scraped through School Certificate Maths, and what a lot of incomprehensible nonsense that was. Shall I tell you about the worst kind of betrayal? It's letters turning up in a maths problem. Just when you think you're among friends, they suddenly turn on you and start behaving like numbers. They should be stripped of their serifs and drummed out of the alphabet with ignominy.

And now to answer a very important question. Can I dance a slow foxtrot? My dear girl – you have to remember of course that my feet last touched a dance floor in March, 1942 – but yes, I can certainly do that. My favourite slow foxtrot number is 'All the Things You Are', a marriage of music and lyrics that could melt the heart of a marble statue. What's your favourite song?

We're getting excited about Christmas here. We'll get a holiday and have a high old time. Don't worry about Len and me. They can't keep two good men down.

In case you don't hear from me before it happens, have a very merry Christmas, and let's hope for a cracking 1944. Take care.

Best wishes,
Freddy.

Sylvia was glad she'd decided to write to him, even when his letters were so cheerful they made her feel sad, and when listening to 'All the Things You Are' on the portable gramophone made her feel even sadder.

5

Sylvia spent Christmas Day in the mess. It was far too cold to go outside, and everyone made the most of the day, including Christmas lunch served by the officers. Will caught her outside the mess and kissed her under the mistletoe, and when she looked up there was no mistletoe. That was typical of Will and his sense of fun, but they'd both have been well and truly in the rattle if a senior rating or an officer had seen them.

It was a shame she couldn't go on leave until the twenty-eighth, and it was just bad luck that she was on watch from 2300 on Christmas Day until 0800 on Boxing Day, especially as the war seemed to have stopped for Christmas. Still, someone had to do it.

She unfolded a letter-form and wrote:

25th December, 1943.

Dear Freddy,

Yes, I'm writing this on Christmas Day because I'm still at work. My family have postponed celebrations until the 29th so that I can be with them, but today is officially the day, so I'm wishing you all the best things at Christmas, and even though you won't get this letter for ages yet, you'll know when it comes that someone was thinking of you.

I couldn't agree more about numbers. When I look at them my brain panics and I can't persuade it to do a thing. I didn't have to do Maths for School Certificate, thank goodness. I scraped through Arithmetic instead, and that was a blessing. My dad's a chartered accountant, and he'd have had a fit if I'd failed that.

You know, I've thought about my favourite song and I agree with you about 'All the Things You Are'. I think it's the most beautiful song ever.

You'd have been a disappointed musician if you'd been here this Christmas. There's been one really good song this year: 'Have Yourself a Merry Little Christmas'. It comes over well and it knocks spots off another one, called 'I'll Be Home For Christmas'.

She read what she'd written and decided that it might be tactful to leave the subject of Christmas. Whatever they got up to in the camp, it could only be a poor excuse for the real thing. Hopefully, he might be back for Christmas 1944 but that was a long way off, so she changed the subject.

I know you like animals generally, but how do you feel about pets? We've always kept them. We currently have an elderly Cocker Spaniel called Peter Ross – trust my dad to name him after a fly-fisherman – and two cats. I kept hamsters as well when I was younger.
I have to start another letter because I'm running out of space. Back soon, Sylvia.

After some thought she added a single seasonal kiss before opening another letter-form.

25ᵗʰ December, 1943.
Dear Freddy,
I'm going to tell you something else about myself now. Most men poke fun when the subject of ballet crops up, but I don't care, and maybe you're more sensitive than some, so here goes. I love ballet; I go whenever I can, which isn't as often as I'd like, and I went to ballet class for years. We had to put on performances for our friends and relations, and everyone had to take part. Once, they gave me a special variation to dance, from 'The Nutcracker'. I'd been looking forward to it so much, but when the day came I felt horribly ill and it was just awful. I must have been the worst Sugar Plum Fairy ever. I was in bed with 'flu the next day. It wasn't always like that though. I just thought I'd tell you about that because it would be boring if I only told you about things I did well.
Now it's your turn to tell me a secret about yourself – if you want to, that is.
I'd like to wish you all the usual things at this time, but that would be silly, so I'm going to wish you a peaceful time this Christmas.
Take care.
Yours, with very best wishes,
Sylvia X

She thought the extra kiss was allowable as it was Christmas.

. . .

Red Cross parcels had arrived in good time, and the kriegies at Tarnowicz had pooled their hard-earned *Lagergeld* to buy some bottles of weak German beer, so Christmas festivities, such as they were, went ahead.

Two days later, however, several of the workforce including Freddy and Len were taken back to the main camp at Lamsdorf for de-lousing and reallocation. The work at Tarnowicz had been relatively easy and they had no way of knowing what the Germans had in store for them so they weren't especially glad to be leaving. They could only hope that they weren't destined for one of the quarries or mines.

When they arrived at the camp they found that instead of being directed to their previous accommodation in the army compound they were to be held in the old RAF enclosure, where they had a clear view through the wire of the Russians in their camp.

With no food parcels and nothing more to sustain them than a pitiful ration of bread and watery soup, their new neighbours were emaciated beyond anything the two men had encountered. They were filthy too, and even from beyond the wire Len and Freddy could see lice swarming over them. Hardly any wore boots, and those they had were close to disintegration. The majority had simply covered their feet with rags that afforded no real protection against the cold or the stony ground. Their clothing was torn and ragged, and wounds were bound with strips of soiled cloth. In all, their physical condition was appalling, but more haunting still was the general sense of utter helplessness and despair.

Despite the cold weather, Freddy and Len spent much of the day walking around the compound. During their journey they had longed for the open air, and having deposited their belongings in the hut, they could now indulge themselves with relative freedom. Most of the time, they walked along the perimeter on the opposite side from the Russian compound, having little stomach for what they had witnessed, but occasionally some disturbance would draw them to the wire in spite of themselves. The worst incident occurred when the guards wheeled a container of soup into the Russian camp and simultaneously lobbed their bread ration over the wire. No one could have ignored the hysteria prompted by the arrival of the food, and Freddy and Len looked on with horrified fascination as prisoners fought and clawed each other like animals for the scraps of bread. In their frenzy they also toppled the container of soup, and within seconds they were on the ground trying to lap the watery liquid before it sank into the soil.

The image returned to them repeatedly and continued to trouble them, and it seemed somehow wrong that prisoners who had been at Lamsdorf for some time could go about their lives as if nothing remarkable were happening in the next camp. Common sense told the newcomers that a degree of desensitisation was both inevitable and necessary in the circumstances, but it still left them in a disturbed frame of mind, and when Freddy turned away he experienced a peculiar sense of guilt that he failed to understand and which plagued him well into the next day.

Late in the afternoon he returned from a walk around the compound and noticed a copy of *The Camp* on the floor beside his bunk. It was a German propaganda newspaper published for the prisoners' benefit and it had proved highly popular in the *Abort*, where there was often a shortage of paper. After some thought he took out his pencil and spent the next hour making notes in the margins of the paper. Sometimes he crossed out one word and substituted another; sometimes he reverted to the original and then changed it again, but eventually his notes led to a single, cogent idea that gave him so much satisfaction that he felt he had to share it. He would need to write the letter in abstract terms; any direct reference to the incident would lead inevitably to confiscation of the letter and a severe punishment for him. In any case he had no wish to share the horror of the previous day with Sylvia of all people, and it was naturally to her that he would write.

The plight of the Russian prisoners had created a distraction on such a scale that neither Freddy nor Len had noticed the air of suppressed excitement in the camp, and the news gleaned from the illicit camp wireless sets that the Royal Navy had sunk the battle-cruiser Scharnhorst came to them almost as an anti-climax.

. . .

The sinking of the Scharnhorst was announced shortly after 0800 on the 27th. Sylvia was working an extra watch at the time, but suddenly everyone had relaxed and become very informal, rather as they had been on Christmas Day.

Another day and an interminable railway journey later, it still felt strange that after celebrating the sinking of an enemy ship they had fallen in on the parade ground for an impromptu service, in which they had sung 'Eternal Father, Strong to Save' and prayed for the souls of those who were killed. Sailors were sailors whatever their nationality, and many of the Scharnhorst's crew had lost their lives. Of course, that didn't mean that God wasn't on the side of the Allies. She hoped he was, because she'd been asking him for rather a lot lately.

But now she was home, dressed once more in her best frock and court shoes and the war seemed far away in spite of the blackout curtains and shortages. The family was together again: Granny Charlesworth, her mother, father, her sister Audrey and her husband David and Audrey's bulge, which was massive because the baby was due in a matter of days. Granny Charlesworth sat between David and her father, saying very little because she was extremely deaf.

'Feast your eyes on the chicken before I carve it,' said her father. 'It's off the ration, a part-payment of a long-overdue bill.' Somehow, he always managed to bring the conversation around to slow payers. It was as if he didn't want anyone to think he had any money in case they asked him for some. There were worse things though, and she was glad that David didn't talk much about his work. He was a doctor and that sort of thing and mealtimes really didn't mix.

It was a magnificent chicken, known for some reason as a 'capon'. Her father had described it as not having 'everything it set out with', but it looked complete to her. It was perhaps not as fulsome as the turkey they'd been used to before rationing but it wasn't alone in that, and she was getting hungrier all the time.

'Who'd like a leg? Don't all speak at once.'

'Give Audrey a leg, Walter,' said her mother. 'She's eating for two.'

'And it shows,' said Audrey. 'Even without the bulge, I've never been as fat as this. Don't worry about me.'

'No Audrey, you shall have a leg, and I'm giving the other to Sylvia.' There you are, love, and welcome home.'

'Thanks, dad.' He'd welcomed her home three or four times already, but that was no doubt a measure of his delight at seeing her.

'It'll be a bit different from what they give you down there,' said her mother.

'You can say that again. We live on corned beef, pilchards, herrings and Spam.'

'Oh, if only I could get my hands on some pilchards.'

'You'd be welcome to my share, but I always manage to eat them. Mind you, the sailors at sea eat better than we do. I suppose they need to.'

'Yes,' said David wistfully, 'they do.'

'Oh David, are you still fretting about that?' Her mother was referring to David's attempts to join the forces. None of them would have him, even as a doctor, because he had one leg a little shorter than the other and he wore a special shoe to make up for it. His eyesight wasn't too good either.

'He never leaves it alone,' said Audrey, 'even with me to come home to every day, he still wants to join up.' She twitched suddenly and then looked more relaxed. 'Just the baby kicking,' she assured them.

Sylvia said, 'I've an idea how you must feel, David.'

'How can you know that?'

'Because I know a sailor who's not allowed to serve at sea any more. His name's Will Hay – actually Ronald Hay but we call him "Will" after the film star – and he's my "sea daddy".'

'He's your what?'

'My sea daddy.' She smiled mischievously. 'That's what they call someone like him in the Navy. He knows the ropes because he's regular RN and a leading telegraphist, and if I need to know anything at all I ask him. He says I'm a good hand, but I think he's just being nice. It's an awful shame, but it bothers him that he can't go back to sea.'

'And why can't he?'

'He was so badly wounded early in the war that he's still not A-one fit, but he's still invaluable in what he does. I'm not the only Wren he's helped out and I doubt I'll be the last. He's worth his weight in gold, and I'm sure that's how your patients see you, David. We're serving, you and I, but in different ways.'

'Well, said David, 'it's something to think about.'

'I believe she's given us all something to think about,' said her father, evidently surprised by his younger daughter's mature observation.

'Now,' said her mother, 'will you all help yourselves to vegetables before they go cold, and there's apple sauce and gravy, and sage-and-onion and sausage-meat stuffing here as well.'

It was a magnificent meal, and when it was over Sylvia and her mother washed the dishes. Audrey had gone to lie down as her back was aching.

'I sent that parcel to Freddy as soon as I could,' said her mother as they stood at the sink, 'but I don't think it'll have reached him yet.'

'Never mind, as long as he gets it eventually. What did you put in it?'

'Well, there were two pairs of socks that I knitted and a pair from Mrs Womersley whose husband died of a heart attack last May. I got her knitting again to keep her occupied. Then there was the balaclava, the gloves, the scarf and the jersey that you sent up, a toothbrush, Dentifrice, shaving soap and ... what else? It'll come to me. Anyway, it didn't come up to the weight limit so I sent a postal order for the Red Cross to make it up with chocolate. The cigarettes have to go direct from the tobacconist and the razor blades are sent by the shop as well.' She emptied the washing-up water and refilled the sink. 'Pass us those pudding bowls, love.' She put her hand to her forehead and said, 'I've just remembered, I used some of his clothing points to get him some underwear, so there you are. He's getting a flannel vest and a pair of long johns as well.'

27

'Mum! You didn't send him long underwear, did you? It's what old men wear.'

'And young men as well if it gets cold enough.'

'It's still embarrassing.'

'Just wait and see what I've given you for Christmas.'

Her mother's eyes were twinkling. Sylvia hoped it wasn't something embarrassing. She couldn't think what it might be, so her thoughts returned to Freddy and the long johns. 'If the weather over there's anything like what we're having, I suppose he'll need those things,' she conceded.

'It's best to be on the safe side, and by the way, I'd get a dry towel if I were you. That one's sopping wet and you've still got the cutlery to do.'

When they had finished washing up they rejoined the others in the sitting room for the distribution of presents. Sylvia felt quite guilty that the four-day postponement had been for her benefit, but no one seemed to mind.

Her mother's present turned out to be a bed jacket with matching socks, and she was thankful rather than embarrassed, because it was freezing in the Wrens' quarters and warmth was more precious than rubies.

Knowing that letter-writing was now an important part of her life, her parents had bought her a fountain pen that wrote quite beautifully. Her presents of initialled handkerchiefs went down well too, but the best present of all began with Audrey's and David's hurried departure at about six o'clock, and culminated in a telephone call from David shortly after midnight to say that Audrey had given birth to a boy.

6

January 1944

Sylvia returned late on the second and found Joyce and Dorothy already in the cabin and about to turn in. There was also an extra bed and locker. When they had exchanged New Year greetings and their personal news, Sylvia asked, 'Who's the new girl?'

'Clarissa.' They uttered the name simultaneously and with equal lack of enthusiasm.

'She's making the best she can of the barbaric bathroom facilities before retiring,' said Joyce.

'I see.'

Dorothy simply snorted.

If any further explanation were forthcoming it was rendered unnecessary as the door opened and the new girl entered the cabin. She was small and fair-haired, with delicate features marred by a pointed nose that seemed to have been intended for a larger face.

'Hello,' she said, looking at Sylvia. 'Who are you?'

'This is Sylvia,' said Joyce. 'She lives here.'

'Oh jolly good. I'm Clarissa. How d' you do?'

'Clarissa's in Signal Distribution,' said Joyce. 'She's on our watch.' It was actually good news because it meant that everyone would be on and off watch at the same time. There were few things worse than someone banging around when others were trying to sleep.

As Dorothy removed her skirt, Joyce asked, 'Are you happy with elastic in the legs of your blackouts, Dorothy? Most of us cut the bottoms off and make them into French knickers. You'll be all right as long as you keep a pair intact for kit inspections.'

'I know, but you know what I'm like at sewing.'

'I'll show you how to hem them up when I use the machine again,' said Sylvia.

Dorothy eyed her warily. 'What are you after this time?'

'I don't know yet but I'll think of something.'

Clarissa, who had been following the conversation said, 'Thank goodness they still had some at Harrods. That's where I got mine.'

'Where else?' Joyce was unimpressed. 'But you'll need a proper pair of blackouts as well, before the next inspection.

'I have a pair somewhere,' said Clarissa. 'Anyway, it's good to know there's a seamstress in the place.'

'We help each other in this cabin,' Dorothy told her sternly. 'You have to be prepared to help as well as be helped.'

Sylvia settled luxuriously into bed in her new jacket and socks, conscious in her pressing need for sleep that the easy-going atmosphere of the cabin was again under threat. She and Joyce had worked hard in their different ways to assimilate Dorothy into their circle, and now Clarissa presented a challenge of another kind. She thought about that as she drifted off to sleep.

. . .

She had the early watch in the morning, and that left her free from 1300 until 1800, so she was able to answer Freddy's letter in the afternoon. Also, she was alone in the cabin and she could write without interruption.

3rd January, 1944.

Dear Freddy,

Thank you for your 26th November, which arrived two days ago.

I'll tell you my big news first. I'm an auntie! My sister had a little boy just hours after leaving us on the 29th. We went to see them both the next day and my mother said straight away that he looks like Audrey with a bit of David (her husband) as well, and I don't know how people can say these things. I thought he looked like a little red monkey, but I naturally kept that to myself.

To answer your question, my birthday's on the 18th of January and I wish I could send you some cake. I know my mother will bake one but we're not allowed to send food. When's yours? I'll send you a special letter as we're not allowed to send cards either. I think you're right about rules and regulations getting together and breeding when no one's looking. It's the only explanation.

I'm sorry it's so cold where you are. The parcel will help when it arrives. By the way, please don't think I knitted all that stuff myself. I had help from two workmates, my mother and an old lady who lives down the road.

She wondered briefly how Third Officer Fuller might feel if she knew she had been described as a workmate.

Tell me what else you need and I'll send it in the next parcel, rules and regs permitting.

Would it upset you if I told you about things happening here? I'd hate to make you more homesick than ever. Do tell me if I say something clumsy, won't you?

I'm running out of space again. Take care.

Very best wishes, Sylvia X.

She reasoned that the X was allowable after the Christmas precedent, and a man needed a bit of affection in his life anyway, so why not?

. . .

The next workplace for Freddy and Len was a construction site at Niwka, building houses and flats for German families as they spread into Hitler's expanding *Reich*. The guards placed them under the supervision of Helmut Grünewald, a corpulent foreman carpenter who soon proved to be lazy and irresponsible. He treated Len to a hostile stare. The civilian population labelled airmen indiscriminately as 'Terror Flyers' and hated them as such. Len's stripes also attracted the foreman's attention.

'Why are you here?' German workers were all aware that manual labour was not compulsory for corporals and above.

'*Lagergeld*,' said Len.

Grünewald gave him a look of disdain and examined Freddy's uniform for badges. Seeing none, he asked, '*Soldat*?'

'*Nein, Ich bin Marineflieger.*'

The chargehand gave him a look of disgust. '*Verdammt Terrorflieger.*'

'You bastard,' said Freddy, feeling his temper rise. 'Your bloody *Luftwaffe* bombed my house and killed my family. Don't call me a bloody *Terrorflieger*!'

'Careful, mate.' Len grabbed his wrist. 'You'll get yourself shot!'

Fortunately, Grünewald seemed to lack the stomach for a confrontation, because he made a palms-out gesture, urging Freddy to calm down, and appeared visibly relieved when he did.

Later, when they were fixing a cast-iron soil stack to the outside wall of a block of flats they discussed the incident.

"We know two important things," said Freddy. "We know that Grünewald doesn't give a damn how the job's done, so he's not going to keep checking up on us all the time, and we know that he backs down when someone stands up to him."

'And we know something else,' said Len.

'What's that?'

'We know that if I don't keep an eye on you, you won't see your twenty-fifth birthday. You really went too far this morning. I had visions of him calling the goons.'

'I know, but the nerve of the bugger, accusing me of doing what those bastards have been doing ever since Guernica.'

'Yes, and you're not even RAF. I've heard you lot drop all your bombs in the sea.'

'Bugger off, but before you do ...'

'What?'

'Pass me that plugging chisel, will you? And thanks for holding me back this morning.'

'That's all right. I thought they might shoot me too.'

'They might do it yet. The RAF's none too popular, although I can't think why when they can never find their bloody target, but listen, I've got an idea.'

'Your first idea and you're only twenty-four.' Len stood a length of soil pipe on end and leant against it to listen.

'These soil pipes have to stand up to strong winds, don't they?'

Len nodded. 'Inside and out.'

'So if we fix a two-metre length of pipe every half-hour ...'

'As often as that?'

'All right, every hour, and if we plug the wall and secure, say, one per length of pipe in three, if my calculations are correct ...'

'The job will take weeks to complete, the first gale will blow this stack apart and we'll have it all to do again. Yes, this building could become famous for entirely the wrong reason.'

'Like Schubert's "Unfinished" Symphony.'

7

The blokes in the flat above are doing a good job,' said Freddy. 'They've laid those floorboards like professionals.'

'Have they now?' Len was studying a length of soil pipe with the look of a man about to make an important decision.

'Yes, they used just enough nails to fix them to the joists.'

'That was obliging of them.'

'They saved the rest to puncture the gas and water pipes.'

Len suddenly motioned Freddy to be quiet. 'Grünewald's coming.' They set about counting nails with methodical slowness.

It was clear from Grünewald's ingratiating attitude that his visit had nothing to do with work and that he wanted a favour, so they each lit a cigarette and waited for him to speak.

Grünewald beamed. "I see you have English cigarettes."

'Players,' confirmed Len.

'Only the finest tobacco," said Freddy, blowing a fragrant cloud for Grünewald's benefit.

The foreman sniffed the smoke longingly and said, 'Please, you will give me English cigarette?'

Both men feigned horror at his request. 'To take Red Cross cigarettes from a prisoner is *verboten*,' said Len, using one of the few words of German he knew.

Freddy drew a menacing finger across his throat. '*Verboten*.'

'But,' said Len, 'we could possibly come to an arrangement.'

'Arrangement?'

'An agreement,' suggested Freddy.

Grünewald looked uncertainly from one to the other.

33

Freddy asked, 'What have you got for lunch?'

'What is lunch?'

'*Mittagessen.*'

Reluctantly, Grünewald opened his knapsack and took out a napkin containing bread and about six inches of sausage. Freddy indicated where he wanted them cut. It amounted to a slice of bread and two inches of sausage each, a welcome supplement to their usual ration.

Grünewald hesitated until Freddy took five cigarettes from a tin of Players and passed them under his nose. Reluctantly, the German opened his clasp knife to cut the bread and sausage.

'*Vielen Dank*, Helmut.' Freddy handed over the cigarettes.

'Nice work,' said Len after the German had left them. 'Now he's broken the rules once he can't refuse to trade with us again.'

'All we've got to do is stay on the right side of our Neolithic friend and we should be all right here.' Fellow kriegies had warned them about Corporal Brunner, a colossus of a man who ruled by fear and insisted on being addressed as '*Herr Gefreiter*'. It seemed that no one had ever refused him that courtesy.

'Meanwhile,' said Len looking down at the pipes waiting to be fixed, 'I've had an idea.'

'Trot out your idea.'

'These pipes have a socket at one end and a narrower bit at the other, Right?'

'I had noticed.'

'And we've been fixing them with the socket end up so as to catch any leakage at the joints, haven't we?'

'Altogether too conscientious of us, Len.'

'But I'm a clerk and you're a photographer, so neither of us can claim expert plumbing knowledge.'

'None whatsoever.'

'So, in our ignorance, what we have to do is fix them with the socket end down, so that when someone eventually pulls the chain, shit and water will fly all over the glorious *Reich*.'

Freddy considered the prospect and nodded approvingly. 'Let's do that.'

'After lunch.'

'Yes, after lunch.' They had that to look forward to.

. . .

Sylvia put her plate of tinned tomatoes and bacon down beside Joyce's and grimaced. ' "Train smash" is a good name for this muck, isn't it?'

Joyce nodded. 'It's not the most glittering example of Jolly Jack's wit but it describes it fairly accurately.' She gathered her skirt to make way for Clarissa, who was similarly unimpressed with the breakfast fare.

'Surely they don't expect us to eat this,' she said. 'It's horrendous.' She stirred the tomatoes derisively with her fork. 'I bet they're not eating this in the wardroom.'

'I expect officers find other things to belly-ache about,' said Dorothy, taking her place beside Sylvia. 'The grub in there can't always be up to scratch and shortages are a pain whoever you are.'

'Clarissa,' said Joyce, changing the subject, 'weren't those silk stockings you were wearing last night?'

'The genuine article, yes.'

Sylvia gaped. 'Where on earth do you find silk stockings nowadays?'

'My mother stocked up on them before the war, silly.'

'That must have been a heck of a shopping trip,' said Joyce.

'Yes, she bought all the essential things that she knew would be difficult to get: stockings, make-up, perfume, cold cream and that sort of thing.'

'Not food?'

'Of course she bought food. She's not stupid.'

'And you've still got several pairs of stockings?'

'I have a few pairs. I look after them. It's the only way.'

Sylvia felt her pulse quickening. 'Would you consider lending a pair occasionally to one of your comrades-in-arms?' There was a dance at Dover Garrison on the twenty-fifth.

'Absolutely not.' Clarissa looked horrified. 'If I did that I'd have half the service coming to me for them. A line has to be drawn somewhere, you know.'

'Well,' said Joyce, 'at least we know now where your line is. It's something we'll have to bear in mind.'

It was a frustrating day, and a spell of squad drill in the freezing wind did nothing to improve it. Their drill instructor on this occasion was PO Wren Shaw, a stern, forbidding woman of mature years – at least thirty – and the kind of martinet the sailors called 'pusser' or 'anchor-faced'. The Wrens knew exactly where they stood.

The PO Wren stood them at ease to speak to them. 'PO Barton regrets he's unable to drill you today, girls,' she announced. 'He is otherwise engaged. There is a scurrilous buzz doing the rounds that you broke his heart, and whether or not that is true, I need hardly tell you that you will not break mine. As some of you who have fallen foul of me in the past know to your cost, I do not possess one. There will be no silly excuses or pantomime performances, and when I give the order to about-turn on the march you will carry out that manoeuvre smartly, neatly and without vocal refrain. Now, squad … squad, shun!'

The only light relief came at the end of the day when they were preparing for bed. Clarissa rubbed her feet and said, 'Where did you get those bed socks, Sylvia? My poor little piggies are frozen silly.'

'My mother made them for me. They're easy enough to knit.'

Clarissa sniffed. 'Easy for you, maybe.' Suddenly she brightened. 'I say, if I paid for the wool and gave you the coupons, would you knit a pair for me?'

For Sylvia, usually so easygoing and good-natured, it was the end of a long, hard day and her patience was dwindling rapidly. 'I couldn't possibly do that,' she said. 'If I did, half the service would want them.'

Dorothy added sleepily, 'The line has to be drawn somewhere, Clarissa.'

. . .

Freddy could scarcely believe what he found in the parcel. The sweater alone would have made a handsome gift, but there were toiletries, a scarf, a balaclava, mittens, socks and – exquisite joy – warm underwear.

Len watched him, enjoying the satisfaction of a job well done. 'It's made all that letter-writing worthwhile, hasn't it?'

'I never expected this, Len. She's really pushed the boat out.' He handled each item again, running his fingers over the clean wool and scenting its freshness.

'And when it gets colder you're going to need it.'

The clothes were marvellous but that wasn't all. He had been writing to Sylvia since October and felt that he knew quite a lot about her. Even so, everything had seemed rather two-dimensional. Now that had changed and it was as if the contents of the parcel made everything much more tangible and Sylvia more real. He was beginning to realise as well that he was dealing with a special kind of girl.

8

The letter was dated the nineteenth of December. It had taken a month to arrive.

Dear Sylvia,

And believe me you are dear, most particularly because you're the only person still speaking to me. Well, there's Len of course, but he'll talk to anyone who'll listen.

All this, if you please, is because of a conversation that took place last night when a certain Seaforth Highlander stated his post-war intention of becoming a pacifist. This prompted the person in the lower bunk, a sapper of limited imagination and entrenched views, to make a challenging comment, a foolhardy act in a hut populated largely by Seaforths and Argylls. Well, the argument raged on with the Jocks scenting a juicy massacre to rival Bannockburn, until I spoke up for the gentle minority and asked the opposing forces to snarl a little more quietly so that the rest of us could sleep. I have to report that I am now marginally less popular than a carol-singer in a turkey run.

Take care, dear Sylvia. I may need a friend after the war as well.

Yours, with very best wishes,

Freddy X

P.S: I was considering a post-war holiday in Scotland but I think Bridlington will be safer. Don't you?

P.P.S: I'm sorry if my letters seem somewhat abstract, nebulous, arcane, abstruse, perhaps recondite and devoid of real information but subject-matter is limited.

Sylvia folded the letter and returned it to her bag. It was good that it had arrived on her birthday, and it was a shame he was worried that he had so little he could tell her. It wasn't his fault, and she enjoyed his bits of nonsense anyway. She knew perfectly well that the story about the silly argument was a gross exaggeration, and she suspected he had used the obscure words at the end simply to give the German censor a headache. As far as she could tell, he was just being Freddy, and that was enough for her. It was a pity he couldn't have a piece of her birthday cake, because it was a beauty. Her mother had made it with real farm butter. One of her father's clients must have been generous or at least made a payment in kind.

With a borrowed knife and several paper bags from the galley, she proceeded to cut pieces for her friends and deserving colleagues. There was a piece for everyone on her watch in the W/T Room, for the watch she was relieving and for Third Officer Fuller because she was a good hand. Dorothy and Clarissa had already had theirs and Joyce would get hers when she returned from the Sick Bay, where she was laid low with tonsillitis. Her bed was one of several that occupied a room in the former hotel's bridal suite but she was too ill to appreciate her surroundings.

Sylvia was more popular than usual when she went on watch a little before 2300 and distributed the cake. Some members of the watch pulled her leg about her advancing years now that she was twenty, and there was an easy atmosphere in the room as the watch commenced.

Signal traffic began to increase after 0200 and before long a flurry of transmissions suggested to Sylvia that the patrol had sighted, and was probably about to engage, the enemy. The signals she received and transmitted were all encoded, so the only indication she had of what might be happening was the precedence prosign that accompanied each signal. 'P' for 'Priority' meant that the signal was important, 'OP' meant 'Immediate', 'O' signified an emergency and 'OU' was 'Most Immediate'. The latter was used to report an enemy sighting. Eighteen months after passing out as a telegraphist Sylvia could still not read the 'OU' prosign without a twinge of apprehension. It was a fleeting sensation because then she had to concentrate on reading the signal accurately, but it was no less unsettling when it occurred.

It was not long before another dreaded 'Most Immediate' materialised and Sylvia's pencil moved rapidly across the signal pad. It was a brief signal, as sighting reports usually were, and having receipted it she held it aloft for the PO Wren, who took it immediately to be decoded.

There was a series of Immediates, all very brief but still requiring prompt attention, and then the circuit went quiet for a spell, during which Sylvia could only presume that the boats were in action. A glance around the room told her that everyone was feeling the same tension. More for something to do than for the need of it, she lit a cigarette, and when she had smoked it halfway down she heard *Wasp*'s call-sign, indistinct and barely recognisable. The calling station's call-sign, however, was completely unreadable. Using 'AA', the 'Unknown Station' prosign, she sent 'ZGF', the operating signal that meant 'Make your call-signs distinctly.'

Something in her expression must have alerted the PO Wren, who switched on the loudspeaker. Sylvia pulled her headphones off to hear the amplified signal as the calling station tried again, and once more she was obliged to send 'ZGF'.

The unknown station's third attempt was successful. His call-sign identified his ship as Motor Torpedo Boat 894, and the precedence of the signal was 'Priority'. With the PO at her shoulder, Sylvia sent 'K', the invitation to transmit his signal.

His Morse was very bad and painfully slow – no more than twelve to fifteen words per minute, and it was also strange that the text of the signal was coming through in plain language. 'ha e s st a ed h vy cas lt s. 8 er ously wounded. eq   med ...'Thereafter, the signal became unreadable, so Sylvia broke in and requested a repetition of everything after 'wounded'. She could make sense of the first two sentences. The PO nodded her approval.

After two attempts, Sylvia managed to make out, 'Request medical assistance on arrival.' The sender gave his Estimated Time of Arrival, which was mercifully easier to read, and she receipted the signal. It now read, 'Have sustained heavy casualties. 8 seriously wounded. Request medical assistance on arrival. ETA 0350.' The PO picked up the signal form and, after a quick word with the Duty Officer, took it to the Signal Distribution Room.

'Either the boat's equipment was damaged or the telegraphist was wounded,' she said on her return. 'Either way, we've done all we can. Good girl. Well done.'

Sylvia had little time to think about it until her next break at 0500, when she agonised over the incident repeatedly before concluding that the MTB's transmitter had not been damaged. The fact that the telegraphist had sent the signal in plain language and in slow, badly-formed Morse was an indication that he was seriously wounded, and she had aggravated his suffering by failing to read his signal the first time. It was too horrible for words.

Having handed over to her relief at 0800, she left the W/T Room, mumbled a preoccupied 'Good morning' to the Royal Marine sentry who was just taking over the watch at the Wrens' entrance, and went up to the cabin.

Her birthday cards were just as she had left them, the remains of the cake were still in their box on the table and the writing case, a present from

39

her parents, lay on her bed. But none of it mattered any more. Slowly, she undressed and slid into bed, turning her tear-soaked face to the bulkhead so that she needn't speak to her cabin mates when they came in.

For some time, she lay in the same position, knees drawn up under her chin, cocooned beneath her bed clothes and detached just for the time being from the horrors of the world. Eventually, she slept.

At about three o'clock in the afternoon, after a shallow and tepid bath, she dressed and went up to the Sick Bay, where she found Joyce weak after her fever, but now able to speak without undue discomfort.

'Happy birthday,' said Joyce. 'Or have I missed it? I've lost all track of time.'

'It was yesterday, and I'm not surprised. You're allowed to ramble when you're running a temperature. There's a piece of cake waiting for you when you're back in the land of the living.'

Joyce winced. 'I'm sure I'll appreciate it but please don't talk about food yet.'

'All right, I won't.'

Joyce was looking at her oddly. 'Are you all right, Sylvia? You look as if you've been crying.'

Tears were threatening again. She wanted desperately to tell Joyce about the previous night but it wouldn't be fair to do that until she was better. Instead she said, 'No, I'm just waiting for you to come back to the cabin. I'm tired of Dorothy complaining about men, and Clarissa boasting about them. You know she's seeing a sub-lieutenant now, don't you?'

'Nothing would surprise me about Clarissa.'

'He's taking her to the Signal Section dance in the Garrison on the twenty-fifth.'

'Good luck to the poor man.'

It was evident that Joyce was feeling weak, so Sylvia made her excuse and left her.

She met Will at the bottom of the stairs. He asked, 'How's Joyce?'

'Improving. She'll be back soon.' She braced herself to ask, 'What's the news about MTB Eight-Nine-Four?'

He grimaced. 'She was badly shot up. There were lots of casualties. The sparker died on his way to hospital, poor devil.'

. . .

Freddy and Len seldom had the opportunity to admire the handiwork of the other kriegies, but Grünewald had been called away on some matter, and the goons, including Brunner, hadn't a clue about building, so they got out of the cutting wind and had a look around inside one of the two-storey houses.

In the kitchen they found the installation of a fireback boiler being carried out under the misdirection of Bombardier 'Bullshit' Bailey of the Royal Artillery. He was tall, with delicate, aesthetic features, and he welcomed them as if into his home.

'Come in, gentlemen. Take a seat and gaze in admiration, because as long as you live you will never see such a display of utter shit masquerading as craftsmanship.' Proudly, he waved an outstretched arm as if at an unveiling ceremony. 'The fireback boiler you now see in the fireplace is connected to a tank that supplies the sink, the wash basin and bath, and of course, the lavatory cistern. With every flush the latter will be replenished with scalding water. Cold water, my friends, will be a thing of the past, and from now on the smallest room in the house will be the place where an overwrought German householder can go, quite literally, to let off steam.'

Freddy and Len applauded.

'It's all right for 'im to talk,' said a Sherwood Forester. 'We're the ones what does most of the work.'

'I do the planning,' Bailey reminded him. 'Someone has to see the overall picture and bring everything efficiently together. It's not given to everyone, you know.'

''E believes all this,' said the Sherwood Forester. ''E's said it so many times he's come to believe it himself.'

Ignoring his colleague, Bailey sat on a stool made of floorboard off-cuts and lit a cigarette. 'I suppose we're all wasted,' he said. 'They asked us what we did before the war and we could have told them anything for all the notice they took. They put bakers to blacksmithing and carpenters to coal-mining. What did you chaps do?'

'I worked in a building society,' said Len, 'and Freddy was a photographer.'

'Good, good,' said Bailey, not really listening. 'I was in the motor car retail business in Edgware. Lovely clientele.'

''E was a second-hand car salesman,' said the Sherwood Forester.

'And a successful one,' said Bailey, deftly turning near-embarrassment to advantage. 'It was a nice living before this pestilential war came along.' He smiled at the memory and said, 'Happy days. I wonder if we'll ever see their like again.' He nipped out his cigarette to save the remainder for later, and extinguished the burning tobacco with the sole of his boot. 'And it wasn't all work, by any means. Sometimes I would take one of the ladies of my acquaintance for a picnic on the river, or we'd go into town and eat at a little place I know in Piccadilly, and then we'd go on to somewhere else and dance the night away.' He sighed. 'Happy days.'

'Very nice.'

'Yes, very nice.'

The Sherwood Forester was unimpressed. 'Some night out,' he said. When did you find the time for a poke in all of that?'

Bailey sighed theatrically. 'Trust the infantry to lower the tone of the conversation.' Turning wearily to the Sherwood Forester, he said, 'It's not the kind of information I divulge, you ribald rifleman. Some things call for discretion, you know.'

The Sherwood Forester shrugged and said, 'I tell me mates when I've had me leg over. You've got to talk about somethin' when you're out for a pint.'

Whether or not there was any truth in Bailey's reminiscence, it had set Freddy thinking.He and Len had escaped twice. The first time was shortly after the Italian armistice was signed. The guards had simply walked out of the camp and gone home, and some of the prisoners, including Freddy and Len, had followed them, only to walk into a German patrol before they could get anywhere near the Swiss frontier. The second occasion was when the train taking them to Lamsdorf slowed down because of an obstruction close to the Czech border. They had slipped quietly on to the track and into the trees, and might well have found shelter and assistance had it not been for Len spraining his ankle, and an alert policeman, who handed them over to the occupying force.

On both occasions they had each had different reasons for escaping. Len's motivation was to get back to Joyce and his home in England. The Air Force had always been a poor third. Freddy, however, wanted to escape captivity, to become free of lice, to use a WC – preferably with a door on it – and to enjoy three normal meals per day. He had no home, no family and no job, his employer's studio also having been destroyed in the Blitz. He would have been happy to fly again and attack enemy shipping; otherwise he had no pressing reason to return to England.

That was how he had felt then, but now things were different. Len had been right when he said that news from beyond the water would be a tonic for him. His correspondence with Sylvia had taken his interest far beyond the wire, and he waited for her letters because he wanted to hear her news. She had made him see that life could still go on in England. He could look forward to that once more, and he wanted to meet her, not just because he wanted to thank her for lots of things, but because he believed he was coming to know her through her letters, and he liked what he knew.

. . .

Sylvia liked herself rather less. She had spent most of her day off avoiding people who knew her, and spending as little time with them as possible when she could not. It was very wearing and she was relieved when her turn came for orderly duty. For once, she welcomed the solitary cleaning tasks.

When she went back on watch she had the luxury of being too busy to think about anything other than what she was doing, at least some of the time, but at the end of the watch the PO Wren waited until their reliefs had taken over, and then beckoned her aside.

'I've been meaning to speak to you,' she said.

'Yes, PO?

'You're like a dying duck in a thunderstorm, Wren Charlesworth. What's the matter?'

Sylvia was about to make an excuse about a headache, but she held the words back when she felt tears forming behind her eyelids. They had never been far away.

'It's about Thursday night, isn't it, the telegraphist who was killed?'

Sylvia nodded mutely.

'I thought so.' She glanced up at the loudspeaker and said, 'I couldn't read his Morse either. That's why I switched the loudspeaker on, to hear what you were struggling with, but I couldn't make it out.'

'But I should have been able to read it.'

'You did what you had to. You sent 'ZGF' until you could read his call-sign, and that's exactly what I would have done.'

'But all those repetitions ....'

'Two repetitions, that's all. If you look at the log you'll find that the whole thing occupied no more than two minutes.'

'He must have been in agony.' Her tears were coming freely now. She tried to stem them with her handkerchief.

'Very likely, but it wasn't your fault, and you've got to stop thinking it was, because unless you pull yourself together you're going to be no use at all to us and those he left behind.'

Everything the PO had said made perfect sense, but logic was of little use to Sylvia. She went up to the cabin as dejected as before.

Over the next two days she tried to act on the PO's advice. Joyce returned from the Sick Bay to provide a ready ear when they occasionally had the cabin to themselves, and Sylvia's misery gradually subsided, leaving only the nagging conviction that, despite all that had been said, she had somehow failed the wounded telegraphist.

There were distractions, one of which was the announcement that watches were to be reorganised forthwith. The Senior Signals Officer gave no explanation, but for Sylvia and her cabin mates it meant that they would be on watch on the evening of the dance at the Garrison.

Ray Hobbs

The other distraction was a letter from Freddy. It was dated the twenty-seventh of December and it struck her initially as strange, even by Freddy's idiosyncratic standards.

Dear Sylvia,

Did you know that the Four Horsemen of the Apocalypse are members of a wider family? I saw some of their cousins recently: Torment, Anguish, Degradation and Hopelessness. I watched them and then I had to turn away. I couldn't help them or even speak to them but I felt guilty. Why? I hadn't mistreated them, I hadn't withheld anything from them, and I hadn't taken their hope and left them with nothing.

I think I've found the answer and I want to share my theory with you. You see, I think children are weaned on guilt, both real and imagined. They waste food while African children starve, they bring shame on their families with their behaviour, and when they long for fine weather in the school holidays they're told sternly about drought and famine. They learn always to question their own actions, and the habit persists even in adulthood. We are brought up to assume guilt and it's a difficult habit to break, hence my dilemma. I'm sorry this has been rather sombre, but do you agree? My next letter will be in the usual mindless, light-hearted vein.

Yours with very best wishes for 1944,

Freddy.

P.S. I may take up psychoanalysis after the war. There'll be no shortage of crackpots, and I reckon quite a lot will need help when the great day comes.

P.P.S. On reflection, I'll keep the photography going as well. I could offer my clients pictures of themselves before and after therapy.

Sylvia read the letter several times before sleeping on it. In the morning she went cheerfully on watch.

9

Clarissa's ball gown hung from the top of her locker. It was made of pale-green satin, the kind of thing no one had seen since before the war. She stroked it and asked, 'What do you think of it?'

'You've gorra ladder in your left stockin',' said Dorothy.

'Oh God, no.' Clarissa looked down urgently. 'Where?'

'Only kiddin'.'

The others didn't trust themselves to speak. While Clarissa was dancing they would be on watch.

'That was cruel, Dorothy, just when I want to look my best.'

Dorothy studied her and said, 'Go on, then. Tell us how you wangled the night off, like.'

'I arranged for one of the other girls to do my watch. There's nothing unusual about that, is there?'

'No, but when are you doin' one for her?'

Clarissa shook her head. 'She never said anything about that.'

Joyce could remain silent no longer. Being married, she wouldn't have gone to the dance anyway, but her friends had been looking forward to it until the SSO changed the watches. 'The custom,' she said, 'is that if someone does a watch for you, Clarissa, it's only right to return the favour.'

'My God,' said Clarissa, stepping into her gown. 'You people put a price on everything.'

Sylvia gave way to her curiosity and asked, 'Who's doing your watch?'

'Is this the Spanish Inquisition or something? Suddenly I feel as if I'm on trial.'

'I was only wondering.'

'If you must know, it's Emily Roberts.'

It made sense. Emily was socially inept and would never have gone to the dance anyway. She was also docile enough to let Clarissa walk all over her. A quick look at the others told Sylvia that they shared her thoughts.

Joyce glanced at her watch and said, 'Shall we go?' They had ten minutes or more before the watch changed but they nodded and followed her to the door.

'Just a minute,' said Clarissa. 'I need one of you to zip me up before you go.'

Dorothy, the last one out, was about to close the door behind her. She leaned inwards and said, 'Sorry, Clarissa. We don't want to be adrift. It wouldn't be fair on the girls we're relievin', but you wouldn't know about that, would you?'

As they walked to the stairs, Joyce said, 'I wonder if she was born selfish or if they taught her that at school.'

'It's what comes of 'avin' servants,' said Dorothy. 'They leave home an' they're helpless. Some of 'em can't even wipe their own bums.'

Sylvia said, 'Does anyone know her first name?'

Joyce frowned. 'We all know her first name.'

'No, Clarissa's her second name. She signs herself E.C. Bonnington, and I just wonder what the "E" stands for.'

'She's kept very quiet about it. Maybe her parents saddled her with something embarrassing. What do you think it might be?'

'Emmeline?'

'Eglantine, Esmeralda?'

'Evangeline,' said Dorothy. 'There was a girl at school called that. She was from the orphanage. The nuns found her on the doorstep when she was a baby an' nobody knew who her mam was.'

'That's tragic,' said Joyce. 'It's bad enough being an orphan, but to hell with going through life with a name like Evangeline.'

They reached the corridor that led to their respective workplaces and found Will about to enter the W/T Room.

'Hello girls,' he said. 'What's the buzz?'

'We've been trying to guess Clarissa's first name,' said Sylvia. 'It begins with "E" and we think it must be embarrassing. Have you any ideas?'

'Is she the one who's applied for officer training?' Will was usually abreast of such things.

They looked at each other in surprise. 'Has she?'

'I think it's her. Fair hair, about five-foot-two-or-three, blue eyes, pointed nose, neat little ....'

'That's her,' said Joyce. 'Do you think she stands a chance?'

46

'By all accounts she's clueless enough, and you never know with the Andrew. They promote some strange people. Anyway, what names have you come up with so far?'

They listed as many as they could remember and added a couple more. Will gave it some thought and said eventually, 'I see her as an Ermintrude.'

'Perfect.'

'Yes.'

'That's just right for 'er.'

Thereafter, whenever Clarissa was out of earshot her name was Ermintrude.

. . .

Freddy, Len and Ernie Houghton, a private in the Durham Light Infantry stood in conversation. They had just eaten their evening allowance of a small piece of hard cheese and a slice of black bread.

'I suppose it's the mint tea now,' said Ernie. 'There's bugger-all else.' No one could get excited about the mint tea the Germans provided. Most kriegies drank a mouthful of it in the absence of anything else and used the rest for shaving.

'I've still got some Red Cross tea,' said Freddy. 'Let's get some water on and have a wet. There's enough for three of us.'

'That's very civil of you, bonny lad. I'll get some water.' Ernie took an empty powdered-milk tin to the pump while Freddy claimed the remains of a wood fire on which two kriegies had been trying unsuccessfully to fry a tin of corned beef from a Red Cross parcel. Len placed his home-made hob over the flames. He had fashioned it from a piece of broken grating and some off-cuts of steel tube from the building site.

'That's a canny hob, Len,' said Ernie, returning with the water.

'Well, it's done all right so far.' Len studied the hob critically and said, 'I wonder sometimes what we're going to do with all this new-found ingenuity when the war's over.'

'I think we'll try to forget it along with everything else,' said Freddy. 'I don't think we'll be all that keen to be reminded of this.'

Whether or not his companions agreed with him he had no idea because a voice from behind silenced them all with a word.

'Brunner!'

Freddy spotted him in the gateway to the compound, still at first, his eyes moving systematically from left to right. He must have been close to six-feet-six, and with his powerful physique he dwarfed the guards who flanked him. As he approached the hut, Freddy noticed his dark, closely-cropped hair and brown, uneven teeth.

The party stopped at the hut doorway whilst Brunner stepped inside, looking around at the prisoners gathered there, and nodding to himself, as if confirming some previous surmise. Eventually, his eye fell on an RAF corporal.

'*Zigaretten*,' he demanded.

The airman patted his pockets to show that he had none. It was a mistake, because the German struck him hard across the mouth with the back of his hand and repeated his demand. '*Zigaretten*!'

Freddy felt Ernie's hand on his wrist, a warning to be still, and he watched the airman reach for his haversack, one hand clutched to his mouth, which was bleeding copiously.

Brunner snatched the haversack and upended it so that its contents fell to the earthen floor. There was a full packet of cigarettes, an opened packet and a few remaining ounces of chocolate from a Red Cross parcel. Brunner threw the opened packet of cigarettes to one of the guards and pocketed the unopened one along with the chocolate. He turned to the door and seemed about to go, but then he paused to look back at the unfortunate airman and appeared to come to a decision. With studied deliberation he re-crossed the hut and struck the man another massive blow. 'Soon I return,' he said, addressing everyone else in the hut. Then, recognising a semblance of a joke, he grinned and added, 'Like the American *Herr General*, I return!'

Someone found a cotton pad in the first aid box and gave it to the injured airman to stop the bleeding, while the others watched Brunner walk away.

'He's a bastard-and-a-half, that one,' said Ernie. 'Now you know why it's a good idea to keep out of the bugger's way.'

Freddy nodded.

'Keep telling him, Ernie,' said Len.

. . .

Sylvia looked down at her soya links and reconstituted egg. 'I prefer pilchards,' she said, 'and that's saying something.'

'It gets worse,' said Dorothy, demolishing hers all the same.

Joyce looked up and said, 'Here's Ermintrude.' She made room for her on the bench.

Clarissa brought her breakfast to the table with a martyr's sigh.

'They're 'avin' porridge an' kippers in the wardroom,' Dorothy told her. 'I heard one of the officers say.'

Joyce nodded. 'Second Officer Bright-Davies, wasn't it?'

Sylvia shook her head. 'No, it was First Officer Finch, I'm sure.'

'That's right,' agreed Dorothy.

Clarissa gave them a puzzled look and cut into a Soya link. 'You may as well all know that I've applied for officer training.'

'We know,' said Sylvia.

'What I don't understand,' said Joyce, thankfully laying down her knife and fork, 'is why you're doing it now. I mean to say, why don't you wait 'til you know a bit more about the job before putting yourself in charge of it?'

Clarissa shrugged dismissively. 'Everyone seems to know what they're doing. As I see it, the job takes care of itself.'

The other three exchanged mystified looks.

'Anyway, how did you all hear about it?'

'First Officer Finch told us,' said Joyce.

'Yeah, when she gave us the forms, like.'

It was Clarissa's turn to frown. 'What forms?'

'We each have to fill in a form about you,' Sylvia explained. 'It's very important, apparently, and all the information gets entered on your history sheet.'

Clarissa's eyes grew wide. 'What sort of information?'

'Oh, just what you're like as a cabin mate and a colleague.'

'That's right,' said Joyce. 'Before they can proceed with the training they need to know that you have certain qualities.'

'What kind of qualities?'

'Selflessness is important.'

'What?'

'Selflessness,' said Dorothy. 'It means not bein' a selfish cow.'

'I know what it means. I'm not stupid.'

'Well then.'

'I just don't see what it's got to do with being an officer.'

'Selflessness,' said Joyce, 'is an officer-like quality. It's about putting the Service and your colleagues first. You'll even have to consider us lesser mortals from time to time.'

'Oh crumbs.' Clarissa looked down at her nails. 'Have you already filled in these forms?'

'Are you serious?' Joyce looked at her watch. 'We've been on watch all night, and I can only speak for myself but I'm doing nothing until I've had at least six hours' sleep.'

'Me too.'

'Me an' all.'

'Oh good, because it doesn't do to be hasty about these things. I mean to say, some things are negotiable, aren't they?'

'Some things are, yes,' said Joyce. 'Emily Roberts would probably agree with that.'

'Emily Roberts? Oh yes.' Memories of the Garrison dance returned. 'I'll arrange to do one of her watches.'

'Good. You know, you're shaping up already.'

'Really? Because, you see, there's something else that's been troubling me.'

'Better get it off your chest, Clarissa,' said Joyce.

'Yes, well, we had a discussion over breakfast not long ago. At least, it wasn't so much a discussion as, well, the subject of stockings happened to arise.'

'Silk stockings,' confirmed Sylvia.

'Yes, and maybe I was a little ....'

'Cow?'

'No, Dorothy. I was going to say I was a little selfish. There, I've said it.'

'You're human after all,' said Joyce.

'Well, we are cabin mates and we've known one another for some time, so I think I can spare three pairs. That's one pair each.' She added, 'They're the finest quality.'

'And so are you, Clarissa.'

'Absolutely.'

'Yeah, you're all right.'

'Oh good.' She looked at her watch and said, 'Well, I'd better see if I can catch Emily. I'd like her to know I haven't forgotten her.'

'Yeah, that's right.'

'That's the spirit.'

' "England expects", Clarissa.'

. . .

It appeared that *Gefreiter* Brunner had been detailed to watch over the hut in which Freddy and Len were quartered, because he turned up again in the morning to march its occupants to their place of work. He looked around for his victim from the previous night and when he was informed that the man was in hospital with a broken jaw, raised his right fist with oafish bravado. Then, satisfied that his awesome power had impressed the prisoners, he formed them up three deep and marched them out of the gates on their half-mile journey to the building site.

It was normal for the prisoners to see members of the local population as they went to work but there was rarely any contact between them. The guards were the inhibiting factor, and it was particularly remarkable that an old woman in the inevitable black dress and shawl should try to give a piece of bread to one of the prisoners that morning.

Freddy saw her offer the bread, he saw the prisoner reach out to take it, and then with a sense of horror he watched Brunner dash the bread from her hand and hit her with the same terrible force he had inflicted on the airman the night before. The woman fell screaming to the ground, and on a reflex Freddy shouted, 'Leave her alone, you evil bastard!' With the corner of his eye he saw Ernie grab Len by the arm, and then Brunner stood before him, eyeing him with a mixture of surprise and amused contempt.

'*Was hast du gesagt?*'

Having come so far, Freddy was not going to back down, and there was just a chance that Brunner might respond to reason. 'The poor woman's done nothing wrong and she needs treatment now. Look, she's in agony!'

Brunner turned to look at the woman, now writhing in the road, before returning his attention to the upstart before him. Slowly, and without taking his eyes away from Freddy, he unslung his rifle and handed it to the nearest guard. It was clear what he was about to do, and Freddy had to dissuade him very quickly.

'Twenty-eight witnesses, *Herr Gefreiter* ...' He continued in German. 'Twenty-eight of us saw a soldier of the *Wehrmacht* strike that woman and leave her to suffer. I wonder what the inspecting officer will say about that.'

Brunner looked again at the woman, who was now on her feet but still howling in pain. He seemed undecided for a moment, and then took his rifle from the guard and ordered him to escort her to the doctor's house. 'She will be cared for,' he told Freddy, shoving him back into line. March!'

When they had reached the building site and were at liberty to speak again, Len said, 'You must be the luckiest bugger in creation.'

'I'll second that,' said Ernie, 'but I reckon you'll be well advised to keep a low profile from now on, marrer.'

10

Ever since joining the WRNS, Sylvia had been familiar with the term 'going ashore'. She had learned that it could mean leaving a real warship for *terra firma* – not that she was ever likely to be given that opportunity – or it could mean simply stepping outside the gates of a naval establishment as she just had. Even so, 'runs ashore' were hardly routine; there was little entertainment apart from the cinema, and screenings of the films she wanted to see had to coincide with her time off. Otherwise, there were only the pubs that had so far survived the shelling, and she had been brought up to believe that no respectable girl would ever enter a pub without a male escort. On this occasion, however, Sylvia, Joyce and Dorothy were ashore in the company of Will Hay and two of the Royal Marines who regularly guarded the Wrens' entrance. They were Norris Turner and Alf Bungay. Norris, a lance-corporal, was a garrulous, self-assured Londoner, who contrasted sharply with Alf in every way. Alf was from Suffolk and had been a farm worker before the war. He was unusually tall – he admitted shyly to being a little over six-feet-five – and with a farm worker's physique. However, in spite of his presence he was shy and said very little, usually allowing Norris to speak for him.

They sat around the fire in the public bar of The Cinque Ports Arms, the lounge bar being frequented by locals, and Sylvia had just taken a sip of cider. She wasn't all that keen on it but she was expected to drink something, and Joyce and Dorothy were drinking the same, so she went along with it. It was the run ashore and the company that were important.

Norris asked, 'Heard any good jokes, Will?'

Will considered the question and said, 'There's the one about the ironing board salesman. Have you heard that?'

'Don't think so. Is it fit for the delicate ears of these young ladies?'

'I think so. Are you feeling broad-minded, girls?'

'Go on,' said Joyce. 'Let's hear it.'

'All right.' Will beamed around at his audience. 'There was a commercial traveller and he was selling ironing boards. Well, he was travelling overnight from London to Edinburgh …'

'He had a big territory,' said Joyce.

'Yeah.' Dorothy was equally surprised. 'My Uncle Dermot's a salesman an' he's only got East Bootle to cover.'

'All right, he had a big territory. Anyway, he was on the sleeper from King's Cross and he had an ironing board with him so that he could demonstrate it. Well, the only place he could keep it overnight was beside him in his bunk, and it was one of those sleeper compartments that you have to share with everybody else …'

'What, even people you don't know, like?'

'Yes, Dorothy. The bunks have curtains on them. It's not that public.'

'Well, I think it's barbaric,' said Joyce. 'What do you think, Sylvia?'

'I don't fancy it at all.'

'Girls, girls,' said Will, 'will you let me tell the story? Anyway, he's in a top bunk and he's got the ironing board with him and he strikes up a conversation with the girl in the top bunk opposite.'

Dorothy sat open-mouthed. 'What, just like that? She lying there in her nightie an' she starts talkin' to him?'

'Yes, and …'

'The hussy. I wouldn't dream of doin' that. Would you, girls?'

'Girls, do you want to hear this joke or not?

'Yes,' said Norris, 'play the game, girls.'

'Right,' Will continued. 'Well, they were getting on ever so well and everyone else was asleep, so he said to her, "Hey, do you fancy coming over and joining me?" And she says, "Yes, but how," because they were both in top bunks, you see, and he could feel his ironing board next to him and it gave him an idea. He said, "I've got something here that's long and stiff and I can lay it between our bunks so you can crawl across." And she said – no, girls, wait for it. Don't interrupt me now – and she said, "That's all very well, but how am I going to get back?" '

Norris and Will became helpless with laughter, Joyce was laughing, although not with quite the same abandon, and Sylvia was relieved to see that she wasn't the only one who hadn't got it. Dorothy looked puzzled and Alf was only laughing politely. Of course, it was possible that he had got it but was embarrassed in mixed company. Joyce noticed their expressions and said, 'I'll explain it to you two later.'

After that, Norris told a joke about a bishop and a showgirl in the blackout, and then in his self-important way called for silence.

'Members of the congregation,' he began, 'I call upon the Reverend Will Hay, leading telegraphist in his spare time, to read The Gospel According to Jack.'

'Oh no.' Will looked at the girls and shook his head.

'Go on, Will,' said Joyce. 'We shan't be embarrassed if you're not.'

Sylvia really didn't mind. She knew that The Gospel According to Jack was a dirty shaggy-dog story that sailors liked to laugh at even though they'd heard it many times, but it would probably be lost on her anyway.

'No,' said Will. 'Not in a public place and certainly not in mixed company.'

'Well, said Norris, 'it looks as if the job's going to fall to the bootnecks as usual.'

'Oh no, it's not,' said Will. 'For one thing, it's not fit for these girls to hear, and for another, you'd get us chucked out of this pub. Let's have a game of darts instead.'

'All right.' Norris was easily led.

'I'll get the darts.'

As Will went to the bar to speak to the landlord, Sylvia realised that Alf was standing next to her and that he had barely spoken a word for quite some time, so she decided to make conversation.

'What made you decide to join the Marines, Alf?'

Alf turned and looked at her uncertainly, possibly surprised by the question or just by the fact that a young woman had spoken to him, and said, 'I didn't decide. They decided it for me.' He spoke slowly and with a strange accent, but she had no difficulty understanding him.

'How did that happen?'

'Well, I went to the office in Ipswich, see, and I told the man I wanted to join the Navy.'

'The Navy?'

'Yes, an' he told me there was no more places in the Navy.' Now that he had started he seemed to have lost some of his shyness. 'They'd all been took up for the time being.'

'I suppose that happens from time to time.' She had only asked the question out of politeness but she was quite interested to hear his story now, and she was not alone. Dorothy was also listening.

'Yes, so I says to 'im, "That's a shame," I says, " 'cause I've always wanted to go to sea. Not for a livin', like, but just for the experience", and he says, "In that case, why don't you join the Royal Marines?" '

By this time, everyone was listening, possibly because it was the most they'd ever heard him say.

'So you got what you wanted in the end.'

'That's right. He eyed me up an' down and said, "You're a big chap. They'll make two Marines out of you." '

There was a laughing snort from Norris, who said, 'And they're still trying to make the first.'

'I'm doin' all right, boy.'

'That's what you think.'

Dorothy was bristling. 'I know who makes me feel safest when he's on our door,' she said, 'so just leave off, right?'

Norris seemed about to say something and then thought better of it. He had never seen Dorothy angry and, now Sylvia thought about it, neither had anyone else. It was quite a surprise.

'Right,' said Will, returning with the pub's darts in his hand, 'we can't really have two teams of three because one team would have one girl and the other would have two.'

'What you're tryin' to say',' said Dorothy, 'is that us girls can't throw darts, right?'

'Well, not in so many words. I'm just trying to be fair.'

'We could take you on, us three against you fellas.'

'No, I'll tell you what. Let's have three teams of two, we'll play three legs, and if two teams get there in the same number of throws we'll have a play-off.

Sylvia decided that it was all very complicated. She wished they were playing dominoes, because she could do that.

'I'll take Sylvia,' said Will, 'Norris'll take Joyce and that leaves Alf and Dorothy, okay?'

The match began. Will scored eighty-five with his first three darts, Norris got twenty-four and Alf scored thirty-two. Then it was the girls' turn. Sylvia managed to get one dart on the board and that made sixteen, Joyce scored twenty-eight and Dorothy threw two trebles and a double top to score a hundred. She and Alf went on to win the first leg. In the second, Sylvia made some improvement and with her first throw got two darts on the board for eighteen. Joyce ran out of form and scored only fourteen, whereas Dorothy excelled again. The second leg went to her and Alf.

'These pub darts are useless,' said Norris. 'The whole world's used 'em. They're not even sharp any more.'

'You know what they say about a workman who blames his tools,' said Dorothy. 'It's to be hoped you're better with a rifle than you are with a dart or God help you.' She crossed herself surreptitiously, realising that she had broken the third commandment, and then concentrated on the final leg.

It was running close, with good scores from Will and Norris. Even Sylvia and Joyce managed to perform reasonably well, but Alf's form had deserted him. He returned from the board with two low scores and in even lower spirits.

Dorothy touched his hand in a motherly way and said, 'Don't you worry, Alf. We're gonna win this leg an' all.' She unbuttoned her jacket and hung it over the newel post of the staircase. 'Right,' she said, rolling up her right sleeve.

'You need seventy-four,' said Will.'

'With her luck she might get it,' said Norris.

'Luck has nothin' to do with it, Clever Dick. Just watch this an' learn somethin'.' Her first dart found treble twenty, her second made eleven, and by that time everyone knew where her third would land.

'And three makes seventy-four,' said Will. 'The drinks are on Dorothy and Alf.'

It was a good night, and it was particularly good to see Dorothy emerging with more confidence than ever before. Her ability to throw darts was a surprise to everyone, but Sylvia's favourite moment was when Dorothy had rushed to Alf's defence. That alone had made the run ashore worthwhile.

As they walked back through the gates of HMS *Wasp* she thought about someone whose runs ashore were suspended for the duration.

11

February

'When you see a picture like that,' said Dorothy, 'it's like eatin' pickled onions. You can enjoy it again and again because memories of it keep coming back.'

'That's very true,' said Joyce, 'although I don't think David Niven and Olivia de Havilland would take kindly to being compared with pickled onions, or burps.'

'Oh, David Niven,' said Sylvia dreamily. They were returning from first house at the Regent, where they had seen 'Raffles'.

'He's handsome all right. He'd have me at his mercy in no time at all, but what about Olivia de Havilland?'

'What about her?' Sylvia wondered where the conversation was going.

'Would you call her a great beauty?'

'I don't know.' Sylvia considered the question. 'She's got great presence.'

'Yeah, but that's not the same as bein' beautiful,' is it, Joyce?'

'I wouldn't mind having some of what she's got.'

'I think,' said Sylvia, 'she makes the most of what she's got.'

'She gets a lot of help from the hairstylists and make-up artists,' said Joyce, 'but, whatever she does to herself or they do to her, she looks lovely on the screen.'

They came to Town Wall Street and caught their first glimpse of the Channel. The night was murky with low cloud and they could see very little so they carried on.

'I don't know about you two,' said Joyce, 'but I'm feeling peckish.'

'Let's get some chips,' said Sylvia, who had long since disregarded her mother's strictures about eating chips in public places.

They came to the fish and chip shop in Snargate Street, bought two-pennyworth of chips each and ate them in the shop, sitting on the stools provided.

Dorothy was intent on pursuing her original topic. 'The thing is, if Olivia de Havilland makes the most of herself, how does she do it?'

'I told you,' said Joyce. 'She has professionals to work on her.'

'Yeah, but how do they go about it?' Dorothy was beginning to sound exasperated.

'Hair, make-up and clothes,' said Sylvia. 'It's the oldest formula in the book, so they say.'

'But do they say what to *do* with your hair, make-up and clothes?'

'What's bothering you, Dorothy?'

Dorothy finished her last chip and gave Sylvia a look of impatience. 'It's all right for you two,' she said. 'You look nice anyway, but we don't all have the head start you've got.'

'So that's it.' Sylvia looked across at Joyce and back to Dorothy. 'Have you got any make-up?' It was a fair question as even the most basic items were unobtainable.

'Yeah, I've got some.' She added dejectedly, 'I don't get to use it as often as you two.'

'Right, when we get back to the cabin we're going to transform you.'

'That's right,' said Joyce. 'By the time we've finished with you they'll have to post two sentries on our entrance, and both of them for your protection.'

'I hope one of 'em's Alf.'

They had been wondering about that.

. . .

The new corporal of the guard read out a list of eight names including those of Len, Freddy, Bailey and Ernie Houghton, and ordered those prisoners to collect their belongings and await transport. They had no idea why or where they might be going. They only knew that if they were being redirected it was a hell of a shame. The building site had been a cosy number by most standards; the work had been mainly light, they had traded with the foreman, and Brunner had been remarkably careful since the incident with the Polish woman. All were good reasons why they should be allowed to remain there. Unfortunately their hosts had other ideas and it was a dispirited group of prisoners that waited in their hut for the promised transport.

'It would be just our luck to be sent to a coal mine,' said Ernie, who tended habitually toward the pessimistic view.

'Or worse,' said Bailey, 'we could be bound for the chemical factory at

Auschwitz. I hope to God we're not, because I've seen more than enough of that bally place.'

More than two hours later, a three-ton lorry arrived and they were told to wait for the guard that was to escort them.

No one had seen their camp leader, the Man-of-Confidence as the Germans called him, for some time, so they still had no idea of their destination.

'Go and ask the driver where we're going, Freddy,' urged Len.

'Why me?' He was becoming tired of acting as spokesman.

'Because you speak their bloody language.'

With a shrug, Freddy walked around to the cab, where the driver sat smoking and reading *Der Völkischer Beobachter*.

'Excuse me.'

The driver looked at him blankly.

'*Entschuldigen Sie mich, bitte.*'

'*Was ist los?*'

'*Wo werden Sie nehmen uns?*'

The driver blew an immaculate smoke ring and said simply, 'Lamsdorf.'

. . .

Two days later, Sylvia was in the Ferry Port Signal Station, a small but cosy hut at the eastern end of the harbour. She had gone to deliver the latest changes to the books in use there but was now chatting with the visual signallers and looking out to sea. It was early morning and the RAF High Speed Launches had been active in the Channel. They could see one of them returning with a long, curving wake and a white bow-wave like a luxuriant moustache, as it headed for the Air-Sea Rescue Station behind them. Rose, one of the V/S Wrens, made the challenge by signalling lamp.

'I'd better get out of the way before they come alongside,' said Sylvia.

Rose said, 'I think you've left it a bit late. You'd better wait here 'til they're ashore.' The HSL gave the reply. It was only about five hundred yards away.

They're very fast, aren't they?' Sylvia watched, fascinated, as the boat approached them.

'They do over forty knots,' said Rose, logging the challenge and reply. 'They're tiny and they've got huge engines. Mind you, they're no good in a heavy sea.'

Her colleague grinned and said, 'Her boyfriend's in one of the MLs at Sheerness. You can tell, can't you?'

The HSL made its approach and came alongside, bumping three times against the jetty. A number of men sprang ashore followed by another two carrying a stretcher case. They lifted the stretcher with well-drilled ease up and on to the pier.

'I think you'll be all right now, Sylvia,' said Rose.

'Good, I'll see you two later. Are you going to the dance at Lympne?'

'Yes, if we're still off-watch then.'

She left the station and made her way along the pier. A small group of airmen stood some distance away, talking with an officer. As she drew nearer she heard one of them say, 'What do you want us to do with the Jerry, sir? The ambulance is taking its time getting here.'

'Leave him where he is. We've fixed him up the best we can and there's no point in moving him until they get here.'

There had been heavy shelling in the night, and Sylvia knew that if the rescue parties were still digging casualties out of the rubble the service ambulance men would be working at full stretch alongside their civilian counterparts. It was hardly surprising they were late, but it still seemed wrong for the RAF men to leave the man alone on the pier, and she couldn't help feeling curious about him as well. She had only ever seen Germans on the newsreels before the war, and here was a real one. What was more, she would have to pass him on her way to the main gate and her transport, so no one could blame her for having a glimpse as she walked past.

The officer had his back to her so she didn't have to salute him. She walked on and then stopped when she reached the stretcher. Glancing down a little nervously, she noticed straight away his slight build, dark hair and narrow features. He was certainly no blond titan. Also, blood had seeped copiously through his shoulder dressing and he was obviously in pain. His eyes opened and he spoke to her.

'Zig ... Zigarette bitte, Fräulein.'

She removed her gloves to light a cigarette and crouched down to hand it to him. It felt very strange. These were the people who had killed James and were holding Freddy prisoner, but the man was suffering and she was surprised to find that she felt sorry for him.

'Danke, Fräulein. Danke schön.' The hand that was holding the cigarette shook and a tear trickled down his cheek and on to the pillow. She felt uncomfortable because she had never seen a man cry. Nevertheless, she crouched by his side. 'Don't worry,' she said. 'Haben Sie kein Angst.' It was a silly thing to say, but she couldn't think of anything else except, 'They'll be taking you to hospital soon. You'll be all right.' He didn't seem to understand, so she searched her memory and said unsurely, 'Jetzt müssen Sie ins Krankenhaus gehen. Alles wird gut.' She hoped that was near enough and tried, 'Verstehen-Sie?'

'*Ja* ...' He seemed about to say something else but was interrupted by an angry shout from behind her.

'You stupid bitch! What the hell do you think you're doing?'

She turned to see a red-faced man in RAF battledress. He wore three stripes and a crown, which made him a flight-sergeant or something equally terrible. He had smoke-stained teeth as well.

'I ... I was only ...'

The man was about to let rip at her again but the officer intervened.

'I'll take care of this, Flight-Sergeant.'

'But sir, I think we can do without the Senior-bloody-Service sending its little floozies to poke their noses into our business.'

'I said I'll take care of this, Flight-Sergeant. I'm sure you have plenty to do.'

'Very good, sir.' The flight-sergeant saluted and walked off.

Remembering her manners, Sylvia saluted him too. He was a flight-lieutenant, and his lapels bore the Volunteer Reserve badges. She wondered if RAFVR officers were generally more human than their professional colleagues. She hoped so, because if this one wasn't, she feared she was in for an almighty bottle, and she wasn't completely sure why.

The officer returned her salute in that funny, elaborate way the RAF, the army and the Marines had, with the palm turned outwards. 'My flight sergeant suspected that you might be fraternising with the enemy,' he said. 'You weren't really, were you?'

'I was just ... I saw he was wounded and in pain, sir. He asked me for a cigarette, so I gave him one.'

'Well, if you can keep a secret, so can I. Don't make a habit of it though, will you?'

'No sir. I'm sorry, sir.' She saw that he was old, maybe forty, but he was really nice.

'We have to keep our distance, you see, and it's worth remembering that he was a gunner in a night fighter. They were stooging around over the Channel, picking off our boys on their way back from Germany.'

'I'm sorry, sir. I didn't think.'

'But you will in future, I know.'

'Oh yes, sir.'

'Good girl.' Suddenly he smiled and said, 'My daughter joined the Wrens two weeks ago.'

'Did she, sir?'

'Yes. How's that for loyalty? Her dad's in the Air Force and she joins the Wrens. Still, there's nothing wrong with the Navy, whatever my flight-sergeant says.' He cocked his head as he heard the bell of an approaching ambulance. 'It sounds as if they're coming for our friend. I must detail two men to go with the ambulance.' He nodded and smiled again. 'Carry on.'

'Aye aye, sir.' She saluted him smartly and went on her way to catch the utility bus back to Admiralty Pier.

Finding the others in the cabin, she took the last three packets of duty-free cigarettes from her locker and placed them on the table. 'You can share these between you,' she said. 'I've given up. I gave my last one to a German airman.'

They gaped as she told them her story, eliciting further details from time to time, and finally Joyce asked, 'But why have you stopped smoking?'

'I never really enjoyed it,' she said, 'but I made the decision when that horrible flight-sergeant was shouting at me. I couldn't bear to have teeth like his.'

'You're right there, Sylvia. You've got lovely teeth and you want to take care of them.' Since her beauty treatment, such matters had never been far from Dorothy's thoughts.

. . .

Before the incoming prisoners could go to their hut the guards marched them to the other end of the camp, where they had to go through the delousing shed. There, they stripped off and handed over their clothes to be loaded into an oven and cooked at a temperature calculated to kill the lice. Meanwhile, the kriegies had to shower in almost unbearably hot water, the theory being that lice were unable to survive in those conditions. The prisoners could only hope that the lice had read the same textbook.

They returned, clean and deloused, to their huts, where they slept on palliasses infested with bed bugs, but at least the authorities had made an effort. It would be noted by Red Cross officials on their next visit.

A summons arrived in the morning from the company sergeant-major who acted as go-between for the Germans in matters of labour procurement. They assembled in his hut, prepared to hear the worst.

'You're famous, lads,' he said. 'You've made a big impression, and I bet you never realised it.'

The prisoners exchanged suspicious looks but the CSM consulted an official memo on his desk and said, 'They're tired of shoddy workmanship and things going wrong at the railway yards. They want workers they can trust. They want you back at Tarnowicz.' He winked and added, 'Don't overdo the funny business, will you, lads?'

. . .

The large envelope contained a letter from her parents and a postcard and two letters from Freddy. Sylvia read her parents' letter and then turned to the postcard, which was more than a month old.

Dear Sylvia,
You're now so dear you're promoted to 'Dearest.' I've just received your 25th December, your 3rd January and the parcel to put all other parcels to shame. Thank you! Thanks also to your lovely mother, your workmates and the lady who lives down the road. Everything is marvellous and the long johns are a blessing in this climate! Please see my two letters. Freddy X.

Both letters bore the same date, so she opened one at random. His writing was even tinier than usual. She imagined it was to facilitate a longer-than-usual letter.

Dearest Sugar Plum,
I don't believe you were the worst Sugar Plum Fairy or the worst anything. You're simply the best and you're piacevole, a lovely person – I learned the word from an Eyetie guard at Veano – and to reinforce my assertion I've written you a song. The music is by Cole Porter – I only work with the cream of the profession – but the lyrics are mine. Stand by.

You're the Best
By Freddy Hinchcliffe

You're the best! You're piacevole!
You're the best! You're the voice of Bowlly.
You're a plaintive tune sung beneath the moon by Bing;
You're the main attraction, the Steinway action, you're ev-ry-thing.
You're the best! You're a foie gras sandwich,
You're superbe in whatever language.
I'm a POW who hates to trouble you, a pest,
But if I'm a nuisance, Dearest, you're the best!

You're the best! You're the morning cuppa,
You're the best! You're champagne at supper.
You're a foxtrot, slow and molto romantico,
You're a gentle rumba to a swaying number played simpatico.
You're the best! You're Sir Walter Raleigh,
You're the best! You're a priceless Dali.

You're a ball gown by Dior, you're Piglet, you're Eeyore, you're Pooh;
But the greatest thing of all, Dearest, is you're you!

You're the best! You're the famous Hallé,
You're the best! You're the Bolshoi Ballet.
You're a joint of pork when it's served with Yorkshire pud;
You're the London Phil, you're Flatford Mill, you're oh, so good!
You're divine! You're num-er-a una!
Oh, be mine, now or even sooner!
In the past, it is true that I've known just a few… and the rest,
But from now on, Dearest, you are simply the best!

Please accept the song in lieu of a Valentine. I'll have to continue the letter in a separate post. God knows when it will get to you.
Totally yours,
Freddy XXX

She read the letter several times before placing it on one side and opening the other.

Dearest Sugar Plum,
Congratulations on becoming an auntie! The same to your sister and brother-in-law, and tell young what's-his-name what a lucky young shaver he is to have you for his auntie. What is his name?
In answer to your question, we had a Labrador who was older than me. He wasn't great company, being elderly and somewhat reserved, but he was a good listener and, oddly enough, I thought about him when I was taking my unscheduled dip in the oggin. There I was, surrounded by the eternal waves and all alone except for my faithful Mae West, and I found myself thinking about dear old Arthur and how he would have enjoyed the swim. I boarded the dinghy eventually, and then other matters competed for my attention, but it's surprising what goes through your mind at such a time.
I've never seen a ballet but, as you suspect, I have an open mind so I'll no doubt give it a try one day.
Please tell me about films etc. It will remind me that pleasanter things await, and please keep writing. You can have no idea how much I appreciate your letters.
Yours and no one else's (in case you're wondering, a Mae West is an inflatable life jacket),
Freddy XXX

P.S. I hope you had a smashing birthday. Mine is the 15th July.

She brushed a tear aside, conscious that Joyce was watching her.

'What is it?'

'Oh, nothing really. It's just that he jokes about most things and then suddenly he turns serious and I feel so sorry for him. I want to help him and I can't.'

'I know,' said Joyce, welling up too. 'I know just how it feels.'

'Look at what he sent me.' Sylvia showed her the first letter.

'No, I shouldn't.'

'It's all right. There's nothing private.'

Joyce read the first letter with tear-filled eyes and then looked up as the cabin door opened and Dorothy walked in.

'What's to do, you two?'

'Freddy's sent her a Valentine,' said Joyce. 'Mine did too but it's not as nice as hers.'

'I'm sure he loves you just the same,' said Sylvia, stifling a sob.

Dorothy took the letter from her, and as she read, her eyes also filled with tears. Eventually she mumbled, 'Worraloovleyfella.'

12

Sylvia finished applying her pencil to Dorothy's eyebrows and stood back to survey the result.

'How am I lookin'?'

'More irresistible by the minute.'

'I hope so. Where is RAF Lympne, anyway?' The name came out as 'Limp-ny.'

'I've no idea. Will says it's less than an hour away in the tilly, and apparently it's pronounced "Lim".'

'Funny. Anyway, thank goodness we've got the tilly. We'd never go anywhere if they didn't let us use it.'

'Mm. Keep still while I powder you.' She looked across at Clarissa, who was studying them with undisguised disapproval. 'Don't you wish you were coming with us, Clarissa?'

'No, I most certainly do not.'

'She's going to the officers' dance down below,' said Joyce.

'How boring.'

'Well, I'm surprised you're going with them,' said Clarissa, 'a married woman.'

'So am I,' said Joyce, 'but I allowed these two to talk me into it, and it's not as if I'm going there to find a man. I just think I'll go mad if I don't have some fun once in a while.'

Clarissa was unmoved. 'I thought you got your fun misleading people.'

'Misleading?'

'Yes, and all for a pair of stockings.'

'Oh, that. We didn't do it for the stockings.'

'Maybe not, but I see you're wearing them all the same.'

'Yeah, and they're lovely, thank you.' Dorothy stood up to look at herself in the wall mirror. 'You're right, Sylvia. It's a big improvement, but you'll have to excuse me while I go to the heads. All these preparations are makin' me nervous.'

Clarissa waited for Dorothy to leave the cabin and said, 'I don't know whom she thinks she's going to impress. She'll put herself out of the running as soon as she utters a word.'

'Oh, now you've gone too far.' Joyce closed her bag with a snap. 'If you're going to be an officer – and heaven help us if that ever happens – you need to know something about the service you've joined. The most important thing of all is that we're all in this war together. As far as most of us are concerned it doesn't matter a damn whether your father's a road sweeper or a stockbroker, whether he catches the bus to work or has a yacht in the Caribbean. We all wear the same uniform and we're all doing what we can to help win this wretched war. Now, if you can't accept that, then you're the one who's out of step.'

'And we're doing this for Dorothy,' said Sylvia. 'because she's good-natured, she's a generous spirit and she's good company, and most of all because she's one of us.'

'And that,' said Clarissa, opening the door, 'is the kind of nonsense I'm only too ready to leave behind.' She left, slamming the door behind her.

Dorothy returned a minute later and asked, 'What's the matter with Ermintrude? She's gorra right cob on.'

'Never mind her,' said Sylvia. 'Let's do something with your hair.'

. . .

The problem of Clarissa dominated the conversation in the back of the utility bus on the way to the dance. Rose, the V/S Wren, asked, 'How did she find out you were having her on about those forms?'

Joyce sighed. 'She asked her boyfriend to find out what we'd written about her, and he tried to worm the information out of First Officer Finch. Of course, she knew nothing about it, so lover-boy put two and two together.'

'Who is lover boy?'

'That wet-looking sub-lieutenant with the thick lips and no chin.'

'Ugh.' Rose grimaced. 'I'd rather be kissed by a fried egg.'

'So would I,' said Dorothy. 'I haven't tasted a real one for a week.'

'Well, I think we ought to forget about Ermintrude for one night,' said Sylvia, 'seeing as we've come ashore to enjoy ourselves.'

'Hear, hear,' said Joyce. 'Ermintrude's a problem for later. Let's concentrate for now on having a good time.'

'Well, an *enjoyable* time,' said Rose.

There were attempts in the front seats to start a sing-song but the girls at the back ignored them for the time being. No one could ever remember all the words anyway.

Sylvia asked, 'What's this story about there not being enough girls at Lympne to go round?'

'It's true,' said Rose. 'That's why the invitations went out far and wide. Apparently the air force boys are starved of female company.' The information prompted enthusiastic noises from the sear seats.

With Will navigating, the Wren driver found her way through the blackout to the aerodrome and thence to the NAAFI hut, from which music was issuing.

The band consisted of a piano, two alto saxophones, a trumpet, a clarinet, bass and drums. The musicians were all in RAF uniform and presumably all serving at the aerodrome. The Union Flag and the RAF Ensign were draped behind them, and elsewhere the hall was dressed with decorations that must have served on various occasions. Sylvia took a seat with the others to see out the number.

Rose surveyed the room with a practised eye and said, 'I reckon the numbers are about even.'

'Let's have a slow foxtrot now,' said the clarinettist. 'It's "Bewitched, Bothered and Bewildered", and here's Irene to sing it for you.'

Suddenly Sylvia was looking into the eyes of an airman so tall that he had bent almost double to speak to her. His breath was quite awful but it would probably not be so noticeable when he straightened up.

'May I have the pleasure?'

She smiled and nodded, and he led her on to the floor. He surprised her by moving smoothly and confidently. It was just her luck that the first man she had met who could dance a decent slow foxtrot was twice as tall as her and had acute halitosis. She fixed her gaze on his second tunic button and followed his firm but gentle lead. It was a lovely number and the WAAF girl had a good voice.

Joyce found her at the end of the number. 'How was yours? I'm feeling benumbed, withered and betrampled. The trouble with those service boots is that it's impossible to feel anything through them, including my feet.'

'Bad luck. Mine was a good dancer.'

'Was he?'

'Oh yes, he did a lovely slow foxtrot but he was nearly as tall as Alf and he had awful breath.'

'At least you got a dancer.' Joyce looked around the room and smiled suddenly. 'Speaking of Alf, have you seen him?'

'No, where is he?'

'Dorothy's cornered him by the bar. She hasn't got him to dance yet but you never know. The night is young.'

'Good for her.'

An airman came to ask Joyce to dance, and then another came and asked Sylvia. The band was playing 'In the Mood.' It wasn't her kind of number but she got up to be sociable.

She danced with several others and then had a lovely slow foxtrot with a sergeant from Ipswich. His accent reminded her of Alf, and at the end of the number she set off in search of Dorothy.

She found her in the crowd, about to leave the room.

'I'm just off to the heads. I'm not kiddin', Sylvia, I've been workin' hard on him but he's too shy for words. I haven't given up yet though.'

Sylvia couldn't help teasing her. 'Do you mean he's not like the rest – only interested in one thing?'

'Interested in it? He doesn't know it's been invented.'

Alf was still at the bar watching the dancers.

'Hello, Alf.'

'Hello, Sylvia.'

'Are you enjoying yourself?'

'It's all right.'

She decided to take the direct route. 'You like Dorothy, don't you?'

He looked away nervously.

'She likes you very much and she'd really like you to dance with her.'

He looked at her uncertainly. 'I'm not all that good at dancin',' he said.

'That won't matter. It's you she wants to dance with, not Fred Astaire.'

'D' you think so?'

'I'm sure of it. Now, when she comes back, just say, "Would you like to dance?" That's all. You can do it, Alf.'

'I don't know.'

It wasn't one of Sylvia's greatest triumphs, but the look of determination on Dorothy's face when she returned told Sylvia that her gentle entreaty had been completely unnecessary.

'All right, Alf,' said Dorothy, 'no more muckin' about. Are you going to ask me to dance or do I have to wait for the Ladies' Invitation Waltz?'

It was good, seeing them take to the floor together, Alf with his ponderous, size thirteen steps and Dorothy weaving around his feet like a doting terrier. Sylvia went in search of Joyce to tell her the news.

'I hope Norris is going to keep his smart-alec remarks to himself,' said Joyce, when Sylvia told her. 'I don't suppose he means any harm but he needs to think before he pokes fun at Alf.'

'That's just the problem,' said Sylvia. 'He doesn't think.'

A loud voice behind the blackout curtain at the entrance distracted them but while the band was playing it was impossible to hear what was happening. After a minute, a group of soldiers entered the room.

'So that's what it was about,' said Joyce.

Will came over and joined them, watchful as ever over his female charges. 'The pongoes just turned up,' he said. 'They weren't invited and they've already been drinking, but the RAF Police have let them in on condition that they behave themselves.

Sylvia thought the RAF Police were being particularly trusting, but it was reassuring to know that they were on watch, duty or whatever airmen called it.

After a while, a soldier weaved his way over to her.

'D' you fancy a dance, darlin'?'

'No thanks, I'm having a rest.'

He tried Joyce, who gave him a similar answer so he wandered off.

Sylvia was dancing when she heard a soldier say, 'Some of these girls are too stuck-up for their own good.' She shut it out of her mind and enjoyed the number.

Eventually, the band leader said, 'Here's a message for the party from HMS *Wasp*. Your transport is leaving in five minutes. Good night, Navy, and have a safe journey home.'

Sylvia and Joyce had just stepped outside and were talking with Will and Norris when they heard angry female voices.

'Bugger off!'

'Get off me, you drunken sod!'

They hurried to the back of the building, from where the voices seemed to be coming and walked into two of the maintenance Wrens from the submarine basin. They were trying to elbow their way past three soldiers, all the worse for drink and clearly unrepentant.

'We just came out of the heads and these pongoes grabbed us,' said one of them, touching her hair where it had become unpinned.

'They're animals,' said the other.

'This is where it stops,' said Will. 'These girls are going back to their transport. Let them through.'

One of them took up the challenge. 'Who's going to make us?' He seemed unsteady but no less menacing.

'We are.'

'Oh yeah? You and whose army?'

'We don't need an …'

'Shut up, Norris,' said Will. 'Let me do the talking.'

'Yeah,' said the soldier, ''cause that's all he can do.' The other three stood behind their colleague, making drunken noises of agreement.

'Send for the RAF Police,' suggested Norris.

'And have us all up before the Commander in the morning? Leave this to me.' He peered into the darkness and called, 'Crusher! Are you there, mate?'

There was the sound of hurrying footsteps and Alf, with Dorothy in close attendance, came to Will's side.

'Allow me to introduce "Crusher",' said Will, noting with satisfaction the effect Alf's appearance was having on the soldiers.

'That's right …'

'Shut up, Norris. Anyway, Crusher thinks a lot of his girls and he doesn't like it when somebody upsets them, do you, Crusher?'

'No, I don't.'

'But he's prepared to let you off with a warning if you go now and leave them alone. That's right, isn't it, Crusher?'

'That's right.' Alf wagged an admonishing finger. 'You leave these maids alone and bugger off now like my oppo says, else I'll really hurt you.'

Sylvia had been fearful of a pitched battle, but something in Will's delivery told her that it wasn't the first time he and Alf had played out this kind of theatre, and that he had been confident from the outset that he could handle the situation. She watched the soldiers shuffle their feet and heard the spokesman say, 'All right. We didn't mean no harm. It was just a bit of fun, that's all.'

One of the maintenance Wrens snorted but the soldiers were already on their way.

'Thanks, Alf,' said one of the girls.

'Yes, thanks, Alf. Thanks, Will.' The girls headed gratefully for the utility, leaving Dorothy to tell Alf how magnificent he was.

''Ere, Will,' asked Norris, 'why do you always have to do the talking? What's so special about you?'

'My mouth's connected to a brain.'

'Charming.'

They boarded the utility whilst Norris pondered the unfairness of life, and when Will had counted heads they set off back to Dover. Because Dorothy had taken up station next to Alf, Will moved to the back with the others.

'Make a bit of room, girls,' he said. 'Remember I'm an invalid.'

'You're a hero, Will, *our* hero,' said Rose.

Sylvia asked him, 'Where were you wounded, Will?'

'You name it, love. Arms, legs and chest. It was like a beetle drive in that hospital, putting me together again.'

71

'No, I meant whereabouts in the world.'

'It was in Narvik Fjord in nineteen-forty, but you don't want to hear about that.'

'Go on, Will, tell us about it,' said Joyce.

'All right. There were five German destroyers in the fjord, big as cruisers, each with five-inch calibre guns, and they posed a threat to our supply ships. All we had to do the job, though, were five old 'H' class destroyers from the last war, each armed with just four ancient four-inch guns. Anyway, we gave Jerry a good old hiding, but he took us by surprise later in the day and turned the tables on us. My ship, the *Hardy*, was damaged as badly as I was and she had to be beached. I got taken ashore with everyone else and they fixed me up as well as they could. They gave our skipper and flotilla commander, Captain Warburton-Lee, the Victoria Cross.'

'I should think so too,' said Sylvia, 'sending him to do a big job with worn-out ships.'

'Ah well, it didn't do him much good, because he was killed in the battle.'

'What a rotten shame.'

'Yes, he was a good hand.'

'So who won in the end?'

Will shrugged. 'I suppose it was a draw, really, but three days later, they sent in another force led by the battleship *Warspite*. The old lady finished the enemy off good and proper, and her aircraft sank a U-boat into the bargain.'

It was a fitting end to a run ashore, thought Sylvia as her head drooped against the window. The dance had been really good apart from the unpleasantness at the end, but that had turned out all right anyway; they had seen the first flicker of romance between Alf and Dorothy and then they had ended the evening with a story. She drifted off to sleep thinking about the aeroplane and the U-boat and wondering if that was the kind of thing Freddy used to do.

13

March

Len was shaking him 'Wake up, Freddy mate. You're drowning again. Come on, wake up.'

There was a murmur of complaint from someone further along the hut and Len swore at him. He returned his attention to Freddy and asked, 'Are you awake yet?'

'Yes.' Freddy opened his eyes. 'Thanks, Len.'

'You're welcome. See you in the morning.' He put one foot on the edge of Freddy's bunk and launched himself upwards into his own.

Freddy lay on his back, still breathless after his nightmare but oddly reassured by the coarse blanket and the ticking of the pillow. It was a recurring dream that never lost any of its vividness.

He remembered the shattering impact as the aircraft hit the waves; he remembered releasing himself from his harness and then realising, as he went over the side, that one leg of his overalls had become hooked on one of the Albacore's canopy catches.

He hung upside down, struggling frantically to kick himself free, and all the time the damaged aircraft was sinking. As it dragged him beneath the surface he tore off his flying boots and ripped open the front of his overalls. His lungs were about to burst but he managed to shed his Mae West so that he could fight his way out of the clinging cotton suit and rise to the surface.

That was the reality of what happened, but he usually woke up from the nightmare while he was still under water.

He remembered surfacing and gasping for breath for what seemed a long time before the pounding in his ears receded and he heard the pilot and the observer calling his name. They had boarded the dinghy and they hauled him

73

on board because he had no strength left. He sat, slumped between them, half-dressed and half-drowned but thankful to be alive.

An Italian merchantman picked them up and Freddy climbed aboard dressed in his cellular drawers and white front. It did nothing for his pride.

The memory returned at odd times throughout the morning, but during the short lunch break he was able to turn his mind to pleasanter things as he read the latest letters from Sylvia.

12ᵗʰ February, 1944.

Dear Freddy,

Don't you dare call yourself a nuisance or a pest ever again! You're neither of those things. You're the only man who's ever sent me a song for St Valentine's Day, and it's a lovely one too. I'm going to keep it in a special place so that I can take it out and read it again and again. My workmates are all envious because they've never had one.

Last Thursday, some friends and I saw a film called 'Raffles', starring David Niven and Olivia de Havilland. Do you know the story? Anyway, it was lovely to see a film set at a time when there was no war, and we bought chips on the way home.

I'm glad you like my letters, because I never thought I was a good letter writer. I tend to jump from one topic to another with no warning, as I'm sure you've noticed, but do you remember a letter you wrote to me shortly after Christmas, about guilt? Well, your letter came when I was feeling guilty about something terrible that wasn't my fault. My supervisor told me it wasn't my fault; she said I'd done everything I could, but still I felt wretched. And then your letter came, and the next morning I felt much better. It was as if you knew all along. Well, I thought I'd tell you that so that you know how important your letters are to me. Not just that one, but all of them, and I wish I could do more for you. Oh dear, I'll have to start a new letter. Back soon, Sylvia XX.

He opened the second, delighted that the two had arrived together.

12ᵗʰ February, 1944.

Dear Freddy,

Back again! We went to a dance last night. The band was good and I thought of you when I heard them. They didn't play 'All The Things You Are' and I'm glad really, because it's rather special, isn't it?

What kinds of books do you read? I'll send you some. We're allowed to do that although they have to go direct from the bookseller.

There's another parcel on its way, and my mother and I have put a lot of thought into it. One thing we've included is some chocolate for Easter. It's my favourite time of the year, and it's on the 9ᵗʰ April, in case you haven't got a calendar, but you don't have to wait until then to eat it.

You asked about my nephew's name. They've called him Bruce after someone who did something special on Boxing Day that you'll find out about when you come home. He has bright blue eyes and dimpled cheeks like his mother's – that's my nephew, not the man who did something special on Boxing Day – and he blows raspberries for no reason when he's lying in his cot. I wonder what or who he's thinking about.

Do tell me something about your life before the war. I'm very interested to know more.I hope the parcel arrives soon. Meanwhile, take care. I think about you often.

Love and best wishes, Sylvia XXX

He was conscious that Len had been watching him. 'It's a really nice letter,' he said. 'I gather they've named the baby "Bruce" after Admiral Fraser. I imagine the old boy's pretty popular back there after the Scharnhorst incident. Apparently little Bruce blows raspberries a lot.'

Len nodded his approval. 'I like a chap to have the courage of his convictions.'

'Yes, the sort of baby who'll stand up in his cot and be counted.'

'Exactly.'

'*Arbeiten! Arbeiten!*' The guards were calling them back to work. Freddy and Len each blew them a surreptitious raspberry before trudging back to the goods yard.

. . .

Sylvia had another opportunity to see David Niven, this time with Ginger Rogers in 'Bachelor Mother'. All three girls thought it was a wonderful film and well worth the trudge through freezing snow to the Plaza and back. As a gesture of goodwill and an attempt to improve the atmosphere in the cabin, they had asked Clarissa to join them. She had been quiet and preoccupied for some time, and they were not surprised when she declined their invitation, or when she showed little interest in the prospect of another run ashore, this time to celebrate Joyce's promotion to Leading Wren. It was one of two promotions worth celebrating, but the other carried with it more than a little sadness. Sylvia heard about it when she relieved her opposite number at 2255 and found Will already on watch.

'Hello, Will,' she said, 'what's the buzz?'

'Only that at long last Their Lordships have recognised my true worth.'

'And so they should, Will.' She signed the log and gave him her full attention. 'What have they done?'

'They're promoting me to PO Tel. I'm joining the course at HMS *Mercury* on the twentieth. Not bad, considering I'm still not a hundred per cent fit.'

'Oh Will, that's terrific, and well-deserved too. You will be coming back here after the course, won't you?'

He shook his head. 'I doubt it. They don't usually allow new senior ratings to rejoin their old oppos. They say it's bad for discipline.'

'Oh no.' She couldn't imagine life without Will but it was wrong to be selfish about it. 'I'm really pleased for you,' she said, 'and it's important to you, being real Navy, isn't it?'

'It is really. I've still got seven of my twelve years to do, although I don't know that they'll let me serve the full dozen now.'

'They'd be stupid not to.'

He smiled. 'They don't know me as well as you do.'

'No, they don't, and I'm going to miss you terribly.'

'You'll be all right, Sylvia. You're a good hand.'

'I've been in good hands, Will.'

She had to leave it there because someone was transmitting *Wasp*'s call-sign, and in any case, she didn't want to make Will feel bad on his red letter day.

. . .

It was quiet in the hut, as it should be on a Sunday morning. A football match was taking place outside, and although there was still snow on the ground there was also a gathering of spectators. Freddy was not a devotee of football. His sporting interests were cricket and rugby league, in that order, and as there was no prospect of either he was taking advantage of the peace and quiet in the hut to write a letter.

12th March, 1944.

My Favourite Sugar Plum Fairy,

Your 12th February arrived this week, and very welcome it was, and still is. 'Raffles' is an excellent story. It's too bad I couldn't be there to see the film, because with David Niven in it, it must have been good. I'm glad you enjoyed the dance too, and you're quite right about 'All the Things You Are.' I'm thinking of making a list of my favourite songs so that one day I can make a nuisance of myself by requesting them at dances. Perhaps you'd like to throw in a few of your own.

I've just realised that I haven't danced a step since 1942 – and another thing I've realised is that I've just stumbled on a possible lyric: 'I haven't danced a step since 1942'. I'll work on it.

We really must meet when I return to England. Now that we know each other so well it would be a tragedy to go our separate ways with never an encounter.

There was fierce excitement outside the hut, and Bailey's cultured tones jolted his memory of an earlier conversation at Niwka.

We could rendezvous for cocktails at some fashionable watering hole and then eat at a little place in Soho that a colleague has recommended. After that we could go on somewhere and dance until dawn. Does the idea appeal?

As you can see, I'm running out of space so I have to leave you for now. Please write soon.

Spurning all other advances,

Freddy XXX

. . .

Everyone was up and about by four o'clock that afternoon, and it was inevitable that the subject of Will's promotion should dominate the conversation.

'It calls for a run ashore,' said Dorothy.

'A big run ashore,' added Joyce.

'Especially as we were already planning one to celebrate your hook,' said Sylvia. The blue-embroidered anchor on Joyce's left sleeve bore the sheen of newness and had been the hot topic until Sylvia broke the news of Will's promotion. 'I think there should be a presentation as well; nothing terribly expensive, just something special that'll remind him of us.'

Dorothy was already giving it some thought. 'Quite a few girls would very likely want to be in on that.' She looked over her shoulder at Clarissa's empty bunk and added, 'Even Ermintrude.'

Joyce raised a sceptical eyebrow. 'Where is she, anyway? Last time I saw her was yesterday at lunchtime.'

'I wonder.' Sylvia walked over to Clarissa's locker and prised the door open with her finger. The locker was empty, as was her drawer. 'Well, goodbye, Ermintrude. She might have said something before she went.'

'And being Ermintrude,' said Joyce, 'she left her bed for someone else to strip.'

'Typical.' Dorothy pulled off the counterpane and blanket, and folded

Ray Hobbs

them prior to removing the sheets, pillow case and mattress cover. 'But where can she have gone?'

They continued to wonder until the next morning, when they went on watch, and Sylvia said, 'I'll ask Will. He'll know if anyone does.'

She found him in the W/T room.

'Will,' she asked, 'what's happened to Ermintrude? Her locker's empty and no one's seen her since yesterday morning.'

'She's on leave.'

'How jammy.'

'I think she'd swap places with you quite happily. She's on leave pending official discharge.'

'Discharge?'

'Yes.' He leaned forward to whisper in her ear,

'Indulging in sexual contortions,
Without taking any precautions,
Dear Ermintrude let a sperm intrude;
Stand by for a change in proportions.'

In a quiet moment she asked the PO Wren if she knew Clarissa's first name.

'Oh yes, the poor girl was called Euphemia.'

Sylvia was beginning to feel sorry for Clarissa, and not just because of her condition. There was much to be said for an ordinary name, such as Sylvia, or Freddy.

14

April

Sylvia hadn't expected leave again, at least until summer, so she wasn't disappointed at having to work on Good Friday and Easter Saturday. Very little had happened during the 'all-night-on', and after breakfast she went to the cabin to re-read Freddy's latest letter in comfort.

The cabin was cold and the wind was rattling the window with rain, so she undressed and made herself cosy in bed before opening the letter.

19th March, 1944.
Dear Sugar Plum,
What a wonderful girl you are! Thank you, thank you and thank you again! Thank you particularly for the chocolate, the shaving tackle, the bootlaces and the underwear and socks, which are always well received. Please thank your mother, and if any other members of your family, your workmates and the old lady who lives down the road have contributed to the parcel, please thank them for me.

My life before the war, since you ask, I spent with the Humber Rumba Boys. That was my main preoccupation, you see. I was determined to be a full-time musician. Only my father's opposition to the idea and maybe my lack of ability prevented it from happening. All the same, I'd like to do something like that again, albeit in a small way. And now I've told you that, it's your turn to bare your soul. Spare no blushes!

Please write and tell me how little Bruce is getting on. Is he still blowing raspberries or has he moved on to old-fashioned looks and disapproving sighs? And how are his proud father and long-suffering mother? If it comes to that, how are all your family, including your Cocker Spaniel and two cats?

I don't know them, of course, but to hear about them helps create a picture of life over there that I can enjoy, and reminds me that the war can't go on for ever.

> *Have a happy Easter and take care.*
> *Love and stuff,*
> *Freddy XXX*

She folded the letter and put it in her bag, feeling desperately sad for a man who asked about her family because he no longer had one of his own.

. . .

The priest from the village who had said Easter Mass for the Catholics had left the camp, and one of the army kriegies, a Baptist minister, was bringing his meeting to its close. Freddy, Len and the others, who represented various denominations, and who had gone along because he was the only minister, thanked him and returned to their hut to enjoy the rest of their day off.

'It was bloody cold out there,' said Len quite unnecessarily but possibly just to air his feelings. The 'other denoms' had vacated the hut so that the priest could use it, and they were now chafing their arms and banging their feet in an effort to restore circulation. Spring had brought with it a reminder of winter. It served as a warning against complacency.

Len settled on his bunk above Freddy's, rolled himself in his blanket and asked, 'What's Sylvia got to say this time?'

'Oh, the usual kind of thing.' Freddy had the letter open in front of him but he was disinclined to give too much away.

'I gather she never stops talking about you.'

'What?'

'So Joyce says. You know what did it, don't you?'

'I haven't a clue.'

'It was that valentine you sent her. It swept her off her feet.'

Freddy looked up sharply. 'How do you know about that?'

'Joyce told me, and I have to say you put me right in the shade.'

'It wasn't all that good, just a bit of fun.'

The bed boards creaked as Len rolled over to communicate more directly. 'A bit of fun it may have been, but she's shown it to half the Wrens in the signal section.'

Freddy looked up at the face that grinned at him over the top bunk. 'So you say.'

'Scouts' honour. I bet she's all over you in those letters she sends you.'

'Your imagination does you credit.'

'OK, Freddy, cards on the table, what's the score with you two? Is it true love or what?'

'Stow it, Len. I've never met the girl. I don't even know what she looks like.'

The bed boards creaked again. Len resumed his dorsal position and yawned massively. 'Come on, Freddy. This is Uncle Len you're talking to, not Big Wet Nellie. You must have struck up some kind of relationship through all that correspondence.'

Freddy sighed heavily. 'Okay, we're on very good terms, quite affectionate terms, really, and I'd like to meet her eventually. I'd like that very much, but it would be bloody silly to make plans when there's every likelihood that she'll have some eager matelot or even an officer in tow by the time I get there.' It was as much as he was prepared to tell Len or anyone else, and if he interpreted the sounds from the top bunk correctly, his inquisitor was falling asleep. He could read the letter again in peace.

15th March 1944
Dear Freddy,
Even if this letter doesn't reach you in time, I'm going to wish you a happy Easter. Christmas apart, it's my favourite time of the year, and I'm only sad that you can't be here to appreciate the things I take for granted. One day I'd like to show you around the countryside where I live, because I think it's the most beautiful place on earth. Naturally I would think that, but I'm not alone.

We saw David Niven and Ginger Rogers in 'Bachelor Mother' on Monday. It was lovely. Do you like Ginger Rogers? I think David Niven is dreamy.

The next paragraph had been obliterated with bright, light-blue opaque pencil. According to Len, that meant that the goons had done it. He understood that the British censors used a darker pencil. Freddy felt the familiar anger rising again. They had taken his home and family, and now they had obliterated a message from lovely, innocent Sylvia. They had laid their filthy Nazi hands on her letter. Their blue scribble was like an obscenity on a lavatory wall and he hated them for it.

When his anger had ebbed sufficiently he tried holding the letter up to the window to see if he could discern any of Sylvia's blue ink from the other side of the page, but without success. The censor had been too thorough. He turned his attention to the next paragraph.

There was another unlikely, if peaceful, collaboration between Peter Ross, our Spaniel, and a puppy my parents were looking after. Well, my mother had left two fresh eggs in a bag in the kitchen, and she returned to find the eggs broken on the floor, and P. R. and the puppy lapping them up. P. R. was in disgrace for a while, but I think it's lovely that he shared the eggs with the puppy.

It was a nice story, but when he read the paragraph again his eyes were drawn to the first line, and he wondered what non-peaceful collaboration could be called unlikely. He could only think of the alliance with Russia, and the more he considered it, the more sense it made. Maybe Sylvia had tried to tell him some encouraging news about the Russians and she hadn't managed to sneak it past the censor. The last news he had heard at Lamsdorf was that the Red Army was advancing rapidly on the Ukrainian front, and the best thing about that was that the next stop on the way to Germany was Poland. Pleased with his minor triumph over the censor, he read on.

One of my workmates is a really nice girl but she's always felt very ordinary. She's not at all pretty, and I know that sounds rotten, but she was the one who said it. Anyway, she's now having a romance with a man in the boot department. He's really nice, not the brightest of souls but honest and good-natured.
Take care and wrap up well.
Love and very best wishes, Sylvia XXX

He thought for a while about the Yorkshire Dales. He'd been to Bolton Abbey, Burnsall and several other places one holiday, but the prospect of exploring the Dales with Sylvia felt too good to be true. The plain girl had evidently taken up with a Royal Marine, and he wondered how long it would be before Sylvia found her ideal man. It was ridiculous to entertain such ideas about a girl he had never met, and she was bound to find someone sooner or later. She was a lovely girl, and it would be awful if she felt under an obligation.

15

There was a soft knock on the cabin door, and the girls looked at one another in mild surprise, gentleness and timidity being almost unknown in a naval establishment. Joyce called, 'Come in.'

The knob turned minutely and then a voice said, 'I'm afraid I can't.'

Sylvia opened the door to find a diminutive Wren struggling with a pile of bedding. She was fair haired, with doll-like features that evoked disturbing memories of Clarissa. 'Here, let me help.' Sylvia picked up the bedding and dropped it on the empty bed. 'I'm Sylvia.' She pointed to the others. 'This is Dorothy and this is Leading Wren Patterson, Joyce to her friends.'

'Oh, how d' you do?' The newcomer sat on the bed, regaining her breath. 'I'm Angela.'

Dorothy was immediately businesslike. 'What's your watch?'

'Baker Watch. I'm Signal Distribution.' Her accent was refined, not unlike Clarissa's.

'Ah,' said Joyce, 'you're Clarissa's replacement.'

'Was she the one who got pregnant?'

'That's right.'

Angela nodded sagely, as if the story were all too familiar in her experience. 'You just can't be too careful, can you?'

'Clarissa certainly wasn't,' said Dorothy.

'The bathroom and heads are pretty basic,' said Joyce. 'These were the hotel staff quarters before the war. The hot water runs out without warning, and when you go into a room always count ten seconds after you switch the light on. It gives the cockroaches time to run for cover.' She examined Angela's features for a reaction and found none. 'Aren't you impressed?'

Angela shook her head. 'I've met cockroaches before. It's just like being back at school.'

Dorothy took over the inquisition. 'Are you thinkin' of stayin' here for some time or maybe goin' on to greater things?'

'Greater things?' Angela gave a little laugh. 'It took me all my time to qualify for SD. Everyone says I'm as dim as a NAAFI candle.' She beamed around at their surprised faces and said, 'If you want some sewing or knitting done that's a different matter, but don't expect ambition.'

'In that case,' said Joyce, 'you're welcome, especially as my husband and Sylvia's boyfriend are POWs in Poland and we have to keep them supplied with woollies.'

Sylvia flushed at her description of Freddy. 'He's not my boyfriend.'

'He's as good as,' said Joyce. Explaining for Angela's benefit, she said, 'He writes her affectionate letters and he's written her a song as a valentine.'

'Oh, that was a lovely song,' said Dorothy.

'How marvellous,' said Angela, 'a man who serenades you. He sounds lovely.'

'He must be,' said Joyce, ignoring Sylvia's protests. 'She's secretly in love with him.'

'Well, if you find the wool I'll knit socks, gloves, and anything else they need. My brother's in the army and he's weighed down with things I've made him.

'Gloves?' For a moment, Sylvia forgot her embarrassment. 'Can you knit gloves?'

'Oh yes.'

'With fingers?'

'Of course.'

'I'll help you make up your bed.'

. . .

Angela had made a timely arrival with her needle skills, as Sylvia discovered on the next day when she was returning from visiting Rose in the Ferry Port Signal Station. She had passed three American patrol torpedo boats on her way out. They were tied up alongside, and two sailors had called out to her. She had come to expect it as normal behaviour but she was surprised when an officer accosted her on her way back. She saluted him and he returned the salute and said, 'Say, honey, have you a minute to spare?'

'Yes sir, of course.' She imagined he wanted directions. He was a long way from home. He was also quite good-looking.

'Will you come on board?' Eyeing her skirt, he added, 'I'll tell my guys to look the other way when you come down the ladder.'

'I'm sorry, sir. We're not allowed to go on board boats. First Lieutenant's Standing Orders.'

'Yeah? Well, I'm Lieutenant Paul Fielding and I say you're welcome on board my boat.' He pointed down to the jetty and said, 'That's her, PT Boat 653, the pride of the ocean!'

The officer was certainly engaging, but much as she liked him Standing Orders had to be obeyed. 'She's lovely, sir, but the First Lieutenant's a lieutenant-commander, he's very fierce and his word is law.'

'You don't say. Well, that's too bad, because we've got a job that needs doing and it's one that a woman does best.'

Despite her misgivings, she asked, 'What sort of job, sir?'

'How handy are you with a needle and thread? We've been out of circulation for some time and, you know, buttons come off, shirts get torn ....'

He was difficult to refuse. 'If you leave your mending at the Lord Warden I'll do it and leave it for you in the wardroom, sir.'

'That's really nice of you, honey, but we're not going to be here for long. Can you get it back to us by oh-eight-hundred tomorrow? I'm afraid there's quite a lot.'

'There are four of us in our cabin, sir. We'll do our best.' She knew the others would understand. 'The only problem is that things like buttons and sewing thread are hard to come by. Have you got any?'

'That's all taken care of. Just wait a minute.' He peered over the edge of the quay and called, 'Kendrick, are you down there?'

An answering voice shouted, 'Here, sir.'

'Will you bring those shirts up here?'

'Sure thing, sir.'

After a few seconds a seaman's head appeared over the edge of the pier. He scrambled over, clutching a bundle of linen. 'Here they are, sir.'

'Have you got the thread and stuff?'

The seaman felt in his pocket and pulled out a paper bag, which he handed to Sylvia, saying, 'We're greatly obliged to you, honey.'

'Right,' said Sylvia, pocketing the paper bag and lifting the bundle. 'By oh-eight-hundred then, sir.'

'If you possibly can, and you're not doing it for nothing, so don't worry.'

'Aye aye, sir.' Transferring the bundle to her left arm, she saluted him very smartly, as she felt she was representing the WRNS, and left them both on the pier. As she walked back to the Lord Warden she heard the seaman say,

'Did you see that, sir? These people think they're on a battleship. Jeez, it's just like the movies.'

'It's all happening for real here,' the officer told him, 'and you don't even have to pay to get in.'

She carried the bundle up to the cabin and dropped it on the table.

Joyce was the first to speak. 'Are you taking in washing?'

'No, mending. It's for the men on one of the PT boats. The officer said I'm not doing it for nothing, and if you'll all help me I'll split whatever he gives me. The only problem is he wants it back by oh-eight-hundred tomorrow.'

'Just look at the quality of this,' said Angela. 'If our boys got shirts like these, they'd think they'd died and gone to Heaven.'

'Buttons an' thread an' all,' said Dorothy, peeping into the paper bag. 'Let's get crackin'. We've only got 'til we go on watch tonight.'

. . .

Freddy and Len had been put on cleaning duties in the station. They were under careful scrutiny because of the obvious temptation afforded by the coming and going of trains, and it also ruled out most forms of mischief, ensuring that life was even more boring than usual. They also had to endure the taunts of German soldiers on their way to the Eastern Front, although the thought of that dreaded destination provided the kriegies with a degree of consolation.

Such an incident occurred shortly before the end of their shift, when a number of troops stepped off a train to answer the call of nature. There were facilities on the platform for both sexes, although it was doubtful that any woman had set foot on the station since the invasion of Poland. Accordingly, and with an accompaniment of crude remarks, the soldiers used both. Even so, some had to wait their turn, and to entertain themselves and their comrades while they waited they shouted insults to the prisoners sweeping the platform.

'Hey, Tommy, what is your wife doing now?' It had become a *cliché* along with the suggestions and sign language that accompanied it. The barrage continued in relays, as others made their exit. One of them, a corporal, spotted Len in his RAF uniform and approached him.

'Hey, *Terrorflieger*,' he said, 'you are not so terrible now. You are *Terrorfeger*.' Laughing at his joke, he said, 'It means "terror sweeper".' He turned to his comrades and said, '*Er ist Terrorfeger!*' They rewarded him with boisterous laughter, which encouraged him to greater efforts. Pointing to a rain puddle on the platform, he said, '*Terrorfeger*, what is this? Come and look.' He waited for Len to look down, and said, 'Look closer, *Terrorfeger*. Get down and look!'

Len crouched down, knowing exactly what was in store.

'Down, *Terrorfeger*, on your knees and look closer.' When Len's face was within a foot of the puddle the corporal stamped hard, drenching him with muddy water. Len remained motionless while his tormentor said, 'There is a very good song. The words are, "With your foot you tap, tap, tap". Do you know it?' He sang the phrase again, stamping in the puddle and laughing stupidly until an officer somewhere shouted the order to board the train. 'You are lucky, *Terrorfeger*,' the German told him. 'I was going to make you lick my boots clean.' He took his place on the train, still laughing.

'Steady, mate.' Freddy put a hand on Len's shoulder. 'Wait until the train moves off.'

It seemed to take an age, but eventually someone blew on a klaxon and the wheels began to turn. Freddy walked beside the corporal's wagon, speaking in German for the benefit of his companions.

'I wonder what your fate will be. Perhaps you will return very soon, bandaged and bleeding in a hospital train. Maybe you will die slowly and painfully in freezing snow. You could be taken prisoner and be at the mercy of the Russians. Otherwise, your deaths may be quick and merciful. Those who return fit only for guard duty tell the same terrible stories.' The train was now moving too quickly for him to keep pace with it, but the soldiers' reactions betrayed their unease as well as their anger. It made Len and him feel a little better.

. . .

Sylvia arrived above the mooring at a little after 1730 with the shirts, mended, washed and ironed. Lieutenant Fielding climbed the ladder to take them from her.

'We're very grateful to you and your friends, honey. Thanks a lot.' He called down to someone on the boat, 'Malone, bring the stuff up for the lady.'

Another face appeared from below and its owner handed Sylvia two large, sealed envelopes that contained something soft and yielding.

'Thank you.' She turned to the officer and asked, 'What are these?'

'Payment for services rendered. Just enjoy them.'

'Thank you, sir.'

'You're very welcome. Carry on, honey.'

She found the others about to go on watch. Dorothy saw the envelopes first and asked, 'What have you got there?'

'I don't know.' She handed one of them over and said, 'You open that one.' Inserting a nail under the gummed flap, she opened the other and took out five cellophane packets. Dorothy did the same.

'I don't believe it,' said Joyce, running her fingers over the cellophane to the accompaniment of gasps around her. 'Nylon stockings. You hear about them but you don't believe you'll ever get your hands on a pair.'

'Ten pairs,' said Sylvia. 'That's two pairs for each of us and two for Doris in the laundry.'

'It's just like the pictures, havin' the Yanks here,' said Dorothy.

'It's all happening for real now,' Sylvia told her, 'and you don't even have to pay to get in.'

. . .

Neither were they required to pay for admission to the Town Hall dance a few days later, because admission was free to members of the armed forces. The band was the Dover Garrison Dance Orchestra and Sylvia, hearing them for the first time, thought they were pretty good. Also, the Americans were back from wherever they had been and were well represented on the dance floor. One of them approached a girl, a civilian, not far from where Sylvia was sitting. He said, 'May I have the pleasure, ma'am?' It sounded old-fashioned and nice, and yet when one of his flotilla mates came to Sylvia he just said, 'D' you want to dance, honey?'

She waited almost until the end of the waltz, because he was a very good dancer, and asked him, 'What's the difference between "ma'am" and "honey"?'

He frowned. 'Excuse me, honey?'

She inclined her head towards where the civilian girl and the sailor were dancing, and said, 'That sailor called the girl "ma'am" but you called me "honey". I just wondered.'

'Oh that.' He screwed up his face in thought and said finally, 'I guess civilians are called "ma'am" and classy navy girls like you are called "honey." Don't worry about it.'

He was rather glib, she thought, but he was nice. He had deep-blue eyes and if she looked at him through narrowed eyes he had a look of Dana Andrews. His uniform was made from soft barathea, very different from the heavy serge that was the lot of Wrens and British sailors. Wrens were not subject to the Naval Discipline Act and were allowed ashore in civilian clothing, but they had been urged on this occasion to 'show the flag' by attending in uniform. It was not a popular decision but the Wrens had nevertheless complied with it.

The waltz ended, and the band leader announced a foxtrot. The sailor lost no time in asking, 'D' you wanna dance again, honey?'

'Only if you call me "ma'am".'

'OK, honey, from here on in you're called "ma'am".' The band started to play 'Yours', and he led her expertly into the foxtrot.

'What's your name?'

'Matthew T. Glaser, ma'am, Matt to my friends.'

'Mine's Sylvia.'

He drew her closer and said, 'That sure is a pretty name, ma'am. It's just a shame I don't get to use it, having to call you "ma'am" now.'

'You can use it if you like.'

'That's mighty nice of you, Sylvia.'

'Not at all. You're an excellent dancer.'

'Thanks, honey. Fred taught me well.'

'You're not trying to tell me Fred Astaire taught you?' She eyed him mockingly.

'No such luck, lady. I mean Fred Muller of Fred and Marjorie's Dance School. That's in Omaha, Nebraska, where my home is. Fred and Marjorie used to run it together but then one day Marjorie ran off with a meat slicer salesman and Fred had it all to do himself. He was real good at taking the woman's part, Fred was. It seemed to come naturally to him, and maybe that had something to do with Marjorie high-tailing it the way she did. I guess she was ready for a little more in the way of excitement.'

They enjoyed the remainder of the dance in silence, and as the last note ended Matt said, 'I guess it would be greedy of me to ask you for the next dance.'

'Yes, it would, but maybe we'll dance again later.'

'You bet, honey … ma'am … Sylvia.' He scratched his head. 'You've got me all confused now.'

'No I haven't. You're just full of flannel.'

'That's what they all say, honey. At least, they say I'm full of something. I can't rightly remember what.'

She danced with a sailor from one of the MTBs, a soldier from the Eastern Arm Battery and two more Americans before Matt found her again. It was just as the band leader was announcing the last dance, 'The Anniversary Waltz.'

'Hi, Sylvia. Is my luck in?'

'Yes, it is.' She let him lead her on to the floor.

'I was hoping I'd catch you before the end of the dance. As we're both heading for Admiralty Pier, will you let me walk you back there?'

'If you want to. There's a whole gang of us going there.'

'OK, I'll join your gang.'

They danced to the end, silent and close, and then after the National Anthem they joined Joyce and the others. It was a party of around thirty that headed for *Wasp*, and it seemed at times that half as many conversations were taking place. Sylvia could see Angela, Dorothy and Alf somewhere near the front, and Rose and two other V/S Wrens behind them. She and Matt walked hand in hand at the back. His hand was lovely and warm. He kept looking around him at the damaged buildings.

'I can't believe I'm seeing this,' he said.

'The shell damage?'

'Yeah. There's hardly any of the town left.'

'They still shell us, you know.'

'No kidding? What do we do when it happens?'

'There are shelters for the civilians and some of them shelter in the caves, but we just carry on. To be honest, most of the civilians do as well.'

'Caves? Are you kidding?'

'No, the chalk cliffs are full of them, but there's no way to dodge the shells really.'

'No?'

'No, if a shell's going to hit you, nothing's going to stop it.'

'You don't say.'

More to take his mind of the possibility of a barrage than anything else, she asked, 'What made you join the Navy?'

'It was mainly the movies. Nebraska's in the Mid West, you see, so the only time I ever got to see the ocean was when I went to the movies.' He added, 'I guess Pearl Harbour had something to do with it as well. How about you? Why did you join the bluebirds?'

'Wrens.'

'Sorry. When I look at you I get all confused.'

'I know. You said so before. Anyhow, it was the uniform that persuaded me. The ATS and WAAF uniforms are not as nice as this.'

'Well, the view's not bad from where I'm standing. When did you join?'

'In 'forty-one. I was seventeen-and-a-half.'

He whistled. 'As long ago as that.'

'Oh yes. I was wearing this uniform before the Dead Sea reported sick.'

'Hey, I like that. "Before the Dead Sea reported sick." That's really good.'

'It's not original. It's just something sailors say. Another one is "When the *Victory* was still in the New Forest".'

He stroked his chin and said, 'No, I don't get that.'

'HMS *Victory* was Lord Nelson's flagship and the New Forest is in Hampshire. It's where they used to get the oak to build warships.'

'Right, I can see now why that might be funny. You just have to know your British history.'

'You do really.'

They walked along Snargate Street, and before long they caught sight of the Lord Warden Hotel. Matt stopped beside one of the ruined buildings and, as her hand was in his, she stopped as well. 'What's the matter?'

He led her gently behind a half-demolished wall and said, 'How's about a little kiss for a lonely sailor who's far from home?'

She smiled knowingly. 'Just a little one. I have to be back on board by twenty-three fifty-nine.'

He took her in his arms and his lips touched hers, lightly at first, and she suspected that might well be the extent of it until she felt herself drawn into a long, sensuous kiss unlike anything she had ever known. She and James had been as inexperienced as each other, and their kisses, though sincere, were artless compared with what she was experiencing now. It was just a little frightening but she thought she could cope; in fact it was really rather nice until one of the hands that had been holding her moved downward and began gathering up her skirt. As she moved to stop him, his hand evaded hers and slid deftly into her blackouts.

'No, Matt, no.' She pulled away from him but he was insistent. 'No!' She tore herself away. 'I've had a lovely time with you but no more of that.' She realised that she was shaking.

'Hell, I'm sorry, honey. It's just been so long, and you're so pretty I couldn't stop myself.' He was also trembling.

'Right.' She straightened her skirt, surreptitiously doing the same with her underwear through the serge cloth. 'We must go.' She was relieved beyond words to hear Dorothy's voice calling her, and then Alf's, bucolic and reassuring.

'Sylvia, are you all right?'

'Yes.' She fought to hold her voice steady. 'Yes thanks, I'm fine. Just coming.'

They walked with Alf and Dorothy to the main gate, where she responded to Matt's shamefaced look by offering a valedictory cheek. 'Goodbye, Matt,' she said. 'Good luck with the war.'

'Goodbye, Sylvia.'

She turned away while he showed his identification to the sentry and walked on to the pier. When he was gone she held up her pay book, hoping that the sentry would not notice that her hand was still trembling, and walked around the building to the junior Wrens' entrance. Dorothy remained behind for a short time with Alf.

· · ·

91

A night's sleep put things more into perspective, but the odd question still occurred to her. She asked Joyce about something that was troubling her. 'What do you think he meant when he said it had been so long?'

Joyce smiled. 'You can be sure he's had some experience. He may even have someone waiting for him at home, perhaps a wife.'

'Surely not.' She stared at Joyce in horror, unable to believe that she might have spent the evening with a married man.

Joyce nodded. 'You can't help being innocent, Sylvia, but you're naïve as well. You have to realise that these things happen.'

She was more than three hundred miles from home and doing a skilled and important job, but she still had much to learn about the ways of men and women. It was quite worrying.

When she came off watch she felt more settled and ready to write to Freddy.

16th April, 1944.

Dear Freddy,

Your 12th March has arrived. It's so frustrating that our letters usually take at least a month to reach us, but it makes it so much more exciting when one arrives.

I'd like to join you with that list of songs. Some of my favourites are the old ones from before the war because they're so much nicer to dance to than some of the new ones and it doesn't matter that I was terribly young when they were written. Let me give you five to begin with. There's 'Embraceable You' (I love that one), 'Deep Purple', 'September in the Rain', 'Love Walked In' (wonderful to dance to) and a waltz for a change: 'I Can Give You the Starlight'. You'll notice that I've left 'All the Things You Are' for you because I know it will be at the top of your list.

I'll have to go on to another letter. These things are so tiny!

Love and best wishes,

Sylvia XXX

She was relieved to find another letter-form in her writing case.

16th April, 1944.

Dear Freddy,

What a shame your musical career was cut short. I'm sure you were being falsely modest. Somehow, I don't think my pre-war reminiscences will compare.

For want of a realistic choice of career, my dad arranged for me to work for a local insurance broker. He knew it would be a mistake to take me into his office, because accountants deal in the one discipline at which I'm truly hopeless. Unfortunately, so do insurance brokers, and it wasn't long before I was looking for something less numeric. In the end, I took a secretarial course, which was much more in my line. I had to learn book-keeping, but the only maths involved was the usual adds, take-aways, timeses and guzzinters, and I was all right with that. All of which brings me to my present job, which I really enjoy. I kept very quiet about my secretarial skills and got the job I wanted, making the sparks fly, and I'm going on an advancement course soon.

As far as my family is concerned, I'm going to write again shortly and tell you all about them. For now, though, let me tell you that I'd love to meet you for cocktails, to eat in Soho and then dance the night away. Of course we must meet. I couldn't bear it if we didn't. Take care.

Yours with love and very best wishes,
Sugar Plum XXX

16

The chaplain was saying something about St Paul and sacrifice, which was confusing, because the parade was supposed to be in honour of St George's Day and Zeebrugge Day, both on the 23rd April. Sylvia listened, only half attentively. It was a gorgeous day with bright sunshine and a cloudless sky, and she was content simply to stand there enjoying the sun on her face.

According to the Chaplain, the ancient Greeks had four different words for love because it was important to them to distinguish between kinds, although with her limited experience Sylvia felt that the usual kind caused quite enough trouble without introducing more. Apparently there was *agape*, which was the brotherly kind that sometimes called for sacrifice; there was *eros*, which was romantic love; *philia* was about loyalty, friendship and that kind of thing, and *storge* was the kind of love parents felt for their children. Oddly, she found herself wondering which of the four she felt for Freddy, because she knew that she felt something for him and she was happy to end her letters to him with 'Love and best wishes.' It was difficult to know for sure.

According to the chaplain there had been a great deal of *philia* and *agape* at the raid on Zeebrugge, which was very nice, but it was frustrating because she wanted him to get on to St George. Zeebrugge was important, fair enough, but the legend of St George was pretty romantic stuff, and knights were special people who deserved to be remembered even when their exploits seemed a little far-fetched.

In the end, the chaplain never mentioned St George. Instead, he went on to the prayers, including the one that always made Sylvia's spine tingle.

'... Preserve us from the dangers of the sea and from the violence of the enemy; that we may be a safeguard unto our most gracious Sovereign Lord,

King George and his Dominions and a security for such as pass on the seas upon their lawful occasions ....' They were beautiful words.

The Lord's Prayer followed, and then the hymn: 'Eternal Father, Strong to Save,' yet more words that had a powerful effect on her, always providing any sailors present could resist the temptation to sing the rude words about the lady who became a prostitute. As it happened, there were very few sailors on parade that day, so the hymn remained unsullied.

At the end of the service the First Lieutenant dismissed the ship's company and Sylvia was able to call at the mail office. She was not expecting anything from Freddy; she had received both of his letters for March, but she thought there might be something from her mother or Audrey.

Joyce came in and spotted a letter from Len immediately. 'Oh, lovely!' She kissed the envelope and said, 'This is just what I need after standing out there for an hour. What have you got there, Sylvia?'

'Just one, from my mum.'

'You might get one from that Matt one day,' said Dorothy, joining them. ''E's got enough brass neck to write to you.'

'No fear of that. I let him know exactly how I felt.'

'If a man started rummagin' in my blackouts he'd get more than a piece of my mind – he'd wake up with a crowd 'round 'im.'

'Sh!'

'Well, you need to let 'em know there's nothin' doin'. You don't want to leave it 'til it's too late.'

'Yes, but let's not advertise it here.'

They took their mail up to the cabin, where Joyce sat on her bed, and Sylvia and Dorothy left her there to read her letter in private.

'What's yours then?' Dorothy pointed to Sylvia's envelope. 'Is it from home?'

'Yes.' There was a short note from her mother and, surprisingly, a postcard from Freddy, which she scanned quickly before scrutinising the photograph on the front. It was of a group of prisoners and it was slightly out of focus. 'What have you got?'

'It's from Alf.'

Sylvia frowned, unaware that Alf had been drafted. 'Where's he gone?'

'He hasn't gone anywhere. He's just practisin' for when he does. I'm helpin' him with his writin', you see. He writes me letters and I mark them and tell him where he's gone wrong an' how well he's doin' an' that.'

'Good for you.'

'Yeah, it's a shame. He used to struggle at school. His mam died when he was a kiddie, you know, an' that didn't help.'

'What a rotten thing to happen.'

'Yeah, I could cry when I think of it, but it's better to do somethin' useful, isn't it?'

'I think so.' This was from Angela, who had a sheaf of mail.

Dorothy looked astonished. 'Is all that lot for you?'

Angela flipped through the envelopes and said, 'There's only four. Two are from home, one's from my brother and the other's from one of his friends who write to me occasionally. I met a few of them at Aldershot when I called to see him last year.'

'You must be popular with his friends if they write to you,' said Dorothy.

'Oh well, there was a dance in the mess, and my brother Paul had no one to take so he took me. That's how I got to know them. They're all in Italy now, so I write to them when I can.'

'Was that in the officers' mess then?'

'Mm.' Angela was riffling through the envelopes again, possibly deciding which to open first.

'The town hall must have been a bit of a come-down for you,' said Dorothy.

'Not at all. I had a lovely time on Saturday.'

'Dorothy's still hung over from Clarissa,' said Joyce, who had finished reading her letter.

'Yeah.' Dorothy nodded contritely. 'Sorry, Angela. I know you're not like that really.'

'I hope not.'

'No, you're all right. You're one of us.'

Noticing some redness around Joyce's eyes, Sylvia asked, 'Is everything OK?'

'Yes.' Joyce smiled. 'Len's letters are rough and ready; they haven't the same style as Freddy's but they reach the spot just the same.'

Sylvia waved her envelope with a bewildered look. 'Freddy's style has deserted him on this occasion,' she said. 'I really don't know what to make of this one.'

'OK,' said Angela, 'spill the beans. Four heads are better than one, even when one of them's mine.'

'By the sound of it,' said Sylvia, 'you're more genned up about men that any of us.' She took the postcard from the envelope again and said, 'We've talked about meeting when he comes home. He sounded keen on the idea and I'd really like to meet him, but then this came.' She read aloud, ' "Dear S, I've enjoyed talking about meeting after the war but I don't want you to feel it's an obligation. I'll understand if you're involved with someone when the time comes. In any case, I'll never forget what you've done for me. L and b w, Freddy." '

'He must have tiny handwriting to get all that on a postcard,' said Dorothy.

'He has, but what do you think he means, and why has he suddenly decided to tell me this?'

Dorothy shrugged. 'He means he'd really like to meet you but you mustn't think you have to keep yourself available for him, and if you find somebody in the meantime he'll understand. There's nothin' tricky about that.'

'I agree,' said Joyce. 'He means just what he says.'

'Men are very basic,' said Angela. 'They're the ones who have to read between the lines, not us. You have to feel sorry for the poor dears really.'

'Do you think so?'

'Affirmative. You know when a man's playing games, even at that distance, and there's not a hint of it in that message.'

Joyce nodded. 'I think he's turned it all over in his mind – and they have no shortage of time for that, believe me – and his conscience has given him a nudge. He just doesn't want you fending off the man of your dreams because of a half-promise you made to him.'

'And that's really decent for a fella,' observed Dorothy.

Sylvia turned the postcard over and studied the picture again. 'I don't suppose Freddy's in this photo,' she said. 'He hasn't said so, and even if he was, it wouldn't mean a thing. It's an awful picture.'

'Let me look.' Joyce took the card and examined it. 'You're right,' she said. 'Len might be on this for all I know, but I'd defy anyone to recognise one of these chaps.'

'It's a pity,' said Sylvia. 'It would have been nice to have a photo of Freddy.' She slipped it back into her mother's envelope and said, 'Still, at least I know now that he doesn't play games. I was trying not to be naïve but I needn't have worried.'

'No, you needn't,' said Joyce. 'There's all the difference in the world between Matt and Freddy.'

. . .

'It's something to do with weather, I'm sure, but it beats me why it comes in bally drums.' Bailey raised himself from the kneeling position in which he had been trying to decipher the stencilled description.

Freddy sighed theatrically. 'You do live up to your reputation, Bailey. Let me look.' He climbed into the wagon and inspected the nearest drum. '*Temperafarbe*,' he read. 'It's nothing to do with the weather. It's distemper, green distemper.'

97

'Germ warfare,' said Bailey. 'I knew it.'

'No, Bailey, it's for painting walls. I imagine there's a shortage of wallpaper in Germany as well as in Blighty.'

'And it's bound for Düsseldorf,' said Len, 'although Berchtesgarten would be more appropriate, considering Hitler's civvy job.'

'Agreed, and we've got small-arms and Spandau ammunition for Milan, and both trains are leaving tonight.'

'Right,' said Len, 'let's get cracking.'

It was heavy work for men on POW rations. The distemper was in twenty-five litre drums and the ammunition boxes were as heavy. Also, they had to be permanently on the lookout for railway workers and guards, which made the job even more difficult, but within ten minutes of the end of the shift they had switched consignments. They were regaining their breath when the yard supervisor arrived.

'*Alles gut?*'

'*Gut* as it'll ever be,' said Freddy.

The Supervisor nodded and consulted his paperwork. '*Düsseldorf,*' he said, pointing to the rolling stock that now contained a quantity of ammunition.

'What?' Freddy feigned ignorance. They had been banking on the train being passed without inspection.

The German pointed to the door of the nearest wagon. '*Aufmachen.*'

Freddy stared stupidly.

'*Aufmachen!* Open!'

'Which one?'

'*Aufmachen!*'

'*Nicht verstehen.*' Freddy spread his hands hopelessly, wondering how much longer he could stall the man. Len was leaning against the wagon and moaning softly. Hopefully he would provide an effective distraction. Bailey was at his side, ready to play a supporting role.

'*Platz machen!* The supervisor ordered him to stand aside and grasped the heavy hasp on the sliding door.

'Hell's bloody bells!' Len clutched his left shoulder, moaning realisticaly.

The German turned and demanded, '*Was ist los?*'

'My shoulder. It hurts like hell!'

'He needs a doctor,' said Freddy. 'Doctor!' He made a pantomime of putting a stethoscope to his ears, and then struck his forehead in recollection. '*Arzt!*'

'I'm in bloody agony!'

'Come on, man,' shouted Freddy. 'What have you got between your ears, a bloody turnip? He needs a doctor!'

The German looked from one to the other. Finally he said, '*Zumachen!*' He motioned Freddy to close the door and muttered something about a doctor, before hurrying away.

'He's going for help,' said Freddy, closing the hasp and inserting the locking pin. 'You'd better get your symptoms right in case he comes back with a real doctor.'

'I *need* a real doctor,' said Len, white-faced and gasping. 'I must have torn a … muscle or something … lugging that … paint. It's bloody agonising.'

. . .

Two years and nine months after joining the service and after the briefest of courses, Sylvia was promoted to Acting Leading Wren. The extra pay would be very handy and it was good to know that someone in authority had recognised her worth. She would have shared the news with Freddy, albeit cryptically, but for one obstacle: letter-writing materials, reading matter, knitting and so on were now excluded from the W/T Room by order of PO Wren Dunn, the replacement for PO Wren Marriott, who had been drafted to Portsmouth. The newcomer was a pale person. She had a pale complexion, light-auburn hair and pale-blue eyes that gave her the appearance of being remote and impersonal. Sylvia was fair-minded in most things but that was nevertheless her impression. She hoped she was wrong, but until events proved otherwise she resolved to treat her new superior with great caution.

At about 2200 one of the coders came in to empty the incoming signals trays. When she came to Sylvia's tray she leaned over her bench to say, 'Congratulations on your hook.'

'Thanks.'

'It's got to be worth a run ashore.' Seeing PO Wren Dunn look up, she gathered up the signals and left.

'What was that about?' The PO Wren had left her desk and was on her way over.

'Nothing, PO. She was just collecting the signals for coding.'

'You were talking.'

'Yes, she'd just heard about my promotion.'

'*Acting* promotion.' The stress was loaded with meaning. 'Whether or not your acting rate is confirmed will be up to me, and you're certainly not going to impress me by gossiping with your friends when you're on watch.'

Argument was out of the question. Sylvia simply said, 'Sorry, PO.'

'Good. Don't let it happen again.'

After that, she left Sylvia alone for a while, and peace was re-established in the W/T Room, at least until Jane Forbes, who had been monitoring the broadcast, began to feel cold and pulled on her jacket. PO Wren Dunn saw what she was doing. She said, 'Take off that jacket.'

Jane looked around, unsure of whom the PO was addressing. 'Do you mean me, PO?'

'Yes, I do mean you. Take off that jacket at once.' She waited for Jane to remove it and said, 'What do you mean by wearing it over rolled-up sleeves?'

Jane put her hand to her mouth. 'Sorry, PO, I wasn't thinking.'

'So you stop thinking when you come on watch, do you?'

'No, PO. I just wasn't thinking then, when I put my jacket on. I was cold so I put it on without thinking.'

'What's the regulation?'

'Shirtsleeves are worn long under the jacket, PO.' Jane's face was bright red.

'That's correct, and if I see you improperly dressed again you'll find yourself on a charge. Do you understand?'

'Yes, PO.'

The incident Sylvia had just witnessed was unbelievable. The sleeves regulation was important in training establishments, and they were probably keen on that kind of thing at the Admiralty, but no one at *Wasp* had ever given it a moment's thought. They were too busy with the war.

At 0200 Sylvia decided to let Jane take first break. The poor girl probably needed it. She called to her and pointed to the clock on the bulkhead, immediately attracting the notice of the PO Wren.

'I decide who goes and when they go, Wren Charlesworth.'

'Yes, PO.'

'You will take first break.'

'Yes, PO.' Sylvia picked up the solitary signal from her box and took it into the Coding Room, where she met Joyce.

'Hi, Hooky.'

'Let's not be premature.'

'What do you mean?' They walked down to the mess together.

'I'm at the mercy of the new PO. I think she's related to Medusa the Gorgon.'

. . .

The Polish doctor examined Len carefully. He knew no English and had to communicate with the corporal of the guard in German, so Freddy eavesdropped on the conversation, learning what he could.

Eventually, with Len's arm immobilised in a sling, Freddy thanked the doctor on his behalf in German, and they made their way back to the prisoners' hut and their meagre evening ration that Bailey had saved for them.

'The doctor mentioned the nerves in your arm and shoulder,' said Freddy. 'I think he was talking about inflammation, but I can't swear to it. Anyway, it could be a chronic condition. I understood that much.'

'Bloody marvellous.'

'It doesn't have to hurt like this all the time, I'm sure.'

'Oh well, that's all right then, just as long as I'm only in agony some of the time.'

'No, wait a minute, mate. It could be just a weakness you'll have to watch, but you'll be seeing the German doctor tomorrow and maybe a British one when they can get hold of one. If the Polish doctor's right, there's just a chance that this could be your Blighty ticket.'

17

May

2nd April, 1944.

Dear Sugar Plum,

Here is a little song for you. I can't send the music – they don't allow enclosures – but I'll play it for you one day when I'm back in England.

I Don't Dance
by Freddie Hinchcliffe

I haven't danced a step since nineteen forty-two,
It may sound unbelievable, but ev'ry word is true.
My dalliance was all too brief at Terpsichore's shrine,
It started at the Palais and ended in the brine.
(Refrain – waltz time)
I don't dance anywhere, any more,
I've no partner, no band and no floor;
And the under-arm turn that took so long to learn
Is no use to a pris'ner-of-war
I don't shimmy, chassé or glissade,
And I've mothballed the gay promenade;
There's no partner for me save a willing KG*,
Or occasional prison camp guard.
(Instrumental)
I've not danced for two years, more's the shame,
Although others must shoulder the blame;
I'm unable to practise, and therefore the fact is,
My foxtrot's become rather lame.

My return to the floor's overdue,
Having waited since March 'forty-two;
Though I'll dance not one measure 'til I've had the pleasure,
Of dancing my next dance with you!

Love and best wishes,
Freddy XXX
P.S. *K.G. = Kriegsgefangene = P.O.W.

She folded the letter because Angela came in and sat down excitedly on her bed. 'Right,' she said, 'are you all ready to hear what I've found out about PO Wren Dunn?'

The others stopped what they were doing and paid attention. The PO Wren's influence extended beyond the W/T Room and several girls now had cause to regret her arrival.

'She came here from the Admiralty, which may explain why she's so pusser.'

'But we knew that already,' said Joyce, keen to find an Achilles' heel.

'Be patient. Before that she was at Fort Southwick, Portsmouth; prior to that she was at Rosyth, and before that she was on her PO's course at HMS *Mercury*.'

Sylvia clapped her hands. 'Well done, Angela.'

'That's not all.' Angela swung her legs up and made herself more comfortable. 'She got on the wrong side of a few people at Rosyth, including the Senior Signals Officer.'

'Never a good idea,' said Joyce.

'No, and they gave her a draft chit to Fort Southwick, where she upset a few more people. Apparently her … wait a minute …' She fumbled in her bag and found a folded message form. ' "Her over-zealous attitude in matters of discipline," ' she read, ' "was found to be prejudicial to morale and the smooth running of the establishment." That's amazing, isn't it?'

'I can't believe it's the Navy sayin' that an' all, because just when you think there's too much discipline they can always find you loads more.'

Sylvia nodded sympathetically. 'That's true, Dorothy, but PO Wren Dunn has an endless supply of it.'

Joyce asked, 'What happened at Fort Southwick?'

'It was the same sort of thing, apparently.'

'So they palmed her off on to us.' Sylvia contemplated the unfairness of it and then asked, 'How did you find all this out, Angela?'

'Ah well, one of the girls in Signal Distribution is having a bit of a fling with a naval officer who has a friend who's doing the same thing with Third Officer Bryant, and she did a bit of phoning around and came up with the goods.' She smiled at the thought. 'It gave them all something to talk about in-between, I suppose.'

'In-between what?' Dorothy spoke for them all.

'The usual.' She looked at each of them in turn. 'Pillow talk. You know.'

But neither Dorothy nor Sylvia really knew, and for Joyce it had been so long she could scarcely remember it.

. . .

The Polish, German and British doctors gave the same diagnosis. Len had neuritis, a condition that rendered him unfit for work, and as he would also be unfit for service in the armed forces there was a strong argument for repatriation. A German specialist and two doctors, each from a neutral country would examine him and make the final decision. He had been waiting three weeks when the order came for the original eight prisoners to await transport to Lamsdorf.

'It looks as if they're going to take you to the quack and bundle the rest of us for delousing,' Bailey told Len.

'For once, Bailey, you may be right.' Out of respect for the other prisoners' sensibilities, Len was trying not to sound too cheerful. It was easy to forget that some of them had been there since nineteen-forty.

'You know,' said Freddy, 'it amuses me that some German kriegie in Britain with chronic piles will be expecting to be repatriated shortly and you're making it possible for him. He'll be looking forward to all the comforts of home, and when he arrives he'll find half of Germany bombed to buggery, a whole nation dreading invasion every bit as much as we're sick of waiting for it, and on top of that, food will be a dim memory. I wonder how long it will be before he wishes he'd stayed put.'

'Well you needn't think I'm coming back, because I shan't miss any of this lot.'

'That's nice, isn't it, Bailey. He's not going to miss his old mates.'

'I know, Freddy old man, and when I think of the camaraderie that used to be, I feel quite choked.'

'I hope you realise,' said Ernie Houghton, looking on the gloomy side as usual, 'food rationing at home will be tighter than it used to be. It stands to reason.'

'Wait a minute,' said Len. 'There was no rationing when you left for France. They only started it in nineteen-forty.'

'Aye well, somebody had to get the war started.' He spat expertly, hitting a beetle that was on a direct course for the hut. 'It's just a bugger that they wouldn't let us go home afterwards. When all's said and done though, I suppose the rations will be better than we get here.'

'Steady, Ernie,' said Freddy. 'If you're not careful you'll be cheering us all up.'

. . .

'Freezin' weather in May. Who'd have thought it?' Dorothy came into the cabin, rubbing her hands with no real vigour.

'Where did you go?' Sylvia had been wondering about the phone message from Alf, asking Dorothy to meet him ashore.

'We just sat in the café, drinking tea. The pub was full and noisy.' She sat on her bed, seemingly reluctant to say more. Joyce carried on with her knitting and Sylvia looked down at her book without reading.

After a while, Dorothy said, 'He's got a draft. They've given him forty-eighters to go visit his dad and his grannie, and then he has to join his ship at Devonport on Wednesday.' She was silent for a moment longer and then said, 'It's wrong to make a fuss, isn't it? He's a serviceman and he has to go where he's sent. I just have to accept it.'

Joyce nodded. 'It's never easy.'

'No, but I shan't make a fuss.' She took out her sponge bag and towel. 'I'll see if there's any hot water left.'

As the door closed behind her, Joyce said, 'I've been expecting this.'

'Why?'

'Alf and Norris were only here on a temporary draft. They're trained for gunnery so it was only a matter of time.'

'And they'd only just met.'

'Some of us were only just married. War does that to people.'

'Yes, I suppose so.'

They both fell silent as the door opened but it was Angela who walked in. 'It's freezing up top.' She was rapidly picking up the nautical lexicon from her new boyfriend, a sub-lieutenant in one of the MTBs.

'Yes,' said Joyce, 'Dorothy just told us.'

'Oh yes, has she said what it was about?'

'Alf's been drafted to a ship,' Sylvia told her.

Angela pulled a sympathetic face. 'Bad luck. They're a nice couple.'

Their conversation stopped when Dorothy returned from the bathroom.

'I'd grab the water now,' she advised. 'It's not quite freezin' yet.' She undressed and got into bed.

. . .

Sylvia woke up during the night. Her shoulders were cold, and as she pulled the bedclothes up to cover them she heard Dorothy crying softly. After a minute she shone her pocket flashlight over the deck to chase the cockroaches away before pulling on her dressing gown and creeping over. Perching on the edge of the bed, she touched Dorothy's arm. 'It's all right,' she said. 'It's only me.' She slipped an arm around her.

The crying continued for quite some time, although she had no idea how long, and an icy draught from the window frame was turning her feet and ankles numb, even through her thick bed socks. She raised them in turn, rubbing them with her free hand but it made little difference. Eventually, she eased herself off the bed, lifted the bedclothes and slipped in beside Dorothy. The sharing of beds was strictly forbidden whatever the temperature, although Sylvia had no idea why. Neither, on this occasion, could she have cared less.

Presently, Dorothy's sobs grew smaller and less frequent, until she was able to say, 'I've gorra hagky … udder de pillow.' Her breath was coming in shudders. She found it and blew her nose. 'I said I wouldn't … make a fuss,' she said, putting the hanky away.

'It doesn't matter.'

'I'd only just … met 'im.'

'I know. Keep your voice down.' The others wouldn't have minded, Sylvia was sure, but she was anxious not to disturb them.

'I just love 'im so much.' Dorothy gave a tiny sob and Sylvia squeezed her shoulder.

'He has to go an' do … his duty like everyone else. It just … came too soon.'

'He'll be back. You'll see.'

'It's a battleship he's joinin'. He should be all right in that.'

'Oh yes, safe as houses.'

'He had to go to that Whale Island place, the gunnery school. Everybody says how hard it is. The discipline's really strict and they go everywhere at the rush. It's all drill an' rushin' around but Alf didn't care. He's been workin' farm machines since he was a kiddie an' he was fit enough to take all that drill an' that.'

'He would be.'

'And he didn't care about the instructors shoutin' an' screamin' an' carryin' on, 'cause he could do all the tasks without any effort. He should be all right. Don't you think so?'

'He'll be fine.'

'Yeah.'

'What ship is it?'

'*Howe*. I'm not supposed to tell anybody but we're all in this together, aren't we?'

'That's right, we are.'

Dorothy raised herself on one elbow and said, 'It's a funny name, though, *Howe*.'

'I suppose so, but it could have been worse.'

'How could it have been worse?'

'It could have been called "How am I supposed to know?" '

'That's right.'

They held on to each other for about a minute, giggling silently, fearful of making a sound, and eventually, Sylvia said, 'Are you going to be OK now?'

'Yeah, thanks.'

'Right, I'll see you in the morning.' She felt in the pocket of her dressing gown for her flashlight before lowering her feet to the deck. 'Good night.'

'Good night, Sylvia.'

. . .

'It's worth going through the delousing shower,' said Freddy, 'for the satisfaction of knowing that the lice must find it as painful as we do.'

'My sentiments exactly,' said Bailey. They stood in the delousing shed, waiting for their clothes to be returned to them, their bodies the colour of boiled lobster from the near-scalding shower.

There was a shout of '*Kleider*!' and a pile of clothing was dumped unceremoniously on the floor.

'You have to admire the goons,' said Freddy. 'They don't waste words.'

'Ah!' Bailey spotted his drawers immediately from the large name tape in the waistband. He plucked them from the pile and began waving them over his head.

Freddy watched him with the tolerance developed over months of living among lunatics. 'What on earth are you doing, Bailey?'

'Cooling them, dear fellow. My faithful friend has already suffered more than he should without being draped in scorching wool for good measure.

A neighbouring kriegie said, 'what's 'e say?'

'He doesn't want to burn his old fella,' said Freddy.

'Why can't 'e say so, then?'

'I don't know. It's defeated the finest medical minds.'

The prisoner looked Bailey up and down and said, 'Poor bugger.'

'Spare your pity for me,' Freddy told him. 'I'm the one who has to go through life translating for him.'

'Do me a favour, Freddy mate?' Len was struggling with his shirt.

'All right.' Freddy drew the sleeve over Len's troublesome right arm and held his shirt while he pushed his left arm through. 'There you are, mate.'

'Thanks, Freddy.'

The kriegie gave Freddy a strange look and joined the squad waiting to be marched away. Freddy pulled on his drawers, wincing as he did so and wishing he had followed Bailey's example.

Early in the afternoon there was a loudspeaker announcement. 'Prisoner 11296 Sergeant Patterson report to the medical centre immediately.'

'Everything's bloody immediate,' said Len, picking up his kit, 'but for once I don't mind.'

'Here, give me your kit. I'll walk across with you.'

'Thanks, Freddy.'

They walked to the medical centre, where Len reported to the orderly and was told to wait inside. Freddy wished him luck and then spent rest of the afternoon walking in the fresh air. He passed the Russian compound again and chose a moment when the guards in the tower had turned their backs, to lob four segments of Red Cross chocolate over the wire. Two Russians found them and called out what were no doubt their profuse thanks without necessarily knowing what he had given them. They would find out soon enough.

He continued on his walk, unable to settle without news of Len's fate and with no idea of how long the process might take. Eventually, however, he could wait no longer. He had only an approximate idea of the time, his wristwatch having been ruined by its immersion in sea water, but he estimated from his most recent enquiry that it must be about five-fifteen, so he returned to the medical centre.

The same orderly was seated at his desk. He looked up when he saw Freddy. '*Was ist los?*'

'I've come for my mate Sergeant Patterson. He came here this afternoon for examination.'

'*Ich spreche nicht Englisch.*'

'Like hell you don't. I want to speak to my friend.'

The orderly merely shrugged.

It went against the grain but Freddy reverted to German. '*Bitte, ich möchte mit* Sergeant Patterson *sprechen!*'

'*Es ist unmöglich.*'

'What do you mean, it's impossible? *Ich möchte mit* Sergeant Patterson *sprechen.*'

'*Es ist unmöglich! Gehst!*' The orderly gestured abruptly towards the door.

'I'm going nowhere until I've seen my friend. Where is he? *Wo ist* Sergeant Patterson?'

A door opened behind the orderly and a man in a white coat demanded to know what was happening. The orderly left his chair and stood to attention, addressing the man in the white coat, presumably a doctor, as *Herr Major*, and giving what Freddy saw as an exaggerated account of their conversation, with the emphasis on Freddy's rudeness to a soldier of the *Reich*.

Freddy saluted. 'I am sorry, *Herr Major*,' he said, 'but I am anxious for news of my friend Sergeant Patterson. He came here to be examined this afternoon.'

The doctor nodded. 'I see. Unfortunately it is impossible for you to speak with Sergeant Patterson because he is no longer here. He was taken this afternoon to the military hospital in Warsaw. He is fortunate that such an appointment is possible.' He took out his pen and ran his eye down the orderly's book.

'Thank you for telling me that, *Herr Major*. Are you able to tell me when I might see him again?'

The doctor made an entry and added his signature. 'If Sergeant Patterson is repatriated he will return eventually to England. Otherwise, who can say where he might find himself?'

18

June

It was Baker Watch's day off, and Sylvia and her cabin mates were discussing how they were going to use the day ahead, when the order came to clear lower deck. The ship's company was to muster on the parade ground at 0800.

Mindful of increased and sometimes deafening aerial activity over the channel and of the imposition of radio silence during the 'all-night-on', but hardly daring to hope, the four made their way to the parade ground to muster with the others. Fortunately, the foul weather of the past few days was no more. Instead, the sky was a welcome blue. They fell into their normal ranks and went through the usual routine, after which, at the Commander's arrival, they were brought to attention, stood at ease and finally told to stand easy.

The Commander cleared his throat and began. 'I have to tell you that early this morning Allied forces landed on several beaches in Normandy. There was some opposition but the Germans were taken largely by surprise, and our forces are now making progress inland.' He paused, no doubt enjoying the moment, and then delivered the announcement, 'D-Day has finally arrived!'

There was an audible reaction which, in the exceptional circumstances, he allowed before going on to read a communiqué from the Admiralty that told them much more. There was a great deal to take in but Sylvia was still digesting the initial announcement. She had barely left school at the time of the Dunkirk evacuation. Four years had passed since then but it seemed a lifetime, and now allied soldiers were once again on French soil. The news from Italy and the Far East was encouraging, more U-boats were being sunk in the Atlantic than ever before, and now the Allies had landed in France. Victory was only a matter of time. At least, that was what people would say. She remembered them saying it after El Alamein, but it wasn't true then any more than it was now. France and Germany were huge; it would take a long time to conquer them both and, more importantly, it would come only at a terrible cost in lives. She was certain of that.

They said the Prayer before a Fight at Sea. It was new to Sylvia and she found it very stirring. During the Naval Prayer, however, instead of experiencing the familiar goose bumps, she found herself thinking again about the awful price men must be paying at that very moment, and tears began to stream down her cheeks, not only for them but for those they had left behind, because she knew all too well how that felt.

PO Wren Dunn caught her as she was about to climb the stairs to the Wrens' quarters.

'Wren Charlesworth, what was that performance in aid of?'

'Performance, PO?'

'You know what I mean – your snivelling behaviour on the parade ground. What was the reason for it?'

'Oh that.' Sylvia noted her superior's reddened nose with some satisfaction, and inspiration came to her again. 'It was hay fever, PO. You know what it's like when the sun comes out.'

'Yes, well, try not to make an exhibition of yourself in future. You need to keep a very clean sheet if you expect to have your leading rate confirmed.'

'Yes, PO.' It pleased her that PO Wren Dunn would never know the true reason for her 'performance'. Some people just had no right to be told anything so personal and intimate. It was horribly frustrating, though, that she couldn't tell Freddy about D-Day.

. . .

It seemed odd to be back at Tamowicz without Len; in fact for him to be absent felt odd altogether. Len had been Freddy's companion since the early days at Veano, where they had first become friends, and the fact that they had chosen to remain together two years later and in the same workforce said much for the strength of their friendship, although neither would have remarked on it.

In the last five minutes of the meal break Freddy took out Sylvia's latest letter to read it again.

26th April, 1944.

Dear Freddy,

It was sweet of you to send that postcard but you mustn't worry. When you come back we're going to do all the things we've written about. I long for the day when we can meet face to face, and then I'll find out if you can really dance! I'm joking! I'll forgive you for anything, just for the joy of having you here. So don't worry!

I've been promoted! It should be confirmed if I stay out of trouble. Hooks have been in short supply but now I've got mine I can do an even better job.

Little Bruce is four months old and has stopped blowing raspberries. Instead, he hums, like Winnie-the-Pooh. My dad can't wait to take him fishing. He says the humming could fool the trout into thinking that there are lots of flies about. He once tried to teach me to cast for trout but I lacked the patience. I was only eight, so I don't see how he could expect very much of me. Are you keen on fishing? My brother-in-law David can't stand it. My mother doesn't mind my dad fishing because it gets him 'out from under her feet.' I think people should be allowed to please themselves as long as they're not hurting anyone. What do you think?

After all that rambling, it's time for me to go back to work, but I'll write again soon. Look after yourself, Freddy, because I do want to see you fit and healthy. Lots of love and best wishes,

Sylvia (or am I still 'Sugar Plum'?) XXXXX

As he folded the letter and put it away he saw Bailey watching him. He said, 'Good news, Freddy?'

'Yes, it's certainly good news.'

'I thought so. I could see it on your face.'

'Really?' There were times when Bailey could be quite intuitive.

'Well, are you going to spill the beans or is it a private matter?'

'No, it's not private. She's just told me she's got her hook.'

'Got her what?'

'She's been promoted to Leading Wren. The 'hook' is the killick, the wooden anchor on her badge.'

'She could easily outrank you when you get home, old man.'

'She could, mate, and we could both be old and grey by the end of the war.'

A great many kriegies shared that sentiment, but when a new draft from Lamsdorf arrived two days later to work at the repair yard they brought the news everyone wanted to hear.

'It's the usual drill,' an RAF corporal told them. 'The goons mustn't get wind that we know, but we heard on the camp wireless that the Allies landed in Normandy on Tuesday morning and they're knocking the living shit out of Jerry.'

Everyone was still, scarcely daring to believe it, and then someone asked,

'Are they there for keeps?' Possibly the speaker had memories of the Dieppe raid.

'Well, I suppose they'll go home eventually, but not until they've made Adolf sign on the dotted line.'

Their jubilation was suppressed but no less real once the news had sunk in, and Freddy relished the moment as much as anyone. He might have enjoyed it even more had he known something of Len's fortunes and whereabouts.

. . .

Since PO Wren Dunn's secret had become known, the question of how best to capitalise on it had occupied several minds, a number of Wrens having fallen foul of her authority. Her latest victim was Jane Forbes, this time for the offence of appearing on watch minus her back collar stud.

'I had to get dressed in a hurry,' she said when she was quizzed by her colleagues. 'I couldn't find the stud and I had to be on watch in five minutes.'

'You've just got to get organised,' said Joyce.

'That's right,' said Sylvia, 'but being improperly dressed isn't your worst crime. Your biggest failing is that when trouble comes stalking, you're the one saying, "Me, over here." You need to learn how to keep your head down.'

It was good advice, and with almost three years' experience Sylvia usually set a good example, so it was all the more unfortunate that she should let down her guard that evening as she went on watch.

She had almost reached the W/T Room when a number of officers, some in RAF uniform, came out of the Operations Room. As they turned to make their way to the front entrance, she recognised the flight-lieutenant from the Air-Sea Rescue launch, and in that same moment he saw her and returned her salute, smiling in recognition as he did so.

'Hello,' he said. 'How are you? Managing to stay out of trouble?'

'So far, sir.' Recalling their earlier conversation, she asked, 'How's your daughter coping with life in the Wrens, sir?'

'Oh, she's two-thirds of the way through her course now. She's training to be a wireless operator, like you.' He smiled again. 'I suppose I should say "telegraphist", shouldn't I?'

'It's the same thing, just another name and a different shade of blue.'

'That's right. Actually, she's finding it quite difficult, getting her Morse up to speed, although I'm sure that's quite normal.'

She nodded. 'Yes, it's all down to practice. She'll get there in the end and it'll seem like second nature when she does.'

He glanced at his wristwatch and said, 'Well, thank you for that. I'll be sure to pass the message on.'

'You do that, and wish her luck for me.'

'I shall. Goodbye and thank you for your words of comfort.'

'It's a pleasure. Goodbye, sir.' She saluted him and turned to find PO Wren Dunn in her path. She looked characteristically displeased.

'W/T Room, Wren Charlesworth, now!'

Sylvia gave a surreptitious sigh and led the way to the W/T Room. She had no idea what offence she had committed but she knew she was about to find out.

'I heard the whole of that conversation,' said the PO Wren when she joined her in the room, 'and I can only presume that you no longer find it necessary to address an officer as "sir".'

Sylvia frowned. 'But I did, PO.'

'Infrequently and very grudgingly.'

Suddenly Sylvia was angry. 'That's not true. I spoke to that officer with respect. I know him. His daughter ...'

'I'm not interested in his daughter, Charlesworth, but I am interested in your behaviour, and I find your attitude slovenly and disrespectful. As far as I'm concerned you can wave goodbye to your leading rate. You're a disgrace to the service.'

. . .

'So that was that.' Sylvia finished telling her story and made room for Angela, who joined them at breakfast.

'Are you talking about Medusa the Gorgon?'

'Yes,' said Joyce. 'She's just put paid to Sylvia's promotion.'

'Oh no, what rotten luck. What was that for?'

'Nothing at all.' Sylvia shook her head dejectedly. 'She makes it up as she goes along.'

Angela made a reluctant assault on her fried Spam and said, 'She's just given me a bottle because I had a button undone.' Her eyes flashed with anger. 'Across the Channel men are locked in battle, U-boats are stalking our convoys, cities are being bombed, and she picks on me because I have a button undone.'

'You know why she does it, don't you?' Dorothy had evidently given the problem some thought and now posed the question, 'What have Sylvia, Jane and Angela got in common?'

'They've got targets pinned to their backs,' said Joyce.

'Yeah, but why?'

'God knows.'

'I'll tell you why.'

'Go on then.'

'It's because they're two things she's not. They're young and they're pretty.' She looked at each of them in turn like a stage detective delivering his final deduction. 'She's jealous and it's made her bitter and twisted.'

'I suppose it makes sense,' said Joyce.

'I should know.' Dorothy looked at them frankly. 'But I've got you lot to boost my confidence occasionally.'

'You're not at all like her,' said Angela, 'but you're right about one thing. She's a frustrated old battleaxe.'

'The lads on sentry duty have a nickname for her,' said Dorothy. 'They call her "Never Been Dunn".' She laughed shortly. 'The same could be said of some of us but it hasn't blighted our outlook on life, has it?'

Sylvia took the disappointment of her lost promotion up to the cabin, where she could at least enjoy the luxury of sleep and a few hours' freedom from unpleasantness.

. . .

Len was beginning to question the German reputation for efficiency and organisation. He had been examined at Tamowicz, at Lamsdorf, in Warsaw, and now he was to be examined again at Luckenwalde, a camp that, according to a communicative orderly, was somewhere to the south east of Berlin. It was as if the Germans had no confidence in their medical officers. Meanwhile, he was heartily tired of long journeys in slow trains that stopped with infuriating frequency. It seemed that allied air raids had damaged the railway system and were therefore responsible for the detours and delays, and in most other contexts the information might have been heartening, but in Len's case and that of his fellow-travellers it was purely academic.

The occupant of the adjacent bunk was an RAF corporal, a wireless operator who had lost his right hand in a mining accident.

'Take my advice, mate,' he said. 'Keep away from those bloody coal mines, whatever you do. It's hell down there.' He waved his bandaged stump in emphasis. 'I'll never complain about striking miners again.'

'I'm still hoping this thing will get me out of here,' said Len, pointing to his now-immobilised arm.

'Don't bank on it.'

'What have you heard?' Every camp had its Jeremiahs but the man might know something.

'A bloke I knew in Lamsdorf had his arm off just below his shoulder,' the corporal told him. 'You'd have thought he was a dead cert for repatriation but they turned him down and passed a bloke with dyspepsia instead.'

'Well, I never.' Len was hazy about dyspepsia but it sounded quite trivial. 'What's your problem anyway?'

'Neuritis,' said Len. 'There are times when I can't move this arm without it hurting like hell, and they say it's most likely chronic.'

The corporal laughed shortly. 'You haven't a hope.'

. . .

Jane Forbes looked particularly relieved at supper and the reason was soon apparent. She asked Joyce, 'Do you remember telling me to get organised?'

Joyce nodded.

'Well, that's what Third Officer Fuller said when I reported to her.'

Dorothy looked up. 'You saw Third Officer Fuller?'

'She was standing in for Second Officer Bright-Davies.'

'That was a lucky escape.'

'Anyway,' said Sylvia, 'what else did she say?'

'Oh, just that I have to establish a routine, to stop being a scatterbrain and to start setting an example to younger recruits when they arrive.'

'Quite right,' said Joyce, maintaining a straight face.

'She says I have special qualities in that respect that I need to develop.' She frowned for a second and said, 'I don't know how she knows that. I mean she hasn't seen all that much of me.'

'Nothing escapes Third Officer Fuller,' said Sylvia.

'Well, I think she's jolly nice.'

'She is, just as long as you stay out of trouble,' said Joyce.

'Oh, I shall.'

'I think you will,' said Angela, joining them late as usual but with a look that promised interesting tidings. 'Take it from me – Never Been's days are numbered, if her number is not already up.'

'But how?' Sylvia, among the rest, wanted desperately to believe it.

'This is just as it was told to me by one of the girls in the Paymaster's office.' She waited for their rapt attention and began. 'Jane came out of Three-Oh Fuller's office after breakfast and Never Been wanted to know what punishment she'd been given. Right, Jane?'

'That's right. She was almost gloating.'

'And when Jane said she'd got a reprimand, Never Been went mad. She went to see Three-Oh Fuller straight away and demanded to know why she hadn't given Jane at least fourteen days' Number One Punishment, and Three-Oh Fuller told her just where she got off. Apparently, the upper echelons have been getting quite bored lately with her unreasonable behaviour.'

'Why didn't they act sooner?'

'I don't know, Joyce, but Three-Oh Fuller passed the ball up to Two-Oh Bright-Davies, who bounced it all the way to the top, and now Dunn is undone, so to speak, and peace is about to return to the venerable pile.'

19

So much for "Flaming June,"' said Joyce, watching the rain through the café window. 'It's nearly flaming July and it's high time the flaming sun came out.'

'Do you remember that song Sam Browne used to sing: "The Sun Has Got His Hat On"? I was about seven or eight when I first heard it but I still enjoy it.'

Joyce smiled. 'I'm sorry, Sylvia. I'm being miserable.'

'You can be miserable in my company if you want to be. We're friends of equal rank. Equal rate anyway.'

'That's true.' Second Officer Bright-Davies had confirmed Sylvia's leading rate two days earlier, and they were relieved to learn that they were allowed to stay in their old cabin as long as they took their turn at the various duties expected of them in their exalted status.

'Have you still not heard from Len?' Sylvia knew Joyce well enough that she could usually put her finger on the problem.

'No, I haven't. I know the mail gets held up sometimes but it's frustrating when it happens.'

'How long has it been?'

'Nine weeks.'

'So the last one must have been …'

Joyce nodded. 'St George's Day, when you got that postcard from Freddy.'

'The mail's very erratic.' Sylvia patted her bag. 'This one came today and it only took three weeks. They usually take at least a month.' An idea occurred to her. 'I'll be writing to Freddy today,' she said, 'so I'll ask him to give Len a shove and tell him to write to you.'

'No, don't do that. If he's written and the letter's been delayed he'll worry about it.'

'Fair enough.' Sylvia looked up to see the café owner coming their way. 'Grub's up,' she announced.

'You sound more like a sailor every day, Sylvia.'

'No, I don't. For one thing, I don't tell dirty jokes all the time.'

'That's not surprising. You don't understand most of them.'

'There you are, ladies.' The café owner put the two plates down in front of them. 'Meat pie and chips.' She shook her head in disbelief. 'I don't know how you girls keep your figures.'

'We don't usually eat as well as this,' said Sylvia.

'Don't you? Well, tuck in then. I'll bring your tea across in a jiffy.'

'Thanks.' Joyce sniffed at the steam rising from her plate and said, 'I don't know what kind of meat is lurking in this pie but I know where it's going.'

'It could be horse or rabbit or squirrel.'

'I don't care.' Joyce cut into it enthusiastically and said, 'Dorothy got a letter from Alf this morning, quite a long one by his standards. I wonder how long it took him to write it.'

'I think it's really sweet, the way Dorothy had him practising before he went away. We'll look back in years to come and remember it as the big romance of the war.'

'Mm.' Joyce tasted the pie. 'It's minced beef all right. I think there's something else in there as well but that's OK with me. Yes, they've surprised everyone but they're certainly good for each other.' She thanked the café lady as she set down two mugs of tea, and said, 'What about you, Sylvia? Do you still think about James as much as you used to?'

'No, I don't. I feel guilty about it sometimes but I can't really help it.'

'I think you're just coping better than you were. You've nothing to feel guilty about.'

'I don't know. It's just that I have so many things to think about nowadays. He's no longer in the forefront of my mind.'

'That's right, and the difference is remarkable.'

Sylvia winced. 'Was I really so awful?'

'No, you weren't awful, but you needed something to take you out of yourself, and I think writing to Freddy helped no end. I expect you think about him rather a lot.'

She was right. Sylvia was thinking about him more than ever before. She had an unopened letter from him in her bag, collected from the mail office as they came ashore that morning, and she was looking forward with childlike eagerness to reading it.

She opened it that afternoon when she had the cabin to herself.

4th June, 1944.

Dear Sugar Plum,

Of course you're still Sugar Plum. I don't bestow temporary titles. It's yours for keeps, and on that subject, congratulations on your promotion. I'm sure you deserve it. The old firm will be all the better for it as well.

You're also my favourite love pot, because I now have copies of 'A Knight on Wheels' and 'The Midshipmaid', and I can read those two repeatedly. Thank you in a great big way for that. I really will put things straight with you when I get back. I've cost you a king's ransom already.

I enjoyed reading about your family, and I hope for your father's sake little Bruce embraces the rod and line. Unfortunately, my interest in fishing extends as far as sitting on a river bank, preferably on a deck chair and in agreeable weather, eating the odd sandwich and drinking pale ale whilst someone else does the angling, dangling and untangling. I do agree with you, though, that people should be allowed to follow their innocent pleasures.

Unfortunately, space is running out, but another letter is on its way, well, almost. Take care, Dear S.P.

Lots of love,

Freddie XXX

Sensible of her friend's predicament, she put the letter away when Joyce came in, and it was late afternoon before she could write to Freddy.

28th June, 1944.

Dear Freddy,

As you can see, your 4th June came remarkably quickly. Let's hope things are looking up in that respect.

What is a 'love pot'? It sounds really nice but it's a new one on me and I've certainly never been called one until now. I'm glad the books arrived. I'd die if I had nothing to read, and don't worry about the money – they're a present from my mum and dad.

Joyce and I saw 'Ali Baba and the Forty Thieves' last week, starring Maria Montez and Jon Hall. It was very exciting and quite funny, but after our recent romantic diet of David Niven and Ginger Rogers I was a bit disappointed. On the way home we ate fish and chips. My mother would have gone mad and blamed the war for our plummeting standards, but we were hungry.

In case this war goes on beyond another winter, and Heaven forbid that it does, I'm going to remobilise the knitting circle, so if there's anything you'd particularly like, just say the word. It can be as difficult as you like, e.g. if you want gloves with fingers you shall have them. We've got a new girl working with us now, a brilliant knitter.

I hope my last letter will reach you in time for your birthday. You'll find a few extra things in your parcel.

Do take care, because you're precious too. Lots of love,
Your favourite love pot (I'm dying to know),
Sugar Plum XXXXX

. . .

Freddy's second letter arrived two weeks later.

4th June, 1944. Part Two
Dear Sugar Plum,
How is Peter Ross these days? He sounds like a venerable old gent, and reading about him reminds me of how comforting it is to think of things gentler than many of those that surround me.

I like to think about the contentment and companionship your dad and Peter Ross must find on that river bank, the benevolent industry of your mother and the knitters, your sister and brother-in-law and their contribution to the next generation, and little Bruce himself, who represents the best things at a time when they're most needed.

Most of all, I think about you and the good things you've come to represent in my life. You've shown me friendship, compassion and concern, and believe me when I tell you they're a powerful remedy for the kind of hopelessness I felt when I arrived here.

I hope this doesn't sound too mawkish – I'd run a mile rather than tell you these things face to face – but I thought you'd like to know.

Take care, dear Sugar Plum,
Lots of love,
Freddy XXXX

Sylvia replied at the end of her next watch.

13th July, 1944.
Dear Freddy,
Of course you're not mawkish, and I'm glad you told me those things. Most of all, I'm glad I've been able to make you feel better. You've done a lot for me too.

Now, in answer to your original question, Peter Ross is well, thank you. He's twelve years old but he's fit and active, and always at his happiest during the brown trout season. Like you, he's a willing spectator, and I heard today that he has a new playmate, a blue roan Cocker Spaniel called Rainbow. She's two years old, and my dad adopted her because she belonged to an ex-client who could no longer look after her. She came with the name Rainbow – nothing to do with the trout, although the association inevitably helped endear her to my single-minded parent – and I think it's a lovely name, a promise of better, brighter things to come. Now, there's something for you to think about!

You must never feel hopeless. It would be awful for a man of twenty-five to feel that he had no future, so if you feel it creeping up on you again, tell me and I'll scare it away.

I hope you got my birthday wishes in time. Take care, because I care about you.

Lots of love,
Sugar Plum XXXXXX

. . .

Joyce also received a letter. It was from Len, dated the 18th May. She learned that he had injured his arm and that the treatment involved a great deal of travel. He said he would write whenever he could.

20

August

Sylvia extracted one podgy hand from the front of her dress. 'No, Bruce, I've told you before; there's nothing in there for you.'

'He'll undress you if you're not careful,' said Audrey. 'I think he just wants something to do with his hands.'

'He's like an American sailor I met at a dance.'

'Really? Come on, tell all.'

Sylvia shrugged. 'He liked to use his hands too. I just let him know there was nothing doing.' They were alone on Audrey's lawn and could exchange confidences that would otherwise have been impossible. Audrey was taller and more generously proportioned than her sister but they were very much alike in character and, apart from occasional disagreements, had an easy relationship despite the four years that separated them.

'All the same,' said Audrey, 'you must have a pretty good time down there.'

'I like the work and we get ashore quite a lot to dances and things, but it isn't all fun and frolics.'

'Don't you get to meet lots of men?'

Sylvia removed Bruce's hand again. 'Not in *Wasp*. Apart from the sailors on the boats the establishment is mainly female.'

'Oh, bad luck.'

'We meet men from other places when we go to dances. There are two RAF stations within about fifteen miles and there's a permanent garrison in Dover.'

'And you've got Freddy to write to.'

Sylvia had been wondering when the subject of Freddy would enter the conversation. 'That's true.' She removed Bruce's hand and held him at arm's length so that he was looking down at her. 'I don't know what to do with you, young man. I really don't. I think I'll hold you up like this all day and you won't be able to do a thing.'

Bruce chortled at the prospect.

'What kind of thing do you find to write to him about?'

'I tell him what I've been doing, what films I've seen and how I feel about things. We have a lot in common.'

'Such as what?'

'Music, dancing, dogs, not fly fishing …' they both laughed. 'And I tell him about us, our family.'

'Really?'

'He's got no family of his own.'

'Of course.' Audrey plucked a solitary daisy while she thought about that. Presently she asked, 'What does he put in his letters?'

'He tells me about things he did before the war, about his little foibles and flights of fancy.' She rose to her feet and held the baby above her head. 'But for now, my friend, you are going to fly!' She began to caper around the lawn, holding him out like an aeroplane on a fairground roundabout.

'Careful, Sylvia. You'll get dizzy and drop him.'

'I shan't get dizzy.' Sylvia subsided on to the grass nevertheless, placing the delighted child beside her.'

'All that ballet training, I suppose.'

'That's right.'

Audrey returned to the original topic. 'I must say, his letters sound a bit unusual.'

'They have to be. If he writes anything about the prison camp or the war, the censor will smother it in blue crayon, so he writes about other things instead.' She smiled as something occurred to her. 'He once told me I was his favourite love pot. I wonder what the censor made of that.'

'I wonder too. What's a love pot?'

'I asked him that. He told me he had a pretend auntie when he was a child. She was a friend of the family but the children had to call her "auntie".' She broke off to tweak Bruce's nose. 'She was quite a kind auntie, Bruce, almost like your Auntie Sylvia except that she wasn't all that keen on little boys.' She returned to the story. 'She used to call Freddy's sister 'Little Love Pot'. I suppose it was like 'honey pot' or something like that, but she never called Freddy that.' She covered Bruce's ears with her hands and said, 'She sometimes called him 'Little Horror' instead, and I think that was a shame, but anyway, someone who is precious is a love pot.'

'And you're precious.'

'So is he.'

'Even though you've never met him?'

'I know him well enough.'

Audrey gave her a straight look and said, 'Be careful, Sylvia.'

'It's a bit late for that.'

. . .

Freddy and Bailey were now responsible for oiling locomotives and rolling stock, a task they carried out with enthusiastic carelessness, their omissions being almost undetectable. In its preference for guns over butter, the Nazi regime had neglected its railways to the extent that breakdowns were the accepted norm. Therefore, as Freddy and Bailey saw the situation, they were only helping to preserve the *status quo*.

At 0700 their supervisor had issued them each with a large pressure oilcan and orders to oil anything that contained a moving part. It was now 1530 and so far nothing had moved, even minutely. All the locomotives and rolling stock in the yard were stationary and therefore oiling was clearly unnecessary.

'When we get back to Blighty,' said Bailey, idly dribbling oil along a length of rail, 'we'll be expected to do an honest day's work. What's the betting that by then we'll have forgotten how?'

'I shouldn't be surprised.' Freddy's response was as distant as his thoughts. Suddenly he asked, 'What's your Christian name, Bailey?'

'It's Gerard, old chap.' He seemed surprised by the question.

'Would you rather I called you that than use your surname all the time?' Actually 'Gerard' sounded like the kind of name Bailey might invent for himself, but it was an amicable gesture that required little effort and now that they were thrown together it would be as well to get things on the right footing.

'No, old man. Let's stick with "Bailey". Nearly everyone calls me that.' He inclined his head thoughtfully for a second and added, 'At least it's better than "Bullshit". I don't know what I've done to deserve that.'

'I can't imagine either.'

They dribbled oil on the rails and between the sleepers for a while longer, until Bailey said, 'I wouldn't give a damn what anyone called me if I could just get a square meal once in a while.'

'Amen to that.'

'One of the civvy workers was tucking into sausage and bread at breakfast.'

'Don't, Bailey.'

125

'I know, old man. It does the same to me, but one of those chaps must be amenable to a spot of barter.'

Freddy nodded thoughtfully. 'It's worth a try.'

'I'm all for giving it a try. A man needs a goal in life, and that sausage and bread looked very inviting.'

. . .

'You're getting keen on Freddy, aren't you?' Sylvia's mother washed the last of the plates and placed it on the draining board for her to dry.

'I suppose Audrey's been talking.'

'Only because she's concerned about you. We all are. You've been hurt once and we don't want it happening again, that's all.'

'I know what I'm doing.' As she dried the knives and forks she dropped them, perhaps a little too noisily, into the cutlery drawer. She was annoyed both with Audrey and her mother for treating her as a child.

'Sylvia, you're twenty years old. You can't possibly know what you're doing. You've never met him, you know hardly anything about him, and for all you know he may be completely wrong for you. Goodness knows, I'm happy enough to do some knitting for him and send him parcels, and it's nice that you write to him, but I do think you're getting carried away with all this.' Having wiped down the sink and draining board, she draped the wrung-out dishcloth over the taps in a deliberate movement that seemed to prohibit further argument.

'You don't understand.' Sylvia pulled out a chair for herself from beneath the kitchen table, determined to make her mother see her position.

'Don't tell me I don't understand. I haven't got to my age without learning a thing or two. You're just starting out and you've got a lot to learn, believe me.'

'But you don't listen.' Tears of frustration were pricking her eyelids. 'I've learned things about him that I couldn't possibly learn about someone I met in the usual way. That's what makes it so special, only you just close your mind to anything I tell you because you don't want to know. You're not prepared to give him or me a chance.'

Suddenly, her mother was furious. 'Now you listen to me, my girl …'

'What on earth is going on?' Sylvia's father stood in the doorway, alarmed by the raised voices in the kitchen.

'I'm trying to explain to this obstinate child that we're only trying to save her from herself and a lot of heartbreak. Unfortunately, she seems to have forgotten her manners as well as her common sense.'

He looked from one to the other, his angry wife and his tearful daughter. 'In that case,' he said, 'that's where we're going to leave it tonight.'

126

'You try reasoning with her,' said his wife, clearly frustrated by his intervention.

'No, I've just said I'll have no more of this tonight. Raised voices never solved anything.' He eyed them both again sternly. 'We'll talk about it tomorrow when you've both calmed down.'

'I'm going to bed. Good night.' Sylvia brushed her father's cheek and headed miserably for the stairs.

For a while, she lay on her bed, sobbing. She hated falling out with her parents, but in this one matter she was determined not to back down. In five months she would be twenty-one, old enough to please herself. It was just awful that there had to be so much unpleasantness in the meantime.

After a while, she heard her parents' voices below. It was impossible to make out everything they said but she could tell that her mother was still complaining about her. Then she heard her father speaking. He was saying something about 'rushing in and causing upset', and then he said something about 'a right way and a wrong way'. He sounded very stern. Quite clearly, she heard him say, 'She has three more days' leave. Goodness knows when we'll see her again, and I come in here and find her in tears …' His voice tailed off, and Sylvia imagined they must have gone into the sitting room. She had no wish to make trouble between them any more than she had wanted the row with her mother, but whether she liked it or not it was all happening now. Wretchedly, she undressed and got into bed.

She had been lying there for some time when there was a soft knock on her door. Wondering quite what to expect, she said, 'Come in.'

The door opened and she saw her father silhouetted against the light on the landing. 'I thought you'd like a cup of tea,' he said, coming in and placing it on her bedside table.

'Thanks.' There was little else she could say.

'Move over and let me sit down.' He let her make room for him and then perched on the edge of the bed. 'The conversation got out of hand tonight,' he said. 'Things were said in anger that should never have been said, and you must never speak to your mother like that again.'

'I know. I'm sorry.'

'Well, you'll have a chance to put things right. You see, your mother's so anxious for you that it makes her a bit on the sharp side, and you have to realise that whether she's right or wrong she has your best interests at heart.'

'I know, but …'

'No arguments tonight. We'll talk later.' He took her hand and held it between his. 'I'm going fishing tomorrow. I'll be taking Peter Ross and Rainbow with me. Would you like to come?'

127

'Oh yes.' Absurdly, she felt like a little girl again.

'All right then. We'll do that.' He leant over and kissed her. 'Good night, love.'

'Good night, Dad.' She sipped the tea before settling down, confident that he would at least listen to her.

. . .

'Which one was it?' Freddy peered at the group of workers who stood at the entrance to the shed.

'The tall one, second in from the right. He walked past me three times, and I'll swear he inhaled a cloud of smoke each time.'

'Right,' said Freddy, 'we'll keep an eye on him.'

Bailey nodded in agreement. 'His name's Stern, but I don't know whether that's his Christian name or his surname.'

'It's a surname. It means "star".'

'And that's what he may turn out to be.'

'If we're careful,' cautioned Freddy. 'Let's not get too eager.'

'Tell that to my stomach.'

'I know, but we've got to box clever. If the goons find out what we're doing we'll end up in a *Sonderlager*.'

Bailey looked mystified. 'I've heard of them,' he said, 'and I gather they're not recommended, but I haven't a clue what the word means.'

'It means "Special Camp", but that's a Nazi euphemism. They're punishment camps.'

Bailey looked at him with undisguised approbation 'I've always admired anyone who can speak a foreign lingo,' he said. 'Not my thing at all.'

'But you told me you were at Eton,' said Freddy, affecting surprise.

'Absolutely right, old thing, but I flunked languages completely.'

'I see.' A pilot of Freddy's acquaintance had once told him that failure wasn't allowed at Eton. It seemed that Bailey was weaving an increasingly tangled web.

In one respect, however, he was entirely genuine, and that was in his determination to obtain food. His chance came the following morning, when Herr Stern stopped to speak to him.

'Ah, you are always smoking.' Stern sniffed the cloud appreciatively. 'English cigarettes are good.'

'And not only that, old fruit. We make dashed good chocolate as well. Ever heard of Cadbury's?'

A frown crept across Stern's face. 'What is Cadbury's?'

'Cadbury's, my dear old soul, is chocolate, finer chocolate than you can possibly imagine.' He took a four-ounce packet from his breast pocket to show him. 'Have a piece?'

Stern shook his head quickly. 'Trading with prisoners is forbidden.'

Bailey smiled indulgently. 'Who said anything about trading, Herr Stern? We wouldn't dream of it.' He broke off a row of segments and tore off the silver paper to offer one to the German. 'A goodwill offering, my friend, a gift.'

Stern looked alarmed.

'*Ein Geschenk,*' Freddy assured him, '*Es ist nicht giftich.*' Turning to Bailey, he said, '*Gift* means "poison". He thinks you're trying to kill him.'

'A mistake anyone could make, old man.' Bailey watched as, reassured, Stern placed the chocolate in his mouth like a gourmet trying a celebrated recipe. Within seconds, his face became a study in ecstasy as the confection melted on his taste buds. Finally, after sucking the last traces from his teeth, he said, 'English chocolate is also very good. It is unfortunate that it is forbidden with prisoners to trade.'

Freddy and Bailey watched him walk away. 'We shall see,' said Bailey.

. . .

Sylvia viewed the sandwiches with surprise.

'Your mum got up bright and early to make them for us,' her father told her. 'And there must be a week's cheese ration in there. Of course, it goes further when you grate it like this.'

'We never get cheese on board,' said Sylvia. 'Pilchards, herrings and corned beef, yes, but not cheese.' Whilst adamant about Freddy, she was still feeling guilty about her previous evening's outburst and it was a relief to be talking about food. She and her father had discussed most things that morning but the subject of Freddy remained so far untouched. It was as if he were waiting for the right moment, whenever that might be, and Sylvia felt unaccountably nervous. There was no reason why she should feel nervous of her father but the circumstances made her so. She took a cheese sandwich from the tin, conscious that Peter Ross and Rainbow were watching her carefully. They both knew there was a limit to their luck, but dogs could dream. It was a dreamy place below Redmire Falls on the River Ure. Her father could not have brought her to a pleasanter place. She just wished he would speak to her about Freddy. She had felt tempted to broach the subject herself but it seemed wrong, somehow, as if by doing that she would be the little girl again, pleading for a treat. No, it would be much better if he spoke first, and she had a feeling that he had been waiting until lunch was over.

When the sandwiches were gone he lit his pipe, and when he was satisfied

Ray Hobbs

it was going well, said, 'Now, Sylvia, tell me why you're so sure that this man you've neither met nor seen is the right man for you.'

Sylvia looked down at her knees, still taken aback after waiting so long. Eventually, she said, 'It doesn't matter that I've never seen him, Dad, because it doesn't matter what a man looks like. It's what's inside that matters.' She plucked a blade of grass and absently tied a knot in it. 'Anyway, my friend Joyce's husband Len says that Freddy looks a lot like him, and I've seen photos of Len and he looks all right to me.'

Her father nodded. 'I can accept that, but what about the fact that you've never met him? That's important, isn't it?'

'No, not in this case. You can see someone regularly over a period of time and still not get to know them properly because there's so much happening all the time, so many distractions.' Something returned to her that she had not considered for some time. 'I saw James regularly for five months,' she said, 'and we got quite serious, as you know, but I never got to know him. Not really. When I met his mother she told me things about him – just funny ways, habits, attitudes and the way he reacted sometimes – that took me completely by surprise. I never knew any of those things because we were always busy finding out what was on at the pictures, when we could go ashore together, where there was a dance we could go to and that sort of thing. I never found out what his favourite songs were or which bands and singers he liked and I had no idea how he felt about the important things in life.'

Her father nodded and blew out a long plume of smoke but said nothing. He hardly ever interrupted her when she was telling him something important, and that was a mixed blessing because, whilst she knew he was listening, it rather put her under the spotlight and she felt exposed. Interrupting was a female thing. Women did it to help each other tell their story. It was a matter of co-operation, and men didn't always appreciate that. For the present, though, it was probably good that he was listening to her.

'It's different with Freddy,' she went on. 'Because we can't write about the war, about what I'm doing or how he's coping in the prison camp, we write about the way we feel about lots of things. We tell each other how we coped with life before the war and sometimes we write about things that happened to us as children.' As she thought of things that had passed between them, her mind returned to his first letter. 'He's very sensitive, you know. I mean sensitive to other people's feelings. After James was killed I got really annoyed when people said silly things. It was obvious they'd no idea how I felt and they just had to say something. Freddy was different. He mentioned it in his first letter – I suppose he thought he'd better get it out of the way – and of course he'd lost his whole family in the Blitz, something I can't begin to imagine, and he wrote about it in such a way that I knew we were on the same wavelength.' She stopped because the dogs were engaged in a noisy tug-of-war with a stick they had found. It was very distracting but suddenly Peter Ross let go of his end and went off to investigate something else. Rainbow lay down to chew the stick.

'There was another time,' she said, 'when I was terribly upset about something that happened when I was on watch. One of the boats was badly damaged and the telegraphist was trying to send us a signal, but he was so badly wounded he couldn't send coherent Morse. I had to ask for several repetitions before I got the complete message, and the poor man must have been in agony. He died on the way to hospital. It was a horrible thing to happen and I felt desperate, but two days later I got a letter from Freddy, written four weeks earlier. He'd seen something awful – I don't know exactly what – and he'd been wondering why he felt guilty about something that was no fault of his, so he gave it some thought and came up with a theory that seemed to explain it. I shan't go into it now, but it really made me feel better about my problem. His letter just happened to arrive when it did – it was nothing more than a coincidence – but isn't it marvellous that he was able to make me feel so much better, even without knowing it?'

'It's a remarkable story.' Her father puffed at his pipe until he realised it had gone out. Putting it on the ground beside him, he said, 'That sailor dying, it was awful that you had to take it to heart.'

'Horrible things happen in wartime, as you know, and however bad I felt, I was still better off than he was.'

'That's true, and it must have been a remarkable letter that Freddy sent you.'

Sylvia sighed. 'I'm glad you can see that but you're not the only one I have to convince.'

Her father replaced the lid on the sandwich tin and returned it to his bag. 'Don't say anything this evening,' he said. 'I believe you're going to see Grannie Charlesworth tomorrow?'

'Tomorrow morning, yes.'

'All right,' he said. 'That's when I'll talk to your mother.'

. . .

Neither Freddy nor Bailey was surprised when Herr Stern approached them the next day. He seemed nervous and kept looking over his shoulder.

'Relax,' Freddy told him. '*Haben Sie kein Angst.*'

'Of course.' Stern nodded nervously.

'Think of cigarettes and chocolate,' said Bailey.

'Yes, it is about chocolate that I wish to speak.'

'The floor is yours, old scout.'

Stern looked puzzled. 'What means "scout"?'

'Don't worry,' Freddy told him. 'Let's talk about chocolate, and please stop looking over your shoulder. You'll have the *Gestapo* here if you're not careful.'

'Yes, of course.' Stern licked his lips and began. 'My children have never eaten chocolate.'

'That's too bad. How many children have you?'

'I have two: a boy and a girl.'

'Lovely, and you'd like to give them some chocolate?'

He nodded vigorously. 'Yes, if I may have some, please.'

Freddy appeared to consider the request. 'It's not easy,' he said. 'The Red Cross send us chocolate because we can't live on the compressed sawdust and cabbage water the Fatherland feeds us. It's very necessary, you know.'

'We'd be buggered without it,' confirmed Bailey.

'What means "buggered"?'

'You really don't want to know. The important thing is that if we give you chocolate you must give us food.'

Stern was sweating now. 'What do you want?'

'Sausage, bread and cheese for both of us.' Freddy held up a finger. 'That's for two weeks.'

'It is difficult.'

'So is chocolate,'

'Especially Cadbury's,' added Bailey.

'Cadbury's, yes.' It was a timely reminder. 'Very well, for three packets of chocolate.'

'Two.'

'Only two?'

'It's very special, and there's only one in each Red Cross parcel.' He was thankful to Sylvia for including extra chocolate in her last shipment.

'Two packets,' agreed Stern.

'Good man. You bring food, we give you one bar of chocolate at the end of the week. More food and you get the second bar at the end of the next week. *Verstehen-Sie?*'

'*Jawohl.*'

'Good. Now bugger off like a good chap and try not to look so bloody nervous.'

Bailey waited until he was out of earshot and said, 'He reminds me of the time I had my first spot of you-know-what. I was as nervous as that.'

Freddy gave him a tired smile. 'I'm sure I'm going to hear about it, Bailey, whether I want to or not. When did this happen?'

'It was when I was at school. I went into town looking for a tart.'

Freddy feigned shock. 'Not in Windsor, surely?'

'No, dear boy. When I say "town" I'm referring to the West End.'

'Of course, just down the road.'

'As a matter of fact it was during the half-term holiday.'

'Right, and you were looking for a half-term treat?'

'Yes, and do stop interrupting, old chap. It's very tiresome.'

'Sorry.'

'Good. Well, I was in Greek Street …'

'In your short trousers and school cap?'

'Freddy!'

'I shall say no more.'

'Good. And a voice said, "'Ello, dearie. Lookin' for a nice time?"'

Freddy stifled a laugh with difficulty.

'Well, she wanted ten bob for the whole business but I managed to beat her down to seven. It was late afternoon and trade was slow. You know how it is.'

'No, I don't.' Freddy had forgotten his vow of silence.

'Do you mean you've never had a tart?'

'Never.'

Bailey stared at him. 'My dear old thing, do you mean you're a virgin?'

'No, I'm not a virgin but I've never paid for it either.'

'Well, I was a kid, so I was obliged to. Anyway, there I was, wearing sunglasses to preserve the incognito …'

'The school cap and short trousers would have given you away, not to mention the catapult in your back pocket.'

Bailey could scarcely contain his disappointment. 'Freddy,' he said, 'there's no impressing you, is there?'

'Oh, I'm impressed, Bailey.'

'Are you?'

'Of course I am. I've never known anyone who could tell a string of elaborate whoppers the way you do, and without a trace of shame.'

Bailey breathed the sigh of one who has been found out. 'Ah well,' he said, 'I suppose that's some consolation.'

21

Sylvia travelled back to Dover in a reasonably contented frame of mind. Her argument had impressed her father, and he must have done a thorough job on her mother, whose attitude, if not entirely softened, was certainly less entrenched.

She was also pleased to find the girls, and particularly Joyce, in a celebratory mood.

'You'll never guess,' she said. 'Len's coming home! They told me today!'

After the initial shock she reacted. 'That's wonderful!' She allowed herself to be caught up in a general hug. 'But how? I mean why?' Her first thought was that he must have escaped, and if that were the case surely Freddy would have escaped with him.

'He's being repatriated.'

'There's somethin' wrong with his arm,' Dorothy told her excitedly, as if it were the latest fashion.

'I'm going to see someone in the Sick Bay tomorrow, to ask about it,' said Joyce. 'It's called neuritis. Have you heard of it?'

'I can't say I have.' Sylvia hid her disappointment that Freddy wasn't also on his way home, and said, 'The lady who brought the milk from the farm suffered from neuralgia and Grannie Charlesworth is crippled with arthritis, but neuritis must be something completely different from either of them.'

'It must be a long-term thing,' said Angela, 'to make him unfit for service in the RAF.' She added quickly, 'But it's not bound to be awful, is it?'

Seeing the alarm on Joyce's face, Sylvia said, 'My brother-in-law is unfit for military service and you'd never think it.'

'What's wrong with him?' Dorothy was never too shy to ask about such matters.

'He broke his hip some time ago and it left him with a bit of a limp.' She left out the bit about his eyesight and one leg being shorter than the other. It was possible to furnish too many details, and what she had said was basically true.

'Yeah, it makes sense,' said Dorothy, taking her cue from Sylvia. 'A lad down our street got turned down by the army 'cause of his flat feet. Mind you, they don't stop 'im doin' 'is civvy job.'

Angela asked, 'What's that?'

'Well, I call it a job. 'E's a bookie's runner.'

'Anyway,' said Sylvia, 'when's he going to arrive?'

'Some time next month. That's all I know but they'll give me a bit of warning before it happens.' She shook her head in joyful disbelief. 'I'm actually going to see him next month, and I know the arm thing must be awful but I'd rather have him back with one arm that works than not have him at all.'

Sylvia could understand that and she was delighted for Joyce's sake, even though Freddy now seemed further away than ever.

. . .

It was so blisteringly hot outside that most of the kriegies had come indoors and were in varying stages of undress. Freddy wore a pair of khaki drill shorts from the Red Cross store at Lamsdorf, whereas the man on the opposite bunk was completely naked. The view was unappealing, to say the least, but kriegie life demanded tolerance and Freddy was as tolerant as most men.

The man lay on his back reading a letter and if the movement of his lips gave a true indication he read with some difficulty, lingering over occasional words and mouthing the syllables. From time to time, his efforts gave rise to an audible whisper until he became conscious of the lapse and retreated into silence. His toil was rewarded, though, when something in the letter appealed to his imagination and caused his penis to stir. Its movement at first was just perceptible, like a tortoise emerging from hibernation and wondering if the effort was worthwhile or better left for another day. Even so, its dilatory progress continued for maybe half a minute before the exertion evidently proved too daunting, whereupon it subsided weakly and resumed its somnolent state. Its owner, who must have been aware of its stirrings, gave it an affectionate pat before returning his full attention to the letter.

Like most men, Freddy found that his thoughts often strayed on the carnal side, but for his peace of mind he usually managed to redirect them along less frustrating routes. Visions of food were torment enough, even allowing for Red Cross parcels and occasional illicit transactions. There was currently no room in his life for more self-inflicted torture. He was fortunate, as well, in that letters from Sylvia were the stuff of purity and therefore seldom stoked his libido. It was true that sometimes he tried to imagine her physically, but that was difficult. All he knew was that according to Len's wife she was 'pretty in a nice sort of way' and that her sister, when swollen with pregnancy, had called her 'skinny'. The evidence, as detectives of popular fiction often said, was thin. It was perhaps as well for the time being.

A gentle breeze had appeared from nowhere and was favouring the occupants of the hut via the open doors and the broken window a few feet from Freddy's bunk. He luxuriated in it for a while, wondering after a while if his 16th July letter had reached Sylvia. It was possible after more than thirty days.

. . .

It had become her habit to save a new letter until after breakfast, lunch or supper, depending on her watch. The latest coincided with lunch so, having stacked her dish and cutlery, she hurried up to the cabin to read it in peace.

> *16th July, 1944.*
> *Dear Sugar Plum,*
> *It was a pity my birthday fell on a Saturday and I had to work. Even so, we had a pleasant enough time last evening, and the whole thing was all the better for your good wishes. As far as I'm concerned, you make everything seem better. That's a fact, not just a possible lyric. It does have possibilities as a lyric though, doesn't it?*

She looked up as Joyce and Dorothy came in but they motioned to her to carry on.

> *I keep thinking about that date of ours. You know – cocktails, dinner and dancing 'til dawn. I expect you've got a posh frock tucked away somewhere. I only mention it because it helps me imagine the scene. There are times, you see, when the work I'm doing falls short of my ideal, and then I distract myself by thinking of that special moment, and I see us dancing close on a crowded floor, oblivious to everyone and everything in the room. That's until we approach the band, and Carroll Gibbons or Bert Ambrose – I haven't decided yet – favours us with a rare smile. They recognise a classic romance when they see one.*
> *At other times I see us in the hills and valleys you call home. I can't*

imagine it too vividly because I haven't seen all that much of it, but that doesn't matter because you'll be there, and that's what really matters.

I'll write again soon. Meanwhile, take care because you're precious.

Lots of love,

Freddy XXXXX

She sniffed and fumbled in her bag for her handkerchief. The others watched her, waiting for her to say something. Eventually, she said, 'It's the usual thing. Just when I think he's joking again he turns serious.'

Dorothy asked cautiously, 'What's he serious about?'

'Me.'

'It's good news, then.'

'When they told me that Len was a prisoner,' said Joyce, 'it was a huge relief, not just because I knew he was alive after all that time, but because I knew he was in a safe place.' She broke off as the door opened, but when Angela walked in she went on. 'As long as Freddy's a prisoner you know he's safe and you know he'll be back one day.'

Angela sat on her bed, swinging her legs and taking in the conversation.

'The last letter I had from Alf came from the Med,' said Dorothy. 'I suppose that could mean anythin'.'

Angela looked up and asked, 'What did he say?'

'Nothin' much. It's not easy for 'im.' She leaned across her bed and pulled out her drawer. 'Just let me look.' With the letter open, she said, 'He's complainin' that he can't get a pint of some beer they brew in Suffolk. Mind you, he couldn't get it here either.'

'What else does he say?'

'It's mainly about that, there's some private stuff, and then …' She narrowed her eyes to decipher his writing. 'Oh yeah, he doesn't know when he'll get a pint of whatever it is. All he has to look forward to is tea.'

'That's funny,' said Joyce. 'He'll get something stronger than tea wherever he's going.'

'Trincomalee,' said Angela confidently.

'Where's that?'

'Ceylon. That's where he's going. "Tea" is the code they all use for Ceylon. I'm surprised the officers who censor their letters haven't cottoned on yet, or maybe they have and they don't think it matters.'

'Are you sure about that?'

'Absolutely, Dorothy. When you've written to as many servicemen as I have you know these things, and I can safely say that your beloved is on his way to Ceylon.'

'Well.' Dorothy considered the information and said, 'That's where the Japs are, isn't it?'

'I shouldn't worry,' said Joyce. 'According to the papers, the Allies are well on top.'

'Let's hope so.'

'What we all need,' said Joyce, 'is a run ashore.'

'There's the hospital dance on the twenty-sixth,' suggested Angela.

Sylvia and Dorothy looked unsure.

'You're talking to three women who've been spoken for,' said Joyce.

'Aren't you being a bit stuffy?'

'Maybe, but you were in on the conversation. Dorothy's missing Alf, Sylvia's in a state about Freddy and mine's on his way home after three years. Maybe The Cinque Ports Arms would be better for us.'

Angela nodded, taking in the argument. Finally, she said, 'Well, I'm going.' She added brightly, 'A doctor would be a nice change.'

Sylvia asked, 'What happened to your subby?'

'Oh him.' Angela wrinkled her nose dismissively. 'He went off to Harwich last week. Anyway, he wasn't really my type.'

. . .

The sausage contained almost as much fat as pork, and the bread was the familiar dry, black crust, thinly spread with *ersatz* margarine for Herr Stern's benefit, but for Freddy and Bailey it represented a banquet.

'You've done well,' Freddy told Stern. 'This is the first real food we've seen since Niwka.'

'Good, and the chocolate comes on Friday?' Stern looked nervously over his shoulder.

'Saturday.'

'Very well.' He looked over his shoulder for possibly the tenth time that morning. 'I must go to work.'

'Good man.' Freddy took out a tin of cigarettes and offered him one.

The man's hand shook as he took it. 'Thank you. I shall smoke it after lunch.'

'You do that. *Auf Wiedersehen.*'

'*Auf Wiedersehen.*' Stern hurried to his place of work.

'I feel quite guilty about twisting the poor bugger's arm,' said Bailey.

'I just wish he'd stop looking so furtive.'

'The poor blighter can't help it, Freddy. I think he's basically a decent chap, and this business is alien to him.'

'He's decent all right, and he's not the only one.'

'I'm sure you're right, Freddy.' Bailey's eyes were on the food.

'Most of the time I have to remind myself that it's the Nazis I hate, not the Germans.'

'Is there a difference?'

'Absolutely. I used to stay with a German family before the war. They were kind, welcoming people. I think the nation was just mesmerised by Hitler.'

'Quite.' Bailey pointed to the sausage and bread and said, 'We're not really going to wait for lunchtime, are we?'

'Certainly not.' Freddy broke the sausage and bread in half, offering Bailey his share. 'A spot of lunch, Bailey, old chap?'

'My dear old soul, I don't mind if I do.'

Each grabbed his share and made short work of it.

. . .

The run ashore was possible once the girls had enlisted the obligatory male company. The off-watch sentries on this occasion were a seaman who was missing his wife and children and was therefore patently harmless, and another who was in love with a Wren at Rosyth, his last draft, and who needed cheering up. The mood was subdued at first but it livened up when Dorothy organised a darts match. By the end of the evening everyone felt much better.

22

September

It was too cruel for words that doodlebugs had caused the train journey from Dover to London to occupy more than three hours with long delays at each station, and that trains on the Northern Line seemed to be operating only intermittently. Eventually though, Joyce arrived at Balham Station and made her way gratefully to the exit. Mercifully, the rain had stopped, possibly for the first time that day, and she would be at the house in less than five minutes. She and Len had given up their rented flat early in the war, knowing they were both going to be away for long periods, and had gone to live in his father's house in Balham, where he had two large bedrooms as well as a small one for Len's brother when he was home. The arrangement had suited them both, Len until his capture and Joyce until now. If Len had to leave the RAF they would have to find somewhere of their own again, but she would worry about that later. For the present, everything could wait.

Her pulse quickened as she opened the gate and hurried up the short path. Her hand was on the knob when the door opened.

She stared, scarcely able to recognise him. His head was shaved and his new uniform seemed too large for him, but then he spoke and she knew the voice was his.

'Joyce,' he said, 'I haven't half missed you.' He held out one arm, his other being cradled in a sling.

'I know.' Suddenly she was blinded by tears. 'I've missed you too.' They clung blissfully to each other, oblivious to passers by, until eventually Len said, 'Joyce.'

'Yes?'

'Mind my arm, darling.'

'Sorry.' She released her hold on him and asked, 'Are you going to let me in?'

'Yes, sorry.' He moved aside to let her into the house.

'Let's sit down.' She pointed to the sofa, dabbing her eyes with her handkerchief in her other hand. 'I'll sit on this side, away from your arm.'

'Yes, sorry to be difficult.'

'Don't be daft.' She took off her coat and draped it over an armchair to join him on the sofa, where they hugged each other again. 'Oh Len,' she said, 'I thought this was never going to happen.' She felt his torso through the coarse fabric of his tunic and said, 'What have they done to you? You're as thin as a pipe cleaner.'

'They've been feeding me up.'

'On what, fresh air?'

'Extra rations. They didn't want us to be an embarrassment to the Fatherland.'

'Embarrassment indeed. I don't quite know how I'm going to do it on civilian rations,' she said, 'but I'm going to feed you up properly.'

'Just give me a kiss for now. I haven't had all that many lately.'

'I should hope not.' She kissed him again less urgently, still mindful of his injured arm, and then, because it was impossible to ignore it for much longer, nerved herself to ask, 'What did the Medical Officer say about your arm?'

'I'll have to see another specialist because I'll most likely get a bit of pension for it. He reckons it's going to be chronic but he doesn't think it'll always be as bad as this.'

'Well, that's something, I suppose. It doesn't explain your funny haircut though. What's that in aid of?'

'Delousing. You can't imagine how it feels to be rid of those little buggers.'

She grimaced. 'I should have realised.'

'The funny thing is, what the MO told me was just what the Polish doctor said when he looked at it in Tamowicz. I've been examined all over Poland and Germany since then, and it seems the Polish doctor was right all along.'

Running her fingers lightly over his bandage, she asked, 'What were you doing for this to happen?'

'We were loading drums of paint on to a train.'

'It's the greatest shame you had to work for the Germans.'

'Oh well, we either worked or went mad with boredom. In any case, anyone below corporal had to do it whether they wanted to or not, and we couldn't just leave it to them.'

'It seems wrong though, getting injured like that for their benefit, and all for the sake of some rotten paint.'

'Oh well, it can't have done them much good. It was bound for somewhere in Germany but we sent it to the Eastern Front. There won't be much painting going on there.'

'I don't suppose so.' She smiled at the thought.

'And it wasn't the only thing. Last year we sent them a consignment of French letters. According to one of the goons who got invalided back from there, it's so cold they think twice before unbuttoning their flies to have a Jimmy Riddle, never mind anything else.'

'It serves them right.'

'Agreed. I'll tell you what though ...'

'What?'

'Are you going to take your cap off and look as if you're staying?'

'All right.' She slid the strap from under her chin and removed her cap. Then, as an afterthought, she unpinned her hair, dropping the pins into her breast pocket and allowing her hair to fall to her shoulders.

'I've really missed that ginger mop of yours,' he said, struggling with his sling.

'What are you doing?'

'Giving my arm a rest.' He managed to remove it from the sling and rested his liberated hand on her knee.

'Should you be doing that?'

'Yes, it's good for it.'

She rested her head on his shoulder, deeply content. Wind and rain were buffeting the windows again but everything inside was once more as it should be. She was aware that Len's hand was about to make a foray inside her clothes but that was reassuring too. It was something else about him that hadn't changed. 'I could put the kettle on,' she said. 'There's half a pound of pusser's tea in my grip.'

'Well done. I take it that means Navy tea?'

'That's right.'

'I thought so. It's like being back at Tarnowicz with Freddy.'

'Well, let's have a cup of tea and it'll like being here with me.'

'We could have one afterwards.' His hand was rediscovering the mysteries of pusser's underwear.

'After what?'

'Don't be a tease, Joyce. Dad'll be back at six o'clock.'

She grinned. 'There's a meal to cook.'

'Mrs Alcock next door made us a pie for my homecoming. There's only the potatoes and runner beans to do.'

'Runner beans? It sounds as if your dad's been busy in the garden.'

'Don't side-track, Joyce. It's been three years.'

'All right.' She stood up. 'But I'll want that cup of tea afterwards.'

'Fine.' He added, 'I brought a dozen contraceptives from the depot.'

'No need to ask what's been at the front of your mind.' She picked up her grip and followed him upstairs. When they reached the landing he put his good arm around her and said a little self-consciously, 'I don't half love you, Ginger.'

'I know, Len. I love you too.' She hesitated for a moment. 'I'm just concerned about your arm.'

'It'll be OK if we keep it out of the way.'

'If we're very careful,' she agreed.

'It should be all right if we sort of change around a bit.'

'What do you mean?'

'Well, the thing is – if I lie on my back, do you mind going in the mid-upper gunner's position?'

She sighed indulgently. 'And you think "pusser's tea" sounds daft. Go on then.' She sat on the bed, undoing his buttons and helping him off with his boots. As they fell to the floor, she grinned at him and said, 'Chocks away.'

. . .

'What news, Freddy?' Bailey was reacting to an involuntary exclamation.

'Len's made it! He's being repatriated!

'Good for him, but by Jove, it's taken some time, hasn't it?'

'Like this letter.' Freddy looked at the date. 'Well over a month.'

'As war approaches its end, chaos proliferates.'

'Well, we hope it's approaching its bloody end. It's had long enough. I'm glad about Len, though. I've kept wondering what was happening to the old sod.' He returned to Sylvia's letter.

I expect you know all about Len's repatriation and you weren't allowed to mention it. He's due to arrive next month, possibly by the time you get this letter. Isn't it marvellous? Joyce is overjoyed and we are all delighted for her. It could only be better if you were coming with him, not that I would ever want you to be injured, but you know what I mean. I just can't wait for this rotten war to end.

'What else does she say, old man?' Bailey seldom received letters from home and he liked to live vicariously. Freddy would have been happier without the interruptions but he reckoned he would have plenty opportunities to read the letter in peace. 'She says she can't understand why we men like to list our favourite things.'

'What on earth does she mean by that?'

'You know the sort of thing: favourite cars, film stars, that sort of thing.'

'It's normal behaviour, isn't it?'

Freddy read further down the letter. 'Not for them, it seems.'

Bailey grunted. 'It makes you wonder what they find to talk about. They spend enough time doing it.'

'I suppose so.' He read another paragraph and said, 'She's humouring me now. She wants to know my top three popular singers. Hers are Bing Crosby, Sam Browne and Al Bowlly. She says she only heard Al Bowlly towards the end of his life but she liked him very much.'

Bailey stubbed out his cigarette and looked up in surprise. 'Is Al Bowlly dead? I'd no idea.'

'Yes, he was killed in the Blitz.'

'Was he really? I missed all that, you see.' Much had happened since nineteen-forty.

I keep thinking about our date just as you do, not because I don't enjoy my work but because it's come to mean something very special to me. The hills and valleys were always special, of course, but will be even more so when you're here.

People I meet in my home town ask after you nowadays as if they know you. It's not often I go into a shop without hearing your name, and as I forgot to tell you that in my last letter, I'll tell you now: they all send you their best wishes. I've persuaded two of them to knit for you as well. Believe me when I tell you that you won't be short of socks this winter! Let's hope it will be our last winter apart.

We saw a film called 'Fanny by Gaslight' recently. I expect you know the story. You usually do. It starred Phyllis Calvert and James Mason. It was very good but a bit of an anti-climax after 'Gone with the Wind' last month.

That's about all I can tell you for now, so wrap up warm and take care. I'll write again soon.

Buckets of love,

Sugar Plum XXXXX

'Anything else, old man?'

'Sylvia and her oppos went to see a film called "Fanny by Gaslight",' Freddy told him absently.

Bailey pondered the information briefly and said, 'I'd say it looks much the same in any light. Wouldn't you, old man?'

'I dare say.' Freddy's mind was distant again.

. . .

The laundry was in the basement of the Lord Warden Hotel, a place of heat, steam and the ubiquitous cockroaches. Sylvia admired anyone who could work in such surroundings, and the object of her respect when she reached the bottom of the steps was Doris Ormondroyd, a lean, ruddy-complexioned girl from Bradford.

Doris looked at the bundle that Sylvia dumped on the floor and asked, 'What have you got there, Sylvia?'

'Woollies, Doris. Nothing special but I imagine they're none too clean.'

'Shouldn't be surprised. Are they for knittin' wool?'

'What else?' Sylvia undid the scarf that held the bundle together, and a collection of pullovers, sweaters and cardigans tumbled apart.

'Won't matter if they shrink then, eh?'

'No, I'll just get some more.'

Doris grinned as she picked up the garments and stuffed them into a huge washing machine. 'Where did you get these?'

'They're from the Salvation Army. They usually have a good jumble sale.'

'I bet they watch out for you an' all nowadays.'

'Oh, they know me all right.' Sylvia had become a seasoned jumbler since her terrifying debut at the YMCA.

'I expect t' wools for that lad o' thine, the POW, eh?'

'Yes, it's knitting time again.'

'Aye well, these'll be ready by fourteen hundred an' I'll still be here an' all.'

'Thanks, Doris. I need to start unravelling as soon as I can and then I can get the others on the job.'

'You're all right, love.' Doris inclined her head towards the load in the machine and said, 'I'm bloody 'opeless at knittin', but I wish t' poor lad all the best.'

'That's kind of you, Doris.' It seemed that Freddy was gathering well-wishers all the time. Sylvia just wondered when she might hear from him.

. . .

Joyce lay with her head resting on Len's sound shoulder, studying the bedroom ceiling. A thin crack had appeared in the plaster since the last time she had viewed it from that angle but she was not surprised. The Blitz had caused cracks to form in a great many houses, and now the Doodlebugs were doing it again. She raised her head to look at Len's face but it was difficult without disturbing him. 'Len,' she said softly, 'are you awake?'

145

'Of course I am.'

'I thought you might be sleeping the sleep of the just-after. You always did.'

'Not this time.' He stroked her hair gently. 'Sorry it was a bit quick.'

'That's all right. You're allowed to be in a hurry when you've waited three years. You'll get the hang of it again when we've flown a few more strikes.'

'*Ops*, not strikes, and you're taking the mickey now.'

'What do you expect?' She made herself more comfortable and said, 'When I was at Lee-On-Solent they used to call them strikes.'

'They were sailors. They didn't know any better.'

'Be careful. You could find yourself without a mid-upper gunner.' She stroked his wasted torso, wincing as she did so. 'We've got to do something about this, Len. Your ribs are like park railings.'

'Yes, I was just thinking about that pie of Mrs Alcock's. I can hardly wait.'

'Oh, you were thinking about that, were you? Very romantic.'

'I was thinking about something else as well.'

'And what was that?'

'I was thinking that we've got time for another op.'

'Oh, you were, were you?'

'Well, you said I needed the practice.'

. . .

So far, Sylvia had offers of socks from her mother, the old lady down the road, the greengrocer's wife, the post office lady, and now Audrey. Angela had offered a pair of gloves, Dorothy was down for a balaclava now that her mother was keeping Alf provided with socks, and Third Officer Fuller had graduated on to a woollen cap. Shamed by the efforts of those around her, Sylvia was about to embark on a seaman's jersey.

Having made the final arrangements with her mother by telephone, she returned to the cabin, where she found Dorothy unravelling a newly-washed pullover.

'Everything's in hand,' Sylvia told her. 'There'll soon be knitting needles clicking all over Wensleydale.'

'Here an' all,' said Dorothy, 'and we'll need to get a move on.'

'We should be all right.' Dorothy was a slow knitter but she had a month to make the balaclava.

'Haven't you heard the buzz?'

'What buzz?'

'It looks as if *Wasp* will be paying off soon. Who knows where we'll all be by Christmas?'

23

'm not happy,' said Freddy.

'Neither am I, old chap. I think our friend may have been indiscreet.' They watched covertly as Herr Stern appeared to be answering to an *Unteroffizier*. He looked characteristically nervous and was shaking his head vigorously.

'I can't think what else it might be,' said Freddy. 'I reckon it's the cigarettes or the chocolate.'

'I suppose it's too much to hope that Stern will keep quiet about us.'

'I don't see how he can. He'll have to say where he got the stuff. Anyway, let's just carry on as normal.' They searched around for something to lubricate, and Freddy was pointing the spout of his oilcan between the spokes of a wheel when he heard the NCO shout. 'You two, come here!'

Freddy stopped and looked around enquiringly.

'You two!' He pointed first to Bailey and then to Freddy. 'Come here!'

Looking puzzled, they approached him. Stern stood miserably by his side.

'This man,' said the German, 'has told me that you have both given him cigarettes.'

'That's right,' Freddy told him, hoping fervently that Stern had not mentioned the food. 'We give him cigarettes occasionally because he treats us as human beings.'

'Do you realise that it is forbidden?'

Freddy's mouth was dry; his tongue was like cardboard, but in his experience a little respect, however counterfeit, often went a long way. 'No,' he said, 'we didn't know that, sir.'

'How long have you been prisoners of the Reich?'

'About a year, sir.'

The *Unteroffizier* was unimpressed. 'In that case you should know the regulations. It is forbidden for a prisoner to make a gift to a German citizen.'

'We're sorry, sir. You see, Herr Stern has always treated us courteously and it seemed quite natural for us to give him the odd cigarette.'

'Just the odd cigarette?'

'That's all, sir.'

'Bailey, who had remained unusually silent so far, said, 'I must say you speak English awfully well.'

'Yes, I was a prisoner in England for three years during the last war.'

'I hope they treated you well,' said Freddy.

'Yes, they treated all prisoners well, but you are changing the subject. You gave cigarettes to this man.'

'We've already said so.'

'And you gave him chocolate also.' Stern was squirming at his side.

'Yes, sir. Herr Stern has children, two little children who had never tasted chocolate in their lives. We have chocolate sent to us from England …'

'All right, I understand what you are saying, but tell me this – has Stern given you anything in return? Think before you answer this question. The consequences could be serious.'

'No, he's given us nothing,' said Freddy.

'Nothing at all,' said Bailey.

'Are you sure?'

'Of course. It's against regulations to trade, isn't it?' Stern was going through torment, but Freddy was beginning to see a speck of blue sky.

'Yes, it is against regulations. I am glad you realise that at least.' The German looked at them both in turn and said, 'I do not trust you. I believe a change of *Arbeitskommando* is called for, somewhere where you will have less time for fraternising. Meanwhile, you must not speak with this man Stern unless a guard is present. Do you understand?'

'Yes, sir.'

'Yes, sir.'

'Very good. You will hear more about this matter.' He spoke briefly in German to Stern before seeing him back to his workplace.

'Well,' said Freddy, 'at least we're not going to be shot.'

'Not yet,' agreed Bailey, 'but let's not get too cocky until we know where they're sending us.'

. . .

A similar question occupied Sylvia's and Dorothy's minds. A buzz was only a buzz. If asked, those in authority would refuse to give it credence whether or not they knew anything, but it had become a major preoccupation on the lower deck.

This was the state of affairs that Joyce encountered when she returned from her eight days' leave, and when the excited questions about Len and her leave were out of the way she gave her decision.

'They're not going to discharge me simply because I have a disabled husband,' she said. 'The only way out is to start a family, and we don't want to do that just yet, so I'm going to request a draft to Whitehall. If I get that I could maybe get the odd weekend and sleeping-out pass.'

'That would be perfect for you,' said Sylvia. 'Do you know anyone who's served at Whitehall?'

'I've met one or two. I get the impression they're a bit pusser up there but it's not surprising.

'It can't be that bad if you keep your nose clean,' said Dorothy, busily sewing up the two halves of the balaclava she had knitted. 'I've lengthened it at the bottom,' she said to Sylvia. 'It'll go under his scarf and keep his neck warm.'

'You're a good hand, Dorothy. That's what Will used to say, isn't it?' With the future of HMS *Wasp* uncertain, Sylvia found herself given to occasional pangs of nostalgia.

'Anyway,' said Joyce, 'what do you have in mind, Dorothy?'

'I don't really know. I fancied Western Approaches at one time but there's not much happening there nowadays. I suppose I can put in for overseas and see what happens.'

'What about you, Sylvia?'

'I don't want to be sent anywhere awful, but if I don't make a request and they send me to the end of the earth I'll only have myself to blame.'

'You could try for Whitehall.'

'I suppose I could.'

Later, they asked Angela, who had already made up her mind.

'To hell with being shelled, doodlebugged and frozen to death,' she said. 'I've put in for an overseas draft. Any place that's warm will suit me.'

After further consideration, Sylvia also requested an overseas draft.

. . .

The Company Sergeant-Major at Lamsdorf had been sympathetic but philosophical. 'You're only human,' he said, 'but you two went all-out to shit your hole full this time.' He went on sadly, 'I hope you like salt with your cabbage soup because you'll find plenty where you're going.'

'In that case,' said Freddy, 'I'm opting out. We don't have to work for the bastards and I don't see why we should have to suffer as well.'

'That goes for me too,' said Bailey.

The CSM shook his head sadly. 'Don't you know you need to give six months' notice to terminate your contract?'

By now Freddy was angry. 'They said nothing about that when we signed the bloody thing. How were we to know?'

'They make up the rules as they go along,' the CSM reminded him. 'Just be thankful they're not sending you to a *Sonderlager*, not that you'll notice much difference. And don't even think about escaping. Hitler's edict is still in force and a dead kriegie is no use to anyone.'

. . .

They stepped down from the lorry and surveyed the landscape that they were sure would be their home until the end of hostilities, and recalled the CSM's warning. Even the upper works of the salt mine presented a forbidding spectacle and one that was seldom out of mind, being in full view of the accommodation block. The latter was a stone-built, barn-like structure with half its roof missing. None of its upper windows was intact.

They were told to stow their kit on the ground floor, the first floor being occupied by Russians. Inevitably, the building was unheated but at least the ground floor windows were intact and the ceiling appeared sound.

They drew oil lamps and pickaxes at the pithead and were shoved into a miniature railway carriage that carried them through narrow tunnels, deep into the mine. At the end of the journey they climbed out and their guard handed them over to a Polish worker, who showed them how to hack chunks of salt from the face and load them into trucks. The air was filled with salt dust that invaded their eyes, noses, ears and mouths, creating intolerable discomfort and a perpetual thirst. Too late, they realised the good fortune they had forfeited at Tarnowicz.

'It's a sobering thought,' said Bailey, 'that some chaps have been working down the mines ever since they arrived in this bally country.'

'Are you in need of a sobering thought? This place is sobering enough for me.' Freddy heaved a chunk of rock salt into the truck, wincing as he did so. Unused as they were to the work, his hands were already forming blisters.

The Polish worker who had set them to work reappeared. He nudged a sorry-looking figure clad in rags that had once been a uniform, and pointed to the pile of rocks. Without a word, the newcomer began loading them into the truck. He was filthy and emaciated, and Freddy and Bailey couldn't even guess how long he had been at the mine.

During a short and unscheduled break, Freddy made contact with him. He asked, 'Do you speak English? *Sprechen-Sie Englisch?*'

The man stared at him for several seconds and said, 'Yes, I speak English.'

'I'm Freddy. This is Bailey.'

The man nodded, the shaking of blistered hands being a painful and unnecessary practice, and muttered something unintelligible.

'Say again?'

He laughed weakly. 'My name is Alexander, but call me Sasha.'

'Glad to meet you, Sasha.'

'Likewise, old chap, but do tell us why you were laughing just now?'

'I laughed because you are the first Englishmen to speak to me.' He managed a smile. 'Maybe the others believe the Germans when they say we are animals.'

'I don't think anyone deserves to be called that,' said Freddy, 'although some of the guards we've met come close to qualifying for it.'

'I agree with you.'

'Back to work,' said Bailey. 'Someone's coming.'

'It is the Pole,' Sasha told him. 'I know from the sound of his footsteps. He is a reasonable man as long as we do not spend too much time in talking. It means more work for the Poles, you understand.'

They fell to work once more and continued until their meal break, which was another new experience. First, British and allied prisoners collected their ration of soup from a large container and received three slices of black bread. The soup turned out to be somewhat thicker than that to which Freddy and Bailey had been accustomed, and they imagined it was because they were now engaged in heavier work than before. The guards watched over the process before supervising the separate allocation of rations to the Russians and Ukrainians. Thereafter, the guards left them to eat wherever they wished, and Sasha naturally sought the company of his British colleagues.

In the privacy of their alcove, Bailey watched him wolf his cabbage water and piece of bread, and said, 'Good Lord. Is that all they give you?'

Sasha wiped his mouth with the back of his hand. 'They do not waste food on barbarians.'

'Come over here with us.' Bailey took him further up the tunnel, away from his compatriots and handed him a piece of his bread. Freddy did the same.

For a moment, Sasha stared in disbelief. Eventually he said, 'Thank you! Thank you, my friends!'

They looked away as he demolished the bread. 'You can have some soup in a minute,' said Freddy.

Bailey asked him, 'Where did you learn to speak English?'

'At school and at university. I studied English, French and German.'

Impressed as always by linguistic ability, Bailey asked, 'What will you do after the war?'

'Nothing.'

'Nothing at all?'

'Comrade Stalin has ordered the execution of all who surrender to the Germans.'

The revelation took them completely by surprise, but eventually Bailey said somewhat pensively, 'A fine comrade he turned out to be.'

24

October

The establishment that Joyce and the others left was very different from the one they had joined. The huge guns at Sangatte had fallen silent, their battery now overrun by the invading army; the Allies had mastery of the North Sea and the Channel, and two flotillas of MTBs based at Dover were about to pay off. HMS *Wasp* had previously housed forty-two Wrens and, at one time, one hundred and thirty officers and ratings as well, but the complement was now reduced to a skeleton. It was a sad moment for the girls when they picked up their movement orders and rail warrants and left the Lord Warden for the last time. There had been tearful farewells; close friendships had developed there that would very likely be maintained long after the war was over, and now Joyce had been drafted to Whitehall, Angela was due to embark for Trincomalee and Dorothy would be at Chatham pending her overseas draft. It seemed that Sylvia's request had been denied. She was to remain at HMS *Wasp* and await further orders.

She was brooding on the absence of mail from Freddy, when the accommodation PO came to her cabin with two girls. Recent departures meant the reallocation of accommodation, so she had been expecting as much.

'I have to put these girls in with you, Sylvia,' said the PO. 'They're on your watch now so I'm putting them in your charge. You all know each other, don't you?' She left without waiting for an answer.

Sylvia had seen the girls about the place but there had been no contact between them apart from occasional preparations for inspections, and her rounds were little more than a formality, so she said, 'Come in and sit down. You know who I am but you'll have to introduce yourselves.'

One of them, a curiously thin girl with mousey hair said, 'You don't mind, do you?' She had a strong northern accent that Sylvia couldn't quite place.

'Don't mind what?'

'Us coming in here like this.'

'It's not my property. In any case, you're welcome.'

Possibly in an effort to move the conversation along, the other girl said, 'I'm Rosemary Cotton. This is my first draft. I've been here eight months.' She had wispy, light-brown hair and a friendly smile.

Sylvia asked, 'Where are you from, Rosemary?'

'Shrewsbury in Shropshire.' Suddenly she laughed at herself. 'I can't usually say that. It's a bit of a tongue twister.'

'Well, you managed it this time.' She turned to the other girl. 'What's your name?'

'Gloria Thompson.'

'Is this your first draft as well?'

'Yeah.'

'When did you join?'

'What d' you mean – t' Wrens or this place?'

'Either. Just tell me something about yourself.'

Gloria bit her lip. 'I've only been here two months,' she said.

'That's all right, it's not a crime. Where are you from?'

'Bolton.' She added helpfully, 'It's in Lancashire.'

'I know.'

Rosemary asked, 'Where are you from, Sylvia?'

'Leyburn in the North Riding.'

'That's in Yorkshire,' said Gloria, like a look-out sighting the enemy.

'That's right,' confirmed Sylvia, 'but don't worry. We're not here to play cricket.' She looked at her watch and said, 'Let's see if the food's improved. As we're holding the fort I think we should qualify for some kind of perk. Don't you?'

. . .

Freddy draped his greatcoat over his shoulders against the October chill. He was trying to write a letter, but the cold draught from the doorway and the relentless pangs of hunger distracted him constantly. He and Bailey had readily given some of their ration to Sasha and would doubtless do so again, but they had little enough for themselves, and Red Cross parcels were overdue. He picked up his pencil again and continued with his letter.

Please excuse the awful writing. My hands are rather sore but it's nothing serious.

He put his pencil down again and blew on his blistered fingers. They were so cold they should have been numb, but they stung like hell.

It was good to hear about Len. He must be home by now. Give the old loafer my best.

He decided to finish the letter later when his hands were in better shape. With any luck, there might be some ointment in the next Red Cross parcel. For the time being he lay on his bed in his greatcoat, trying to think about anything but food.

There had been a distraction that morning but it had been far from welcome. It began when the guards arrived to shake them with their familiar shout of '*Aufstehen!* Out of bed!' Two of them went stamping upstairs to do the same for the Russians and in no time the ritual became a screaming rant. As far as Freddy could make out, someone had failed to leap out of bed and was now paying a severe penalty. A number of Russian voices had joined in the din, and that was exceptional, because a prisoner who raised his voice to a guard could expect at least a severe beating. A Russian usually fared much worse.

The row continued as Freddy laced up his boots and fastened his greatcoat to attend the hated early *Appell*. Quite suddenly, the shouting ceased, and he caught the words '*Er ist todt.*'

So one of them had died, presumably in the night. No wonder the poor bugger had been slow to get out of bed.

It was not until the start of work that Sasha was able to tell them the full story. It appeared that the man had been suffering from congestion of the lungs and had been in a poor way for several days. He had simply lacked the strength to get up when he was ordered, and the guards had beaten him with their rifle butts. 'He was almost dead before they began,' Sasha told them. 'They took what remained of his life.'

. . .

'We've no idea how long we're going to be here,' said Sylvia over the corned beef, tinned tomato and chips, 'but life has to go on. I suppose you two have men tucked away somewhere?'

Rosemary shook her head glumly and Gloria looked down at her plate.

'Well, we don't have to do things together but as we're all in the same cabin it would be nice if we could. Don't you think so?' She took in their nodded agreement and went on. '"Lady Hamilton" is on at the Plaza next week.'

155

Rosemary nodded eagerly. 'My brother saw it in London. He says it's very good.'

'Good. What about you, Gloria? Do you fancy it?'

'What's it about?'

Hiding her surprise and trying not to meet Rosemary's eye, Sylvia told her, 'It's about the romance between Lord Nelson and Lady Hamilton.'

That seemed to clinch it for Gloria. 'OK,' she said, 'I like a love story. You can count me in.' She picked up her empty plate and cutlery to stack them and asked as an afterthought, 'Has it got a happy ending?'

'It depends on how you look at it,' said Rosemary. 'Everyone has to die sometime, but not everyone becomes a national treasure and has a monument and a square all to himself.'

'I know about Nelson.' Gloria sounded scornful. 'I just wasn't sure about the love story, that's all.' Transferring her gaze to the dishes laid out on the long side tables, she said, 'Whatever it is has custard on it. I'm going to get some before it all goes.'

When all three had returned with their fruit tart and custard, Rosemary said, 'There's a dance at the Town Hall on Saturday and it's our night off.'

'I'm not exactly footloose and fancy-free,' said Sylvia, 'but I'm game. I just enjoy dancing.' She looked across at the third member of the group, whose face betrayed no enthusiasm. 'What about you, Gloria?'

'I can't dance.'

'Why not?' She wondered for a moment if perhaps Gloria belonged to some funny religious sect that frowned on enjoyment, but the reality turned out to be less intriguing.

'I don't know how. I've tried to learn but I always get the steps wrong.'

It was more than a challenge; it was a sacred duty. 'Rosemary,' said Sylvia, 'are we going to stand by and see one of our number play the wallflower for the rest of her life?'

Gloria's eyes widened in alarm, but Rosemary replied without hesitation, 'Absolutely not.'

'We have until Saturday.'

'Ample time.'

'And we have four hours before we go on watch,' said Sylvia, now confident in her role as matriarch. 'Let's make a start.'

. . .

Sasha had just returned with his cabbage water and bread when the fight started in the Russian queue. 'Bread,' he said shortly. 'It is the only thing worth fighting for.'

Freddy and Bailey watched as more prisoners clawed and grabbed at the bread, elbowing others aside and being elbowed and trampled in their turn.

Sasha looked on, sickened. 'Someone thought his comrade was getting more than his share.'

'Now they'll all get more than they bargained for,' said Bailey, watching the guards attack the brawling mass with their rifle butts.

'Here comes Vogel,' said Sasha. 'God help them.' He was referring to a *Feldwebel*, a sergeant, who was yelling at his men to detach themselves from the mêlée. His next order was as sickening as it was inevitable, and Freddy closed his eyes as shots reverberated in the tunnel. When he reopened them the Russians were silent. Those who were unharmed stood shocked and still; others lay dead at their feet and one writhed on the floor, his bloodied hands clasped to his abdomen. Vogel fired another shot and the Russian lay still.

'Let's go back to work,' said Sasha softly. 'We stay out of Vogel's way if we can.'

'I don't blame you,' said Bailey grimly. 'He'd certainly be black-balled at my club.'

Freddy said, 'Didn't they hang buggers like him after the last war?'

'A few, I think,' said Bailey. 'As I recall, it was a good idea that didn't seem to catch on.'

'Maybe it'll be more popular after this one. At all events, I think it's time someone started keeping a record, because I don't think Vogel's finished with us yet.'

. . .

'Daa-da-da-daa-de-de-daa-daa …' Uncertain of the words, Sylvia kept up the rhythm and melody of 'Yours', while Rosemary and Gloria danced around the cabin, nimbly avoiding the beds and Sylvia's canvas grip, which she had placed strategically to simulate a crowded dance floor.

'Slow, quick-quick, slow,' prompted Rosemary.

'I know. I'm getting the 'ang of it now.' Gloria was even enjoying it, as her rare smile showed.

Sylvia tapped Rosemary on the shoulder but without success. 'Go away,' said Rosemary. 'Find your own partner.'

'This is an Excuse Me.'

'No, it's not.'

'It's a Leading Wren's Excuse Me. All right?'

'OK.' Rosemary relinquished her partner and took over the vocal refrain. It worked better that way, as she could remember the words and had a nice singing voice as well.

At the end of the number they all subsided breathlessly on to Gloria's bed, well satisfied with their afternoon's work. Gloria was the first to speak.

'I never thought I'd be able to do that,' she said. 'I never could before.'

'You can do most things if you do a little bit at a time,' said Sylvia, 'and if the people who are showing you don't make it sound impossible.'

'I suppose so.'

'It's true. Whenever my dad set out to show me something, whether it was algebra or fly fishing, he always started by telling me how difficult it was, and that put me off straight away.'

'Just like my maths mistress,' said Rosemary, wrinkling her nose at the memory.

'Whereas Gloria has learned the foxtrot this afternoon, haven't you, Gloria?'

'Aye, an' it were nothing like as hard as I thought it would be.'

'I must say,' said Rosemary, 'I was expecting you to teach her the waltz first. It's so much easier.'

'We'll do that tomorrow.' The foxtrot was Sylvia's favourite, and Freddy's too. She wished he would write. It had been three months since his last letter.

. . .

The shift continued with Freddy, Bailey and Sasha now alternately loading the drying machine with wet salt and then hacking out the dried and caked residue. The fire was fuelled with coal dust and slack, and the interior of the drum became so unbearably hot that the prisoners were obliged to emerge, faint and gasping for air after only a few minutes. Their respite was brief and water was strictly rationed, so they were forced to work on in spite of the fainting, dizziness and injury-proneness caused by dehydration.

25

November

The noise of tumbling rock echoing through the tunnel alerted everyone working on the dryer, and they were the first to hear the muffled screams. Freddy's first thought was that the roof had fallen in, and he and the others dashed into the tunnel.

They could see nothing at first; the tunnel was poorly lit and the ever-present dust made it impossible to discern anything beyond twenty yards or so, but as they progressed they were able to make out a pile of rocks and then the derailed truck on its side. More urgent, though, were the cries from beneath the avalanche.

They were working frantically, flinging the rocks back along the side of the track when Vogel arrived with a squad of men.

'*Was ist hier los?*'

Without pausing from his task, even though his hands were cut and bleeding, Freddy told him, 'There's a man buried under these rocks.' Then, remembering that Vogel understood no English, he repeated the information in German and, as he did so he uncovered one bleeding and lacerated arm. Turning to the others, he shouted, 'Here! He's here!' For the moment, Vogel was forgotten in the rush to free the buried man.

'His foot is trapped,' Sasha told them, translating the man's frenzied cries. 'It is trapped under the truck.'

'We have to get him out.' Freddy spoke to Vogel again urgently in German. 'We must lift the truck.' He reckoned that the prisoners and the guards should be able to right the truck between them and he leant against the steel chassis, ready to heave. Vogel, however, was unmoved. He merely asked, '*Russisch?*'

'Yes, he's Russian.' Freddy knew then what Vogel was about to do, and he knew there was nothing he could do to stop him. The Russian was still yelling in torment when Vogel gave the order to shoot. Freddy braced himself. The guards, though, seemed uncertain; two of them had unslung their rifles but even they hesitated. Clearly angry, Vogel repeated his order, but it was only when the guards raised their rifles that Bailey seemed to realise what was happening. Suddenly he erupted, yelling at Vogel, 'You murdering bastard! You can't shoot him!'

Freddy grabbed his arm. 'For God's sake, Bailey! You'll get yourself shot!' As he struggled to pull his friend back, something hard struck him on the back of his head and he fell to the ground, stunned. Through a crimson mist he saw Bailey go down beneath a welter of blows from the rifle butts of the guards, and he saw Sasha hurl himself at them, snarling and screaming, his arms flailing. Thereafter he knew nothing.

. . .

As he regained consciousness he was aware of a great deal of noise and the fact that his head ached horribly. He struggled to bring his eyes into focus. After some time, he realised that the noise came from a gang of prisoners loading the fallen rocks into the truck, which was now back on its rails. He raised his head with difficulty and looked around him but there was no sign of Bailey or Sasha. He'd last seen Bailey falling under the guards' rifle butts. There was little hope for him and none at all for Sasha. Assaulting a German was normally a shooting offence for anyone, and Vogel would show a Russian no mercy at all. Freddy just hoped that in his insane fury Sasha had been able to exact some kind of rough justice before the goons overpowered him.

After some time, one of the Polish workers spoke to him. 'You okay? I think you dead.' He offered Freddy a drink from his bottle.

'Thanks.' Freddy took no more than a sip to moisten his dry mouth. Water was precious, even for the free workers. He handed the bottle back and asked, 'What happened? Did the guards kill my friends?'

The Pole said flatly, '*Russky* dead. He fight and Vogel shoot.'

'Bugger.' It had been inevitable but that didn't make it any easier. He braced himself for the worst. 'What about Bailey? Did Vogel do the same for him?'

The Pole studied him doubtfully, and Freddy realised that he mustn't have understood the question.

'Bailey,' he repeated. 'British soldier.' He traced two imaginary stripes on his arm. 'Did Vogel shoot the British soldier?'

Comprehension dawned and the Pole said, 'No, British soldier not die.'

. . .

Freddy handed Bailey a can of tea. The leaves had cost him five cigarettes but he considered it currency well spent now that Bailey was back in the hut, battered but alive.

'I can't work these people out,' he told Freddy. 'They break half my ribs, batter me senseless and then send me to the doctor to be reassembled.'

'They're thorough,' agreed Freddy. He decided to change the subject to something more cheerful. 'A new lot of prisoners arrived today,' he said. 'They're Yanks.'

'I'm glad they could make it. Have they brought any news?'

'Oh yes. I only had a quick word with one of them – they're all in the new hut on the other side – but the news was worth hearing. The RAF have sunk the Tirpitz.'

'What's the Tirpitz?'

It was another reminder that Bailey had been a prisoner since nineteen-forty. 'She was the biggest battleship in the world, sister ship to the Bismarck. It seems they dropped bloody big bombs on her. Their bombs are much bigger than ours. They've got the machines to carry them.'

'Well, good for the RAF. I could almost forgive them for giving northern France a miss in nineteen-forty when we needed the blighters.' He sipped his tea like a gourmet tasting a rare wine and said, 'Every time I taste real tea it's a reminder that dear old Blighty is still there. It's just a shame this bally war is dragging on.'

'I know.' Freddy's two years and eight months seemed an age, but four years were beyond his imagination.

Bailey said quietly, 'They shot the poor blighter under the truck.'

Freddy nodded. 'His future wasn't looking too promising when I got my knock on the head.'

'Maybe Vogel did him a favour, putting him out of his misery like that. They'd never have treated him.'

'True.'

'Of course, the pity of it is that we can talk so dispassionately about this kind of thing. I sometimes wonder if we're still human or if we've had all that knocked out of us.'

Freddy took his empty can from him and put it with his own. 'There was nothing dispassionate about the way you rounded on Vogel,' he said. 'Insane, maybe, but certainly not dispassionate.'

'You were quite well known for it yourself at one time, Freddy.'

'Maybe I've learned my lesson.'

Bailey winced. 'I think I've learned mine now.' He closed his eyes tightly, possibly in pain or perhaps reliving some part of the experience. Eventually, he said, 'Poor old Sasha. The goons held him while Vogel shot him in the head with his pistol.' He screwed up his eyes at the thought. 'Sasha did it for me, you know, and I wish to hell he hadn't. He just went berserk with no warning at all. It must have been coming for some time, but who could have known?'

'It must have been a combination of things,' Freddy agreed. 'He hated the goons, he'd suffered the worst kind of treatment and he'd become our mate as well. That's important. Maybe he thought he owed you something.'

'He didn't owe me his life.'

'But he had nothing to lose.'

'Oh, that. Do you think Stalin was serious about shooting ex-kriegies?'

'Sasha believed him.'

'That's very true.' Bailey felt at his battledress blouse and winced with pain. 'I say, old man, would you mind lighting a gasper for me? The effort's too much for the old ribs, you know.'

'Of course.' Freddy lit two of his own and handed one to him.

'Thanks, old man.'

'I'll make sure Vogel answers for this, you know.'

'How will you do that, old scout?'

'I've got his name, rank and regiment. All I need now is his official number and I'll report the bastard at the first opportunity.'

'Be careful, Freddy.'

'I shall. There'll be no more heroics, believe me.'

'Good.' He closed his eyes again weakly. 'I'm going to finish this smoke and then if my ribs will give me half a chance I'm going to indulge in the sleep of the innocent and totally buggered.'

Freddy had plans too. The next day was Sunday, a day of gentle pursuits. He was sick of violence and he was going to turn his mind to something clean, decent and honourable. He had written another song for Sylvia, an important one because it would tell her something that, with all his light-hearted nonsense, he'd never had the nerve to say.

26

December

Sylvia's torment might have been even more acute had it not been for her frequent correspondence with Joyce, who reminded her from experience that long periods without mail were far from unusual.

Relief came, however, when she returned to the billet after the all-night-on to find a letter from her mother. The envelope was unusually thick, and when she managed to open it with trembling hands she was overjoyed to find six letters from Freddy. They were date-stamped July to November, so she opened the most recent one to find that each ruled line contained two lines of his miniscule writing, and that the letter appeared to be in the form of a song.

19th November, 1944.
Dearest Sugar Plum,
Here is my combined Christmas and twenty-first birthday present to you.

You Make Everything Better!
Music and Lyrics by Freddy Hinchcliffe

Into every life, they say, a little rain must find its way,
To mask with temporary gloom all thoughts that otherwise illume.
A kriegie has his share of rain, although you'll not hear me complain.
I don't need a hat and coat. I've got the perfect antidote.
(Refrain - foxtrot)
You make everything better! No matter how gloomy the day,
A line from you makes the sky turn blue and the sun finds an extra ray.
You put the 'joy' into 'joyful' and the 'hope' into 'hopeful' as well.

163

In the Hollywood vernacular, you're something quite spectacular!
You're ritzy! You're sensational! You're swell!

Yes, you make everything better! You put a twinkle in the eye of despair;
You could even bring a smile to the Sphinx on the Nile,
An accomplishment, they tell me, that is rare.
(Instrumental)
A pickaxe feels like a feather, a shovel weighs nothing at all;
A letter with your name upon it rivals Shakespeare's greatest sonnet,
Making every task appear small.
Each paragraph acts like a tonic, every adverb, conjunction and phrase.
I must confess I feel quite heady every time I read 'Dear Freddy';
Kisses leave me lost in a daze.

You make everything better! You really show those stars how to shine,
You put to lowly shame the comet and its flame,
And the shooting star might just as well resign.
You make everything better! It's a fact – believe me – it's true!
And that, by the by, is the reason why I love you as much as I do!

I hope you get home for Christmas and have a wonderful time.
With love (about a ton for now. More later), Freddy XXXXX

She read the song again, lingering over the last line and reading it repeatedly until her tears made it impossible. He'd joked in the past, calling her 'precious' and his 'favourite love pot', and everyone wrote 'Lots of love' and put kisses on letters, but this was saying it properly. She wanted to dance around the room, and might have done so had it not been too small for that. It was all so exciting that she had to share it with someone. She didn't want the girls to see her in that state – she had to think of discipline – so that person had to be Joyce. She was jaded after the all-night-on, but sleep could wait. It was too bad she couldn't speak to Joyce on the phone, but a letter was almost as good. She took out her writing things and started on it straight away.

. . .

Freddy had also received a letter. He had read it that morning and such was his surprise that he took it out again to read during his mid-day break.

15ᵗʰ November, 1944.
Freddy old mate,

How's it going? I'd have written before but life's been hectic here, what with getting back to work and married life – not that I'm complaining about that! Joyce sends her best, by the way.

I got my medical discharge fairly quickly. It must have been obvious that I was no longer any use to them. Anyway, the old firm is happy to have me back. Just as well, really.

We had a visit from Sylvia last month. Well, she came to see Joyce, really, and stayed here over the weekend. Let me tell you, mate, that's a peach of a girl you've got waiting for you, and I don't just mean she's pretty. As a matter of fact, she is rather pretty, but I mean in other ways as well, if you follow me. She's a lovely girl in all sorts of ways and she's serious about you, you lucky devil.

You'll find things a bit strange when you come home. I did, and it wasn't easy for a while, but I soon settled down. Come and see us when you can. It'll be nice to sink a few pints and shoot a line.

Keep your chin up, mate.

Len.

It was good to hear from Len. His news about Sylvia was particularly welcome, and the knowledge would keep him warm inside through many a cold night. Also, clever old Len had casually invited him round as if it might happen in the next few days, and that was as good as saying that the war was nearing its end. He'd done well to sneak that one past the censor. Good old Len.

He pocketed the letter when he heard the familiar call to return to work. '*Arbeiten! Schnell!*' It would sustain him for the next few hours.

He and Bailey had a new workmate in the dryer, a serious American who only spoke to complain. He had introduced himself as Randy and been surprised at their reaction until they explained why they found his name amusing, but he had said very little since then beyond acknowledging whatever instructions Freddy or Bailey gave him. He was clearly very unhappy, having been taken prisoner early in his involvement in the war. He was also very young.

'We have to do something about him,' Bailey said when Randy had gone to answer a call of nature. 'The miserable blighter will have us both ready to cut our throats by the end of the week.'

'He certainly won't survive if he goes on like this,' agreed Freddy. 'He says he was taken prisoner a month ago. He can't believe some of you have been here since nineteen-forty.'

'I can.' Bailey rammed his chisel into a chunk of salt for emphasis. 'And he won't last another month if he doesn't buck up. He's doing himself no good and he's having the same effect on the rest of us.'

165

'So we'd better have a word with him. Here he comes.' One of the guards was escorting Randy back to his workplace.

'He looks a trifle disgruntled, if you ask me.'

Freddy stopped scraping to speak to the newcomer, 'What's on your mind, Randy?'

'Bastards. They even watch us going to the goddamned bathroom. Is there no privacy in this place?'

'Not a scrap,' confirmed Bailey, 'but if it makes you feel safer, it's not because they have designs on you – the *Reich* tends to frown upon that sort of thing – they just don't want you trying to escape.'

'Realising as they do,' added Freddy, 'that you're not overwhelmed by the warmth of their hospitality.'

'Holy Moses.' It was almost a wail. 'How can you guys joke about it? This place is hell!'

'It's not ideal,' said Freddy, 'but there are worse places. You should ask the kriegies who've worked in the coal mines or the stone quarries. Those places really are hell, so I've been told.'

'And as for the merry quip and ribald jest,' Bailey told him, 'it's all we have left. It's our way of coping with kriegie life. Take it from me. I joined this club in nineteen-forty and I intend to be in my right mind when I take my leave of it.'

'So you see,' Freddy told him, 'you can go out of your mind with misery or you can join the worshipful company of clowns. We recommend the latter.' He picked up his chisel and nodded in the direction of two guards who were watching them. 'For the time being, though, we'd better get back to work.'

'But the conditions! This is slave labour, and we don't even get enough to eat, goddamn it.' He pressed his hands against his stomach. 'I hurt with hunger!'

'So do we, old scout, and we're old hands at going hungry.'

'Work,' Freddy reminded them. 'The goons are watching us.'

'Of course,' said Bailey, chipping at the salt, 'you could always share your reservations about this country retreat with Vogel. That would get you moved.'

'Where would he send me?' Randy was rightly suspicious.

'It depends on your religious belief,' said Freddy. 'Suffice it to say, the last kriegie who tried it got a bullet through the head.'

'And the next to the last can still feel the beating.' Bailey touched his chest at the memory.

'He shoots Russians without a second thought,' warned Freddy. 'He'd give a Yank maybe a moment's consideration but the result would be the same. Now, for goodness' sake, get scraping.'

'*Arbeit!*' One of the guards was pointing his rifle at Randy.

'Okay, okay.' Randy began scraping and the guard lowered his rifle.

'Most of the goons are either unfit or too old for active service,' said Freddy, 'but don't let that fool you. They can still make your life pretty uncomfortable.'

'Oh, my hands.' Randy dropped his chisel and leant helplessly against the wall. 'Oh, sweet Jesus, I can't do this.' The guards approached again with their rifles levelled until they saw, from their point of view, the humour of the situation. One pretended to cry on the other's shoulder, but only for a few seconds before they both collapsed into laughter.

'For goodness' sake,' said Freddy, 'don't let the goons see you in that state. You must *never* show them you're down. Come on, get back to work.'

'I can't help it. My hands are so sore.'

'You'll bally-well have to help it,' Bailey told him. 'We haven't spent all this time keeping our end up to have our reputation set to nought by a walking tragedy like you.'

'He's right,' said Freddy. 'Now pull yourself together before you give the Allies a bad name.'

The remainder of the shift was uneventful, but when they reached the surface Freddy spoke to a corporal from the American hut.

'Randy?' The American searched his memory.'

'A tall, thin bloke with sandy-coloured hair,' Freddy prompted. 'From New Jersey, I think he said. He needs watching, believe me.'

'Oh, you mean Adams.' He nodded. 'He's just a baby. Forget him.'

· · ·

Freddy had plenty to occupy his mind that night, but he spotted Randy the next morning as Vogel dismissed them from a lengthy and freezing roll-call.

' Good morning,' he called.

'Oh, hi.' The response was as lacklustre as Freddy had expected.

'You're going to remember what we told you, aren't you?'

'I guess.'

'It's more important than you realise, both for your morale and to make those bastards realise that we're not finished yet. Don't you see?'

'I guess.'

He was wondering what to say to him next, when he heard the roar of approaching aircraft. They were Dorniers and, as far as he could tell, they were heading west. He remembered seeing them earlier when he fell in with the others for roll-call. He'd counted six and the same number had returned. 'Just a minute, Randy,' he said. Turning to the nearest guard, he asked him for the time. The guard looked grudgingly at his wristwatch and muttered, '*Zwanzig nach fünf.*'

'*Danke.*' Turning to his companion, he said, 'It's five-twenty. Those bombers were heading east at oh-five-hundred when we fell in, so they've been gone twenty minutes.'

'What of it?'

'They're Dornier two-one-sevens and they cruise at about two-hundred-and-fifty miles an hour. Now, what's two-hundred-and-fifty divided by sixty?'

'About four. OK? We're missing breakfast. At least, that's what they call it around here.'

'Right, so they do four miles a minute. Twenty minutes multiplied by four is eighty.'

'Correct. Now can we go?'

'Wait.' He caught Randy's arm and held him, conscious that Vogel was watching them. 'They've done eighty miles in twenty minutes. Don't you see? It means that the Russians are only about forty miles away. They're closer than we thought, and it's just a matter of time, a very short time before they arrive.' He shook Randy by his arm. 'Doesn't that make you feel better?'

Before Randy could answer, Vogel stood beside them, demanding to know what they were discussing, so Freddy told him readily in German and was gratified to see a reaction. It was a tiny reaction, only the twitch of a facial muscle and a shifting of the eyes, because Vogel was a professional soldier and a man of discipline, but it gave Freddy great satisfaction because it meant that for the first time Vogel was scared.

. . .

Sylvia had written to Joyce about the letter. She had also told Rosemary, and Gloria, and she was still elated two days later, when she heard a pipe ordering her to report to her Divisional Officer.

She found Third Officer Fuller in a sunny mood.

'You've done an excellent job,' she said, 'helping to hold the fort, and your reward has finally arrived.'

'My reward, ma'am?' She wasn't expecting anything.

'Yes, you're to report to the Regulating Office to collect your movement order, orders for embarkation and your leave pass. You've got eight days' embarkation leave because your request for an overseas draft has come through. You're going to sunny Malta.'

27

January 1945

After an unusually long leave, Sylvia and nine other Wrens had embarked in the light cruiser HMS Carnforth, and were on passage to Malta.

Sylvia and her colleagues were accommodated in the gun room; its usual inhabitants had been allocated temporary space in various parts of the ship, and the Wrens' appearance on board had given rise to conflicting reactions among members of the ship's company. According to one of the Wren officers, the older hands disapproved strongly of their presence and maintained that no good ever came of steaming with women on board, whilst the more junior ratings displayed a predictably healthy interest in their female passengers. Any ambitions on their part remained unrealised, however, as the sexes were kept strictly segregated throughout the passage. In any case, it was unlikely that any of the girls would have been at all interested in male company during the first leg of the journey, heavy seas having rendered them helpless with seasickness.

A long-awaited improvement in the weather and the prospect of a run ashore in Gibraltar improved their spirits in no time, even though they were first ordered to muster on the upper deck to be 'told off'. They quickly learned that a telling-off was not a reprimand, at least in navalese, but a briefing. The briefing officer in this case was Second Officer Bentham, a formidable woman of great age – at least thirty-five – who had once been games mistress in a minor school for girls. She was tall and commanding, but, despite her pre-war calling, clearly nervous when called upon to speak of matters of the flesh. A stony-faced PO Wren stood beside the girls.

'You will shortly be going ashore,' Miss Bentham told them, 'and you will find that Gibraltar is a fascinating place with much to see. There are, however,

169

certain things you need to know. That is to say, there are possible, er, dangers of which you have to beware.' It seemed that Miss Bentham was steeling herself to speak of the unspeakable, and the girls were wondering when she was going to get to the point. Sylvia's attention had already begun to wander, and it wasn't long before she spotted two seamen working on the afterdeck above them. One was shaking his head dismissively at the second officer's warning. The other winked at Sylvia, and she forced herself to keep a straight face.

'The danger to which I am referring,' said Miss Bentham eventually, 'is namely and principally that most fatal combination of strong drink and male company.'

The sailor who had winked at Sylvia was pursing his lips and wagging a finger in disapproval of his friend, who pretended to be drunk.

'Have I said something to amuse you?'

Sylvia thought for a moment that the second officer was addressing her, until the girl next to her spoke.

'No, ma'am, not at all. I was screwing my eyes up against the sun.'

'Then perhaps you will remember in future to keep your sun glasses about your person. You possess a pair of sun glasses, I presume?'

'Yes, ma'am.'

Sylvia silently gave full marks to the girl for quick thinking. The officer merely continued with her talk. 'Now,' she said, 'it is necessary, in a hot climate, to maintain our intake of fluids. Some are tempted to drink alcohol, and that is all very well in moderation. I should say that it is relatively harmless in small quantities. The danger occurs when alcohol is taken to excess, because that is when the unsuspecting female is at her most vulnerable.'

Sylvia kept her eyes lowered, afraid even to glance at the two sailors. She doubted, as she was sure everyone else did, that Miss Bentham had ever been vulnerable.

'Now, to speak plainly, each of you girls possesses something that the unscrupulous male regards as his greatest trophy, and that is, not to put too fine a point on it, your, er, well … your *honour*.'

A minor convulsion swept through the line, but Miss Bentham seemed oblivious to it.

'Under no circumstances must you ever, as single girls, allow your honour to be compromised. The designing male will plead, cajole and beguile you; he will use all the wiles at his disposal. Our colleague Jolly Jack has quite a reputation in this regard.'

Out of the corner of her eye, Sylvia caught sight of the two sailors dancing an approximation of a hornpipe.

'But you must resist all attempts on your honour.' Miss Bentham delivered the last phrase and then cleared her throat self-consciously. 'Enjoy your time ashore, girls, and remember that the last boat leaves at seventeen-forty-five hours. Carry on, PO.'

The PO waited until the officer was out of earshot before addressing the Wrens. When she did, it was to give them a summary of Miss Bentham's talk. 'So there you have it,' she told them. Don't let Jack get you plastered, and in any case keep your hands on your ha'pennies. Especially,' she added, inclining her head towards the afterdeck, 'when Laurel and Hardy are about.'

The two sailors acknowledged the mention with an elaborate bow.

. . .

Sylvia and her two companions had walked miles and seen as much as they could because it was a shame not to. Gibraltar was an ancient port that had much to offer. Oddly, though, the dolphins playing outside the harbour had fascinated them most of all, and their aquabatics held the girls spellbound until their aching feet prompted them to head for the Star Bar in Parliament Lane. They were relieved to find three vacant stools, which they quickly claimed.

Ruth tasted her cider and nodded her approval. 'This is all right,' she said. 'It just doesn't seem right to drink beer, but cider's OK and it tastes quite nice.' She was nineteen, with auburn curls and freckles that seemed already to have multiplied in the sunshine.

'I know what you mean,' said Sylvia. 'Beer's a man's thing when all's said and done.'

'In times gone by,' said Gwendoline, 'both men and women drank beer. It was usually unsafe to drink water.' She was a quiet, solitary girl, who might have stayed on board had Sylvia not insisted on her joining the party.

'Speaking of men,' said Ruth, who did so frequently, 'the officer who saw us off in the boat was dreamy, wasn't he?'

'Not bad at all,' agreed Sylvia.

'Masterful too. "Lower away handsomely",' she mimicked. 'I don't know what he meant by that but I like to think that when I meet my ideal man, he'll treat me handsomely.'

'It's just an outmoded word for "elegantly" or "smoothly",' said Gwendoline.

Ruth nodded eagerly. 'That suits me. I want a man who will lower me handsomely on to satin sheets.'

'But what about your honour?' Sylvia grinned at the memory of Second Officer Bentham's warning.

Ruth snorted good-naturedly. 'It'll be a bit late for that. I left my honour

171

in an Anderson shelter in Dulwich.' She smiled at her colleagues' reaction. 'You have to get your fun while you can,' she said. 'After all, there's a war on.'

'The war, of course,' said Sylvia, relieved that Gwendoline was blushing for them both.

'It was a bit tricky at first,' Ruth went on. 'We had two goes at it before we got it right.'

'Did you really?' Sylvia was curious in spite of herself.

'We might have done it again if his dad hadn't come down the garden looking for him. It was a close thing, I can tell you. He only just managed to pull his trousers up in time.' She smiled again. 'I put my blackouts in my bag. It was easier than trying to put them on in a hurry.'

'Quick thinking,' was all Sylvia could say.

'Yes, and I had to stay to tea with his family, and me with nothing underneath.' She laughed shortly. 'Not even my honour.'

Sylvia looked at her watch. It was four-thirty. 'We should get down to the jetty,' she said, relieved in a way to be able to change the subject, if only for Gwendoline's sake, the poor girl having suffered acute embarrassment throughout Ruth's revelation.

As they walked towards the harbour, Ruth said, 'I wonder why the Navy uses such funny language. I'm sure no one else says "handsomely" nowadays.'

'I've wondered about that,' said Sylvia.

'There's a very simple explanation.' They were the first words Gwendoline had uttered for some time, and both Sylvia and Ruth turned to look at her in surprise.

'When the Navy was founded,' she explained, 'we were speaking a mixture of Anglo-Saxon, Old Norse and Norman French. Modern English, you see, only began in Shakespeare's time. By that time the Navy must have developed its own language, and as ships spent years at sea sailors continued to communicate in the same way.' She shrugged at the simplicity of it. 'It was almost like being in a foreign country and it was inevitable that their vocabulary should develop independently.'

'That's fascinating, Gwendoline.' Impressed though Sylvia was by her companion's reasoning, she could see why Gwendoline spent so much time alone. It was a shame, really, because she needed friends, although it was still a relief when they reached the jetty and found a boat waiting there.

A seaman greeted them. 'Three more for the Skylark? Climb aboard, girls.' He offered a hand to each of them, steadying Gwendoline as she stumbled over the gunwale, with the advice, 'Don't do the splits whatever you do, love. Think of your honour.'

. . .

It was 0510 and the prisoners had fallen in on the frozen snow for roll call. The Man-of-Confidence had told them they were going to hear something of great importance but Vogel was taking his time, as he usually did. Freddy wriggled his toes in a forlorn effort to ease the numbness. A piercing wind penetrated his greatcoat and the four layers beneath it, so that he longed for shelter. Even the mine would have been welcome.

Eventually the guards completed the count, the Russians and Ukrainians were marched away and the *Unteroffizier* came out of his hut to speak to the prisoners who remained. He was wearing thick gloves and a fur cap with the ear flaps turned down and tied under his chin. Freddy wondered for a moment if they had been part of a consignment that he and Len had diverted from the Eastern Front. He remembered then that they had sent the entire load to Hohenfels or some other place that sounded warm.

'Today, you will all return to Lamsdorf,' the *Unteroffizier* told them through his interpreter. 'Transport has been arranged and you will leave in one hour's time. You will take two blankets and such belongings as you can carry. That is all.'

When Vogel had dismissed them, Bailey said, 'That was short and not so sweet. It was hardly worth his while dressing up like that. I wonder what game the blighters are playing.'

'Listen,' said Freddy.

'To what?'

'The guns.' He inclined his head again. 'A bombardier should be able to recognise artillery fire.'

'Not me, old man. Haven't you noticed I'm a shade hard of hearing? Gunfire did that to me long before I was taken prisoner.'

'Now you mention it, I suppose, but it's getting louder. I reckon the goons are going to do a bunk before the Russians arrive. For my money, they're going to herd us all into Lamsdorf and let the Russians liberate us while they all make themselves scarce.'

'I sure as hell hope not.' Randy had arrived beside them, as curious as the rest. 'The last thing I want is to be caught by those guys.'

'They're our allies,' Freddy reminded him, although he, too, wondered a little about the treatment allied prisoners might receive from them.

'They're commies, for Pete's sake. They're not regular people.'

'Maybe,' said Bailey, 'they're going to use us as hostages. Our people could be nearer than we realise.'

Randy snorted. 'Last time I looked, they were still the other side of the Rhine.'

173

'Well,' said Freddy, 'we'll find out soon enough. Meanwhile, breakfast beckons.'

'Yeah,' agreed Randy, 'a whole piece of black bread. Some breakfast.'

They had not long to wait before they learned their fate. Within two hours of their arrival at Lamsdorf, they were each given a Red Cross parcel and ordered to join a large party of prisoners preparing to march west. The camp guards were abandoning occupied Poland, as Freddy had suspected, but they were taking the prisoners with them. It seemed to him that it was literally the first step towards freedom and his long-overdue return to England.

28

Thanks to one of Second Officer Bentham's briefings, Sylvia had been able to identify a number of Valetta's landmarks as she and the others mustered on deck with their kit. There were the steep fortifications of the Knights of St John, the imposing Barraca Battery and, high above them and dominating the harbour, the Castille Signal Station, a towering and magnificent reminder of Malta's place in history. Evidence of the island's most recent siege was everywhere; the yellow, sun-bleached buildings bore the scars of incessant bombing, but for Sylvia, who had witnessed Dover's worst agonies, the damage seemed only to emphasise their magnificence.

A proper appreciation of Valetta had to wait, however, because the girls had been ashore only a short time before they were collected and transported to their accommodation in the former Imperial Hotel in Sliema.

'This is all right,' said Ruth after a brief inspection of the cabin.

For Sylvia, it was a somewhat more luxurious reminder of HMS *Wasp*. 'It's almost like Dover,' she said, casting a wary eye, 'hopefully without the cockroaches.'

They had elected to stay together and had been fortunate to be allocated a four-berth cabin, although so far, there were only three of them. The third occupant was Gwendoline, who arrived at that moment.

'What was that about cockroaches?' She was struggling to move herself and her kit through the doorway.

'I was just saying I hope there aren't any,' said Sylvia, watching her efforts with some curiosity.

'They say the biggest problem's the mosquitoes,' said Ruth, 'although I haven't seen one yet.' She was also watching Gwendoline with detached interest until the latter solved her problem by entering the room and dragging her kit behind her.

'As a matter of fact, the mosquitoes are relatively harmless.' Gwendoline sat on a bed to recover from her exertion. 'They don't carry malaria, if that's what is worrying you.'

'It was, but we shan't worry about it any longer,' said Ruth, 'but how do you get to know about these things?'

'One simply reads about them.' She shrugged dismissively and then asked, 'Does either of you know where the heads are?'

Sylvia pointed. 'Down the passage and it's either the third or the fourth door on the left.'

'Thank you.' Gwendoline stood up and stumbled over her kitbag, grabbing Ruth's proffered arm as she went.

'Careful,' said Ruth. 'Remember your honour.'

'Yes. Thank you.'

When Gwendoline was safely in the heads, Ruth said, 'I don't think I've ever met anyone as clumsy as her, but at least we've got entertainment as long as she's around.'

'We can't cure her clumsiness,' said Sylvia thoughtfully, 'but we've got to do something about her general awkwardness. She's got no friends, and she'll never have any as long as she sounds like a talking encyclopaedia.'

'She's hopeless among people,' agreed Ruth. 'I suppose we'll have to do something.'

Sylvia was about to make a suggestion when a voice with a pronounced Liverpool accent came from the doorway.

'I thought I was seein' things when I saw your name on the watch bill, but it really is our Sylvia!'

Sylvia looked up, and disbelief became joy as she greeted the newcomer. 'Dorothy!'

· · ·

Like many others, Freddy had expected the guards to march them to Lamsdorf railway station, where they would presumably start out on a cold and uncomfortable but welcome journey west, but so far all they had done was walk. They had walked for hours through snow and in agonising cold until some of them began to droop with fatigue.

Long after nightfall, they reached a village, where the guards allowed them to fall out. There was a distribution of two slices of bread per prisoner, which Freddy and his companions ate immediately along with what remained in their Red Cross parcels, and the guards pushed them into a huge barn with orders to sleep there.

'They even tell us when to sleep,' said Randy. 'They think we need to be told.' He placed his pack behind him as a pillow and wrapped himself in his blankets. 'Did anyone notice the name of this place?'

No one had, but someone asked sourly, 'Are you thinking of coming back after the war?'

'I'm sure as hell never going to come back to this goddamned country as long as I live. I just wondered because I may want to tell my kids about the place it took us six hours to find and where they fed us two pieces of black bread and made us sleep in a goddamned pig sty.'

'Can you take a piece of advice from an old hand?' Sleep was about to overpower Freddy but he was determined to stop Randy before he antagonised every man in the column.

'I guess.'

'Well, this is no picnic for any of us, least of all the blokes who've been here from the beginning, but don't make it worse for yourself than it is already.'

'Okay, and how am I doing that?'

'By carping and belly-aching all the bloody time as if you're a special case who deserves better. You're just one of thousands, believe me, and you're not going to survive if you don't get a grip on yourself and stop moaning. Now, do yourself and everyone else a favour by accepting the fact that it's the same for all of us, and by going to bloody sleep so that we can too.' He rolled over, and the crackling sound of Sylvia's letters in the lining of his greatcoat made him feel a shade warmer

. . .

Life at HMS *St Angelo* was a subterranean existence, but with the benefit that its personnel could usually look forward to their time 'up top' with blue skies, sunshine and gentle warmth. It was very different from the British winter. The signals section operated a four-watch system as well, which meant a regular day off, a real luxury.

One of Sylvia's first off-watch jobs was to write to Freddy. She couldn't tell him where she was but the sooner a letter reached her home in Yorkshire the quicker her mother could get it off to him, and it had to go from there. Also, by her reckoning, her quarterly parcel should reach him soon. She had been particularly worried about him since her conversation with Len and she wanted to send him what luxuries she could. It was just an awful shame she wasn't allowed to send food but she understood the reason for the rule.

It would cause awful problems if one prisoner got more than the others. Of course, there were the Red Cross parcels. After what Len had told her, she hoped they were getting through.

His last letter was dated the third of December and it ended on an optimistic note.

Because of the time it takes for letters to arrive, I'll wish you the best twenty-first birthday ever. I only wish I could celebrate it with you.

We'll be preparing for Christmas soon. Lift that Christmas tree! Haul that sleigh! A white Christmas is odds-on favourite as well. Last time I was in the main camp I heard a song called 'White Christmas'. It was sung by Bing Crosby and I'm sure you'll know it. I liked it, but prefer 'All the Things You Are' because it's about you and me.

All my love, as ever,
Freddy XXXXX

It was so typical of Freddy to make light of things. She took out her writing things and began.

27th January, 1945.
Dearest Freddy,
I know I've already thanked you, but I've hardly stopped reading your song since it arrived. Everyone I've told about it has been terribly impressed.

I had a lovely birthday, thank you, although I don't feel at all different. Did you feel different when you were twenty-one?

Little Bruce is walking well now. He sometimes staggers a bit like a drunken man, usually when he has to turn left or right, but he's improving all the time. He's not talking yet though. He just burbles complete nonsense. My dad says only women can understand him because we talk nonsense as well.

Do you remember my telling you about the girl who started a big romance with a chap in the boot department? Well, she transferred to one of our other branches for a while, and now I've changed branches too, and guess what? She turned up here, so we're working together again. What luck!

I hope you get your parcel soon so that you can take advantage of the extra woollies. I'll write again when I have more to tell you. For now, just let me tell you that I love you to bits, because that's the most important thing of all. I wish I could tell you in person. One day soon ... In the meantime, take care and wrap up well.

Heaps and heaps of love,
Your Sugar Plum XXXXXX

It was too bad she couldn't tell him about all the things that had happened to her recently. She would have lots to tell him after the war, but that was of no immediate help. She worried at the problem until Dorothy came into the cabin.

'Whatcha doin', Sylvia? Writin' to Freddy? Send him my love.'

'Right, I will.' After 'What luck!' she inserted the words, 'She sends her love too.' It was a small thing, but a man in Freddy's situation needed all the good wishes he could get.

'Did you write that just now, like?' Dorothy tried not to peer over Sylvia's shoulder.

'Of course. I've been fast for things to tell him, so every little helps.'

'What do you mean, you've been "fast"?'

'At a loss, I suppose.'

'And they say Scouses talk rubbish.' Dorothy perched on the end of Sylvia's bed and looked wistful. 'I write loads of rubbish to Alf but he says he's just thankful for the letters. He doesn't care what they say as long as they're from me.'

'That's nice. How's he keeping?'

'He's doin' all right. He's not taking any lip from Norris nowadays. I told him not to. Alf's worth ten of 'im.'

'He certainly is, and good for you. You did right to tell him that.'

'Yeah.' Suddenly Dorothy became animated. 'I know what you can do,' she said. 'Join the revue.'

'What?'

'You say you're stuck for somethin' to tell Freddy about, so come an' join us in the revue. You'll love it an' it'll keep you in things to tell him about from now 'til he comes home.'

'I don't know what you're talking about.'

'Rather than leave it all to ENSA,' she explained patiently, 'we put concerts and revues on to entertain the others. There's singers, comedians, dancers an' all sorts. You'd be surprised. I do a Gracie Fields act. D'you want to hear it?'

'Maybe later.' She remembered when Dorothy was shy and awkward, and marvelled at the transformation that had taken place since she and Joyce had taken her in hand. Gracie Fields, though, wasn't really her cup of tea. She could wait for that.

'You'll think about it, won't you?'

'I don't know' It was happening rather too quickly for Sylvia, who never liked to be rushed into things. 'I don't know what I could do.'

'You can dance. The chorus could do with some talent.'

'I don't know.'

'An' you've gorra lovely voice. Do you remember how we used to sing on the way home from the Plaza?'

'When we weren't eating chips.' They both smiled at the memory.

'Come to the rehearsal this afternoon, just to see, like.'

'All right.' It was as far as she was prepared to go for the time being.

. . .

The night had been so cold that it was almost a relief to be on the march again, and there were even sporadic attempts at humour. Recognising the guards' anxiety to stay ahead of the advancing Russians, some prisoners had been unable to resist the temptation to break into song.

'*Ei, ukhnem!* Yo, heave ho!' They had heard the Russian kriegies singing it but it was as much as they could remember, which was possibly as well, as the guards became increasingly angry, shouting and pointing their rifles, so that all singing ceased abruptly.

'Miserable blighters,' said Bailey. 'I thought they were a musical race. Maybe a spot of Wagner would be more to their taste. What about "The Ride of the Valkyries"?'

'Maybe not,' cautioned Freddy. 'They're nervous enough to start shooting.'

'Well,' said Randy, who had been unusually quiet that morning, 'I like the idea of those sons of bitches pissing in their pants with fright. It was high time, and with the Russians behind us and our boys ahead of us, they're too damn' right to be scared.'

'It's a comforting thought,' agreed Freddy.

'Ah yes, comfort. Whatever happened to that?' Bailey shifted his kitbag from his left shoulder to his right. 'I've been trying to think of a better way to carry this confounded thing, and I think I've found it.'

'Expound,' invited Freddy.

'It was fairly obvious, really, and I'll try it when we stop. You just roll up a blanket and use it as a strap-arrangement to carry the kitbag like a knapsack. Do you see what I mean?'

'You amaze me, Bailey. I'd say you have a future of some kind.'

'If you only knew, old boy.'

It was clear that Bailey had been giving the matter some thought, because the next time he spoke it was to ask, 'What's your future, Freddy?'

'Do you mean work? I suppose I'll go back to photography. It was a good life until this *fracas* interrupted it. How about you?'

'I've often thought I'd like to tread the boards.'

An Act of Kindness

Freddy was surprised but he nodded approvingly. 'I could see you doing that.'

'Why not? I've been acting a part most of my life. I don't see why I shouldn't do it as a career.' He slithered dangerously on the icy road and acknowledged Randy's supportive hand. 'Thanks, old man. These boots are not the best thing in this kind of weather.'

'You're welcome, and I think you'd do okay as an actor. Damn it, I reckon you'd go down big in Hollywood with that upper-class English accent of yours. You could be another Ronald Colman or David Niven.'

'My dear old thing, I'm quite touched.'

'If you don't mind my asking,' said Freddy, who had been pondering the matter for some time, 'how did you acquire that accent?'

Bailey looked uncharacteristically modest. 'It's not difficult to ape the ways of the leisured classes when you rub shoulders with them every day,' he said. 'I sold them motor cars and they unwittingly gave me lessons in drawing room manners and all that went with them. It was as simple as that, and it came in jolly useful for an elementary school lad with no prospects to speak of.'

Freddy was so impressed that he became quite thoughtful for a while, but Randy was planning Bailey's thespian career. 'I guess there'll be opportunities for ex-servicemen after the war. I'm thinking of college courses, acting school and suchlike.'

'I imagine so,' said Bailey, 'and I can't imagine they'd take too unhealthy an interest in a fellow's past. Not at a drama school, surely.'

'I shouldn't think so,' agreed Freddy, sensing that another confession might be imminent. 'I'd say it's most unlikely.'

'You see, I did have a minor *contretemps* with the forces of law and order. It was more a misunderstanding than anything else really, but it still earned me a sojourn on the sunny Isle of Wight.'

Randy stared at him. 'Do you mean they gave you a vacation?'

'He means Parkhurst prison,' translated Freddy.

'A penitentiary, huh?'

'Not to put too fine a point on it, old man, yes.'

There was a pause as Randy digested the information, and then he said, 'Well, I don't think you're a bad guy, Bailey. Not at all.'

For the second time that morning, Bailey was touched. He said, 'You don't know what that means to me, Randy. I must say I'm a heartened man.' After a moment, he added warmly, 'You know, you're a decent sort of chap yourself.'

Their conversation had given Freddy much to consider, and there would

181

be ample time for thought during the journey. So far, none of the guards had mentioned transport of any kind, and that seemed to point to a long walk.

. . .

Sylvia sat on a folding chair in the hut that until recently had been a makeshift canteen, its predecessor having been destroyed in the bombing. A stage had been erected at one end, with ingeniously-contrived curtains, tabs and a plain backcloth.

She had heard some impressive singing, and some of the novelty acts were particularly good. It was just unfortunate that the dancing was so awful, a flaw that was evidently lost on Dorothy.

'What are you pullin' that face for, Sylvia? You look as if somebody's made a rude noise at a tea party.'

'It's the dancing. Who's in charge of choreography?'

'Now you're asking.' Dorothy searched her memory and then gave up. 'I don't think anybody is. They just make it up as they go along.'

'It certainly looks that way.'

'Aren't they very good, then?'

'I'm afraid not.' They were doubtless doing their best but it really was a shambles.

'Hang on a minute.' Dorothy left her seat and went to speak with a buxom and statuesque PO Wren in the wings. She returned with her a minute later.

'This is Sylvia Charlesworth, Daisy. She's done years of ballet an' she's really good at dancin' an' that.'

Sylvia was mortified. 'It's not for me to criticise, PO. I only ...'

'Nonsense. We obviously need all the help we can get. Do you think you can sort us out?'

Sylvia bit her lip and made her decision. 'I'll do my best, PO.'

'First class. I'm Daisy Watson. Come and meet the company.' She led Sylvia to the front of the stage, where they waited until the end of the number. When it came, the accompanist, a bored-looking Wren cook, played an elaborate final arpeggio, lit a cigarette and accepted a mug of tea, all with the same fluid action.

The dancers looked expectantly towards Sylvia and the PO Wren, who clapped her hands quite unnecessarily. 'This is Leading Wren Charleston,' she announced. 'What's your Christian name again, dear?'

'Sylvia, and it's Charlesworth, PO, not Charleston.'

'Call me Daisy. We're very informal here.' Returning her attention to the dancers, she said, 'Sylvia is a professional dancer and she's going to be in charge of dance. It will be her job to transform you.'

29

February

Even the guards were finding the going difficult. One of them, an East Prussian, admitted to Freddy that it was the worst winter he could remember. Others were less communicative, except when prisoners crept into the fields to find root crops. Fearing a mass escape, they forced them back into the column under threat of death and kept careful watch for any further excursions. Meanwhile, the prisoners went hungry. Usually, they had one meal per day of a little bread and, if they were fortunate, some soup. There were occasions, though, when they simply went without, sometimes for two days at a time. If they were able to steal vegetables from the farms where they spent their nights, they did, and on one occasion they found some grain in a cellar.

'Chew it,' Randy told them, grabbing a handful. 'Chew it for long enough and it'll make you a meal.'

The others followed his lead without hesitation. Bailey asked, 'Where did you learn this?'

'At summer camp. We learned all kinds of things there, like how the Indians hunted and tracked. It was good.'

'It's a pity you can't shoot a buffalo for us,' said Bailey, but this stuff is very welcome.'

'It seems odd,' said Freddy, 'to hear you talk about "camp" like that, considering what the word's come to mean to us.'

Bailey nodded sagely. 'It's one word that's not going to be too popular after the war.'

'I can't imagine how some of you guys have survived five years of it,' said Randy.

'It certainly hasn't been easy,' Bailey told him, 'although you see worse things when you look around.'

The others knew he was referring to the Russians who had been unable to keep up with them on the march that day. The guards had taken them away, and now no one knew where they were, although most suspected the worst.

'I saw unspeakable things at the I.G. Farben factory,' said Bailey.

Freddy nodded, reluctant to pursue the subject, but Randy asked, 'What kind of place is this I.G. Farben joint?'

'It's a chemical factory near Auschwitz, and there's a camp attached to it.'

'A POW camp?'

'No, it's an internment camp for civilians but it's worse than anything we've ever known. We're hungry all right, but those poor devils are literally starving to death.'

'So why are they there?'

'Because they're Jews.' Bailey visibly curbed his impatience at Randy's ignorance. 'The goons are forever on the lookout for them.' Did you have to go through a short arms parade, Freddy?'

'Yes, when they brought us from Veano. The first thing we had to do was drop our pants.'

'I imagine you'd have some fast talking to do, old man.'

'You've been peeping.'

'No, but seriously, I've seen far too many of the poor blighters pulled out of the line with their trousers still round their ankles, and then taken away and never seen again. You think you'll get used to it but some things just stay with you.'

'I don't get it. I know lots of Jews back home in the States, and they're just regular people. I can't see what these guys have against them.'

No one spoke for about a minute although it was clear what everyone was thinking. Then, to break the silence and the mood, Freddy said, 'I've sometimes wondered about Jews and the circumcision thing. I mean, I wonder if they have a system like ours. You know how a kiddie gets a threepenny bit for a tooth. Well, maybe they have a fairy too …'

'I don't think so,' said Randy, involuntarily crossing his legs. 'They do it when they're babies and money means nothing to them. How old were you, for Pete's sake?'

'Seven days. I'll never forget it.'

'Funny man. But say, how much is this threepenny thing? I never could get used to your money.'

'About five cents.'

'Well, I'd sure as hell want more than any nickel if they did that to me.'

There were no boundaries where conversation was concerned, except when, as a body, they opted for silence. Often, they trudged without a word, alone with their thoughts. At such times, Freddy thought about Sylvia, because every painful, frozen footstep was taking him closer to her, and she, after all, was his reason for wanting to survive.

. . .

To swell the numbers, Sylvia had conscripted Ruth and Gwendoline into the chorus. Ruth was willing enough but Gwendoline had to be coaxed, and only relented when Sylvia assured her that her role on stage would be basically a static one. Nevertheless, mixing with the rest of the company had been good for her, as she pointed out to Sylvia during a break in rehearsal.

'I'm enjoying it enormously. They're so welcoming.'

'Most of them are.' The concert party had been formed only recently but Sylvia was already aware of a bitches' coven.

'Why did you introduce me as "Gwen"? No one's ever called me that.'

'Don't you like it?'

'I really don't mind. I just wondered why.'

Sylvia tested her tea and found it drinkable. The pause gave her time to think how best to explain it tactfully. Eventually, she said, 'It's less formal than "Gwendoline".'

'Obviously, but I still don't understand.'

Sylvia tried again. 'This is an informal group. That's why we all get along so well regardless of rank or rate, so I introduced you informally.'

'I see.' The principle that might have been obvious to most was evidently new and appealing for Gwendoline. 'My father says there's a place for informality.'

'Does he really? What does your dad do?'

'He's a clergyman. He's Rector of St Oswald's in Harrowfield.'

'Ah.' It explained quite a lot.

'Why did you say that?'

'Why did I say what?'

' "Ah", like that.'

'Because I'm impressed.' She was too, but her dad was a chartered accountant and he could be stuffy when he wanted to be. It might take a little time, but she reckoned she had the background and the intuition to set Gwendoline on the right road. Before she could begin, however, she noticed that Daisy was on her way over. There was just time to give Gwen a quick piece of advice. 'Stay informal,' she told her.

'Ideas,' said Daisy, waving her arms for no obvious reason. 'We need ideas.'

'Ideas for what?'

'Think on a big scale, Sylvia. Think of Busby Berkeley, think of Broadway!'

'All right, Daisy, but what do you want?'

'I'm talking about the grand finale, Sylvia. It has to be big!' She stood with her arms suddenly outstretched like the sails of a windmill, presumably indicating the size she had in mind.

'All right, I'll think about it.' Whilst she could possibly appreciate Daisy's vision, she was unable to share her excitement.

'It's terribly important. This is a big revue and it needs a spectacular finale.'

'I realise that, Daisy, and I'll think about it.'

'Urgently, I hope.'

'I'm thinking about it already.'

. . .

Freddy reckoned they were covering about fifteen miles per day. He based his calculation on an estimated walking pace of one mile per hour, which was the most the column could manage. It was pitifully slow progress.

His chief preoccupation, though, was with Bailey, who was in bad shape, stumbling along with the rest but quieter and more subdued than Freddy had ever known him. Randy was also sensitive to Bailey's condition.

'How's he doin', Freddy?' A newcomer to kriegie rations, the American was sprightly compared with the others.

'He's had five years of relative starvation,' Freddy told him. 'It's a wonder he's come so far.'

They trudged on for another hour, during which the snow abated but the temperature fell alarmingly. Even with a scarf over his head and his balaclava pulled down over that, Freddy's ears and head ached agonisingly, and his throat and lungs burned with every breath.

After a while, the East Prussian guard with whom he'd spoken earlier drew level with them. He was in a more cheerful mood than before and he leaned towards Freddy and said in German, 'Five kilometres.'

'What?'

'Five more kilometres to Stalag Eight A. There we rest.'

'I don't believe it.'

Randy said, 'What's he say?'

'He says it's five more kilometres to Stalag Eight A. We're going to rest there.'

'Holy shit! Where's Stalag Eight A?'

Freddy asked the guard and then relayed the information to Randy. 'Görlitz. It's full of Yugoslavs, apparently, but maybe they've got room for us.'

'I've never heard of the goddamned place but, Holy Moses, lead me there!'

Freddy shook Bailey by the shoulder. 'Chin up, mate. We're nearly at Görlitz, wherever that is, and we're going to stop for a rest. It's a POW camp, so there's got to be food as well.'

Bailey trudged on, barely able to reply.

'Give us your pack, Bailey. Come on.' Freddy slid the blanket straps off Bailey's shoulders and shouldered the kitbag. Taking his cue, Randy crossed over to Bailey's side, gently taking his arm. 'Lean on me, buddy. Come on, take it easy. We'll soon be there.'

A voice from behind asked, 'What's happening?'

'Görlitz,' Randy told him. 'Five kilometres ahead of us. We're stopping for a rest and food. Pass it on.'

The message passed rapidly down the column, creating a buzz as it went and lifting everyone's spirits for the first time since leaving Lamsdorf.

. . .

Sylvia was giving the finale a great deal of thought. She thought about it on her way to and from HMS St Angelo, in the cabin when she was dressing and undressing, and during the all-night-on when things were quiet. Eventually she was able to put her suggestion to Daisy at the next rehearsal.

'It hasn't been easy,' she told her.

'I'm sure it hasn't, but you've got a plan?'

'I think so.'

'Well, go on then.' Daisy's enthusiasm was seldom absent for long.

'The finale needs to be rousing. I mean emotionally rousing.'

'Oh yes, that's the whole ...'

'No, listen.' No one who knew her could have called Sylvia bossy, but there was something about Daisy that prompted assertiveness, if only as a strategy for making one's voice heard. 'I was only fifteen when the war began,' she said, 'but I remember some of the patriotic songs of the time, and frankly ...'

'Oh, yes. There was "Sing As We Go", "Wish Me Luck" and what else?'

'Well, we can't use them.'

'Why can't we? They're wonderful songs.'

187

'They were terribly popular five years ago but we can't use them now.'

'But why not?'

'Because we're going to perform this revue to an audience of servicemen who have just had five years of hard reality, and anything that smacks of, you know ... "bull," will get hissed off the stage immediately. Mention the Siegfried Line and they'll all walk out, believe me.'

'So what do you suggest?' For once, Daisy seemed almost subdued.

'We need a song that radiates optimism, one that looks forward to peace and reunion. They are the things servicemen want, not songs about marching and hanging out washing.'

'Are you sure?'

Sylvia tried to remain patient. 'Daisy,' she said, 'what have you been doing for the past five years?'

'When I've not been working as a secretary I've been producing entertainments, and pretty successfully, I might say.' She sounded hurt and cross at the same time.

'I'm sure you've been successful, Daisy, but look at it from a different point of view. I don't think my aspirations are all that different from most people's, and chief among them is keeping a date with a man who's currently a POW in Poland. Most people have a date with someone or other, whether it's a man, a woman or a family, and winning the war is just a means to that end. The politicians talk about making the world a better place and bringing Hitler and the rest to justice, but the average sailor, soldier or airman just wants a satisfactory end to it all so that life can go on as before.'

'I see.' Daisy was now very subdued. 'I'm sorry. I didn't know about your friend being a POW.'

'That's all right. I only told you about him to make my point, and you do see what I mean, don't you?'

'I think so.'

'Good, so let's take a leaf out of Irving Berlin's book. The song I have in mind is "It's a Lovely Day Tomorrow", because that's what we're looking forward to.'

'Yes.' Daisy brightened immediately. 'I know the song, but how will you stage it?'

'I've been working on that. One thing I'll need is a huge calendar with pages that can be torn off on stage to mark the passage of time. Each page will represent a year, starting at nineteen-thirty-nine and ending in nineteen-forty-five. The chorus will form wheels that will engage and rotate like the mechanism of a clock as the clicks come from the orchestra and the pages are torn off.'

'It's a stroke of genius!' Daisy was jumping up and down in a way that was downright reckless with a bosom like hers.

'Thank you.' Sylvia preferred to think of it simply as a good idea, but exaggeration was Daisy's trademark and her enthusiasm, though irksome at times, was no less valuable. 'Two dancers will form the axles – or whatever they're called – of the wheels, and pirouette until the wheels stop moving for the final chorus. There are only two dancers, apart from yours truly, who are capable of doing it properly, and they are Cynthia Watkinson and Mary Williams. I'm sure they'll agree to it. Anyway, I'll choreograph the whole thing and you'll see how it works.'

With that done, she would have quite a lot to tell Freddy.

. . .

Mercifully, the guards let them eat before delousing, and Freddy was able to see that Bailey received his ration of soup and black bread. Between them, he and Randy then helped him through the scalding shower, at the end of which he was fit only for bed.

After food, the kriegies' greatest need was rest, and the two quickly followed Bailey's example by sinking gratefully on to their respective palliasses. Neither believed the rumour that their stay at Görlitz was likely to be more than an overnight stop, but they were both determined to make the most of what time they had.

Freddy was returning from the laundry next morning, when a familiar voice greeted him.

'Ah, the Englishman who speaks German.'

'Good morning, *Feldwebel* Vogel.'

Vogel looked almost friendly. He drew Freddy aside and asked, 'Have you everything you need?' His breath carried the mixed odours of garlic and dental decay but Freddy tried to ignore it.

'No, *Feldwebel*.' The question was quite unexpected but Freddy nevertheless gave a truthful answer. 'There are no Red Cross parcels, there's never enough food and water and there's no mail collection from here. Also, men are exhausted and as yet we have no idea where we are going.'

The *Feldwebel* nodded in a way that might have suggested sympathy had Freddy not known him better. 'We are marching west,' he said. It was the guards' stock answer, but then Vogel added, 'It is true that there is a shortage of food but maybe I can find a little more for you.'

Hiding his disbelief, Freddy said, 'I should be grateful for that, *Feldwebel*. My friend is very weak through lack of food.'

189

Vogel nodded again slowly. 'I am sorry to hear that,' he said. 'Meet me here in one hour.' He continued his journey and Freddy did the same, speculating on what might have brought about such a change of attitude on Vogel's part.

He shared the conundrum with Randy, who had now forsaken the American block by day for the company of Freddy and Bailey.

'He wants something,' he suggested.

'The same thought had occurred to me, but what could he possibly want from me?'

'Maybe he wants you to be a stool pigeon,' Randy suggested darkly.

'A what?'

'An informer. You speak Kraut, and maybe he thinks you're friendly. You never know.'

It seemed the likeliest explanation. For a minute or so, Freddy considered how he might play such a game, delivering false information in exchange for desperately-needed food. He would have to be very careful in case his fellow-kriegies suspected he really was an informer. The prospect was terrifying.

'When are you meeting him?'

'In an hour's time.' Freddy looked down at his exhausted comrade and his decision was made.

He spotted Vogel as soon as he left the hut. The *Feldwebel* was on the other side of the compound, talking with two other guards. After a minute or so, he appeared to dismiss them and stood for a while, gazing around the compound. Meanwhile, and with his stomach taut with apprehension, Freddy walked slowly towards the spot where they had met earlier.

'*Komm!*'

The summons caused Freddy to turn with a start. If he had been unsure how Vogel might greet him the question was now answered. He doubled across the compound and stood to attention before the NCO.

Without relaxing his expression, Vogel felt in his greatcoat pocket. 'Here,' he said quietly, pushing something into Freddy's hands. 'Take this and meet me at the same time tomorrow.'

'Thank you, *Feldwebel* Vogel.' It was almost an anti-climax after the trepidation of the past hour, and Freddy heard himself ask, 'Could we meet somewhere else? It would be safer.'

Vogel nodded briefly. 'Come to the orderly office.'

. . .

At last Sylvia had a letter from Freddy. She hurried to the cabin after breakfast so that she could read it before the others arrived.

6ᵗʰ January, 1945.

Dearest Sugar Plum,

We had a white Christmas after all, and very enjoyable it was too. All the same, I'm looking forward to hearing about Christmas in Leyburn.

I'll tell you what – let's defy this month-long time-lag and do something together for once. Let's make a wish on a new moon. I believe one is due next week, so the next one will be early in February, and this letter might not have reached you by then, so let's go for March to be on the safe side, OK? On the night in question, we both make the same wish on the new moon – that this global insanity will end very soon and that we can be together. Also, why don't we decide where we're going to meet? I imagine circumstances may well intervene before the great day, but for now I'll suggest Trafalgar Square. We could rendezvous at the foot of Nelson's Column. It's much less hackneyed than under the clock in Waterloo Station, and it has infinitely more gravitas. What do you think? The Immortal Memory and the Grand Romance!

Keep me posted about your folks: your parents, little Bruce, Peter Ross, Rainbow and the rest. I'm looking forward to meeting them all. Meanwhile, take care and remember the new moon!

Barrow-loads and buckets of love,

Freddy XXXXX

PS I got a letter from Len! It was good to hear from him. He told me you'd been to visit. You made a big impression on him.

The new moon thing was typical of Freddy, and what a lovely idea it was. She found it in her diary; it was the fourteenth of March and she wrote Freddy's name across the page.

Increasingly, his letters made her tearful, and a few minutes went by before she could begin her reply, even though she knew just what she was going to tell him. There was the revue and the grand finale; Cynthia and Mary had both sent home for their *pointe* shoes and everything else was going well. She would tell him about all those things, but there were other things she wanted to say that were infinitely more personal and naturally more important.

· · ·

It seemed that the rumour that they were to stay at Görlitz was true and Freddy was determined to get as much out of it as he could, whatever Vogel had in mind.

So that he could give Bailey the cheese and sausage he had brought back from his meeting with Vogel, he had waited until most of his fellow-kriegies were resting in their huts before taking him for a discreet walk around the compound. It was Freddy's greatest fear that someone would see the food and start a riot but, whilst they had seen a few Yugoslav prisoners from the main camp, none had come close enough to see what they were doing.

He was no less anxious the following morning when he knocked on the door of the orderly office. No one had seen him arrive, at least as far as he knew, but he was still uneasy.

When a voice from within told him to enter, he pushed the door open to find Vogel at a desk and with a corporal, most likely an orderly clerk, at his side. Vogel looked up without giving any sign of recognition and handed a document to the clerk, telling him to take it to the pay office.

'We shall leave this camp in four days' time,' he said when the clerk had gone. His eyes were fixed, impassive as ever, on Freddy's. 'I am confident that the *Reich* will be victorious in the end. There is no doubt about that.' He paused to underline his assertion and then continued. 'Even so, things could be awkward for me if I were to be taken prisoner, however briefly, by the British or Americans. Certain prisoners may imagine they have some grudge against me.' As he shrugged at the foolishness of such a notion, Freddy began to have an inkling of what Vogel was after. The *Feldwebel* went on, confirming Freddy's suspicion. 'I need a letter stating that I have always treated prisoners well, as I am treating you well. Do you understand?'

'Yes, *Feldwebel*.' Freddy nodded as gravely as he could. The news that all Vogel wanted from him was a note was a massive relief. At the same time, he was amused at Vogel's discomfiture and excited at the same time, because his request was a fair indication that the Allies were not far away.

'If you will write such a letter for me, I shall give you extra food for your friend for as long as I can.' The *Feldwebel*'s pale-grey eyes showed neither compassion nor remorse. He had looked much the same when he had refused Sasha and the victim of the derailment a Christian burial.

'Very well,' said Freddy, 'I'll write that letter.'

Randy was waiting for him when he and Bailey returned from their short, lunch-time walk. 'Come on, Freddy,' he said. 'What gives with Vogel?'

' *"What gives?"* Freddy ushered him discreetly outside. 'It's the greatest shame that you colonials seized independence before we could teach you to speak English. It makes communication with you impossible at times.'

'I'd say it was just typical British disorganisation.'

'In that case, let me tell you what I organised this morning.'

'Go right ahead.'

'OK, Vogel wants me to write him a certificate that he can show to the Allies if he's taken prisoner, to the effect that he's always been kind to kriegies, and all the stories about him being a sadistic, murdering bastard are the product of an over-active and mischievous imagination.'

Randy whistled. 'And what did you say to that?'

'I agreed.'

'What?'

'You heard.'

Randy gaped. 'He had one of the Yugoslavs beaten half to death this morning. Doesn't that mean anything to you?'

'Of course it does. I also got him to agree to keep the letter sealed and to show it to no one in case the idea catches on and there are so many that the Allies stop taking them seriously.'

'And I guess that makes all the difference, huh?'

'That's right, because that way he won't find some English-speaking goon who'll tell him what I've really written. It must remain a secret until he shows it to the Allies, and that day can't be all that far away, because we're moving out of here in four days' time.' He glanced back at the hut they had left, and added, 'I just hope we can get Bailey fit by then.'

30

The source of extra food ended when the column left the gates, as Vogel seemed to have found business elsewhere. Freddy made several discreet enquiries but no one knew of his whereabouts. Fortunately Bailey was very much stronger after his improved diet and week's rest, so Vogel's disappearance was not the disaster it might have been, although food was still generally scarce. Other factors also continued to add to the kriegies' misery. Temperatures remained well below freezing by day and found new depths at night so that morning often came as a welcome relief, as walking generated a vestige of warmth. By contrast, there was no escape from the ubiquitous and numerous lice that populated the warmer parts of the body, such as the waist, the neck and under the arms. Another horror was dysentery, incurred from drinking water that had run off the fields. Old hands such as Bailey and Freddy knew that the crops were fertilised with human waste from the camp latrines and they were quick to warn the others, but many still drank the water. The result was painful and debilitating for them, and to add to their suffering, the hard-pressed guards were not always sympathetic to their frequent requests for roadside relief.

At night, those who were unaffected usually found a place some distance from the more malodorous members of the column, even if it meant sharing animal quarters.

'There's shit whichever way you turn,' said Randy, leading the way into a stable, 'but I sure as hell prefer the good old animal kind.'

Bailey asked, 'Are you going to give us the benefit of some more of that summer camp lore, old thing?'

'Sure. For one thing, you can't catch anything from a horse.'

'I wasn't planning on getting so friendly with one,' said Freddy.

'I mean you can't catch their vermin, dummy.'

'We don't need to.' Bailey was scratching industriously. 'We've got plenty of our own.'

Randy ignored the levity. 'Another thing that makes the horse the ideal stable companion is that he'll keep you warm.'

'Be especially nice to him,' said Freddy as he buried himself in straw, 'and he'll wake you with a cup of tea. I've asked mine for a shake at oh-five-hundred.'

'Scoff as much as you like,' said Randy. 'You'll learn soon enough on a night like this.'

He was right. Such was the outside temperature that Freddy and Bailey soon began to appreciate the proximity of their equine hosts.

They were on the move again by six hundred hours the next morning. Freddy and the others marched in silence, each no doubt thinking about the two lifeless bodies they had discovered half-an-hour earlier. Already weakened by hunger and dysentery, the casualties must have frozen to death during the night. It was a fate that stalked everyone in the column, as they all realised.

After a while though, men began to think and talk of other things, and it was on such an occasion that the subject of nicknames arose.

'The Americans took to calling me "Limey" back at Görlitz,' Randy told them. 'It was because I was spending so much time with you guys, and who can blame me?'

'I must confess I've wondered about that, welcome though you are to our little band of wayfarers.'

'That's kind of you, Freddy.'

'Not at all. As a matter of fact, we've been thinking of making you an honorary British kriegie. We'd have to do some work on your English and you'd have to acquire the taste for tea, but we have time in abundance, so why not?'

'Even tea would be an improvement on that *ersatz* stuff the goons used to serve.'

'We have progress already. Seriously, though, what's the problem with the American contingent?'

'Ah, you don't know what it's like back there. Arguments all the time. Ever since we were taken prisoner they've been arguing about whose goddam fault it was. Weeks and weeks of arguing and buck-passing. I got sick of it.'

'I can imagine.'

'Let me tell you, Freddy, I could care less whose fault it was. I'd own up to it myself if it would get us back to civilisation.'

'Our ambition in a nutshell, eh, Bailey?'

'Agreed, old thing, and a chap can be called worse things than "Limey". I speak from harsh experience.'

'They used to call him "Bullshit",' said Freddy, 'and he could never imagine why.'

'It was an unwarranted slander, a vile calumny. I'll have you know, there were times when I could have sued.'

'Never mind, Bailey.' Randy patted him on the shoulder. 'We think you're a good guy, don't we, Freddy?'

'No question about it. He's a good egg, maybe a little creative with the facts but a stout fellow notwithstanding.'

'I owe you chaps a huge debt,' said Bailey, 'looking after me the way you did back at Görlitz. I don't mind telling you, I was ready to throw in the towel.'

'Let's hear no more about it,' said Freddy. 'It was nothing.'

Randy was more inclined to pursue the topic. 'We're all in the same hole,' he reminded Bailey, somewhat unnecessarily, 'and we're buddies. Buddies help each other, right?'

'Right,' agreed Freddy, 'but let's not labour the point.'

'You British are just not happy talking about the things that matter, are you?'

'I suppose it is basically a British thing, and it's certainly one of the chief characteristics where I come from,' Freddy told him. 'It's a fair bet that there's more emotional constipation north of the River Humber than anywhere else in the known world. We even emerge from the womb refusing to discuss the experience.'

'Say,' said Randy, 'that's some kind of hang-up.'

Not all conversations along the route were so revealing; some were contentious and others quite trivial. More often than not, men trudged over the snow in silence, often with their eyes closed against the driving snow, preoccupied with their common craving for food and rest.

. . .

Sylvia found Dorothy sewing a button on her shirt preparatory to going on watch. She asked, 'Can you spare a minute?'

'A minute's all I've got. What's to do?'

'It's Gwen. She's upset about something, and your name cropped up in the conversation. Will you come and have a word with her?'

Dorothy finished sewing on the button and snapped off the thread. 'Oh, I know what it'll be,' she said, putting the shirt on. 'Let me finish dressin' an'

I'll be with you. I've only got a few minutes though. The transport'll be here any minute.'

'That's all it'll take.' Sylvia returned to her cabin, where Ruth was doing her best to placate the sobbing Gwen. 'Dorothy's coming,' she told them. 'I'm going to sort this out once and for all.' She realised that with her new-found authority she was beginning to sound distressingly like her mother.

The door opened and Dorothy said, 'I'm sorry if whatever I said upset you, but you're goin' to have to stop bein' so touchy or you're in for a really hard time.'

'It's not just ... you,' Gwen protested between sobs, 'it's ev ... eryone.'

Sylvia was wondering how many had been involved, when Dorothy said, 'I can't speak for the others, so let's deal with you an' me, an' then I can go an' do what I'm paid for, right? As I remember, we were waitin' for the transport, an' I said, "Fancy meetin' you here," or some such nonsense, an' you said, "I don't know about you, but I'm waiting to avail myself of the utility," an' I said somethin' like, "Do you have to sound like a flamin' headmistress all the flamin' time?" Is that how you remember it?'

'Yes.' The word was almost lost in a shudder.

'Well, like I said, I'm sorry if that upset you, but I grew up around the Liverpool docks, an' when someone annoys us there, we tell 'em. It's easier than playin' games. Now, you annoyed me by talkin' like I was some street urchin who'd had the brass neck to look up when you were passin', so I let you know.' She looked pointedly at her watch. 'An' now I'm goin' on watch before I upset a lot more people about somethin' that really matters. All right?' She gave Sylvia a raised-eyes look as she opened the door to go.

'Thanks for coming in, Dorothy. We'll have a chat later.'

'All right, Sylvia.'

When she had gone, Sylvia said, 'I've known Dorothy since her first draft, and let me tell you she's the salt of the earth. She's direct and outspoken and sometimes quite dry. When she says something like, "Fancy meeting you here", it's just her way of saying "Hello". She wasn't really asking you what you were doing there. It's like my relief saying to me, "We have to stop meeting like this." Irony doesn't just happen in English lessons, you know.'

'I'm afraid it was that sort of day,' said Ruth. 'She'd already had a disagreement with someone else.'

'Who?'

Gwen blew her nose vigorously. 'Mona Tebbitt.' It still sounded like 'Boda Debbid.'

It was a relief that Gwen's 'everyone else' had been a ridiculous exaggeration, even when the girl in question turned out to be the dominant force in the coven. 'Don't worry about her,' said Sylvia. 'I'm more concerned about the thing with Dorothy.'

'You're just od her side because you're friedds.'

'I hope you and I are friends too, Gwen, and do blow your nose again.' She waited for the fanfare to end, and when she was satisfied that Gwen's nasal consonants were restored she went on. 'When you said you were availing yourself, you were trying to be clever, weren't you?'

'Well, the way she said it, she made it sound as if I'd no right to be there.'

'Even so, you're not going to make yourself popular taking that attitude.'

'I'll never be popular anyway.'

'Oh dear.' Progress was slow indeed. 'Were you bullied at school, Gwen?'

'Yes, all the time, and this is just as bad.'

Sylvia wasn't at all surprised. 'I'll tell you what. Ruth, be yourself and I'll be Dorothy, OK? You're waiting for the tilly.'

'All right.' Ruth stood by the window and adopted a bored expression.

Sylvia went to her side. After a moment, she said, 'Fancy meeting you here.'

Ruth shrugged good-naturedly. 'You know what they say about the service. It's a big family and a small world.'

'There.' Sylvia turned to Gwen. 'You see? No offence at all. Let's try another one, Ruth. We'll be ourselves this time.'

'Oh.' Ruth adopted a look of dismay. 'I want to be First Officer Fanshawe.' She stamped her foot. 'Why can't I be First Officer Fanshawe?'

'You have to be able to do joined-up writing and long division to be an officer.'

'Oh.' Ruth stamped her foot again and then recovered her spirits immediately. 'Right, what are we going to do?'

'I think we've just done it.'

'Fine.'

They both turned to face Gwen, who seemed confused. 'I don't understand,' she said. 'Everyone can do joined-up writing and long division.'

31

March

Although the obstruction was some way ahead it was not difficult to imagine what was causing it. The furious shouts and screamed insults could only be aimed at the prisoners in RAF uniform. Their route had been planned so as to avoid major towns, but angry civilians were turning up almost everywhere and the guards were usually obliged to turn them away at gunpoint.

'When they brought us here in nineteen-forty,' said Bailey, 'the civilians were quite harmless, as I recall. It was the goons we had to watch out for. Now they're protecting us.' He shook his head at the wonder of it all.

'Hostages,' said Randy. 'That's why they want us and that's why they're protecting us. It's obvious.'

The same thought had occurred to Freddy but his attention was momentarily drawn to some pieces of animal hide that lay on the field by the roadside. They were possibly off-cuts that were only fit for fertiliser. They would take an age to rot down and would be much more useful, he imagined, lining the worn-out soles of his boots. He looked along the line towards the village and saw that the guards were all transfixed by the commotion taking place. A glance over his shoulder told him that those behind him were similarly distracted. Quickly, he slipped into the field and picked up two pieces. Then, seeing several more, he took half-a-dozen and re-joined the column.

Randy was saying, 'You can understand how they must feel. I've never seen anything like the other night.'

Randy was not alone in that. No one had seen anything quite like the sky over Dresden that night. The Blitz had been terrible but the spectacle of Dresden, even from a distance, had left its mark on all but the hardest in the column. Even Freddy, who had seen the wreckage of Hull and who had as much cause as anyone to hold a grudge, had been sobered by it. He was surprised to find that he even felt some sympathy for the local population. There were two sides in every war and, as he had told Sylvia, people did terrible things to one another in wartime.

'What have you got there, Freddy?' Randy's question brought him back to the present.

'Insoles.' He gave him two pieces of hide. 'Furry side up, disgusting side down, they'll keep the water out for a while and they should be quite comfortable when they're bedded in.'

'A touch of luxury, and just when it's needed,' said Bailey, accepting his share of the bovine remains.

'It looks as if we're moving again,' observed Freddy. He had been hoping to try out his new insoles but that would have to wait until the column stopped for the night.

They trudged on, eventually reaching the village, where a few diehards still watched the column and shouted threats whenever they caught sight of an item of RAF uniform, despite the presence of the guards.

As they passed, Freddy recognised *Feldwebel* Vogel, but the German showed no sign of having recognised him.

After a few minutes, Randy asked, 'What did you write in that letter you gave him?'

'I said that I was writing the note in exchange for food for a fellow-kriegie who was suffering from exhaustion and malnutrition and that Vogel believed it to be a note of exoneration, whereas he was actually guilty of numerous acts of brutality and murder.'

'I'd sure like to be there when he hands it over.'

'So would I. I intend to give evidence against the bastard.'

'I imagine a whole lot of justice will be done after the war.'

'It's inevitable.'

'It's inescapable,' said Bailey, somewhat pensively.

. . .

Dorothy sat on her bed and leaned comfortably against the bulkhead. She asked, 'Somethin's botherin' you, isn't it? Have you heard from Freddy recently?'

Sylvia shook her head.

'It's not surprising when you think about all that's happenin' over there. The Germans won't know which way to turn, what with our lads advancin' all the time an' the Russians knockin' on the back door an' all. My Uncle Jack's a postman an' he says he wouldn't want to be deliverin' letters over there with all that goin' on.'

Sylvia had to smile. She didn't believe that Dorothy's Uncle Jack had said anything of the sort but it made her feel a little better, if only because that was what Dorothy had intended.

. . .

Their resting place was a farm outside Eisenach. 'For what it's worth,' Freddy told his companions, 'this was the birthplace of Johann Sebastian Bach.'

Bailey was sceptical. 'How do you know it was here?' His finger pointed downwards.

'I'm not saying he was born at this farm, but Eisenach was his birthplace, so it was somewhere around here.'

'Who was this guy anyway?'

'Some say he was the greatest composer of all time, although he wasn't valued too highly in his own time, certainly by his employers. He was always complaining about being hard up.'

'He couldn't have been as hungry as we are.' Bailey spoke for the entire column, which had received no rations for forty-eight hours. Even the guards were hungry.

'What we have to do,' said Randy, 'is get into the grain store.'

'When the goons are out of the way,' Freddy reminded him. Hunger had a way of banishing caution. 'Until then we'll just have to think about something else.'

'Like the close shave we had this morning,' said Randy.

'If you like,' said Freddy. 'I prefer not to think about it.'

'How can you not think about it? When that son-of-a-bitch dived on us I thought my time had come.'

'I think we all did,' said Freddy, seeing again the muzzle flashes as the aircraft strafed them, and then the markings on the underside of its wings as it passed over them , confirming that it was 'friendly'. It was likely that the khaki and RAF greatcoats alerted the pilot to his mistake and caused him to break off his attack. Even so, it was better not to think about it.

. . .

The first performance was better than anyone had expected. There were some unusual turns, including a fine soprano and an electrical artificer with a glorious baritone voice. They sang some of the duets Nelson Eddy and Jeanette MacDonald had made famous. It wasn't the kind of music that usually went down well with service audiences, but the quality of their singing soon calmed the restive spirits.

At all events, Sylvia now had something quite unusual to tell Freddy, and the thought reminded her of their covenant, almost forgotten in the evening's excitement. As she stepped outside the theatre the new moon was clearly visible between the clouds.

. . .

More than a thousand miles away, at the farm outside Eisenach, Freddy lay cocooned in his blanket and surrounded by straw. The night was cold, but he, Bailey and Randy had found some grain, so they were spared the worst of the habitual stomach cramps, at least for the time being.

With the morning's horror dominating his thoughts, the new moon had escaped his memory too, but he could see it now through the open side of the barn. The sky was clear and it was as if the stars had also turned out to reprimand him for his lapse. Suitably chastened, he honoured his part of the pledge.

32

The engine coughed twice before lapsing into silence. 'He's OK,' Angelo called to his passengers. 'I make him go in one minute.'

Gwen fanned herself with her cap and waited patiently. It happened quite frequently.

'It is the petrol,' said Angelo. 'The engine doesn't like it.'

'Never mind, Angelo,' Dorothy told him from her seat at the front, 'Nobody's blamin' you.'

A voice from behind said, 'Gwen will know what's wrong with it. She knows everything.' The voice was Mona Tebbitt's but the giggles that followed came from her followers who sat on either side of her.

Angelo's efforts with the self-starter were suddenly rewarded and the engine coughed uncertainly into life. There was a cheer from the passengers.

'It can't just be the petrol,' said Mona. 'You'd better let Gwen look at it, Angelo. She'll tell you how to mend it but you'll need a dictionary.'

'For heaven's sake give it a rest,' said Gwen. 'You're being very childish and you're annoying the others as well.'

'Annoying the others, am I?' Mona feigned surprise and turned to one of her cohort. 'Am I annoying you?'

'No.' Her neighbour giggled.

'Or you?'

Her other companion shook her head, laughing. 'Not me, no.'

'You're annoyin' me though, an' it's not the best idea you've had today.' Dorothy had left her seat at the front and was making her way to the back where Mona and her friends were sitting. 'You're annoyin' me by pickin' on somebody who doesn't deserve it, an' you're annoyin' me again by not knowin' when to keep your poisonous gob shut.'

203

As she turned in her seat, Gwen saw Mona staring, red-faced at Dorothy, who had not finished speaking.

'First of all,' she said, pointing to Gwen, 'you can stop pickin' on her, an' then you can keep your nasty remarks to yourself, otherwise one of us is goin' to wake up with a crowd round her, an' it's not goin' to be me. Right?' Then, receiving no response, she asked again, 'Right?'

'All right, keep your hair on.' Possibly Mona intended her reply to carry a measure of defiance but instead she merely sounded sulky.

'I've given you fair warnin'.' Dorothy turned her attention to Mona's friends, who were looking suitably chastened. 'An' the same applies to you two,' she told them before taking the seat next to Gwen.

'Thanks, Dorothy.' It was inadequate but Gwen really didn't know what to say. She was surprised, relieved, grateful and confused. Dorothy was the last person she had expected to take her side.

'It's all right. It was high time somebody sorted her out anyway.' As the utility stopped outside the Imperial, she asked, 'What are you doin' later on today?'

'Nothing much. Why do you ask?'

'A few of us are goin' swimmin'. Why don't you join us?'

Gwen watched Mona and her friends get off the bus without looking at her. She asked, 'Swimming in March?'

'Why not? The sea's warm enough. Anyway,' she shrugged, 'it's up to you.'

'Well, yes, I'd love to come. Thank you.'

'There's no need to thank me. You're one of us.' She stood up and straightened her skirt. 'Now, let's get off this tilly before Angelo takes us back to work. I don't know about you but I've had enough for one night and I'm ready for me breakfast.'

. . .

It was an eventful morning. First, the column had another encounter with friendly aircraft. Thankfully, their pilots realised their mistake before firing a shot and so no harm was done, but everyone was still shaken.

The second event was more a piece of news, and it did much to cheer them after the morning's experience. It seemed that they were heading for another camp and a period of rest, although Freddy was sceptical until he received confirmation from the friendly East-Prussian guard.

'Seigenheim,' he told Freddy.

'Where's that?'

'Near Göttingen.'

'I don't know it.'

The guard thought again and said, 'Also near Kassel.'

'Now I know where we are. Have we really come so far?' Incredibly, by Freddy's reckoning, they had covered about five hundred miles since leaving Lamsdorf. He shared that information with the others, adding modestly that he could easily be wrong.

'But it feels like five hundred miles,' said Bailey, who was more in need than the others of the respite. 'That's what matters, old man.'

Another kriegie, who had taught geography before the war, estimated the distance at approximately five hundred and thirty-five miles.

'The five miles are important,' said Randy. 'Five-thirty or five-forty sounds like guesswork but that extra five miles make it sound like the answer in the back of the teacher's book.'

'And he's a geography teacher,' said Freddy with a kind of latent awe.

'It wasn't my main subject,' the kriegie told him.

'What was your main subject?'

'Mathematics.'

That clinched it for all of them.

Five hours later, they walked through the camp gates. They had expected the usual drill but they found that things were far from routine. To begin with, no matter where they looked, there wasn't a German in sight.

Randy looked over his shoulder and asked, 'What about the Krauts who came with us?'

'They've gone,' Bailey told him. 'I saw some of the blighters sloping off shortly after we arrived. They evidently know something we don't.'

It was difficult not to form the most welcome conclusion, but Freddy wanted to know more before taking part in any premature celebration. He spotted an RAF flight-sergeant coming out of one of the huts and approached him, working on the principle that those who should know everything must know at least something.

'Excuse me, Flight.'

'What's the matter, son?'

'We've just arrived and we're wondering what the score is with delousing, accommodation and so on. There don't seem to be any goons around to organise things.'

The flight-sergeant's expression suggested that he'd been asked the same question many times. 'You'll have to help yourselves to a shower,' he said, pointing to the end of the row. 'The oven's still working as well, so you should be able to delouse your kit if you get a move on. After that, grab yourselves a bunk where you can. As for food, you'll have to forage like everyone else. The goons have all scarpered, so there's no point in looking for them.'

'So the bastards really are on the run?' Like so many long-awaited events, it was difficult to believe that it was happening.

'That's right, son. Our lads can't be all that far away. We arrived five days ago and the goons were chafing at the bit then.' He smiled and patted Freddy's shoulder. 'All this could soon be a bad memory.'

'Thanks, Flight. I'll go and tell the others.'

'Good lad.'

Tired though he was after the day's march, Freddy couldn't help feeling elated by the news. More than anything, he wanted to tell Sylvia, but there was no way. He'd last written to her when they were still at Lamsdorf, and had no way of knowing when he would be able to write again. She would have heard nothing for about two months. He hoped there would be news at home of what was happening in Germany, because that might explain the interrupted mail. Otherwise, she would be desperately worried.

He returned to tell the others the news and found Bailey guarding their packs. He had already heard.

'We spoke to some of the others,' he said. 'Randy's gone foraging for food. He left me to guard these things and find three beds, although how the hell I'm supposed to do both jobs at once is beyond me.'

'Me too, Bailey, so if you don't mind guarding them a bit longer, I'll check on the bed situation.'

'Suits me, old man.'

Freddy checked several huts and eventually found one with some vacant beds, of which he claimed three. The hut's other occupants were all RAF, and they welcomed the newcomers readily enough. They all had their stories of the march, and Freddy was surprised to learn that his experiences and those of his friends could have been much worse. With the exception of Vogel, it seemed their goons had not been so bad after all.

Bailey spotted Randy two huts away and hailed him. He arrived with two large potatoes, two carrots and a cabbage, which he dropped on his bed.

'Some of the guys have found meat,' he said, 'but I wouldn't like to say what animal it came from. I played safe and kept it strictly vegetarian. These things will be okay if we can find something to cook them in.'

Freddy nodded approvingly. 'You're a hero, Randy.'

'A good scout,' agreed Bailey.

'You can use this.' A corporal handed Randy a bowl made from tins that had once held dried milk. 'Give it a wash and it'll be all right. Look after it though – it's the only one we've got.'

'Thanks, buddy. I'll take real good care of it.'

'You'll find wood in the goons' quarters if you're quick about it,' the corporal told him. 'We've been dismantling the place ever since the bastards left.'

Within the hour they were eating boiled cabbage, carrots and potatoes. It was the best meal they'd had in a long while and there was also the promise of better things to come.

. . .

Sylvia read the last paragraph of Joyce's letter again.

Len had a reply to his November letter, and he wrote another one that should have reached Freddy in January but he's had no reply to that. Mail must be completely disrupted over there, so there's probably nothing to worry about. Len says the chances are next time you hear from Freddy he'll be in England. Do bring him to see us when you can. After everything you and Len have told me I can't wait to meet him, and Len misses his old mate too.

Unfortunately, references to chaos in Europe did nothing to soothe Sylvia's imaginings. It was the upheaval she feared most. If the situation for the Germans really was desperate they were unlikely to care much about the welfare of their prisoners. She had no idea what was happening to him and even if she had she was utterly helpless.

When their off-watch periods coincided Dorothy was always ready with a diversion, her favourite one being swimming in St Paul's Bay. It was such a novelty to be able to swim in warm water during March that it had become a favourite with many at the Imperial.

It was good, as well, to see Gwen mixing more easily with the others. Dorothy's intervention had been crucial in making her feel included, and Sylvia found some satisfaction in the knowledge that, threats of violence apart, she had been able to do it because of what she and Joyce had done for her. Such were the distractions that prevented Sylvia from going mad with worry.

. . .

Liberation began in a quiet, almost matter-of-fact way when a jeep and several lorries with US Army markings appeared at the main gate of the camp at Seigenheim. Freddy and the others were taking a turn around the compound and were among the first to greet the newcomers.

A youthful lieutenant returned Randy's salute from his seat in the jeep and said, 'American, huh?'

'Yes, sir.' Randy gave his name and unit, adding generously, 'My friends are British, sir.'

'Good to see an American liaising with our allies, soldier.' He nodded to Freddy and Bailey. 'Nice to meet you guys. How are you both?'

Freddy shook his hand. 'All the better for seeing you, sir.'

'Absolutely top hole, sir.'

'I guess those were your guards we met back there. You'll be pleased to know they're our prisoners now.' He looked at his watch and said, 'We have to be moving now. It's been good to meet you guys. I'll talk to base and they'll lay on some transportation for you.' He spoke briefly with the sergeant next to him. 'I'll get these guys to leave some "K" rations with you as well. I guess the catering's not so hot around here.'

'Thank you very much, sir.' Prisoners were converging on the American convoy in gathering numbers, and Freddy had to ask, 'About those Germans you took prisoner, sir, do you recall a *Feldwebel*, a sergeant, called Vogel? He had a note that I wrote for him. I just wondered …'

The lieutenant was trying not to smile. 'You wouldn't believe how many of them had notes from prisoners, soldier, and not one of them knew what their notes really said.'

In the general uproar, Freddy could barely hear himself or the lieutenant. He raised his voice to say, 'What will happen to them, sir?'

'Don't you worry about that.'

'It's just that if Vogel goes to trial …'

The officer and the sergeant exchanged knowing looks. 'Just leave them to us, soldier.'

'Aye aye, sir, and it's "Leading Airman", by the way.'

'Nice talking with you, Leading Airman. See you around.' The lieutenant left to speak with the soldiers in the first lorry, who were distributing rations.

'You know what that means,' said Bailey.

Freddy nodded. 'Summary justice.'

'Unfortunate for some, old man. The fortunes of war, eh.'

'It was no worse than the treatment he gave Sasha and the others, but I'd have preferred a fair trial all the same.'

'It's not an ideal world, Freddy, but it's just begun to improve.'

33

April
Leyburn, Yorkshire

Walter Charlesworth brought the post into the dining room and picked out a small, buff envelope from the Borough Treasurer's office. 'About time too,' he muttered.

'What's that, Walter?' Jessie set the plates down, eager as ever to see if there was a letter from Sylvia.

'The receipt from the Treasurer's department. I paid the rates nearly three weeks ago.' He put the envelope beside his plate. 'If we ran the firm like that we wouldn't last two minutes.'

'Don't let your breakfast get cold, Walter. It's a real egg this morning.'

'Oh good.' He buttered a piece of toast thinly and then flicked through the rest of the mail. 'There's nothing from Sylvia,' he said.

'Oh well, it's only been just over a week, I suppose.'

'Yes, that's all. I'm sure she'll write as soon as she has a ... good grief!'

'What is it?'

'A postcard addressed to Sylvia. It has a Portsmouth postmark.'

'Let me see.' Jessie took it from him. 'It's Freddy's writing. I shouldn't ....' she said, reading it.

'Well, now that you have, what does he say?'

' "Dearest S. P." – I really don't know why he's calling her that – "as you can see, I'm back. I'm travelling to Hull tomorrow to see my solicitor. Staying at a seamen's hostel for now." He gives a phone number that I can just about read – his writing is ever so tiny. He says, "Please phone me if you can. I've got a month's leave. Sorry I couldn't write earlier – will explain." '

209

She stopped reading and said bleakly, 'Of course, the poor lad doesn't know, does he?'

'Not unless she's dropped a hint in one of her letters.'

'No, she said that was too risky.'

'She was probably right.'

'Anyway, I'll write to her straight away and tell her. She'll be thrilled to bits.'

Walter smiled and said, 'I think this piece of news warrants a telegram, Jessie.'

'Right, I'll go to the post office after you've gone to work. I'll telephone Freddy tonight as well.'

. . .

The Americans had flown Randy to a staging camp in Antwerp to be medically examined, debriefed and kitted out, but not before he and Freddy had arranged to keep in touch. Strong friendships had to be maintained.

He and Bailey had been debriefed at a camp in Brussels. From there, they had travelled to England in the same transport but had then parted. Bailey had gone to an army depot in Andover, and Freddy to Royal Naval Barracks, Portsmouth. They were likely to meet again quite soon, though, as Freddy had agreed to appear in court as a character witness on Bailey's behalf. It transpired that the police had been keen to interview him in nineteen thirty-nine about 'a small omission', when he had left for France.

Freddy spent a week in barracks being deloused, examined and assessed, kitted out in temporary uniform, given double ration coupons and finally sent on leave.

It was after seven-thirty in the evening when his train arrived in Hull. He stepped on to the platform still feeling strange in his ill-fitting uniform and with his cap firmly covering his closely-shaven head, a legacy of the de-infestation process at Portsmouth. He was also uncomfortably conscious of his emaciated appearance. Apparently he had lost sixty-three pounds in captivity, which was even more alarming when he converted it into stones – four-and-a-half of them. Even in food-rationed Britain he felt uncomfortably conspicuous, although none of his old acquaintances would recognise him. He was quite relieved when the elderly taxi driver gave him no more than a glance as he said, 'You know there's nowt left there, don't you?' This was in response to Freddy's request to be taken to the street that had once been his home. After five years of bombing, Hull was also unrecognisable. Many of the buildings he remembered from before the war were now anonymous piles of rubble.

As they approached the site where the house had stood, he asked the driver to stop and he stood on the pavement for several minutes, examining the expanse of debris that was almost identical to those around it, except that here and there he noticed something heart-breakingly familiar: a scrap of painted wood, a soiled and sodden shred of curtain material, intimate reminders that summoned the old hatred and despair as if they'd never been absent.

After a while he was able to bring his feelings under control and he returned to the taxi.

'All right, lad?' The driver had been watching him.

'Yes, thanks,' he said heavily. 'I used to live here.'

'I thought so. I'm sorry, lad. Is it t' first time you've seen it like this?'

Freddy nodded.

'You must have been away a fair while.'

'More than three years.' He took one final look at the remains and asked, 'Do you think you can find Plimsoll House?'

'Aye, lad, I can do that all right.'

The devastation was increasingly evident as they approached the docks but the driver picked his way confidently between the ruined buildings and found the hostel for him. 'You see,' he said, 'the buildings that have been knocked down make it easier to see them that are still standing.' He took his leave then, refusing to accept payment for the waiting time.

Freddy thanked him and checked in at reception.

'There's a telephone message for you,' the porter told him, handing him a slip of paper. 'The lady rang about an hour ago, thinking you'd be here.'

'Thank you.' Freddy took the folded note, controlling his excitement and telling himself that it would be too much of a coincidence for Sylvia to be on leave as well, and that the call couldn't possibly have been from her.

'She was keen for you to get the message,' said the porter.

One glance at the note confirmed Freddy's doubts, but it was no less disappointing. It was from a Mrs Charlesworth. Sylvia's mother, he supposed.

'I'd better give her a ring,' he said.

'Help yourself.' The porter pointed down the passage.

Freddy found the telephone and asked the operator to connect him. The phone rang a few times before a woman's voice answered.

'Leyburn one-oh-four.'

'Hello, is that Mrs Charlesworth?'

'Yes. Who's calling?'

'Freddy Hinchcliffe. I'm sorry I wasn't here when you rang. My train was delayed.'

'Freddy, it's lovely to hear from you! Have you got somewhere to spend your leave?' Her accent owed something to Yorkshire, but it carried a hint of the north-east as well. It was very pleasant.

'Not really. I'm here to see my solicitor, and then I suppose I'll go back to Portsmouth. I'd really like to see Sylvia, but if she's not at home ...'

'I'm ever so sorry, Freddy. You couldn't possibly have known – she's been serving overseas since Christmas.'

For a moment, Freddy was stunned into silence. It was the last thing he'd expected. Eventually, he said, 'I didn't know that. I only knew she'd been drafted. The censors, you know ...' After all the pent-up anticipation he felt horribly empty.

'I sent her a telegram this morning. She's been terribly worried about you. Listen, Freddy, you mustn't stay in that place any longer than you have to. Have you got money for a train?'

'Yes, I've got plenty for that.'

'Then you must come and stay with us.'

If he were honest, he had no idea what he wanted to do. He'd thought no further than simply getting in touch with Sylvia. He'd been sure she would be granted leave, and then they were going to make plans. Instead, after eighteen months she was still beyond his reach. 'No,' he said wearily, it's very kind of you but I couldn't, really.'

'Fiddlesticks. I've made up the bed in the spare room and we're all dying to meet you. When can we expect you?'

. . .

PO Wren Stubbs placed her hands on Sylvia's bench and leaned forward confidingly. 'Your new divisional officer's arrived,' she said. 'Chances are you've met already. She was at Dover too.'

'Oh, what's her name?'

'Second Officer Fuller.'

Sylvia's eyes opened wide. 'Really?'

'It sounds like good news.'

'And she's a two-oh now?'

The PO Wren gave a little shrug. 'Everyone has to grow up sometime.'

'Excellent. Thanks for telling me.'

'Don't mention it. I thought I'd let you know in case you need her help with this.' She took a small buff envelope from her pocket and handed it to Sylvia. 'I'll leave you with it, shall I?'

'No, there's no need.' Puzzled, Sylvia slit open the envelope and took out the telegram. It read:

FREDDY ALIVE AND WELL STOP STAYING WITH US STOP LOVE MUM AND DAD.

She stared at it for several seconds before she was able to speak. Eventually, she managed to say, 'I can't believe it! It's just wonderful!'

'I know. Do you want to see Second Officer Fuller?'

Dabbing at her eyes with her hanky, she nodded. 'Yes, please.'

'I thought you might. Fill in the request form and I'll see she gets it.'

. . .

At the end of the watch, Sylvia came to attention inside the DO's office.

'Stand easy, Leading Wren. How are you?' Miss Fuller offered her hand.

'Very well, thank you, ma'am. Congratulations on your promotion.'

'Thank you.'

'I'm glad they posted you here, ma'am.'

'And I'm pleased to find you here too. They must be sending all the best people to Malta these days.' She leaned back in her chair and asked, 'Now, how can I help you?'

'Well, ma'am, do you remember knitting a scarf for a POW about two years ago?' It was already beginning to feel like the good old days at HMS *Wasp*.

'I do. Do you want me to knit another?'

'No, ma'am, I just wanted to remind you because there's been a development.'

'I'm only joking. The telegram came through my office so I know why you're here. I imagine you want a draft home. I know I would.'

'Yes, please, ma'am. You see, when I applied for this draft I honestly thought I'd be home before him. There didn't seem to be very much happening in the Med, and I just thought that things would tail off here before the army reached Germany.'

Miss Fuller nodded. 'It was an easy mistake to make, but you must understand that it's not my decision. I'll put your case forward as strongly as I can but I can't promise anything. I'll do my best.'

'I know you will, ma'am. Thank you.'

. . .

When two of the merchant seamen from the hostel joined Freddy at the bar he was glad of their company. He disliked drinking alone, especially when he was unhappy, which he undoubtedly was, and he wasn't a man of solitary habits anyway.

One of them, a man of around forty with a Midlands accent, was called

Cyril. The other was of mixed race and might have been partly West Indian, but his dialect, when he uttered more than a few words, was local. His name was Geoff. They had both sailed on Atlantic convoys, and Freddy spent a fascinating half-hour listening to their stories. After a while, Cyril pointed to Freddy's category badge and asked, 'What's your trade, then?'

'I'm aircrew,' Freddy explained, 'telegraphist-air-gunner.'

'In that case,' said Cyril, 'we're glad to meet you, aren't we, Geoff?'

'Yeah,' said Geoff, waving the barmaid over.

'When we saw a Swordfish out on patrol we knew the U-boats were keeping their heads down. You lads are all right with us.'

'Yeah,' said Geoff, whose purpose seemed to be to endorse Cyril's opinions.

'I'm afraid I never flew on Atlantic convoys,' Freddy told them. 'I was in the Med from 'forty-one with an Albacore squadron. That was until we ditched.'

'Oh, bad luck, mate. Shot down, were you?'

'No, it was engine failure, but it came to the same thing. An Eyetie merchant ship picked us up and we were taken to POW camps in Italy.'

'So what happened when the Eyeties threw the towel in?'

'Yeah,' said Geoff, 'what happened then?' It seemed that, eventful though their lives had been, they were eager to hear someone else's story.

Freddy gave them a much-abbreviated version of the past two years in Poland, glossing over the forced march because it was too recent and too painful to be put into words. Even so, they listened intently and the drinks kept coming. Eventually, Cyril asked, 'So what are you doing in Hull?'

'I live here. At least, I did until my house was bombed.'

'Oh, no. Was there anybody at home?'

Freddy nodded.

'Same as Geoff here. They bombed your house an' all, didn't they, Geoff?'

'Yeah.'

'Lousy luck, that. I've been torpedoed twice and that's no joke, but losing your house and your folks, that's bloody awful. I can't think of anything worse. What are you going to do now, Freddy?'

'I don't know. I'm going to stay with some people in the North Riding for a while. After that, I don't know.'

'Have you got friends up there, then?'

'I've never met them.' He hadn't intended telling them about Sylvia, but beer had washed away inhibition, and before long he was telling them about her and how he'd built up on finding her in England, only to learn that she was overseas.

'Rotten luck, mate,' said Cyril.

'Yeah,' said Geoff.

'What we need now,' said Cyril for no obvious reason, 'is a toast.'

'Yeah,' Geoff seemed uncertain but prepared to give it a try.

'Here's to Sylvia.'

They drank to Sylvia.

'And Freddy.'

'Yeah.'

'Freddy and Sylvia.'

They drank the toast and found their glasses empty, so they recharged them.

'Sylvia and Freddy.'

Seeking to move things on, Freddy suggested, 'The Merchant Navy.' At least, that was what he thought he said, because his speech was becoming slurred, or his hearing was. It was one of those two.

'The Royal Navy,' proposed Cyril.

'Yeah,' agreed Geoff.

'The Fleet Air ....'

Freddy remembered them helping him back to the hostel and draping him across his bed, where he made the final descent into profound and drunken sleep.

. . .

As soon as Sylvia entered the DO's office she knew the answer wasn't going to be the one she wanted to hear.

'I'm terribly sorry,' said Miss Fuller. 'I put your case to First Officer Fanshawe and pressed her as hard as I could but she was adamant. There are Wrens who've been here longer than you, and most of them have good reasons to return home too. She just won't hear of it.'

Sylvia's voice came out as a whisper. 'Thank you for trying, ma'am. I appreciate it and I'm sorry I put you to the trouble.'

'It was no trouble. If there's anything else I can do, come and see me.'

'Yes, ma'am. Thank you.' She swallowed hard to keep her voice from wavering. 'Am I allowed to send a telegram?'

34

Freddy's hangover had persisted from the first agonising minutes on waking, through the meeting with his solicitor and for most of the train journey up the east coast. It had done nothing to soften his mood.

He had learned that his inheritance was safely invested in War Bonds and earning interest of more than three per cent. That was fine, and he was content to leave his money where it was, at least for the time being. It would be of little use to him in the Navy.

The reason for his displeasure was the sequestration of part of his pay to reimburse the Nazis for the wages they claimed to have paid him. According to his solicitor, international law allowed the opposing sides to make such transactions through a neutral power. It was a civilised arrangement that might have worked well with both sides acting in good faith, but that was where the problem lay. By Freddy's reckoning, he could have spent ten years working for the Nazis and still earned only a fraction of what they had claimed. He had returned to Britain a free man, to find that his former captors still had the last word.

Changing trains provided the distraction he needed and after a while he began to see the problem in a more sober light. For the time being, he decided, there was nothing to be done, but the argument must be taken up after the war, because thousands of cheated ex-kriegies would surely make their voices heard.

As the train moved ever westward, he began to take more notice of the view from his carriage window. This was the beautiful countryside of Sylvia's letters, and he'd been so preoccupied with the injustice of his plight that he'd given it no more than a glance.

Early signs of spring were everywhere; leaves were beginning to shoot and the first blossom couldn't be far away. He remembered the great matrices of dry-stone-walls from the holidays of his boyhood, and that wasn't all. The countryside he knew in the East Riding was soft and pleasing, but the grass hereabouts seemed to be of a fresher, richer shade. He had no doubt there was a scientific reason for it but he was content simply to enjoy the spectacle. A geography teacher had once told him that aesthetic wonder was the product of an unscientific mind. It was a formative time for Freddy because that was when he decided in his twelve-year-old way that he was firmly on the side of the poets.

In a surprisingly short time, the train entered Leyburn Station and Freddy stepped on to the platform with his kitbag. Only a few passengers had left the train, and he looked around the half-empty station in fascination. After the bomb-wrecked buildings of Portsmouth, London and Hull, it was like a scene from before the war. The waiting room, ticket kiosk and stationmaster's office were clean and well cared-for and the few people on the platform seemed to be going about their lives in a calm and unhurried way. It was a welcome in itself.

He walked out to the front of the station, rested his kitbag on the ground and waited, as arranged, for Mrs Charlesworth. It was a pleasant, sunny day, not especially warm but comfortable enough after his recent experience. He imagined that winter weather would never seem so harsh again, and now that spring was here he intended to enjoy it.

Thoughts of spring led naturally to flowers, and he looked around for a florist or greengrocer. As he did so, a man dressed smartly in brown tweeds and with a neat pencil moustache stepped out of a Rover by the entrance and spoke to him.

'Are you Freddy Hinchcliffe, by any chance?' His complexion bore signs of time spent out-of-doors.

'That's right.'

'I'm Walter Charlesworth,' he said, although the fishing flies in his tweed hat had already betrayed his identity. 'My wife sends her apologies. She's been called away on urgent WVS business.' He smiled good-naturedly. 'A knitting crisis, I fancy.' He shook Freddy's hand. 'Let's put your kitbag in the car.' He gave a guilty smile and said, 'I suppose I could be criticised for using petrol for such a journey but I really don't care. I have a game leg, and I imagine from various accounts that you've done quite enough walking lately.'

'More than enough, and I'm glad to meet you, Mr Charlesworth.' Freddy lifted his kitbag into the opened boot. 'I wonder, is there a florist on the way? I'd like to get some flowers for Mrs Charlesworth if I can.'

Walter looked at him in surprise. 'That's very civil of you, Freddy, very civil indeed. Let me see.' He thought for a moment and said, 'There's a greengrocery not far away, clients of mine. They may have some. There are not many flowers about, you know. Everyone's been growing vegetables, but let's see what we can find.'

Freddy lowered himself on to the leather upholstery, relishing the sensation and trying to remember how long it was since he had last travelled in a car. He was fascinated, too, with the square, three-storey stone buildings that lined the main street like an immaculate guard of honour. Mr Charlesworth was more interested in Freddy's journey and the general disruption of rail travel, however, and so they chatted on the way until presently they arrived at the shop.

Walter greeted the woman behind the counter. 'Good afternoon, Mrs Holmes. My young friend is looking for some flowers. What have you got?'

Mrs Holmes looked at Freddy, taking in his uniform, and her mouth opened in surprise. She beamed at him. 'You must be Freddy!'

'That's right.' Surprised, he offered his hand.

'I knitted some socks for you last year. I hope you got them all right.'

'I did, and I'm very grateful to you. Those socks were more precious than you can imagine.'

'I'm glad, an' I'm pleased to see you back safe and sound. Now then, I've got some daffies you can have. Just bear with me a minute.' She disappeared into a back room and returned a minute later with a bunch of daffodils wrapped in newspaper.

'Thank you, Mrs Holmes. How much do I owe you?'

'Don't worry about that, love. Take 'em and enjoy 'em. It's good to see you. Is Sylvia back as well, Mr Charlesworth?'

'I'm afraid not.'

'That's a shame. Have you heard from her lately?'

'Yes, she's very well, thank you.'

'Will she be home soon, do you think?'

'That's anybody's guess, I'm afraid. This war seems to drag on and on.'

As they walked on, Freddy said, 'That was generous of her. First a pair of socks and now a bunch of flowers.'

Mr Charlesworth laughed. 'They're among the slowest payers on our books, but you're right – she's a kindly soul.'

There was a question Freddy had been itching to ask and had only waited so as not to appear indecently eager. He decided he could wait no longer. 'Mr Charlesworth,' he said as they took their seats in the car again, 'I understand that Sylvia's serving overseas, and I realise that Mrs Charlesworth had to be guarded on the telephone, but where is she exactly?'

'Of course, you'd no way of knowing. She's in Malta.'

'Good heavens.'

'Is something the matter?'

'Not at all. It's just that I was based on Malta in 'forty-two, when we ditched.'

'Is that so? Well, Sylvia tells us that the Navy is a small world and a big family.'

'It certainly is.'

They turned into a narrow passage, one of several that led off the High Street, and his companion said, 'Nearly there.'

Suddenly Freddy felt awkward about the hospitality he was about to enjoy, his first for more than four years. 'It's very kind of you to have me stay with you, Mr Charlesworth,' he said, 'but I don't want you to be out of pocket. I'm quite prepared to chip in with the housekeeping and I've got double coupons.'

'Don't you worry about the housekeeping, my lad. You're our guest, and it's a poor job if we can't extend a bit of hospitality to a friend of our daughter.' They had stopped outside the gates of a substantial, double-fronted house. 'Here we are,' he said, switching off the engine and opening the car door. 'I'll put the car away later.'

They entered the house and Freddy stopped suddenly inside the doorway, conscious of the faint aromas that make a house unique. Most dominant among them was the smell of baking.

Walter was waiting to help him off with his coat. He asked, 'Is something wrong, old chap?'

'No, nothing at all. It's just a shock.'

Walter smiled uncomprehendingly. 'A shock?'

'Well, this is the first house I've been in for four years and it's all so new again.'

'Of course it is. I should have realised.' He put a hand on Freddy's shoulder. 'Come and take the weight off your feet while I put the kettle on and let the dogs out.'

'Actually, I'd be grateful if you'd point me in the direction of the usual offices first.'

'Of course. The cloakroom's just here.' He pointed to the door. 'You can leave your kitbag here for now. I'll show you to your room later.'

Freddy closed the door behind him, enjoying the luxury of privacy. He wondered if he would ever take it for granted again, and the feeling was the same when he washed his hands. Toilet soap had been a Red Cross luxury for too long.

He let himself out to the sound of excited dogs and a woman's voice. The dogs found him first, bustling around him as dogs do when they expect something to happen.

'Hello, hello.' A quick look at their hind quarters helped him distinguish them. 'So you're Peter Ross and you're Rainbow. I'm Freddy. You've possibly heard my name thrown into the conversation at some time.'

'They certainly have.'

Freddy looked up to see a neat, smartly-dressed woman in the grey-green flannel WVS summer uniform. 'Hello, Mrs Charlesworth. I'm Freddy.'

'I thought you might be.' She shook his hand. 'My husband said you'd had a good journey. Come and sit down. You'd like a cup of tea, I expect.'

'Yes, please. I'd like that very much.' He followed her into the sitting room, conscious of the unfamiliar carpet beneath his feet, and sank into a deep armchair, overwhelmed by the whole experience.

'This came for you.' She handed him a small brown envelope. 'We got one as well.'

'Thank you.' Freddy slit open the envelope, knowing what was inside but eager to read anything from Sylvia. The telegram read: WONDERFUL NEWS BUT DRAFT AND LEAVE DENIED STOP WILL WRITE STOP ALL MY LOVE SYLVIA

It was the first communication he'd received from her since January and he read it several times. It was frustrating that they had refused to send her home but he wasn't surprised. POWs were coming home in their thousands; the services couldn't accommodate everyone.

He put the telegram with its envelope into the inside pocket of his jumper and because there was nothing else to do he looked around him at the comfortable furnishings, the drape curtains and the large fireplace with its basket grate and high wooden mantelpiece. In one corner of the room was a glass-fronted cabinet displaying a few pieces of decorative china, but it was the framed photographs on top that caught his eye. He walked over to look at them more closely. The largest was obviously taken on the Charlesworths' wedding day as they stood outside the church. Mrs Charlesworth looked very elegant, if a little nervous, as might be expected. Mr Charlesworth was in army uniform with his lieutenant's pips, and Freddy wondered for a moment how he must feel about his daughter corresponding with a mere rating. He dismissed the thought immediately, telling himself that a man like Mr Charlesworth would have little time for that sort of nonsense. He put the photo down, and his pulse quickened as his eye fell on another. It was of a girl in civilian clothing. She looked very pleasant; in fact she was rather attractive, and he wondered for a moment if he might have happened on a picture of Sylvia, until he saw another of the same girl in a nurse's uniform and then one obviously taken on her wedding day.

He looked up when he heard his hosts come into the room. 'I'm just admiring your photographs,' he told them.

Mr Charlesworth peered over his shoulder. 'That's Audrey,' he said, 'our other daughter. Of course, Sylvia wasn't allowed to send you a photo, was she?' He picked up another and handed it to Freddy. 'This is Sylvia. It was taken shortly before she went to Harwich. It was only three years ago, so she hasn't changed all that much.'

Freddy took it from him, conscious that his hand was trembling with anticipation.

'It's a good one of her,' said Mrs Charlesworth, taking the tea things from her tray.

He held the photograph in both hands to prevent them from shaking, because the girl with whom he'd been exchanging letters for the past eighteen months, and with whom he was unquestionably in love, now had a face. It was a lovely face; not in a particularly glamorous way – he remembered her telling him that – but in a way that was infinitely more special. Her hair was pinned up in accordance with service regulations; her eyelashes were long, her complexion clear, and her mouth was … well, she was smiling. She had told him that people said she smiled a lot, and it was good that she did, because she had a wonderful, open smile, the kind that could bring cheer to the most determined pessimist.

'Pretty in a nice way,' he said.

'What do you mean?' Mrs Charlesworth seemed puzzled.

'Her friend Joyce said that. Joyce's husband and I were prisoners together, and she told him that Sylvia was "pretty in a nice sort of way". Len didn't understand that at first, but I knew what she meant.' He continued to study the photograph. 'She's lovely.' Almost to himself he murmured, 'Pretty on the outside and lovely inside, where it really matters.' He'd always known that.

.   .   .

Sylvia was not smiling. Common sense told her that it was the only decision First Officer Fanshawe could have made in the circumstances, but that was of no help. All she knew was that she had waited eighteen months to see Freddy and now that he was safely home the distance between them was even greater than before. She sat in Dorothy's cabin, berating herself for requesting a foreign draft in the first place.

'You're not Gypsy Rose Lee, Sylvia. You couldn't have known he'd get home before you, or that the war would change into bottom gear the way it has.'

For the first time that evening, a suggestion of a smile crossed Sylvia's face. Dorothy's conversation had contained references to driving ever since Angelo had explained the basic principles to her. 'You're really keen on learning to drive, aren't you?'

'I'm keen on anythin' that'll help me get a decent job after the war. I'm going to have drivin' lessons as soon as I get home, an' Alf's goin' to show me how to drive a tractor an' all. That'll get 'em talkin' down Salthouse Dock if anythin' will.'

Mention of Alf was a cautionary reminder. 'I feel guilty now,' Sylvia confessed.

'Wharrabout?'

'Thinking about you and Alf reminds me I'm not the only one with this problem.'

'That's right. Some girls have been waitin' four or five years. Mind you, knowin' that doesn't stop me gettin' impatient sometimes. I don't mind tellin' you, there's goin' to be no end of a hoolie when my Alf comes home.' The thought evidently triggered a memory, because she asked, 'Do you remember that night in Dover when he told me he'd been drafted overseas?' She shook her head at the memory. 'I made a right fuss, didn't I? I still don't know what I'd have done if you hadn't come to me when you did. I'll never forget that.'

'It was no effort.'

'Good. Neither is this, now I think about it, an' you're starting to feel better, aren't you?'

'I am really.' It was difficult not to feel better in Dorothy's company.

'Yeah, 'cause we all feel like that sometimes. You've just got to keep things in proportion. Not all that long ago you were worried to death because you hadn't heard from him, but now you know he's safe. We'll all go home one day soon, an' you'll find him waitin' for you an' things will go back to normal. They might even improve. Leastways, if they don't, this war will have taken a lot of precious lives for nothin'.'

. . .

Freddy's first day in his new wonderland was approaching its close. Since his arrival at the railway station, one curiosity had followed another: flowers from a stranger, the best kind of hospitality, tea in a china cup and saucer, dinner at the family table, a room and bed to himself – and all this had begun with a memorable encounter, not with a white rabbit but with a kindly and genial man.

He burped as he sat on the bed to remove his boots. He'd eaten precious little meat in the past three years, and Mrs Charlesworth's rabbit pie had been a new experience, if a trifle daunting for his shrunken and unsuspecting stomach.

The room was furnished by a woman's hand; the curtain material and floral wallpaper were testimony to that, and none of it surprised him. The room had apparently been Audrey's. He was looking forward to meeting Audrey, David and Bruce, and especially Bruce. He suspected that they would get along very well.

He folded his trousers meticulously along their seven horizontal creases, and placed his boots on top of them. All that would change when he received the automatic promotion due to a returning POW. As a Petty Officer, he would wear fore-and-aft rig, with its vertically-creased trousers, double-breasted jacket, collar and tie and peaked cap, all much easier to maintain than the junior ratings' square rig.

As he removed and folded his white front, he allowed himself a recollection of the most significant event of the day, which was that of seeing Sylvia's photograph for the first time. He had tried not to think of it too often, being anxious to preserve the initial impression that had meant so much to him, but he knew he was worrying unnecessarily. In time to come, he would photograph her as many times as she would allow, and each picture might well be a technical improvement on the original, but none would give him the joy he had experienced that afternoon when he held her photograph in its silver frame for the first time.

He lay for a while, waiting for sleep. Unfortunately the bed was softer than anything he had known in a very long time and was proving such a distraction as to make sleep impossible. After a while, he pulled off the bedclothes and lay on the hard floor, where he slept soundly.

Over the next few days, Freddy began to adjust gradually to his new surroundings. In compliance with rationing regulations, he registered with local traders, and used some of his points to buy a few items of civilian clothing. Some shopkeepers, like Mrs Holmes the greengrocer, had knitted various items for him, and he was now able to thank them properly, not that any of them could ever imagine the conditions in which their offerings had proved so vital.

He also met Audrey, David and Bruce. The last of that trio appealed to him immediately. He was still tottering, as Sylvia had said, like a drunken man, and was reluctant to speak, relying rather on sign language to make his feelings known. His irreverent grandfather saw a future for him as a bookmaker, a prospect for which Mrs Charlesworth showed little enthusiasm. Whatever his destiny, though, the young fellow was affable company and Freddy was content with that. In contrast, David was pleasant but shy and therefore not the easiest person to get to know. Audrey, who bore some physical resemblance to Sylvia, was spirited and charming, except when she referred to Sylvia – somewhat patronisingly, Freddy thought – as her 'little sister', although he suspected himself of being particularly sensitive where Sylvia was concerned. In his new life, he was becoming sensitive about a great many things.

35

As temperatures on Malta continued to rise, swimming became the most popular pastime, and St Paul's Bay was the Wrens' favourite destination. Sylvia was never sure why this should be, as it was a half-hour journey from the Imperial and it lacked a sandy beach, but she went along with the others and enjoyed herself all the same.

After a particularly euphoric swim in the bay, she arranged her towel strategically and changed out of her bathing costume. Gwen and Ruth sat beside her, gazing out to sea.

'It's a funny thing,' said Ruth absently.

'What is?' Sylvia was struggling into her underclothes but was nevertheless prepared to be sociable.

'We all complain about things from time to time,' explained Ruth, 'but I'm not the only one who'll be sorry to leave all this behind when the time comes.'

'Swimming in the sea,' agreed Gwen. 'I'll be sorry to leave that behind.'

'I mean all of it.' Ruth looked down at Sylvia and said, 'I know you've got problems, Sylvia, but I'm speaking generally. I think most of us will look back at this time and see it as, well …'

'Our "Finest Hour"?' Sylvia had just broken a fingernail and she felt she was allowed to be facetious.

'Well, yes. I think for some of us it'll be the best time of our lives.'

Sylvia was surprised to see Gwen nodding cautiously. 'For some of us,' she agreed, 'but there are things we haven't experienced, and I think we need to be careful not to talk about it as if it's been a great party.'

'What do you mean?' The question came from Ruth, but Gwen looked equally surprised.

'Do you remember the message on the posters? "Join the Wrens and Free a Man for the Fleet." Well, we may have done that, but let's not forget the job they've been doing. It hasn't been a party for them, and I can't imagine they'd be all that impressed to hear us talking about having the time of our lives.' Now fully dressed, she rolled up her swimsuit inside her towel and laid them beside her. 'There was a chap I met in Harwich,' she told them. 'He was a seaman on one of the minesweepers. I got quite involved with him, and then his ship hit a mine and he was killed.' She held up a hand to forestall their expressions of sympathy. 'That was what first brought the horror of war home to me.'

Ruth nodded slowly. 'Fair enough,' she said. 'I'm sorry about your boyfriend, and it's true that we'd be sensible not to offend anyone, but we can't help the way we feel.'

'True.' Sylvia smiled, realising that she'd maybe been a little severe. 'Anyway, will you be going back to your chap in Dulwich after the war?'

'Absolutely not.'

'Your mind's made up?'

'I should say so. Do you know what he told me before I left?'

'Go on.' Both Sylvia and Gwen were listening.

'He told me that when he got married it would be to a virgin.'

'No, really?'

'After what he'd done to you?' Gwen was shocked enough to comment.

'*With* me, not *to* me – it takes two, remember. But yes, that's what he said, so I told him where to go.'

'Quite right.' Sylvia shared Ruth's feelings entirely, but Gwen was gazing out to sea again. 'I've never had a boyfriend,' she said.

'Well, what's stopping you?' Forthright as ever, Ruth went to the centre of the problem. 'You just need to make something of yourself and get on with it. What are you waiting for?'

'I'm not pretty like you two.'

Sylvia recalled a similar conversation long before, in a fish-and-chip shop in Dover. 'Talk to Dorothy,' she said. 'She'll sort you out.'

As Gwen and Ruth continued to chat, she took out Freddy's telegram, now dog-eared and creased from handling, and read it again.

SORRY COULD NOT WRITE STOP WENT WEST WITH GOONS STOP NO MAIL STOP WILL WRITE STOP LOVE YOU FREDDY.

He'd spared no expense. By her reckoning, it must have come to one shilling and twopence. Now she thought of it, her telegram to him had cost her a shilling and had been worth every penny, but it would be much better when the letters began to flow again.

As for the content of his telegram, she had asked around, and no one at the Imperial had any idea what 'goons' might be. She could only imagine it was a slang name for the Germans. It sounded disrespectful and therefore quite likely. And 'went west' had a sinister ring, although he was alive and well so there was clearly no need to worry about that. Freddy's letters could be cryptic but his telegrams were indecipherable. It was anybody's guess when they would meet face to face and have a proper conversation.

· · ·

It was Tuesday the eighth of May, the first of the two national holidays to celebrate the German surrender, and Freddy awoke to the familiar soft knock on his bedroom door. Struggling to open his eyes after a night of little sleep, he heard Mr Charlesworth put a cup of tea down on his bedside table. 'Thank you,' he mumbled.

'It's my pleasure.' Mr Charlesworth perched on the chair by the wall and said, 'I was about to ask if you'd slept well, but it would have been a silly question. You look terrible, old son.'

Freddy's eyes were now open and he managed to focus on his host. 'It's nothing,' he said. 'I hope I didn't disturb either of you last night.'

'No, not at all. We're both sound sleepers.' He inclined his head towards the tea on the bedside table and said, 'Your "gunfire" will get cold, Freddy. I'd drink some of it if I were you. It's the best medicine I know for a troubled night.'

Freddy raised himself on one elbow to comply. He asked, 'Why do you call it that?'

'It became a habit in the last war. Each day in the trenches began with the sound of gunfire and the smell of tea. The association was difficult to break.'

'I never knew that.' He'd also never seen anyone else wear a spotted handkerchief, tastefully arranged, in the breast pocket of his dressing gown, but it wasn't out of place with the neat moustache and carefully-groomed appearance. He asked, 'What outfit were you in?'

'The Eighth Battalion, the Nineteenth Green Howards.'

Freddy nodded although he knew little about the army and its regiments. 'A bad dream, was it?'

Freddy nodded again.

'There's no shame in it, my boy, and it's not surprising in the circumstances.' He stood up to leave. 'The bathroom's free. We got up early, thinking we'd let you have a lie-in.'

227

Now he knew he'd woken them in the night. 'Thank you,' he said, 'but I'll get up now.'

'Come down when you're ready. It's a big day for the WVS, so I'm in charge of breakfast.'

When Freddy went downstairs he found Audrey and Bruce in the dining room but Mrs Charlesworth had already left for the market place, where the festivities were due to take place.

'She's a great organiser,' Audrey told him. 'She'll be organising tables, chairs, bandstands, husbands, shirkers …. You name it and she'll have it on her list.'

'But not breakfast,' said Mr Charlesworth. 'That's my domain.' He set a plate down in front of Freddy. 'That's your second real egg of the week. I thought I'd push the boat out in honour of the day. They're real sausages too.' Mrs Charlesworth had been scrupulously careful about giving Freddy the double rations issued to him as a returning POW, and her husband was no less meticulous. 'This,' he said, passing the butter, 'was a gift from a grateful client. I'll get you some toast.'

Freddy looked around him and said, 'I don't deserve any of this.'

'Hand it over then,' said Audrey. 'We'll eat it, won't we Bruce?'

'I mean this kind of treatment. You're all being so good to me.'

'Oh well, you can blame Sylvia for that.'

'I shall.' He meant to write to her later if he got a chance, or he might delay it for a day or so because he was still feeling pretty awful. Also, he'd had an idea for a song, and it would be nice to include it in his next letter. He would make the decision later.

At that point, Bruce decided to take his mother's suggestion seriously. Pointing to the egg on Freddy's plate, he uttered his first word. 'Tookie!'

'Clever boy!' Audrey seized his hand before it could inflict damage on the egg. 'Did you hear him, Dad? He said "Chookie"!'

'Yes. Good boy!' His proud grandfather beamed at him. 'And it's not as if he's seen all that many lately.'

'I'll tell you what,' said Freddy, 'I'll cut it in half and he can have some.'

'No, Freddy, you mustn't. You need your rations.' Audrey stood up to move Bruce away from the table.

'Tookie! Tookie!' It seemed that having learned the word Bruce was determined to get some use out of it.

'No, Bruce. You had your chookie-egg this morning.'

'Tookie!' He let out a piercing cry of anger and frustration that earned a sharp reprimand from his mother, but its effect on Freddy was infinitely more devastating.

For a moment, the room and its occupants merged into a general haze before the light was blotted out. It was as if the horrors of the past had returned to reclaim him, and that the room had become a fearful place filled with the din of small-arms fire, the cries of the wounded and the acerbic stench of cordite.

And then, inexplicably, he was back at the table, breathless and drenched in clammy sweat.

'Freddy, are you all right? He's as white as anything, Audrey.' Walter's hand was on his shoulder. Somewhere in the room Bruce was crying.

'It's all right,' Audrey was saying. 'Mummy's not cross any more – take him, Dad – Go with Granddad, Bruce. He's got something for you. I bet it's a sweetie.' And then she was crouching beside Freddy, asking him if he felt faint.

'I don't know.' He was vaguely aware that his voice sounded tremulous.

'All right, turn round and face me, OK? Now put your head between your knees.'

He sat like that for some time, and then Audrey held his wrist and studied her watch.

'Now,' she said, 'sit up and let me look at your eyes. Look straight at me.' She examined them in turn whilst feeling his forehead, and said, 'I think you'd better take it easy for a while, at least until David arrives.' Then, as if she were embarrassingly conscious that things had become too serious, she smiled and said, 'You'll have to buck up, you know. I'm looking forward to dancing with you later.'

'I'm terribly sorry.' His voice was still unsteady.

'Don't be silly.'

'No, this is awful. I don't understand it.'

'You'll be all right. Just take it easy.'

'I hope I haven't frightened Bruce. Is he all right?'

'He's fine. He was only crying because I told him off.'

Mr Charlesworth's voice came from the next room. 'David's here.'

'Oh good.' Audrey got up to go and meet her husband. Freddy heard the front door being opened and then closed; he heard David's voice in the hall, and then Audrey's. He heard her say something about his pulse being over a hundred and fifty and his pupils being dilated, and then Mr Charlesworth said something he couldn't catch.

'Hello, Freddy.' David was at his side, lifting his eyelids to peer at his eyes. 'What have you been up to?'

'I really don't know. I think I'm going mad.'

'I gather you had a bad night.'

Freddy nodded.

'Okay, let's take your temperature and pulse.'

Despite his natural preoccupation, Freddy decided he preferred the feminine touch, especially when having his pulse read, but he was currently grateful for any treatment, and David's quiet manner was very calming.

The latter noted his temperature with a nod of satisfaction. 'Not bad,' he said. 'Your heart rate's down as well. Tell me what happened.'

'I don't know.' Freddy struggled to make sense of it. 'Is it possible to have a nightmare when you're wide awake? I was in the middle of breakfast when it happened.'

'It's quite possible.'

'It was like being in the mine again.' He hesitated. 'It was so realistic I really believed it was happening.' He stopped again, at a loss to describe the experience.

'Go on.'

'There was an incident involving some Russian prisoners, a murderous business.'

'And is that what you saw just now?'

'Not exactly. I heard firing and I think I saw faces. I could feel the cold air. I could even smell gun smoke.' He winced at the renewed recollection. 'The awful thing is that I thought I'd left all that behind. Tell me, David, am I going round the bend?'

'No, you're not. This sort of thing is more common than you think. You've suffered a nervous reaction, no doubt prompted by the excitement of yesterday's news. I don't suppose today's merry-making will help either, so I'd advise caution if you're thinking of going out there. I'm going to give you something to calm your nerves, and I want you to take a dose now and another tonight when you turn in. More importantly, though, I think you should see your medical officer when you report again. I'll give you a letter.'

'Do I have to report it?'

'That's my advice. It's the only way you'll get treatment.'

'I'll bear it in mind. Thanks, David.'

'You're welcome.' David picked up his bag. 'Now remember – no excitement for the rest of the day. You must take things easy.'

'Just as I told him,' said Audrey, following Walter into the room.

Although he would never say so, Freddy wasn't all that sorry to miss the festivities. Peace had been inevitable after the discovery of Hitler's body, and VE Day was almost an anti-climax. In any case, whatever the medical advice, he really needed some time on his own.

'Here's something that should aid recovery,' announced Mr Charlesworth.

'In all the excitement yesterday, no one seems to have looked at the second post.' He handed Freddy an envelope. 'Now take care. We'll bring you something for lunch and one of us will call in later, so just take it easy.'

When they had all gone to the market place, Freddy opened the envelope. The letter was dated two weeks earlier; about the time he had arrived.

Dearest Freddy,

You can't imagine how thrilled I was to hear you were home safe and sound, or how disappointed I was that I couldn't be with you. It will happen one day though!

I expect my family are looking after you and making you feel at home. Don't believe anything Audrey tells you about me!

Please explain what you meant by going west with goons. I'm curious to know. There are lots of things I want to know. When did you last get a letter from me? Did you get the Christmas parcel we sent? Have you been to see Len yet? Have you a photo of yourself that you can send me? I don't really care what you look like – I'm just curious.

If you get to the pictures, do tell me what's on – you know, the way I used to tell you when you were in the camp. We don't get to see films very often. We spend most of our off-watch time swimming.

Did you get my letter about the revue? There'll be a lot to talk about once we've sorted out what we don't know, if you see what I mean. For now, though, just let me say I love you to bits and pieces. It's one of the few things that are off the ration, and I'm thrilled to know you're back, so why shouldn't I?

Take great care,
Your Sugar Plum XXXXXXXXX
P.S. I wished on the new moon. Did you?
P.P.S. Let's find another new moon. The last one only did half a job.

Sylvia hadn't lost her touch: he was feeling better already, still somewhat disturbed about the waking nightmare thing but certainly feeling better.

. . .

Spoken for or not, Sylvia was never going to miss the Victory Dance. To cater for all watches, several dances had been arranged and she, Ruth and Gwen happened to be off-watch on the night of the eighth. Gwen insisted that she was no good at dancing and that she was there simply to celebrate with everyone else. It sounded quite illogical to Sylvia but she kept her thoughts to herself for the time being.

The dance was held in the old canteen, where they had performed the revue, but the interior was unrecognisable because of the bunting draped over the walls and ceiling. Where the stage had been there was a small bandstand and behind it against the backcloth the White Ensign, the Union Flag and the RAF Ensign formed a symbol of unity. After all, there was no knowing when they might receive a visit from the other services. The floor was pretty crowded, so it was possible there were some there already.

The eight-piece band sounded superb, as did the Wren and the leading seaman who provided the vocals.

'You can bet they were all professionals before the war,' said Ruth, 'like the Blue Mariners.'

Sylvia nodded, equally impressed, but somewhat distracted by an ache in her right ear. It had begun as an annoying itch and had persisted throughout much of the day despite numerous applications of heated cotton wool, there being no olive oil to be found. Even so, she wasn't going to let it spoil her enjoyment of the evening and when a rating asked her to dance she agreed readily. Appropriately, the band was playing 'I'm Going to Get Lit up When the Lights Go on in London'. Her partner was a signalman from one of the destroyers in Sliema Harbour and he was quite a good dancer, if a trifle invasive.

'Take it easy, Jack,' she told him, easing herself away from him. 'Give me room to breathe.'

'I was only being friendly.'

'I know you were. That's the trouble.'

'Have you got a party on the island, then?'

'Not on the island. He's at home.'

'Officer, is he?'

'No, he's an air-gunner.'

It made no difference to the sailor, who merely snorted and said, 'Some blokes have all the luck.' When the number ended, he thanked her politely enough and re-joined his shipmates. Sylvia found Ruth and Gwen. Ruth asked, 'How was yours?'

'A bit friendly but okay to dance with.'

'At least yours could dance. I got a bootneck with two left feet. He thought a foxtrot was a hunt on foot.'

'Bad luck. Still, the night is young.'

Gwen simply looked bored.

The band leader announced a waltz. It was 'The Boy Next Door', and the rating who came to ask Sylvia to dance might easily have met that description.

He was very young and diffident, and it was clear that he found the process daunting.

'I wondered, I mean, you know, if ...'

Sylvia threw him a line. 'If I'd like to dance?'

'Mm,' he nodded. 'Yes, please.'

'Why not?' She let him lead her nervously on to the floor, and she knew after a few steps that he was struggling. After a while, she said, 'Let's just shuffle.'

His young face was crimson. 'I'm sorry,' he said, 'this is awful.'

'No it's not. Keep shuffling and we can enjoy the music. It's a lovely song.'

'I feel so awful. I've been practising all day.'

'Who have you been practising with?'

'No one. Just on my own. I did it in the clothing store where I work, where no one could see me.' He was almost in tears.

'But how did you learn the steps?'

'I got them out of a book.' The words came out in a whisper, rather like a confession.

'Don't worry about it.' She squeezed his left hand. 'What's your name?'

'Andrew.' He whispered that too, and she wasn't surprised, given the naval connotation. She could imagine him as the butt of a great deal of mess-deck humour.

'Don't worry, Andrew. Mine's Sylvia, and I'm telling you that because I want you to come to our table after this dance. There's a nice girl I want you to meet, and she won't make you feel at all awkward, because she's still learning to dance too. Will you do that?'

'If you want me to.'

'Listen, Andrew, I don't dish out invitations lightly. Will you come and join us?'

'Yes, please.' He was like a child being offered a treat after a bad experience.

'That's the spirit. With any luck, your evening may be about to take an upward turn.'

The number reached its close and she took him back to meet the others. 'This is Andrew, girls. Andrew, this is Ruth, and this is Gwen. 'You two would do well to dance together.' She answered Gwen's shocked expression with a smile and a wink.

They sat out 'Sentimental Journey', during which Sylvia managed to draw Andrew and Gwen into something that was almost a conversation, and then Ruth got up to dance to 'In the Mood'. The next, though, was 'Moonlight

Serenade', a number that was ideal for reluctant dancers. Sylvia gave Andrew a meaningful look and, taking his cue, he led Gwen on to the floor.

'In certain countries,' said Ruth, 'parents pay people like you to do what you've just done. I only mention it in case you find yourself at a loose end after the war.'

'I just felt sorry for them both, but mainly Andrew. He's been practising his dance steps on his own in the clothing store.'

Ruth shook her head in disbelief. 'Poor little scrap. They sent him away to war and he couldn't even dance. What was the Navy thinking?'

There was a succession of swing numbers, during which Andrew and Gwen became much more at ease with each other, and when the band turned to music of a softer kind they got up quite naturally to dance together. Ruth took to the floor with a petty officer, but Sylvia smiled apologetically at his friend, saying, 'Sorry, I've got a bit of a headache.' It sounded more credible than earache, and it was only an excuse anyway. The number was 'All the Things You Are', and that dance was reserved for one man. In her current situation, it was the last song Sylvia wanted to hear.

The girl singer was good, and Sylvia was unable to listen to more than a few bars of the refrain before wishing she were anywhere but in that hall.

She blinked desperately, knowing that if she left the room and went to the heads she would most likely give way altogether, and that would be awful. Victory might be in sight but discipline still had to be upheld, and she must never let the girls see her in tears. Wretchedly, she heard the song through to the last lines that seemed to mock her in her misery.

36

Freddy was no more interested in fishing than he had been at the time of his correspondence on the subject with Sylvia, but Mr Charlesworth's suggestion that he join him on the river for the day had sounded like a coded message. Also, he needed the peace and the fresh air, lowering skies notwithstanding. In any case, he enjoyed the older man's company so he accepted the invitation readily. The extra pair of gum boots that stood beside his host's waders in the hall suggested that he might be expected to take part in the activity, but he really didn't mind.

On the river bank below Redmire falls he felt more relaxed than he could remember. Staying with the Charlesworths was very pleasant, but the experience of living with a family and adapting to its way of life was still a new one that presented him with awkward constraints. For now, though, they were simply two friends out for the day.

He watched the water spill over the brown rocks whilst Rainbow and Peter Ross played on the bank, inventing new diversions with inexhaustible canine ingenuity. Their noses had quivered at the scent of wild garlic all the way down the steep hill to the river bank and now they chased each other with joyful abandon. He wondered if he would ever see a more glorious sight.

His host was content too, standing in the river and casting sideways to avoid the overhanging branches of the trees that lined the bank. Freddy wondered what special pleasure it gave him, considering his catch had been quite modest so far.

At length, Mr Charlesworth reeled in his line and joined Freddy on the bank. 'What do you think, Freddy? Isn't it the greatest place on earth?' He unbuckled the straps of his waders and extricated himself from them.

'It's magnificent, Mr Charlesworth.'

'Even on a dull day like today?'

'I've never seen the river in sunshine.'

'Then you've another treat in store.' He unfolded a stool and sat down. 'I'll make no bones about it, Freddy; I brought you out here for a purpose.'

'I've been wondering.' Freddy had an awful feeling that his soul was about to be laid bare.

Mr Charlesworth found his pipe and lit it. 'Of course you need the peace and quiet. That goes without saying, but the main reason I've brought you here is that I'm the only member of the family who has a clue about your state of mind – apart from David, of course, and he's never experienced it for himself.'

'There's really no need to worry about me. I've caused you all enough trouble already.'

'You've been no trouble at all, and there's no need to feel awkward. You and I have more in common than you think.'

Freddy picked self-consciously at a head of wild garlic. 'Why do you say that?'

'Because when I came home after the last war I was disturbed and confused, just as you are. I had troubled nights and daytime horrors too.'

There was no way Freddy could stop the discussion so he lit a cigarette and let it continue.

'I got this on the Somme,' said Mr Charlesworth, tapping his knee with the stem of his pipe, 'but it was the lesser of my problems. In one sense, it was a stroke of luck because it was my Blighty wound.' He smiled awkwardly. 'I don't know if they call it that nowadays, but I'm sure you know what I mean.'

'Yes,' said Freddy. 'It got you home. It was an odd kind of luck, wasn't it?'

'It was.' Mr Charlesworth lit his pipe again and blew out a stream of smoke before saying, 'I don't mind telling you, Freddy, that whole episode was hell on earth.' He was silent for a few moments, no doubt in painful recollection, the only sounds coming from the river and from the dogs as they chased in and out of the trees. 'There are many things I'd prefer to forget,' he went on, 'but it's not always possible to do that. I think we have that in common.'

Freddy nodded silently. The images of the previous day were still painfully fresh in his mind.

'It's odd, though, that the worst horrors are not memories of what we suffered, but of what we saw inflicted on others.'

Freddy sat with his head bowed, hardly trusting himself to speak.

'And, as if that's not enough, we're consumed with guilt because we survived and others didn't.'

Freddy said nothing. He had no need because it was as if his companion could read his thoughts.

'I know it's not easy to talk about these things, Freddy, but you have to know that you and I are speaking the same language. Do you see?'

Eventually Freddy said quietly, 'It was the shock of it. There was liberation and repatriation, the long-awaited homecoming. Everything was going to be fine and then ....'

'I know.'

'And the bugger of it is that there's no hiding place.'

'Ah, but there is.'

Freddy looked up for the first time at the hint of optimism.

'This is my hiding place and you'll agree with me before long that it's the best hiding place a man could have.' Pipe in hand, Walter pointed to the features that meant so much to him. 'Look at these trees, Freddy. They were around before Hitler, Hirohito, or, for that matter, the Kaiser. Believe it or not, when some of those beeches were saplings, Germany was no more than an unassembled jigsaw of states, Japan meant little beyond its own shores, and it's fair to say that the good old Ure was splashing over those rocks long before man learned to stand upright and covet his neighbour's land. It's better than all those things, Freddy. It's a place for a man to hide, and you're always welcome to join me in it.' His pipe had gone out but his enthusiasm had made him temporarily unaware of the fact. 'I came here in nineteen-twenty after I was discharged,' he said, 'and it made me whole again. It took a while but it did the job. Jessie knew that. She'd no idea what had been haunting me but she noticed the difference all right.'

'Did she come here with you?'

'Sometimes, and she knew when I needed my own company as well. A lot of women might have struggled with that but she had her wits about her and she coped magnificently.'

'I couldn't imagine her not coping.'

'You're very astute, Freddy.' Mr Charlesworth opened the basket beside him and took out a tin of sandwiches. 'I believe some of these are Spam and some are cheese, but I imagine that's academic as far as you're concerned.'

'You're right there, Mr Charlesworth.' Food was still a novelty, and all sandwiches were equally welcome. He took one from the proffered tin. It turned out to be Spam. 'Thank you.'

'I heard Bing Crosby on the wireless some time ago.' Mr Charlesworth smiled at Freddy's surprise. 'Oh yes, even accountants turn to light entertainment sometimes. Anyway, he was singing a song called "Accentuate the Positive". If you haven't heard it yet I'm sure you will, and I think you'll agree with me that it's good advice. It's what you need to do, Freddy. Concentrate on the good things and they'll drive out the demons eventually.'

'Is that what you did?'

'Of course. That's why I'm so confident it'll work for you. Just take stock. You're a free man again, the war's over in Europe, you have a standing invitation to stay with us and enjoy the Dales countryside at any time – including this place – and of course there's the other matter.'

'What other matter is that?' He thought he knew.

With a mischievous smile his companion said, 'Sylvia won't be in foreign parts for ever. You've got that to look forward to.' He picked up the tin of sandwiches again. 'Come on, Freddy, dig in. And when we've eaten, perhaps you'd like to try a few casts with the rod and line.'

. . .

The ache in Sylvia's ear developed gradually into a pain that kept her awake throughout the night and became so acute that she was at the head of the queue at sick parade the following morning.

The surgeon-lieutenant peered into each ear through a strange-looking instrument and registered his concern.

'That's a nasty infection you've got in your right ear. When were you first aware of it?'

'It was about mid-day yesterday, sir. Some of us had been swimming and I thought I mustn't have dried my ear properly. It was as if there was water in it, but then it started itching and I thought it might be wax, but it just got worse. I've never had anything like it.'

'I see.' He made a note on her form. 'Have you brought your small kit?'

'Yes, sir.'

'Well then, we'd better have you in hospital so that we can keep an eye on you.'

Later that morning, the Principal Medical Officer, a grey-haired and affable surgeon-commander, examined Sylvia's ear and reacted much as his junior colleague had. 'That's quite an infection,' he said. I understand you spent yesterday forenoon swimming in the sea.'

'That's right, sir.'

'In that case, I shouldn't be surprised if the culprit happened to be some microscopic miscreant you encountered in the bay.' He consulted his notes and said, 'The sulphonamide tablets the surgeon-lieutenant prescribed for you should do the trick, and we'll give you something to lessen the pain as well.'

'Thank you, sir.' She welcomed anything that would give her some relief.

The PMO handed her notes to one of the nurses. 'Chin up, my dear,' he told Sylvia. 'You'll soon feel better.'

The analgesic eventually dulled the pain so that she was able to sleep, albeit intermittently. The sulphonamide tablets had to be taken with numerous glasses of water, with the inevitable result, and the need to rouse herself and make frequent journeys to the heads added frustration to her woes. Eventually, though, her system adjusted to the new regime and rewarded her with a few hours of oblivion.

. . .

Freddy was surprised that he'd taken so readily to fly fishing. He'd only tried it out of gratitude and as a matter of courtesy, and already he was hungry for more.

'I suppose we might go again on Sunday,' said Mr Charlesworth, who was naturally delighted by his pupil's enthusiasm. 'Of course, I'll have to speak nicely to the lady of the house but I believe she's doing something with the WVS anyway, so I doubt if she'll mind.'

'I'll need to buy some equipment at some stage and I'd be grateful for your advice on that.'

Walter smiled at his boyish zeal. 'You really are keen, aren't you? Of course I'll advise you.'

It was an inviting prospect and one that Freddy took to bed, with the result that he spent an untroubled night and emerged the following morning in a particularly resilient frame of mind. It was as well, because he came downstairs to find an envelope addressed to Acting PO Airman F.W. Hinchcliffe. It contained a movement order, a rail warrant and orders to report to HMS *Kestrel*, the Royal Naval Air Station at Worthy Down, near Winchester, by 0800 hours on the fourteenth of May.

'That's next Monday,' observed Mrs Charlesworth. 'They might have given us a chance to fatten you up a bit.'

'You've done me a power of good,' Freddy told her, 'but I'm afraid the war won't wait.'

Mrs Charlesworth snorted. 'I thought it was as good as over. Now Hitler's out of the way, surely the Japanese can't go on much longer. In any case, I don't see why they need you after all you've been through.'

Freddy just hoped he would get to see Sylvia before they drafted him.

. . .

239

Ray Hobbs

Five days had passed, the medication had done its work and the pain was an unpleasant memory. Sylvia had just one preoccupation, and that was that she could hear nothing at all with her right ear.

The PMO inserted his otoscope and examined the ear carefully. 'The infection is gone,' he told her, 'but there is some damage. I'm afraid the reason for your deafness is that the ear drum is perforated.'

37

The medical officer made a note of the result. 'No sugar, slight acid,' he commented as he poured away Freddy's urine specimen. It seemed almost a shame after the effort Freddy had put into providing it. The mug of tea at breakfast had barely had time to work, and he had been obliged to whistle the whole of 'I Can't Get Started', much to the surgeon-lieutenant's irritation. To be fair, it wasn't one of Freddy's favourite numbers either.

'You're malnourished, but then it's hardly surprising,' the doctor told him, writing again.

'But I've been on double rations for the past month, sir.'

'It's going to take more than a month to counteract the effects of three years' malnutrition.' He finished writing and screwed the cap back firmly on his fountain pen.

'Maybe shipboard rations will help,' suggested Freddy, not wishing to appear feeble.

The surgeon-lieutenant looked at him as he might regard a half-wit. He asked, 'What on earth gives you the idea you're going to sea?'

Freddy shrugged. 'I just thought they might appreciate a helping hand in the Far East, sir.' He stopped short of reminding the doctor that Great Britain had been at war with Japan since 1941. He had to remember which of them was supposed to be the half-wit.

'It's unlikely you'll be going to sea, PO, and you're certainly not going to the Far East. You're unfit for flying duties.' He tapped Freddy's medical record sheet. 'It's official.'

And that was that. Freddy had made no mention of the nightmares and daytime horrors. It had never been his intention anyway. He had no wish to be labelled 'lacking moral fibre', which would have been the likeliest outcome.

He felt a kind of guilt that his colleagues were fighting in the Far East without him but he reminded himself that he'd done his share, and his unfitness was no fault of his. All that remained was to find out what his duties were to be. Then he would be free to write to the Charlesworths and, as importantly, to Sylvia.

. . .

'I'm delighted you've recovered from the infection,' said Second Officer Fuller, 'but it's rotten luck about the perforated ear drum, and it leaves us with a problem too. You see, you may think you're capable of doing the job with only half your hearing, but regulations say otherwise. You understand that, don't you?'

'Yes, ma'am.' Sylvia was taken by surprise. Whilst she had been trying to come to terms with the knowledge that her hearing loss might be permanent, she had not begun to consider the implications it might have for her service in the WRNS.

'A short time ago you requested a draft home.'

'Yes, ma'am, I know what you're thinking, and I'm as keen as ever to go home. It's just a shame that I have to be discharged while the war's still going on.' She hoped she was making sense. The whole business had come upon her very suddenly.

'Do you really feel that you'd be letting the side down?'

'Yes, ma'am.'

'I think you can stop worrying about that.' Miss Fuller consulted Sylvia's service documents. 'After almost four years' exemplary service, your commitment is beyond question. You served with complete satisfaction at Harwich and Dover and you've more than justified your leading rate since you arrived here.' She smiled. 'I think you can leave the service confident that you've made a sound contribution to the war effort.'

'Thank you, ma'am.' Sylvia had naturally been aware that her service record was a satisfactory one, in spite of PO Wren Dunn's machinations, but she had been completely unprepared for the unsolicited praise she had just received.

'Don't imagine, though, that the powers-that-be will discharge you immediately. If I know the service they'll find something for you to do while someone at the Admiralty prepares the relevant forms and then holds up the job because they've run out of carbon paper.'

'In that case, ma'am, I don't feel too bad about it.'

'Good, then I'll set the wheels in motion.'

. . .

Freddy had to be retrained, presumably so that he could then train others for a war that must surely end within a year or so. It made no sense at all, as he pointed out to the course instructor.

The Chief PO Airman was not at all surprised. 'What did you expect? They've promoted you to PO so they've got to get their money's worth out of you somehow. Be thankful you're not going to the Far East. Some very nasty stories have come back from that place.'

Freddy found he had a great deal to learn because so much had changed since 1942. To begin with, there was a new alphabet. 'Able' and 'Baker' had replaced 'Apple' and 'Beer'. 'Charlie' and 'Dog' had escaped the axe but many other old friends had gone. There were also new Wireless Telegraphy and Radio Telephony procedures, and the more he used them the more sense they made. He always felt better when things made sense, because he knew then that if there was a fault, at least it was not his.

Before joining the others for a drink at the end of the first day, he wrote a letter to the Charlesworths, thanking them for their generous hospitality and reassuring them that all was well. When he had done that he wrote to Sylvia.

38

Freddy picked up an envelope two weeks later, addressed to him in Sylvia's handwriting and with a Northallerton postmark. He wondered, controlling his excitement as he slit it open.

30th May, 1945.
Dearest Freddy,

I'm at home, as you can see, but only until tomorrow. They've only given me forty-eighters from arrival in England because I'm being discharged soon, and I had a horrible journey that gobbled up part of my leave. We must be able to meet soon. My draft is Whitehall, next door to our trysting place – remember? For once, we shan't be too far apart, but that's just until they throw me out. I'd better explain that I'm being medically discharged because I have a perforated ear drum. You'll have to whisper endearments into my left ear because I can't hear a thing with the right! Oh, why do our paths never meet? It's too frustrating for words. If I'd arrived home when I was supposed to we might have been able to talk on the phone, however briefly. It would have been wonderful to hear your voice.

I'm sorry this is so short. I'll write as soon as I know where I'm billeted. In the meantime, take care. I love you.

Your Sugar Plum XXXXX

P.S. Congratulations on your promotion!

P.P.S. I've heard you're a convert to fly fishing. Another one!

Things were happening at last. It was awful news about her ear drum but a stroke of luck that she'd been drafted to London. Whitehall was a stone's throw from Worthy Down, at least compared with the distances that had separated them in the past. It was early to be requesting leave but the time would come.

. . .

Another benefit in being drafted to Whitehall was that Joyce was there, and Sylvia's recent parting from Dorothy and the others had been a tearful reminder, if it were needed, that true friends were very special. Joyce had been her best friend since joining HMS *Wasp*, and the prospect of seeing her again came second only to meeting Freddy.

She was overjoyed when she found that not only were she and Joyce on the same watch but her new billet was in Upper Norwood, a relatively short bus ride to Joyce's home in Balham. Suddenly things were going her way again. At least she certainly hoped they were.

After another long and frequently-interrupted journey, she reported to Whitehall, learned that she was due to commence duties in twenty-four hours' time, greeted a startled Joyce in the Coding Room and made arrangements with her for an off-watch meeting.

When she arrived at her billet she had a good look around to familiarise herself with the place, and when she was satisfied she unpacked and took out her writing things.

'Palace View',
Central Hill,
Upper Norwood,
London SE19.

31st May, 1945.

Dearest Freddy,
I've just arrived after a long, long journey, and very soon I'll be unconscious, but not before I've given you my address and passed on all good wishes from Mum, Dad, Audrey, David, Bruce, the Post Office lady and Mrs Holmes the greengrocer's wife.
I saw Joyce today. Of course, I couldn't tell you before that she's been at Whitehall since October. We're on the same watch, believe it or not, and when I see Len I'll give him your regards. Mind you, there's no reason why you shouldn't see him soon, is there?
The girls in this billet seem a pleasant lot. It's a funny name, though – 'Palace View' – when you think about it, because it must have been impossible to see the Crystal Palace from here even before it was burned down. Maybe

the original owner's imagination ran away with him. Apparently it belongs to an actor, but no one knows who he is. Maybe he's not at all famous, but wouldn't it be grand if he turned out to be Lawrence Olivier, John Clements or someone like that? It's a lovely house, too. I'd say it's early Victorian. It's double-fronted, with a big staircase and high ceilings. There are four storeys but I'm on the first floor, thank goodness. I don't know how long I'm going to be here – the whole thing's ridiculous – but at least I've got a nice billet.

I've got a bit of time tomorrow, so I'll look up trains to your neck of the woods, in case for some reason you can't get away.

Take care. Oceans of love,

Your Sugar Plum XXXXX

. . .

Freddy received the letter next morning, but before he could reply to it he had to endure a day of W/T and R/T practical procedure and familiarisation with the wireless equipment of the Fairey Barracuda, the torpedo bomber that aircrew called 'The Bloody Barra' because of its questionable safety record, and he was particularly careful to learn all he could about its equipment. Communication was vital in the event of a ditching, and such knowledge might save lives.

Eventually the class secured for the day and he was able to write to Sylvia.

Dearest Sugar Plum,

Believe me when I tell you that you grow dearer by the minute, especially now we're in the same country at last.

I'm horrified to hear about your ear drum, even though it turned out to be your Blighty wound. Is it likely to heal, or must I always murmur endearments exclusively to your left? That seems too unfair for words.

My last letter to you with all my latest information is probably on its way to Malta, so I'll tell you now that I've been grounded, as our RAF colleagues say. I'm classified medically unfit for flying, and all because I've lost a few pounds. What have they got against slim people?

There's a chance I may get up to London before long. I have to speak up in court for a kriegie oppo of mine. It's nothing awful – just a difference of opinion with the tax man – and he's a good bloke or I wouldn't be doing it. Anyway, he's pleading guilty so his case should come up soon. Fingers crossed.

I'm in an instructional class of three here. The other two are decent blokes. They were both shot down over Norway in 1940, which puts my three-year inconvenience into perspective. They say I'm lucky, as well, because I wasn't shot down. I don't see what was so lucky about coming down in the oggin through engine failure. Some people just have to show off.

On to happier things, though. I had a marvellous time staying with your folks. They were unbelievably kind, and as for the countryside there – well, you did your best to describe it but I still couldn't believe it. That place below Redmire Falls where your dad goes fishing must be the most beautiful and peaceful place on earth, and with Pen Hill and Bolton Castle overlooking the Dale like benevolent sentinels it's the perfect refuge for an ex-kriegie. Can you believe it? I'm telling you this and you live there!

Two nights earlier, drenched with sweat after a hideous nightmare, he had scattered the demons by concentrating on Redmire Falls. It was a huge step forward.

I'm glad you've got a decent billet and you're reunited with Joyce. I know you were in Dover together. It seems ages ago that your letter came and Len told me about you. It'll be good to see him again. Best of all, though, will be seeing you at last, and that can't happen soon enough. You still make everything better, even though things are so much better than they were.

I'm sending you a huge love bubble. It's rather like a barrage balloon, but invisible and much friendlier. We'll burst it together when we meet. What a moment that will be!

All my love for now,
Freddy XXXXXX

. . .

It was the greatest luxury to receive a letter from Freddy only a day after he'd posted it. Sylvia had read it several times during the watch. Her new job afforded frequent opportunities for private correspondence, and she saw no harm in taking advantage of them. As she saw it, they were taking advantage of her, so yah-boo to them.

Joyce joined her on the pavement outside the station while she was re-reading Freddy's letter.

'What's he got to say, Sylvia?'

'He's been grounded, and that's the best news. It means he won't be going to the Far East. He says it's because he's lost a few pounds, but I don't care as long as it's nothing awful.'

Joyce nodded knowingly. 'Shall we have a cup of tea?'

'Yes, let's.' They walked together to the café favoured by some of the station's personnel, near the top of Whitehall. The pavement was crowded, and they were obliged to walk behind a lieutenant in the Pay Corps and an ATS officer, whose conversation they were unable to ignore.

He asked, 'Did you get the key to the flat, Cynthia?'

'Oh yes,' the ATS officer replied with a hint of excitement in her voice. 'She'll be away for some time, so we've got the place to ourselves.'

'Oh, good.' The lieutenant was also excited. 'We could go there now and leave the shopping until later.'

'Why on earth would we want to do that?' It was clear from her tone that she was teasing him.

'You know, darling.'

'No, why?'

'Well,' he said with a hint of embarrassment, 'We could have a spot of rumty-tumty-tiddley-tum.'

'I suppose so,' said Cynthia, 'and won't it be fun to see if you can get as far as "tiddley-tum" this time?'

The back of the lieutenant's neck was brick red, and the girls were about to descend into laughter, but fortunately they reached the café and watched the lovers disappear.

'Oh glory,' said Joyce, 'I couldn't hold on a moment longer.'

'I know,' said Sylvia, also laughing. 'What a pair of twerps. It's just as well they've got the likes of us to run the war for them.'

'Did you know what they were talking about?'

'Oh yes.' She ordered a pot of tea because it worked out cheaper than two cups.

'My word, Sylvia, you're coming on. You were too innocent for words in Dover.'

'I'm still innocent, just not as naïve. I teamed up with a girl called Ruth on the way to Malta. She was a mine of information.'

'Good,' said Joyce, making space for the tea things. 'Is she married?'

'No, but she left her honour in an Andersen shelter in Dulwich, not far from where I'm billeted, apparently.' She told the story while Joyce stirred the tea and poured it out.

'Good for her. We used Len's bedroom while his dad was at the pub.'

'Before you were married?'

'Don't look so shocked. It's not a crime.'

'Well, no, I suppose not.' Sylvia hid momentarily behind her cup.

'You just take care your parents don't find out.'

'Heavens, no. That would be awful.'

'Seriously though, and away from the subject of "rumty-tumty", there's something I should warn you about.'

248

Sylvia put her cup down. 'What's that?'

'Relax. It's just that, well, do you remember what Len looked like when you came to see me?'

'He was very thin.'

'He was huge compared with how he looked when he first came home. Honestly, I could have used his rib-cage as a rubbing board.'

Sylvia smiled. 'Poor old Len.'

'Yes, and the short hair wasn't a new fashion either. His head was shaved when he came home. It was to get rid of lice, apparently. It's growing nicely now but I hardly recognised him at first. You said Freddy hadn't sent you a photo from Yorkshire and maybe you can understand why.' She finished her tea and said apologetically, 'I just thought I'd better warn you.'

. . .

Freddy was unusually conscious about his appearance, because his long-anticipated visit to London was about to happen. A letter had arrived in the morning's mail, instructing him to report to the City of London Magistrates' Court on Friday the eighth of June as a character witness in the matter of Gerard Bailey.

Because the hearing was scheduled to begin at ten o'clock on the morning of the eighth, Freddy was granted leave to travel up to London on the seventh, and because his request for leave was partly on compassionate grounds his commanding officer had granted a seventy-two-hour pass. It meant that he would not have to return to Worthy Down until the following Sunday. A flurry of letters followed.

28th May.
Dear Len,
I'm a bloody nuisance, I know, but can you possibly put me up from 7th June until the 10th? I have business in London and I'm determined to meet Sylvia if I can.
Yours,
Freddy.

28th May.
Dearest Sugar Plum,
I have to be in London, on 8th June to speak up for the chap I told you about. I'm coming up on the 7th and staying at Len's place until the 10th, when I have to return. Can you get a stand-down? I'm in court on the morning of the 8th, but it shouldn't take long. Thereafter, I'm all yours.

All my love,
Freddy XXXX

29ᵗʰ May.
Dearest Freddy,
We're all working extra watches because of a tummy bug at one of the wrenneries, but I'll get a stand-down if it's the last thing I do. I'll put my request in before I go on watch. They're bound to understand. This is wonderful! And you're staying with Len and Joyce! Surely nothing can stand in our way now!
All my love,
Sylvia XXXXX
(Sorry – I mean 'Your Sugar Plum.' The excitement made me forget).
P.S. I can't wait!

29ᵗʰ May.
Freddy, my old mate,
If you don't mind kipping down on the sofa, of course you can stay here. Sylvia usually has the spare room, and I've no doubt she'll end up here at some stage. I'm sure you don't mind that. I haven't seen Joyce to tell her yet – she's on some silly duty, watch, or whatever you old sea-dogs call it, but I know she'll be thrilled to bits.
All the best, mate. See you soon,
Len.

Freddy packed his new number one uniform and previously unworn white shirts meticulously. He was still uncomfortably aware of his emaciated appearance, and his hair had only grown about an inch. Wearing his cap flattened it to some extent, but otherwise there was nothing he could do about his hair or his weight. He was determined, however, that if he looked a mess it would not be for lack of grooming. Sylvia would surely understand and not take fright when she saw him.

39

As the two men left the court building and stepped into Queen Victoria Street, Bailey beamed at his companion. 'What would you say to a pre-prandial noggin, Freddy?'

Freddy consulted his recently-purchased wristwatch, still conscious of its novelty. 'I'd call it a good idea.'

'Splendid.' Bailey raised his arm and within seconds a taxi drew up beside them. 'The Savoy,' he told the driver.

'You're incorrigible,' said Freddy, joining him in the taxi. 'You just have to do everything in the grand manner.'

'I'm a reformed character,' Bailey protested. 'From now on I'm strictly above board. I just prefer to do things with a little style.'

'But the Savoy, for goodness' sake.'

'It's the ideal place for a celebration, my boy, and for the odd helpful wrinkle as well.'

'The odd what?'

Bailey held up his hand to forestall further negative comment. 'Like you,' he said, 'I want your forthcoming rendezvous to be a total success, and to that end I'm placing the Bailey *savoir faire* at your disposal.'

With a sense of inevitability Freddy turned away from watching the streets retreat past his window. 'I have a feeling, Bailey, that your advice could turn out to be the shortest-ever route to Queer Street.'

'Oh, you of little faith. What I have in mind will not break the bank. You can trust me.'

Freddy snorted. 'I told the beak I'd trust you with my life. I never mentioned my bank account.'

'That's true, old man, and I have to say I was touched by what you said in there. It made all the difference.'

'It was no trouble.'

'It got me off with a fine and an earful from the beak.'

'I'm sure your five-year stretch in Poland helped sway him. It wasn't all down to me.'

'It's possible, old man.' The taxi drew up outside the Savoy and the doorman held open the taxi door. 'But, you know, you had the poor old soul almost in tears with your description of the salt mine.' He hopped out and paid the driver before Freddy could put his hand in his pocket for the fare.

They saluted two naval officers who had emerged from the hotel in time to claim the vacated taxi. 'Once we're inside and our caps are off,' said Bailey, 'we can forget about saluting. In any case, we're all patrons and I think that makes us all gentlemen.' He led the way from the Front Hall, through the American Bar lounge and into the bar itself, where they took their seats. Freddy looked around him at the magnificently-appointed room with its bright, broad-striped carpet and opulent furnishings, wondering how his companion could afford such a lifestyle. He suspected he would never know.

'I was last here,' announced Bailey, 'in July, nineteen thirty-nine.'

'Has it changed a lot?'

'Hardly at all. I'd say it's reassuringly the same.'

One of the bar staff came to them, and Bailey glanced across at Freddy, who asked for a gin and tonic. He felt that a request for beer might be out of place.

'The same for me, I think.'

'Very good, sir.'

Bailey leant forward confidentially. 'When exactly are you seeing the lovely Sylvia, Freddy?'

'At about fifteen-thirty this afternoon.' He tried to sound casual but excitement and anticipation were seldom far from the surface. 'She has to be back on watch at eighteen-thirty, though, and then she's on again until eight tomorrow morning.'

'Good Lord.'

'I know. She must be exhausted. There's a gastric thing doing the rounds at one of the wrenneries, and the others are all working extra watches. The daft thing is that she's due to be officially discharged next weekend.'

'The timing could have been better.'

'You can say that again. At all events, she's off-watch from oh-eight-hundred tomorrow until fourteen-hundred on Sunday. It means we can meet tomorrow evening and not worry about the late night.'

'That's good. So we'd better address the question of what and where.'

'Have you any ideas, Bailey?'

'Yes, I have. I'm not suggesting you eat here, old man; that would really leave the bank balance groaning, but it would be a good idea to bring her here for a drink. It will create a sense of occasion without over-facing the poor girl. I mean she won't get the idea that you're driving beyond your tankful on her account, if you see what I mean. Then, as the weather is decidedly unsettled, you can take a short taxi ride to Soho, to an intimate but inexpensive place I can heartily recommend. As a matter of fact, I was there only last evening.'

Freddy stared at him in mild disbelief. 'You really have thought about this, haven't you?'

'My dear chap, of course I have. I've given some thought to the remainder of the evening as well.'

'I'm speechless.'

'It's important, old man. You said you wanted to dance, and I know the very place for it. It's called "The Glass Slipper" and it's a short walk from the restaurant. I renewed my membership only yesterday, so I can't lend you my card, as they know me. You'll need to take out short-term membership but it shouldn't be too expensive.'

'Forgive my provincial ignorance, but why is it necessary to be a member?'

'It's a respectable night club, old chap, a place where you can foxtrot the night away, but they don't let just anyone in. I'll take you there and introduce you, and then perhaps we can drop in for lunch at the place I told you about. Time spent on reconnaissance is never wasted.'

'I'm indebted to you, Bailey.'

'Not at all, my friend. The boot's entirely on the other foot.' He motioned to the barman and ordered the same again. 'Just a quick one before we go,' he told Freddy, 'a bracer against this wretched climate.'

'You must admit this climate is a damned sight friendlier than the one we left behind in Germany.'

'Absolutely, old man. I'm simply reasserting myself as an Englishman in the most characteristic way, by moaning about the weather. I'm sure there are things that irritate you now that starvation and exposure no longer dominate our lives.'

'There is one thing.' Freddy had been giving the matter some thought.

'Trot out your thing, old man.'

'It's the music.'

'How do you mean?'

'Well, it's changed so much. At one time we had little gems like "A Nightingale Sang in Berkeley Square", "You've Done Something to My Heart", "Moonlight Becomes You" – that was the last song I heard before I was taken prisoner – and there were all those marvellous songs from before the war, but now it's as if music has somehow lost its innocence and become grown-up and sophisticated. I was listening to one of the American bands the other day, all squealing trumpets and blaring trombones. The softness and intimacy we used to know have gone out of fashion.'

'The world has moved on in our absence, and not entirely for the better,' agreed Bailey, but I think you'll find the music at the Glass Slipper more to your taste.' He paused in recollection and said, 'I remember your telling me about a song that meant an awful lot to you and Sylvia. "All the Things You Are", wasn't it?'

'That's right. When did I tell you that?'

'One night when we were both freezing to death in a stable in Saxony.' Bailey finished his drink. 'We should move on,' he said. 'We have things to do.'

. . .

As she emerged from Spring Gardens, Sylvia saw someone through the drizzle, standing at the foot of the plinth that supported one of the Landseer lions. He was looking in her direction too, but in spite of her excitement she forced herself not to hurry. She would feel an awful fool if she rushed to greet him and it turned out that he wasn't Freddy after all.

As she drew nearer, however, his face relaxed into a huge smile and he hurried towards her.

'Hello, Sylvia.'

'Freddy?' Her heart was beating so hard it made her breathless and she could barely speak. 'How did you know it was me?' As she spoke, she knew it was a silly question but she didn't care. He had kind eyes that softened his gaunt features, and laughter lines at the corners of his eyes, which was remarkable, considering where he'd been. In all, she was pleased that he didn't look dramatically different from the man she'd imagined. He was just very much thinner.

'I recognised you from your photograph.'

'Of course.' Her hands touched his and she felt unaccountably shy.

'Let's find somewhere where we can shelter from this stuff,' he said.

'There's a café in Whitehall that we use, or there's a Corner House in the Strand. It's just – Oh dear, I was going to say "around the corner".' She was nervous and it was making her say silly things.

'That's very reassuring. The war's changed so many things you just never know where you're going to find them next. Which is nearer?'

The rain was beginning to fall more heavily and she made a quick decision. 'The café.'

'That's all right by me if you're game.'

'Oh yes.' A cup of tea might help her calm down.

As they set out towards Whitehall, Freddy asked, 'Have you eaten recently?'

'Say again?' He was on her deaf side, and the traffic noise added to her problem.

'I asked you if you'd eaten recently.'

'I had half a corned-beef sandwich about two hours ago. We're so busy that they only let me out this afternoon because the PO Wren on my watch offered to cover for me.'

'Good for her.' With a look of apology he said, 'I'd offer you my arm, as a gentleman should, but we're bound to meet an over-zealous officer.'

'Bound to what?'

'I said we're bound to bump into at least one officer.'

'You're right,' she agreed, 'we mustn't disgrace the King's uniform.' As they crossed the road and entered Whitehall, she said, 'Freddy?'

'Yes?'

'Do you think we could swap sides? You're on my deaf side and I can hardly hear you.'

'I'm sorry.' He moved to her left. 'How's that?'

'Strength five.'

'Excellent.'

They reached the café and hung their coats on the stand. There were several tables free so they took one by the window. Freddy studied the menu with an air of growing excitement. Suddenly he said, 'I haven't had cottage pie for years. Right, I've decided. How about you?'

'I think I fancy that as well.' Now that he had removed his cap, she was studying him discreetly and she realised that if anything his hair was a little longer than she had expected. It was also heavily flecked with grey.

When the waitress had taken their order, Freddy said, 'Actually, I had lunch only a couple of hours ago.'

'And you're still hungry?'

'I'm permanently hungry. It's a kriegie characteristic.'

'Oh, I'm sorry, Freddy. That was clumsy of me.' The thought of him, starved and ill-treated, made her reach across the table to touch his hand. But then she hesitated, unsure in the circumstances.

'We must agree on some rules,' he said, taking her hand and clasping it between his. 'You must never feel shy when referring to my grand tour of Europe, and I shan't be embarrassed when you ask me for repetitions because I've addressed the wrong ear.'

His accent was less pronounced than she'd expected and his voice had a warm, soothing quality. She was pleased he'd taken her hand, although it troubled her that his felt rough and calloused. She was suddenly noticing those things, like the way he had looked around him with childlike pleasure at the white tablecloths and pre-war decor, features that must once have been commonplace but which had been absent from his life for so long.

Something else that troubled her was her appearance. 'I must look an awful sight,' she said.

'What makes you say that?'

'The circles under my eyes, for one thing.'

'Like the canary in the song.'

The waitress brought their tea and Freddy thanked her.

'I was a little girl when I heard the song about the canary,' said Sylvia.

'Ah, but I'm almost twenty-six, and I say that in my adult opinion you look truly wonderful.'

'Even in uniform and with my hair pinned up?'

'Particularly so. I can understand why you feel uncomfortable about having to turn up in the rig and without war-paint, but you have to understand that I'm looking at the image I've carried around since I first saw your photograph. Seeing that picture meant an awful lot to me. Even though you were in Malta and still beyond my reach, it seemed to bring you closer.'

'I'd no idea.'

'You'd no way of knowing. But, you know, you're a sight to gladden the heart of a bewildered ex-kriegie, clad as you are in pusser's serge, with your face pink and shiny and your hair pinned up in accordance with King's Regulations and Admiralty Instructions. That's why it was worth spending three years behind barbed wire, just to see you walking towards me in Trafalgar Square.' He broke off to thank the waitress as she put their food on the table. 'I hope I've convinced you,' he said when she had left them, 'because I speak as a son of Kingston-Upon-Hull, where the baring of souls is as rare as daffodils in December.' He sniffed the aroma that rose from his plate. 'Let's eat,' he said. 'This smells good.'

Sylvia hardly trusted herself to speak, so she made a start on the cottage pie and it braced her to some extent, as well as reminding her how ravenous she was. When she eventually spoke, she said, 'You always do that, Freddy.'

'What do I always do?'

'You joke about things and then you're suddenly serious, and I think about you in that horrible place, and it's too awful for words.'

'But it's all in the past.'

'I know. I just have to keep telling myself that.'

'That's right. Concentrate on the good things.'

'You sound like my dad. He's always saying that.' It was good advice, though. Certainly, Freddy seemed quite relaxed. Maybe he was a naturally relaxed sort of person and she was worrying alone. Now, to her annoyance, she found herself worrying about that. It was awful.

'A penny for them.'

'What?'

'You were lost in thought.'

'Yes, I was.' She had to ask him. 'Don't you feel awkward too?'

'Not as awkward as I did half-an-hour ago, but yes, to some extent. I suppose it was inevitable. We know each other so well from our letters, but now we're face to face it's all strange and new. We'll get over it.'

'I hope so. It's as if we have to be terribly distant and polite until someone gives the word. Do you know what I mean?'

'I know exactly what you mean.' With a smile, he said, 'It doesn't happen like this in the pictures, does it?'

'No, it doesn't. I imagined at one time that we'd be like Greer Garson and Ronald Colman in *Random Harvest*, but that was just me being soppy.'

'I'm afraid you have the advantage of me there.'

'Of course. I saw it in Harwich when it first came out. It was less than two years ago. I'm sorry.'

'Don't worry. Tell me about it.'

'All right.' She pushed her empty plate aside and leaned forward to tell the story.

'It's about a girl who befriends a soldier at the end of the last war.'

'Is the girl Greer Garson?'

'Yes. The soldier is Ronald Colman and he's lost his memory. Anyway, they get married and go to live in a village in Devon.' She smiled as he took her hands and held them again. 'And then one day, he goes to meet someone in Liverpool and he's knocked down by a taxi and when he regains consciousness his earlier memory has returned but he remembers nothing of his life with Paula.'

'That's Greer Garson?'

'Yes, and all kinds of things happen until Paula, who's now his secretary, goes on holiday and visits the village where they lived, and Smithy – that's Ronald Colman – goes to Birmingham, but a chain of associations leads him to the village as well, and they meet at the cottage, where his memory returns and the film ends with them in each other's arms.' She studied him through narrowed eyelids. 'Freddy, you're laughing at me.'

'You evidently enjoyed the film.'

'It was lovely. I cried buckets.'

Still amused, he asked, 'Is that a good thing?'

'Oh yes, you can't beat a good cry over a happy ending.'

'Well then, it must have been a good film. I imagine it lost something in the telling.'

'All the same,' she said wistfully, 'it was very romantic.'

As he held her hands he stroked them with his thumbs. It was comforting and it made up for him being sniffy about *Random Harvest*.

'Our story's pretty good too,' he told her. 'And it's going to get even better.' He gave her hands a squeeze. 'You must have a proper sleep tomorrow, but then I want you to meet me at the Savoy at seven o'clock.'

She gasped, 'The Savoy? We can't eat there.'

'No, but we can have a drink there. I'm told the American Bar is the best place to start a special evening, and this one's going to be very special. For one thing, our friend the new moon has promised to drop in.'

40

She looked around her uncertainly as she came through the door into the front hall, and then beamed when she saw him.

'Now I know how Al Bowlly must have felt,' he said, kissing her cheek.

'About what?'

'Having a date with an angel.'

'Get away.'

'I mean it. You look wonderful.'

Her expression softened. 'Thank you.'

'I'm just afraid you might turn into a scullery maid at midnight.'

'What have you got against scullery maids? I hope you're not a snob.'

'Not at all. I just prefer you as you are.'

'Actually,' she said, taking his arm, 'I'm staying at Len's dad's place tonight, so you'll be stuck with me, scullery maid or not.'

'Excellent.'

They made for the doorway to the American Bar and descended the short flight of steps into the bar lounge.

'Let me take your jacket,' said Freddy.

'Thank you.' She let him ease it from her shoulders. 'I'll keep it with me,' she said, draping it over her chair.

Her dress was dark purple, with a round neck and short puff sleeves, and she wore a matching velvet topknot, from which her hair fell in loose curls to her shoulders. Freddy had no idea what the angel in the song looked like but he was enchanted with his.

She stroked his sleeve with her fingers. 'It feels silky,' she said. 'Is it doeskin?'

'It's similar to doeskin, apparently. I don't know the first thing about cloth,' he confessed. 'I just told the tailor I was looking for something special and he found this stuff buried in his back room.'

'It's lovely.'

'I'm glad you like it. What would you like to drink?'

'Oh dear.' She looked at the people around her and said, 'I've no idea. This is a new experience for me.'

'Well now, if we were doing things in the grand manner we would probably have an "Eight Bells". That's the cocktail created specifically for the Senior Service. However, I would suggest a pink gin. It's unostentatious, yet still in the naval tradition.'

'That sounds lovely.' She glanced nervously at a Wren first officer and a major of Marines at a corner table, and leaned forward to whisper through scarcely-moving lips, 'That Wren officer keeps looking at us.'

'Let her. She looks as if she needs some fun in her life. Anyway, it's your stockings she's looking at, and I have to say I'm pretty impressed too.' A barman came to them and Freddy ordered two pink gins.

'I've been saving these stockings since last Easter,' she confided. 'I worked hard for them.'

'Oh?'

'I got them from the crew of an American torpedo boat.'

'I'm not going to ask.'

'Not for anything awful, silly. The other girls and I did some mending for them and they paid us with stockings.'

'I'm glad they did, because you look proper *chic* in them.'

The compliment was lost for the moment on Sylvia, who glanced nervously at the major of Marines. 'He's looking at your PO's badge,' she whispered.

'And so he should. They're not easy to get, and I have to say he doesn't look all that bright.' To distract her from the scrutiny of envious senior officers he took her hands and examined them. It was a successful ploy because she watched him with amusement. After a moment she asked, 'Do they pass muster?'

'They're exquisite.'

'Thank you. I've never been complimented on my hands before.'

'Petrarch would have immortalised them.'

'Who's he?'

'He was a lyric poet who wrote sonnets about the woman he loved, and I know how he felt.'

'You're full of flannel.'

He concentrated his scrutiny on her nails. 'Do you polish them?'

'My nails? I just buff them with a pad. I haven't been able to find any nail varnish for ages.'

'You'd only be gilding the lily.' He released her hands and asked, 'What shade is your lipstick?'

'Why do you want to know?' She sounded amused but a little unnerved by his close attention.

'Professional curiosity. I'm a photographer, remember.'

'All right, it's called "Battle Red".'

'What a silly name.'

'I'm sorry you don't like it.'

'I like the colour, and you look exquisite in it. It's just a daft name.'

'Well, maybe when you're a famous photographer you'll think up a better name.'

'You never know.'

Possibly to avoid further scrutiny, she changed the subject by asking, 'Have you been here before?'

'I came here for the first time yesterday with Bailey.'

'All right,' she said, 'I'll take back what I said about flannel.'

The barman put their drinks down and Freddy thanked him. 'Here's to us, Sugar Plum,' he said raising his glass.

'Yes, to us.' She touched his glass with hers and said, 'That's the first time you've called me that since we met.'

'I told you things would improve.'

'You did, and you were right.' She smiled, now visibly more relaxed. 'I'm sorry I was such a wet lettuce yesterday.'

'It was only natural. I must confess I feel uneasy sometimes.'

'Do you really?'

'Now and then. When things seem too good to be true I wonder if I'm going to wake up in a Thuringian farmyard, having dreamt it all.'

'Oh, Freddy.' She reached across the table and squeezed his wrist. 'That's all behind you now.'

'I keep telling myself that.' He smiled again. 'And you weren't a wet lettuce at all. A drier, crisper, more appetising lettuce I've yet to see.'

'If that's a compliment, thank you.' She sipped her pink gin and gave a look of surprise. 'This is really nice. It's a lovely place too.'

'It is, isn't it? One of the officers I flew with told me his parents used to bring him to the Savoy for half-term treats. I thought at the time it sounded rather grand.'

'Did Bailey come here with his parents?'

'No, but he did tell me about a half-term treat he once had in Soho. I don't think his parents knew anything about it.'

'Oh?'

'I should tell you that he left school at fourteen and led a shadowy life until the war intervened. He also spent six months in prison for false representation. His airs and graces are the result of careful observation and practice.'

Her eyes widened at the mention of prison.

'He's a rogue, but a kind-hearted one. You get to know your fellow-wayfarers on a five-hundred-mile hike through the worst winter anyone can remember.'

Her shock at Bailey's past quickly forgotten, she asked, 'Did you really walk five hundred miles?'

'It was five-hundred-and-fifty, actually. I was breaking the news gently.'

'It must have been awful.'

'It had its lighter moments,' he said, attempting to reassure her, 'but I have to say that it shattered one illusion.'

'What was that?'

' "Winter Wonderland" will never appeal to me in quite the same way again.'

'Oh, Freddy.' Her tone suggested that words failed her.

'Let's not talk about that. Instead, I'll tell you what I have in mind for this evening. I thought we'd go to a restaurant in Soho that's particularly good.'

'How do you know about it?'

'Bailey and I had lunch there yesterday as a try-out.'

'And then you had cottage pie at the café in Whitehall.'

'I did, and excellent it was too, but to continue …'

'Sorry.'

'That's all right. Anyway, I thought we might go on afterwards to dance at a place that's strongly recommended because it still favours the dreamy number and the slow foxtrot.'

'That sounds perfect. You know, I'm glad your tastes are cosy and old-fashioned.'

'So am I. It comes of being an air-gunner, trained to face aft and view the world in retrospect.' He saw off the last of his drink. 'Shall we move on?'

He paid the bill and they went down to the hotel entrance. After a few minutes a taxi drew up. 'Marcel's in Greek Street,' he told the driver.

'Are we going to the place where Bailey had his half-term treat?' Her curiosity about that occasion was undiminished.

'Not exactly, although I believe it wasn't far away.'

He found her hand in the dark and held it during the short journey to the restaurant, relishing again the novelty of its softness. Her perfume, too, was a reminder of something long forgotten, and he inhaled deeply to enjoy it all the more.

She asked, 'What are you doing?'

'I'm basking in your scent. What is it?'

'Nothing grand, just the last drop of something I was given when there was still some in the shops. It's a familiar story, I'm afraid.'

'It's lovely.'

'Do you really think so?' She sounded surprised.

The taxi pulled up outside the restaurant. 'I haven't known anything like it for at least three years,' he assured her, offering his arm.

When they entered the restaurant they found a number of tables already occupied, and Freddie recognised the uniforms of several nationalities including the United States. Americans were still a novelty in his life and he was noticing them everywhere. He was already familiar with the superior quality of their uniforms and it pleased him that on this occasion his was at least as fine. He felt that, in a sartorial kind of way, he was flying the Union Flag. Had he needed a heartening thought it would have served him as well as any, but he was cheerful enough when he gave his name to the elderly waiter who greeted them.

'Mr Hinchliffe? I will tell Marcel you are here, sir.'

Freddy looked around at the French influence in the décor and the seascapes that lined the walls, pleasantly surprised that Marcel should wish to welcome them. 'I think we may be more important than we thought,' he said.

'Do you know Marcel?'

'We met yesterday for the first time.'

'Here he is, I think.' Sylvia nodded towards the door, which had opened to allow an immaculate, silver-haired man into the room.

'Mr Hinchcliffe, Mademoiselle,' he said, hesitating for a moment in his pronunciation of Freddy's surname. 'Welcome.' He shook Freddy's hand and kissed Sylvia's. 'Let Albert take your coats and I will show you to your table.' He left the waiter with their coats and led them to a secluded corner. 'I hope this table is to your satisfaction. Albert will bring the menu and wine list to you in a moment.' He lit the candle, adding in a lower voice, 'There is an addition to the menu that I am pleased to offer. It is saddle of hare in a cream sauce. If you need anything at all, please speak to Albert or to me and it will be our pleasure to assist you.' He made a shallow bow and left them.

'I don't think I've ever eaten hare,' said Freddy.

'Oh, I have. It's lovely.'

'It must be very special or he wouldn't have made such a secret of it. Maybe it's in limited supply.'

'And he's saved it for us. Isn't that grand?'

After a little thought, Freddy said, 'I detect the hand of Bailey in all this.'

'Do you think he provided the hare?'

'No, but I'll lay odds that the VIP treatment is his doing.'

'He must have a lot of influence.'

'He has a lot of something. He treats every place he visits as if he's just bought it. He was the same at Niwka and Tarnowicz, although, I have to say, less so at the mine. That would have been a hard one to pull off, even for Bailey.'

The waiter brought the menu and wine list.

'You know,' said Sylvia, 'I'm not much of a drinker; in fact I'm still feeling a bit woozy after that pink gin.'

'Alcohol isn't compulsory, you know. You could always go on to goffers.'

'I will,' she agreed, 'I think I'd like tomato juice if they have some.'

Freddy ordered tomato juice and a white Bordeaux, having already decided on the hare as his main course, and with that settled he turned again to the menu. 'Good grief.' His eye fell on the first item. 'The last time I had oxtail soup, Chamberlain was Prime Minister and I was too young to vote.' He put the menu down and said, 'Right, that's my decision made.' He began to observe the other diners. 'The Yanks all have an intrepid look about them,' he remarked.

Sylvia followed his gaze and said, 'Don't you think that with a bit of practice you could look intrepid too?'

'Not for one minute.'

'Even in your aeroplane with your machine gun and things?'

'Especially with a machine gun. I always kept both eyes tightly closed when I fired it, even in training.' He held her hand across the table as he had so often, because she was smiling in amused disbelief and because the candle's glow made her more irresistible than ever. He wanted quite badly to hold her close, but that was an indulgence that would have to wait, even if the evening progressed as they hoped. It had gone well so far, but he wasn't convinced that the awkwardness of the previous day was completely behind them.

'It's my turn to offer you a penny for your thoughts,' she said.

'All right.' He thought quickly, 'I was wondering what nonsense Len might have told you about me.'

'What makes you think he told me anything about you?'

'Mr Patterson told me last night in the pub, when Len was out of the room.'

She teased him, regarding him through half-closed eyelids. Eventually she said, 'He told me … just the usual things.'

'What usual things?'

'He said that you snored, that you never changed your socks, that you slurped your tea and, oh yes, he said you were a terrible philanderer. Apparently you were forever writing to a girl in Dover and then to one in Malta. I was quite shocked.'

He sighed with resignation. 'You're not going to tell me, are you?'

'I will, one day when you need cheering up.'

Freddy was bound to agree, particularly when she put her hand on his for the first time. It felt so good it was almost a shame when Albert arrived with the wine.

. . .

It was a magnificent meal, and they agreed that neither of them had eaten as well since the onset of rationing, but eventually they had to leave, taking with them the good wishes of their host and his head waiter.

'It's not far,' said Freddy, offering her his arm. For the time being at least, the weather was on their side; the drizzle had stopped and stars were clearly discernible in the breaks between the clouds.

'What are you looking at?' They had both stopped, and Sylvia was trying to follow the line of his gaze.

'Wait a second … Look, there.' He pointed to a patch of clear sky.

'Where?' She positioned herself at his shoulder to see where he was pointing.

'There, look, between the clouds.' For no reason he could think of, he was whispering.

It was her turn to whisper. 'It's the new moon!'

'I told you he was coming. I imagine he wants to see the job through.'

She pressed herself closer to him as if they were peering through a crack in a door. 'I'm sorry I criticised him,' she said.

'Don't worry, he's used to it.'

'How do you know?'

'We spent a freezing night together in a farmyard outside Eisenach. We have no secrets from each other.'

Because they were so close, he put his arm around her waist and they walked the fifty yards or so that remained to the Glass Slipper.

When they arrived, Freddy showed his membership card to a doorman in a dinner jacket and black tie, who spoke briefly with someone behind a curtain. A moment later a young man in similar garb emerged.

'Good evening, Mr Hinchcliffe. Good evening, miss. Welcome to the Glass Slipper.' He motioned to the doorman to take their coats, and when that was done he held back the curtain for them. 'Please come this way and I'll show you to your table.' He opened a door to invite them into a large, softly-lit room furnished principally in wine red. Beyond the tables, which were set discreetly apart, were a small dance floor and a band consisting of a piano, bass, drums and an alto saxophone. They were playing 'Bewitched', a song Freddie remembered from before his capture. It was a good start.

The manager led them to a table in one of several discreet alcoves built around the seating area. 'I believe you're a society photographer, Mr Hinchcliffe,' he said, lighting the candle on their table.

'Really?'

'Mr Bailey told us all about you.'

'Oh, I see.'

He gave Freddie the wine list. 'Shall I leave it with you for a few minutes, sir?'

Freddie looked across at Sylvia and asked, 'Are you ready for a drink, S. P?'

'Mm,' she nodded, 'I think so.'

'Good.' He scanned the list, which looked remarkably comprehensive after six years of war. 'No, don't go,' he told the manager. 'I'd like a bottle of the Veuve Clicquot, the 'thirty-seven, please.' He'd tasted champagne only twice in his life but he'd promised Sylvia a special evening. Also, Mme Clicquot's widowed status had appealed immediately to his compassionate nature. He had selected the 1937 vintage because its grapes had been picked before the global descent into insanity, and that alone made them worthy of his choice. Too much knowledge, he suspected, hindered decision-making.

As the manager retreated, Sylvia asked, 'What have you ordered?'

'Champagne.'

'Champagne?'

'It's a special occasion and I thought I'd spend some of my back-pay. I've waited a long time for this.'

The band began 'I'll Be Seeing You,' and that prompted the question Freddy had waited so long to ask. Rising to his feet, he offered his hand. 'May I have the pleasure?'

She gave him a beaming smile. 'Of course.'

There were only three couples on the dance floor, so they had lots of room, and he wasn't surprised to find that she moved easily and gracefully.

After a while, and with a suggestion of surprise in her voice, she said, 'You really can dance a slow foxtrot.'

'And I kept my promise.'

'What was that?'

'To dance not one measure 'til I'd had the pleasure ...'

'Of dancing your next dance with me.'

'You know it by heart.'

'Of course I do.'

They continued without speaking, merely applauding the band at the end of the number.

They found the champagne in an ice-bucket beside their table. An envelope stood propped between the two glasses. It was addressed to Freddie in an elaborate hand, so he opened it and read it in the candle's glow.

My dear old thing,

I trust the evening has been a success so far and that you have not found my small gestures too intrusive. One tiny surprise still awaits you, and then I shall interfere no more. I simply had to lend a helping hand after the service you performed for me yesterday.

We both know, however, that you did infinitely more for me on the road to Görlitz. I owe my life to you and I'll never forget that.

All that remains is for me to wish you and the dear lady the greatest happiness because you both deserve it.

Your grateful chum,

Bailey.

Sylvia had been watching him. She asked, 'What is it?'

'Just a note from Bailey.'

'What does it say?'

'Nothing really.'

'Is it very private?'

'No, it's not. Read it, by all means, but don't take any of it seriously. Bailey spends his life exaggerating.'

She read the note. 'So the VIP treatment really was at his request.'

'And maybe in response to a hint that I might take a year's membership here and possibly give the club some free publicity in *The Illustrated London News* or *The Tatler*, being the society photographer I am. Bailey can tell such whoppers quite plausibly and with absolutely no effort.'

'He sounds fascinating, and I don't know what you did for him on the road to Görlitz but I'm glad you did it.'

'Oh, let's have some champagne,' he said, reaching for the bottle and conveniently changing the subject.

267

'Are you going to close your eyes when you draw the cork?'

'I'm afraid so.' He removed the foil and the wire cage, screwed up his eyes with theatrical exaggeration and eased out the cork. There was a satisfying report and he caught the initial surge of foaming liquid in a glass. Finally, with both glasses filled, he raised his. 'Here's to us, Sugar Plum.'

'To us.'

'Yours' beckoned, so, after a sip, they returned to the floor.

'Nineteen forty-one was a vintage year for songs,' observed Freddy.

'Mm.' It was the response of a girl keen on dancing but unimpressed by detail. She had noticed, however, that there were more couples on the floor than before. 'It's getting crowded,' she said, dodging the elbow of an enthusiastic Free French officer. 'Let's just shuffle.' It was a wise suggestion. He buried his face happily in her hair, luxuriating in her scent and softness and wondering for maybe the hundredth time how long the dream could last.

'Remind me about that Ronald Colman picture,' he said as they returned to their table. 'How did it all begin between those two?'

Hesitantly, she asked, 'You're not going to poke fun, are you?'

'Not in the least. I'm genuinely interested.'

'All right,' she said, finishing her champagne. 'For what it's worth, he'd walked out of the asylum when no one was looking, and she hid him from the asylum people when she realised he was harmless.'

'So it began with an act of kindness,' he said, refilling her glass. 'Rather like our story, really.'

'I suppose so.'

'And it ended at the cottage where they used to live?'

'Actually, it was on the garden path. The gate creaked when he opened it, as it always had, and then he had to bob under an overhanging branch, and that was another clue. Anyway, he'd just opened the cottage door when he heard Paula calling him "Smithy", and that was the clue that finally unlocked his memory. He saw her standing by the gate and recognised her.'

'It must have been quite a reunion.'

She wrinkled her nose in embarrassment. 'I told you I was just being silly when I thought of us like that.'

'No, you weren't at all silly, and I'm sorry I didn't take it seriously.' He gave her hand a reassuring squeeze. 'You know,' he said, 'of those clues, I favour the creaking gate.'

'Why?' She seemed surprised, possibly less by the observation than by the change in his attitude.

'I'm not Sigmund Freud, but I find dodging under the branch of a tree a shade nebulous as memory-joggers go, and I can't imagine how hearing his name would do the trick either. My maths teacher used to bellow my name with alarming frequency, and I still couldn't remember a thing about differential calculus. No, the creaking gate wins every time for me. It's a strident, tangible thing that must have got on his nerves at one time. He'd remember that all right.'

'All right,' she conceded, 'I imagine he would.'

' "Taking A Chance On Love," ' he remarked on hearing the opening bars of the new number.

'I know. Shall we dance?'

The club and its band were evidently popular, because the floor was now very crowded, and they only just managed to claim a space on it. Even then, they were pushed very close together by the press of bodies around them.

With his mouth almost touching Sylvia's right ear, Freddy said, 'I don't think this was such a good idea.'

'I can't hear you. You're on my deaf side.'

'Sorry.' He moved his head so that his left cheek was in contact with hers. 'Some people have more sense than us,' he said. They're dancing between the tables where there's more room. Shall we join them?'

'Do you think we can?'

'Follow me.' Still keeping her in hold, he reversed slowly and firmly until they were out of the crowd and able to return to their table.

'You've done that before,' she remarked as he took her in hold again.

'As I told you, we air-gunners go everywhere backwards. It ensures that life is always full of surprises.'

'Aren't you tired of surprises? I thought you might be waiting for life to return to normal. It's what most people want.'

In the moment of quiet that followed the brief applause at the end of the number, he said, 'My 'normal' did a bunk some time ago, Sugar Plum. I shan't see that again.'

'Oh Freddy, I'm sorry,' she said, clutching his arm. 'I wasn't thinking when I said that.'

'It's all right.' He hated to see her guilty and apologetic. 'Come and sit down.' He poured the last of the champagne and placed the empty bottle in the bucket. 'There's going to be a brand new 'normal' after the war, starting the moment I'm demobbed.'

'What are you going to do?' Her gaffe quickly forgotten, there was amusement as well as curiosity in her voice.

'General photography to begin with, just to pay the bills, but that's only until I make my reputation as an animal specialist.'

'Oh yes, I remember – those cows with large, appealing eyes.'

'Well remembered, S.P., but that's not all. I'm going to photograph gossiping budgerigars, omniscient owls, condescending cats, fawning spaniels, hen-pecked cockerels, narrow-minded ferrets, woolly-minded sheep and – I have to mention them – naughty-minded bulls.'

Her smile had grown wider with each item. 'I love you, Freddy,' she said at last.

'I know. I love you too, S.P., more than I can tell you, and it's just as well we're agreed on that, because I'm going to need your help.'

'I was about to ask if there was a place for me in your grand plan.'

'There'll always be a place for you.' He had been keeping the conversation light-hearted so far but there was something he had to tell her simply because she had the right to know. 'Without you,' he said, 'there'd have been no grand plan; in fact I might never have returned.'

Suddenly she was as serious as he was. 'What do you mean?'

He wondered quite how to tell her without being too explicit. Eventually he said, 'I don't know how many died on the way back from Poland, and I'll spare you the worst details, but the fact is that when a man is exhausted, frozen to the marrow and wracked by hunger pains there's the most awful temptation to give in and let nature end the misery. Some mornings we found men lying where they'd slept, frozen to the ground, and I reckon most of them had simply let go because they no longer had a reason for wanting to survive. Some had lost their relatives, as I had, in the Blitz; others had learned that their wives and girlfriends had grown tired of waiting and found someone else. It happened all the time. I really was one of the lucky ones.'

'I'd no idea it was so awful.'

The dismay in her eyes made him feel suddenly guilty. 'I only told you that,' he said, 'to let you know how important you are to me, so please don't be upset. Think of what you've achieved. You didn't just "Free a Man for the Fleet," you put a broken man together, brought him safely home and made him unbelievably happy.' He could see tears threatening and he knew it was time to end the serious talk. It had been a moment of rare intensity by Freddy's guarded standards, so he said brightly, 'I'm also going to need an assistant.'

'I see.' She nodded, composing herself again. 'What will my duties be, exactly?'

'The usual things: loading cameras, setting up studio lights, dispensing tea and dog biscuits, and so on. Oh, and the thing you do best.'

'What's that?'

He shrugged as if the answer were obvious. 'Making everything better.'

'Oh, that old thing.'

'You'll be invaluable with the portrait subjects.'

'Putting a smile on the face of the Sphinx?'

'The Sphinx,' he confirmed, 'and other animals. There are times when "watch the birdie" falls on deaf ears, unless the subject is a cat, of course. They're not usually averse to a spot of bird-watching.'

'All right, I'll do my best with the dogs and sheep. If what you say is right, the Sphinx shouldn't be too much of a challenge.'

They sat out the next number, simply enjoying each other's proximity and only dimly aware of the music. All awkwardness was forgotten, and they might have remained like that for some time had the band leader not captured their attention by announcing a request.

'It's for Freddy and Sylvia,' he said, 'and the song that's been requested for them is the sublime "All The Things You Are".'

Neither of them spoke as they got up from their table. There was no need, because they both knew it was Bailey's final surprise.

After waiting so long they held each other very close as they moved imperceptibly to that song of all songs. Then, with a profound sense of journey's end, Freddy kissed her neck, her cheek and finally her parted lips. She responded readily until, conscious of her surroundings, she broke away, saying, 'People can see us.'

Without a word, he leaned sideways and blew out the candle. Then, in the security of the darkened alcove, he held her close and kissed her again unhurriedly and oblivious to everything, because he knew now that there would be no brutal awakening in a frozen farmyard. Veano, Lamsdorf, Tamowicz, Niwka, Brunner, Vogel, the salt mine and the forced march would all become distant memories. Only the present was real.

After a while, Sylvia murmured in his ear, 'The music's stopped.'

'I hadn't noticed.'

'And I'm the one who's supposed to be deaf.'

'There's nothing wrong with my hearing,' he assured her. 'As a matter of fact, I'll swear I just heard a gate creak.'

THE END